W9-BKR-905

BLACK WIDOW

This Large Print Book carries the
Seal of Approval of N.A.V.H.

BLACK WIDOW

RANDY WAYNE WHITE

THORNDIKE PRESS
A part of Gale, Cengage Learning

GALE
CENGAGE Learning™

Detroit • New York • San Francisco • New Haven, Conn • Waterville, Maine • London

GALE
CENGAGE Learning

Thorndike Press® Large Print Basic.
The text of this Large Print edition is unabridged.
Other aspects of the book may vary from the original edition.
Set in 16 pt. Plantin.
Printed on permanent paper.

LIBRARY OF CONGRESS CATALOGING-IN-PUBLICATION DATA

White, Randy Wayne.
  Black widow / by Randy Wayne White.
    p. cm. — (Thorndike Press large print basic)
  ISBN-13: 978-1-4104-0575-3 (hardcover : alk. paper)
  ISBN-10: 1-4104-0575-3 (hardcover : alk. paper)
  1. Ford, Doc (Fictitious character) — Fiction. 2. Marine
biologists — Fiction. 3. Suicidal behavior — Fiction. 4. Extortion
— Fiction. 5. Computer crimes — Fiction. 6. Florida — Fiction.
7. Windward Islands (West Indies) — Fiction. 8. Large type
books. I. Title.
  PS3573.H47473B57 2008b
  813'.54—dc22
                                                    2008000671

Published in 2008 in arrangement with G. P. Putnam's Sons, a member
of Penguin Group (USA) Inc.

Printed in the United States of America
1 2 3 4 5 6 7 12 11 10 09 08

*For Wendy, again,
and my pal, Dr. Brian Hummel*

AUTHOR'S NOTE

I called upon experts in various fields who kindly provided information used in writing this novel. I take full blame, in advance, for any misunderstandings that may have led to factual errors.

Thanks to Dr. John Miller for the ingenious idea of using shrimp as weapons of terror, and to Dr. Brian Lapointe for many years of advice related to marine biology and Marion Ford. Capt. Peter Hull and dolphin expert Kim Hull of Mote Marine once again provided valuable counsel.

For insights into massage, and the massage industry, I called upon several people, including old friends Nick Swartz, head athletic trainer, Kansas City Royals (and MLB American League All-Star selection); Dr. Brian Hummel, M.D., FACS; and Dr. Dan White, DC. Jean Baer, consultant to spas and resorts in Florida and the Bahamas, provided valuable information that was

not available through conventional sources
— but should be.

For information on Freemasonry, I called upon Col. Gerry Bass, Ralph Benko, and Matt Hall of Captiva, as well as Barry Thrasher at Tropical Lodge #56, Fort Myers, Florida, where, in 1985, I was raised as a Master Mason.

For general information on fishing, life, and interesting beverages, the following people were incredibly helpful: Mark Marinello, Marty Harrity, Greg Nelson, Dan Howes, Brian Cunningham, Kevin Boyce, Steve Carta, Stu Johnson, Scott Fizer, Gary Terwilliger, David Osier, Capt. Jeffrey Cardenas, Capt. Chico Fernandez, Capt. Flip Pallet, my uncle Phil Byers, my sister, Kay White, and Bill Spaceman Lee.

I would especially like to thank Nick and Karolin Troubetzkoy and the staff at Jade Mountain and Anse Chastanet, Saint Lucia, in the Eastern Caribbean. It is among the most beautiful and brilliantly designed nature-oriented resorts I have seen. While I was writing there, Della Thornille, Jondel Bailey, and Peter Jean-Paul were unfailingly helpful, as were my friends Karyn and Michael Allard.

As usual, I wrote parts of this novel while on the road, and I want to thank staff at

8

Dave Taylor's Cypress House, Useppa Island, and Doc Ford's Sanibel Rum Bar and Grille for their input, kindness, and forbearance: Jean, Lindsey, Rachel, Michelle, Liz, Allyson, Matthew, Alex, Khusan, Millie, and Kevin.

Finally, I would like to thank my sons, Lee and Rogan White, for once again helping me finish a book.

For a great bachelorette party, try planning a weekend getaway at a spa or tropical resort. Get pampered, go sightseeing, dance with dashing foreign men who don't speak English. Pack a survival kit . . . including a disposable camera. The pictures you take at the bachelorette party will come in handy when you need to blackmail the bride later!
— ADVICE TO MAIDS OF HONOR
www.ForeverWed1.com

"My grandfather was a powerful Houngan, a vitch [voodoo priest] known from Nassau through the islands. Now I'm a Houngan, keeper of that knowledge. I will tell you about assault obeahs, blue stone, fire, blood spells, and the lost Books of Moses. But you cannot write everything I tell you."
— VICTOR SMITH
Free & Accepted Mason,
Queen Esther Chapter #2
Cat Island, Bahamas
(in conversation with the author)

1

It was a simple exchange. Clean. So why did things go so wrong for the determined young bride?

I flew to the Caribbean on a Wednesday, and Thursday morning gave the blackmailer's bagman a routing number to an account containing $109,000. The bagman gave me a video shot secretly at a party thrown by my goddaughter, Shay Money, for her bridesmaids.

In the sepulchre chill of a cubicle provided by the Bank of Aruba, I popped the cassette into a minicamera long enough to confirm its contents before nodding at the teller.

Yes. She could transfer the funds.

Bagman and teller conversed in patois French as I stowed the cassette in a briefcase, focusing on details to mitigate my nausea. Inside the men's room, I filled a marble sink with water, then lathered face and hands, but the taint was subcutaneous, associative. Soap couldn't cut it. I had helped Shay with high school homework. I'd fielded her homesick letters when she was a college freshman.

After leaving the bank, I pulled my rental around the block, waited, then followed the bagman's Fiat to a waterfront bar. Big round man, big round head. I battled the urge to snatch him from the parking lot, then drive to a secluded place.

I'm no longer authorized to do that sort of thing.

Eight hours later, I landed at Miami International, then caught a commuter flight to Fort Myers Regional, a forty-minute drive from my home and laboratory on Sanibel Island, southwest coast of Florida. Shay, now twenty-six, with a master's in business, was waiting.

"Did you check luggage?"

I was carrying the briefcase and a recent issue of *Journal of Invertebrate Pathology.*

"Never."

"Ah . . . I forgot. All those research trips, studying fish in foreign countries. What's the secret to packing light?"

"Simple. Wear dark clothes, and always save your second pair of socks for the flight home."

The girl laughed as we hugged. "Doc

Ford, the mysterious biologist. I picked the right guy."

I said, "It's been awhile. We'll see."

Shay had her arm around my waist, shoulder wedged into ribs, thumb hooked to my belt. She was her usual affectionate, alpha-female self, body docked to mine so she could steer me efficiently toward baggage, or her awaiting car. But there was an intensity to the way she hugged close. This was a frightened women desperate for asylum. Had I provided it?

Life may be a chemical-electrical process, but living is a procession of uncertainties, one damn thing after another. Somehow, that truth makes lying easier.

"Did everything . . . go okay?"

"Couldn't have gone smoother."

"You feel good about it?"

"Better than expected. Very businesslike. We've been dealing with pros."

"The money transferred from my account fast enough. I checked. Geezus, one hell of a chunk. Were you . . . surprised by the amount?"

Not surprised, shocked. But I replied, "A lot of money."

"My entire savings."

"You've saved that much since college?"

"Well . . . plus Daddy's life insurance."

15

"Insurance? He didn't seem like the type."

"I know, I know — a man like him being thoughtful was as unexpected as him dying. I thought I told you about the check. After the honeymoon, Michael and I could've —"

"It's done. You said you weren't going to beat yourself up when I got back. I'm back."

"You're right. You know the way I ought to see it? Like it's an investment in the future. I have to keep reminding myself. Our future, Michael and me."

We exited the terminal into the sodium glare of asphalt and Everglades heat. It was a Thursday in June, a little before midnight, less than ten days until the girl's wedding. There were stars up there above palm trees.

"So he gave you the . . . thing."

"Yes." The briefcase was on my opposite shoulder, and I tapped it. "In here."

I felt her body stiffen. "The only copy?"

"I don't know. That's the deal you made. But it's his game, his rules."

"Do you know why . . . why I paid the money?"

"I have a pretty good idea."

"So you watched."

"Just the beginning. You and your brides-

16

maids were on a patio by a swimming pool, a view of the ocean below. With three men I assume were locals — so the party was just getting started. That was enough."

"Really?"

"Really."

Another lie. The video had been queued to footage that was unambiguously graphic. I'd watched for a few seconds, skipped ahead, then couldn't hit the power button fast enough.

Yes, we had been dealing with a pro, but there were also symptoms of pathology. Voyeurism plus cruelty. Her blackmailer enjoyed humiliating his victims.

Shay laughed to disguise relief. "Thanks for being a gentleman. Not that there's anything really *bad*. Just stupid. The sort of things we did in college — smoke grass, smooch with strangers. But Michael wouldn't have understood. None of our guys would, even though it seemed harmless at the time. We tried to turn the clock back — Liz, Corey, Beryl, and me — and have one last fling . . . only now, I wish we'd never heard of that damn island. By October, we'll all be married. And we've got professions. We're grown-ups now, not sorority girls."

I'd just lied to Shay, so why did I find it so irritating that she was lying to me? My own moral code varies with time zones and border crossings, plus I do not accept the premise that human behavior can be separated neatly into columns of right and wrong. So who the hell am I to judge? But I am neither so jaundiced nor naïve that I don't know the difference between a kiss and a blow job.

"Aren't grown-ups also supposed to accept responsibility for their behavior?" I said.

The woman stopped walking for a moment, her expression indignant, then sped ahead. "I don't care for your tone, buddy boy."

"Then stop treating me like I'm stupid."

"I have no idea what you're talking about!"

"Really? You didn't pay a hundred thousand dollars to spare your future husband seeing you smoke dope and kiss a stranger."

"I just told you: Michael's the jealous type. Like most guys, there's a double standard. It doesn't matter if it was innocent fun. He wouldn't have understood."

"I flew halfway to the equator and back because of innocent fun? Knock it off, Shay. I know better."

"Damn it! You said you didn't watch the video!"

The woman slowed enough for me to catch up, eyes searching. The footage I'd seen was disturbing. What I had not seen was there in her eyes, and it sickened her.

I said, "I don't give a damn what's on this tape. Whatever perceived sins, your girls' weekend couldn't have been any worse than a lot of bachelor parties. Okay? And it sure as hell doesn't compare to some of the things I've done in my life." I cut her off before she interrupted. *"Don't* ask. We're all entitled to our secrets. The point is, I'm your friend. As of today, I'm also your partner. So no more evasions.

"When you asked me to fly south and make the exchange, I did — no questions asked. Now I expect the truth. Because there's a chance we're going to hear from him again."

Shay stopped and faced me. She took a shuddering breath, and in a voice I hadn't heard since she was a teen, she whispered, "Oh . . . Ford, I hope . . . I so hope you're wrong."

I swept the girl into my free arm and held her, thumping my hand on her back. "Me, too, Shay. But if it happens, no surprises, okay? Because it's started."

"What? *What's* started? I don't understand."

I meant the lie we'd created. It now had a life of its own. Unlike the truth, lies can't

19

survive independently. They're quasi matter, like something sewn together in a lab, and require monitoring.

"If we're not straight with each other," I told her, "our friendship will be the first casualty. Your marriage could be the second."

"My God, Doc," the girl said, pushing away, "don't even say that. Damn it! I did what I was supposed to do. I paid the money. I'm safe now, aren't I? We deserve to be safe!"

"This has nothing to do with what you deserve. Fairness isn't bankable. Right now, the guy may be rethinking your payment schedule because fear has an *exact* dollar value. He's a pirate, not an entrepreneur."

I put my arm around her waist, and we continued toward the parking garage. "You're saying he'll want more money after the wedding."

That's what I was thinking. She was marrying Michael Jonquil, a third-generation Swiss-American whose family was regal, Lear jet–wealthy, and politically connected — Michael was running for a state house seat in the fall.

I replied, "Possibly. Depends on the fear factor. That's why you have to be honest. I don't need details. Just a realistic understanding of how much leverage the man has."

"Fear, huh?"

"Isn't that what business negotiation is all about?"

"Guilt's more like it. Or shame." She was talking about herself.

I said, "Then let's hope he didn't keep a copy of the tape."

2

It wasn't until we were in Shay's toy-sized convertible, traveling west, top down, that she spoke again. The long silence suggested a prelude to confession — not without reason.

"Remember the first e-mail demanding money? I told you he sent video samples as an attachment."

I remembered. It was eight days ago. Less than a week after Shay and friends returned from Saint Arc, an island only a few miles from Saint Lucia, off the coast of South America. Shay had downloaded the video files, but the files were corrupt, she said. The clips wouldn't open.

I'd urged her to contact the FBI, but she refused. I should've insisted. I didn't.

I asked, "What about the files?"

"They weren't corrupt. What he filmed was corrupt — things the girls and I did on Saint Arc. I trashed the clips because I knew you'd want to see everything when I asked for help. Like it was evidence."

"It was that bad?"

"Bad enough. Michael and I won't be getting married next week if he gets hold of the tape. Beryl and Liz's wedding plans will be wrecked, and Corey's husband — he's such a violence freak — he'd kill someone if he finds out. Maybe he'd kill Corey. And she didn't even do anything. Not really. Just the fact she was with us, he'd go orbital."

Shay paused to turn south, downshifting as she slalomed between slower vehicles, picking lanes then accelerating: a decisive female whose driving mirrored her personality — not always good in an overpowered, undersized car. I no longer lectured her on the dangers of tailgating and accelerating through intersections. Putting my hands on the dash had become my way of saying *Slow the hell down.*

When traffic thinned, though, she lost her edge. She sat back and let the night sky tunnel above us, thinking things through before giving me her attention.

"Who'm I kidding. Of course you're right. I wouldn't let someone con that much money if all we'd done was smoke and play kissy face with the local cabana boys — which would've been bad enough as far as Michael's family is concerned. I was too embarrassed to give you the details. Sorry."

"Don't apologize. It was the smart way to deal with it. At first."

"Really?"

"Sure. There was no reason for me to know. But now — "

"Okay. So that's why I'm telling you. Truth is, the three guys in the video? We all ended up in the swimming pool. Naked — except for Corey, but even she took her top off. The cameraman must've been hidden on the hillside above our rental house. It looked like jungle, but that's where he had to be." Shay lowered her voice to a whisper. "Doc, you've got to swear you won't tell a soul about Corey. *Ever.* Vance is nuts. Seriously."

I'd never met Corey's husband. He was a bodybuilder; a sometimes actor. I'd heard the stories of his steroid rages and cocktail-party dramas. His temper had gotten him fired from his job as a firefighter.

I said, "Don't worry."

Shay nodded, concentrating on her driving again. "There were only a couple shots of Corey, but enough to make him crazy. Beryl and Liz took their suits off, too. But most of the close-ups are of me. In fact, the asshole cameraman made me the star."

Before I could catch myself, I said, "If your

girlfriends were nude, why pick on you?"

If the question offended her, she didn't react. Or maybe she was confident enough to be unfazed. Shay was no longer the pinch-faced teen I'd met eight years ago. The adolescent brown hair was now a luxurious maple, the baby fat was gone, the clothes stylish. She was attractive in a solid, assertive way, but our instinctual perception of beauty has to do with symmetry and proportions. Shay's facial proportions were off — nose a little too thick, lips too thin, and the columella, the divider that separates her nostrils, was creased.

Her maid of honor, Beryl Woodward, though, was an auburn Grace Kelly who radiated ice when she entered a room, then slowly filled the space with heat. Her bridesmaid Liz made extra money modeling swimsuits. Corey was about to sign a film contract when she met the domineering man who became her husband. Yet the voyeur had singled out Shay?

"Maybe it had something to do with the guy I was with," she said. "He was the leader . . . that was my impression. He wore a pirate bandanna and was a little too good-looking. Like a fashion model, but nice — or so I thought. He was younger . . . twenty-one. We flirted. He was a good dancer, and dancing is something I never get to do since I got engaged.

"In the pool, he and I . . . the two of us drifted off into a corner and . . . we played around for a while, then . . . and then the three guys got dressed and left. And that's all that happened."

She was having second thoughts. This amended version had been assembled as she talked.

There was a bottle of water in the cup holder. I took a long drink, then opened my briefcase and began to separate travel documents from travel trash. We were on Summerlin Road. The causeway that links the mainland with Sanibel was ahead, the new skyway bridge arching into summer darkness. To the south, Estero Island was a yellow necklace of condo lights. We were through the tollgate, halfway across the bay, before Shay broke the silence.

"Why don't you say something?"

"I was waiting for you to finish."

"I did. That's the whole story. Nothing sexual happened because that's a line we didn't cross. None of us girls did. Not technically sexual, I'm saying."

"Technically sexual," I repeated.

"You know what I mean."

"Nope, I'm a biologist, and I wouldn't at-

26

tempt a guess. But it doesn't matter. If the blackmailer kept a copy of the video, how much power does it give him six months from now? Or a year from now if Michael's elected to the legislature? Or in six years if you start a company, and it's about to go public?"

"Jesus Christ, what a nightmare even to think about."

"Maybe. But it's better to deal with it now."

"Why? I just told you — we didn't do anything wrong."

"All right. In that case, there's no reason to worry."

"You say that like you don't believe me."

"I *choose* to believe you because you're too smart to risk giving me bad information. I just explained what's at stake."

"You *don't* believe me!"

"I'm discussing security. You're fixating on morality. Why? That's not my engagement ring on your finger."

"Don't be nasty."

"I'm not."

"Bullshit, buddy-ruff. If you want to draw blood, you need heavier ammo. Maybe you forget I come from redneck country, the toughest and nastiest sort. I'm not bulletproof, but the small-caliber

27

stuff bounces off."

I smiled. "Oh, I see. So now I'm talking to the *real* Shay Money. Not the faker who earned scholarships, graduated cum laude, won umpteen awards, and is fast becoming the administrative darling of a Sanibel clothing company."

"That Sanibel clothing company," she replied, her tone icy and impatient, "happens to be an international company listed on NASDAQ."

I said, "Sorry. The founders of Chico's used to keep me updated. We've lost touch."

"Is that another jab about how I got my job? Maybe I haven't thanked you enough. Okay, I'll say it again: *Thanks.*"

I was still smiling. "Do you realize your piney-woods accent comes back when you're mad? File that tidbit away so all the people you think you're fooling don't stumble onto the truth about the real Shay Money. Or have you gone back to using Shanay?"

The woman growled in frustration. "Don't call me that. You can be such an asshole."

"It's the only way I can relate to anal-retentive friends."

Bridge lights shadowed her scowl in rhythmic panels as we descended onto the island. "Okay, *okay.* So I'm not proud of what's on the video. I've spent the last seven years trying to become someone I'm not. Maybe the mask finally slipped when we were on Saint Arc. White trash, that's what the camera captured. Me. Yeah, the *real* me, and cameras don't lie. What do you expect from the daughter of Dexter Ray Money?"

The late Dex Money, Shay's father, was one of the foulest men I'd ever met.

"Excuses," I said. "Self-pity and excuses — that's what I'd expect . . . if I didn't know you so well."

I watched the girl straighten. After a moment, she whispered, "My God, that's what I'm doing, isn't it? I'm acting just like *him*."

I pretended not to hear.

A moment later, she said, "Thanks. Thanks for the boot in the butt. Doc, you *are* right. I may be the daughter of . . . of —" Her voice thickened, then she slapped the steering wheel. "I may be his daughter, but I sure don't have to behave like that sad, dead son of a bitch."

I nodded and sipped my water.

"All his life, he did nothing but get trickier and cuter when he was in trouble. He hurt the people who cared for him, and he made excuses — mostly to cops. And you're no cop. I owe you a lot. You and your sister. The way you two helped when you had no reason in the world to help. I've been lying

29

to you, and Ransom, too. If I can't tell you two the truth, who can I trust?"

Ransom Gatrell is my cousin, not my sister, but I no longer bother correcting people.

Shay sniffled, her voice still shaky, but she got the words out: "Sorry, Doc. Give me a sec?"

I said, "Relax. It's no big deal." Then, for some reason, I had to add, "Everything's going to be okay. I promise."

3

On Sanibel, Shay downshifted and turned onto Periwinkle, the island's main drag. She drove in silence, tilting her head so wind could find her hair. The road was narrowed by tree shadow, and I gulped air that tasted of saltwater and asphalt-scented rain. When returning from an airport, after a long flight, the dulled intimacies of home become fresh again. So why did I feel restless?

I'd missed something. Not long flights . . . but elements that were associated with travel.

It had been a while, as I told Shay.

Until that moment, I'd considered the trip an interruption. June's a good month in Florida. Squalls and heat begin their metrical interplay. Tourism slows, fishing's superb, mangoes are ripe. The old fish camp marina where I live is at its quirky best because the reduced population allows locals to focus on their own small dramas.

My personal dramas had taken a pleasant turn. A love interest from the past had returned, and I'd been weighing the pros and cons of resuming the relationship. I had unusual projects under way in my lab. My son was healthy, my daughter was growing, and the mothers of each child were happily occupied with their own lives, so rarely caused trouble in mine. And vice versa.

Summer is a favorite time of year, and Florida's personal little secret. So why travel?

But friendship isn't a recreational vehicle. It is a covenant. I take the obligations seriously. So I dropped everything when the girl yelled *help*.

Now I pretended to concentrate on my briefcase as Shay wrestled with the decision to tell me the truth, or stick with her story.

"Okay . . . I'll start at the beginning and tell you what really happened."

"I'd appreciate that."

"Jesus, Doc . . . this is so damn embarrassing. We were so stupid! It isn't easy to talk about."

I said, "I'll match my personal stupidities with anyone's. You're safe with me."

"Humph." It was the sound of reflection. "True. Always have been with you. I remember the first time I laid eyes on you. You were soaking wet, all dressed in black,

and I thought you'd come to rob us —"

Patiently, I said, "We were talking about your girls' weekend in the Caribbean."

"Oh, yeah. Sorry. Well . . . my bridesmaids deserved a break. Michael and I are having a huge wedding. I've delegated a lot of the work to those ladies. Plus, planning a wedding — and this may come as a surprise to a guy like you — but planning a wedding is one of the most stressful things you can imagine. I've read it ranks up there with buying a house or dealing with a friend's death. I was about crazy, and we all needed a break."

I said, "You've always been generous," letting her get to the truth in her own way.

"I decided on a surprise vacation, just the four of us. I asked around for travel tips, narrowed it down to a couple of islands, then asked around until I found the perfect girls' hideaway. Our own seaside house, secluded but with shopping, lots of books, yoga, and a private beach for topless sunbathing. A really wicked beach. That's the way I described it in the invitations. Unfortunately, it came exactly as advertised."

It wasn't their first trip. She and her friends liked exotic destinations, away from local gossips.

"We've had our secret fun, sure. We trust

each other not to blab. The saintly, girly-girl types are a pain in the ass — after all those years in Catholic school? But we are *not* sluts. And we never came close to getting as wild as we did on Saint Arc. I swear to God, I still don't understand how it got out of control."

When Shay sensed me looking at her, she huffed, "I mean it. It was our last night on the island. The last time we'd ever be together free and single since finishing our master's degrees, and we'd been bawling all day. Life changes so damn *fast.* We wanted to cut loose and have some laughs. But it was a Sunday night, nothing going on.

"That's when the men appeared. Three strangers.

"They came strolling onto our private little beach, looking for a party some movie people were throwing. Supposedly. They were polite and funny. We invited them in. They made special margaritas. A little later, we put on music and started dancing. But we didn't pair off right away. It was more of a group thing."

Shay told me the guys brought a couple of joints, local grass. She hadn't smoked since college.

"Because I was high, the whole scene seemed hilarious. But innocent. Us with these good-looking dudes with French or Caribbean accents, passing around a joint. Maybe because they were younger, we felt in control. They didn't even realize we were laughing at *them,* so cool-acting. But then it got to be more like a dare between us girls when the guys said they wanted to get in the pool. Who'd be the first to say 'stop'? Beryl or Liz, Corey or me?"

No one said stop. The night kept going.

Shay leaned toward the steering wheel, no longer guarded. "It was my party, and I let it go too far. I don't know why, and it's driving me nuts."

I said, "You didn't force your friends. They're older than you. Beryl's, what, three or four years older?"

"Four. And she's the queen of Ice Queens — usually — and she was the first one with her suit off. But it doesn't matter. I was in charge. I didn't stop it when I had the chance. Everything felt slow and dreamy. They told us the grass was really strong shit, but man, I don't know."

"You think they slipped you something else?"

"I've wondered about it. If they did, I hope I never get the chance to buy the stuff because I don't think I could pass up the chance. The feeling was incredible. Like someone hit the happy switch, and all my stress was gone. It was also like . . . like I got a dose of aphrodisiac down where it counts."

I turned to her as she turned to me. "You wanted honesty? I'm being honest. Maybe it was the dope. Maybe it was the guys — all muscles and curls. The other girls, they'd have to speak for themselves. But I lost control. What I did was wrong. I knew it, but I couldn't stop myself. The way my body reacted . . . it was like riding a slow wave. The sensation was *unreal.* How clinical do you want me to be?"

I was shaking my head as I replied, "You can still be blackmailed, that's all I need to know —" But she interrupted, saying, "No, I want to tell the rest. I'm not embarrassed now. I don't want you to be. Maybe a man can make sense of what happened, because I'm driving myself nuts with guilt, trying to figure it out. I love Michael. I'm monogamous by nature. I didn't even fantasize about other men after we started dating. But now . . . after the way it was that night on the island. My *God.*"

I interrupted. "Ransom's from the Bahamas. Why not wait and talk to us both?"

"What? Now you *don't* want the truth?"

We'd turned right on Tarpon Bay Road, and were pulling into a mangrove lane, bay

36

side, feeling air humid and dense descend on the convertible. The gate to Dinkin's Bay Marina was locked. Nearby, the path to my laboratory was marked by a glimmer through the trees, and also a friend's bicycle: a fat-tire cruiser, peace signs painted on the fenders, and a basket on the handlebars that read, FAUSTOS — KEY WEST.

"Tomlinson's here. Must be something important if he's ashore this late." I spoke as if surprised, but I expected him to be waiting. Tomlinson is a boat bum, a Zen teacher, a womanizer, a hipster academic, and my neighbor. He and Shay were close, but not confidants. It was a welcome intrusion. I was interested in assembling data about the woman's blackmailer, but I didn't want to hear her confession. It would include admissions, I felt sure, that would later distance us.

I asked, "Can we talk tomorrow?"

"*Tomorrow.* The wedding's only nine days away. I don't have time to breathe. But . . . okay, if that's what you want, I'll make time. What I don't understand is, what does Ransom and the Bahamas have to do with —"

I said, "Saint Arc and the Bahamas have some similarities — cultural, I mean. She might pick up on things I'll miss."

"Like what?"

"Don't know. But those guys didn't come to your beach house accidentally. A cameraman wasn't positioned with a view of the pool accidentally. What you felt, how you felt — maybe it was the drugs. Maybe it was you. We're human. Ransom will have a better read on that, too. Either way, you were targeted. That's why I'd like to wait awhile before we destroy the tape."

"In case the cops get involved? Look, I don't care what happens, no one can ever see that damn video —"

"No. I want a closer look at the cassette. The brand; how it's wrapped. Maybe I can learn something. I'll keep it locked. You can trust me."

"I *do* trust you. But . . . you absolutely have to swear you won't get curious and —"

"I didn't watch it when I had a reason. I'm not going to watch now."

"Okay . . . okay. When you're ready, we'll burn the damn thing and drink cheap champagne to celebrate. Doc . . . ?"

"Yeah?"

"I'm sorry I got you into this . . . made you fly to that damn island when you'd rather be here, messing with fish and your test tubes and books. I know how much you love that old house and lab. I tell everyone about the place."

"When you asked me to be your unofficial godfather, I said *yes,* remember? It comes with the job. You also happen to be worth it."

"That's not how I feel. I feel like a tramp."

"Don't. When I told you to accept responsibility, I didn't know the story. You were set up by someone who is very, very good. So stop punishing yourself. It's what victims do — even when the guilt belongs to some asshole who gets his kicks preying on weaker people."

"I've never been called weak in my life."

"That's not the kind of weakness I'm talking about."

"Then why would I do something so damn stupid and destructive so close to my wedding?"

I didn't reply. The question wasn't mine to answer. I waited in the chirring silence of frogs and mosquitoes until she made an attempt.

"I worry that . . . no matter how good I get at pretending, I can't change the blood that's in me. I'm *afraid,* Doc. Scared that I'll go back to being what I was born to be, no matter how hard I fight. What's the term? Self-sabotage?"

"Don't be silly."

"The voice inside a person's head may be wrong, but it's not silly. It tells me I can't change where I came from. Especially when I pull some crazy stunt like this. Your house and lab — that's who *you* are. You told me that once."

Had I? I didn't remember the conversation, so I said, "We identify with all kinds of things. But we don't come preprogrammed. We make choices."

"It wasn't by choice I grew up believing I was redneck trash. That little voice knows. Sometimes it tries to drag me back into the hole where Daddy lived."

"A panther would be easier to drag into a hole. That's what I think."

We were out of the car. Shay stood facing me. I couldn't see her clearly in the car's parking lights, and for a moment I thought I'd made her laugh. No . . . she was crying. I let her lean into my arms and held her, face buried in my chest. As she sobbed, I stroked her hair until the spasms slowed.

"You're too stubborn to go back to that world. You're also too smart — take my word."

"I wish I was as confident. I've worked so hard to get where I am, but that damn little voice is real. It keeps reminding me I'm Dexter Money's daughter. It's like a curse."

I gave her a little shake. "Women with master's degrees don't waste time on superstitious crap. They aren't afraid of witches and dragons and trolls — unless you count the insurance adjuster you dated from South Beach."

The girl snorted, hiccupped, and began to sniffle. "Oh, God! Don't remind me."

After a minute, I said, "Why don't you come inside? Have some tea, lie in the hammock, and look at the stars until you calm down."

"Can't. I have so damn much to do. Planning the wedding is pressure enough. Three hundred people, half of them speak French, and the only woman that ever impressed my future mother-in-law is a dead virgin named Mary. The perfect Catholic girl — kept her knees together but still gave birth to a saint like Michael. And Joseph actually *believed* her. Now I have to deal with this bullshit."

"She's that bad, huh?"

"Michael's mother? Her name's Ida. As in *'I'd'a* rather never met her. Ida is a ballbreaker, especially when it comes to other women — maybe because she has six sisters. Michael says they're ball-breakers. Lots of family money, but still serious overachievers. All five are coming to the wedding. Now do you see why I ran away to the Caribbean?"

"All six sisters, you mean."

"No . . . just the five. One's an invalid; lives at a facility near Paris because of some kind of birth defect. His mother doesn't talk about it — probably because it would be admitting her family's not perfect."

I smiled. "Have you been getting any sleep?"

"You've got to be kidding. Even if I take a couple of Xanax, I wake up in the middle of the night, my heart pounding so hard it shakes the bed. Sometimes I feel like I really am going insane."

"When did you start taking Xanax?"

"It's one of my prescriptions. Everyone takes Xanax. Or something like it. They're mild."

"*One* of your prescriptions?"

"Yes, Dr. Ford, I have more than one prescription. Do you even realize what a prude you can be? They're for when I get overwhelmed. Like right now."

"Instead of taking a pill, stay here. I'll be up most the night anyway, working in the lab. You're not crazy; I think you're having panic attacks. Talk to Tomlinson. He can discuss both from personal experience."

It got a chuckle, but her tone said, *Why do I bother?*

Shay gave me a squeeze, pulled away as

she wiped her eyes, then added a smile to prove she was under control. "Thanks, but I can't stay. Beryl's dad will be worried if I'm not home soon. You know how he is."

No, I didn't know. Shay had been unofficially adopted into Beryl Woodward's family during college, but all I knew about the father was that he'd made a pile of money buying floundering hotels and turning them into five-star resort spas. He would be giving Shay away at the wedding. For some reason, Shay found the topic awkward, so seldom mentioned it.

I asked, "Does he know what happened on Saint Arc?"

"Bill? Good lord, he wouldn't believe it, anyway."

"What about Beryl?"

"About being blackmailed? I told you, my bridesmaids don't know anything."

"That was before we agreed to be straight."

"I *am* being straight. There's no reason to drag the girls into this."

"If you haven't discussed it, how do you know they weren't sent the same video samples?" It wasn't the first time I'd asked.

"Because I would *know*, okay? I'm the one who rented the beach house, so my personal information's all over that goddamn island by now. And there was no reason for the girls to give out their e-mail addresses. So why involve them?"

"I can think of a hundred and nine thousand reasons. You paid the whole tab."

"I told you right off the guy wanted money. I told you I was negotiating."

"You didn't tell me it was six figures."

"Maybe I'd have done it different if it wasn't for the life insurance. At first, the jerk wanted a quarter million. We settled for what I had in cash."

"That's very thoughtful. You have lucky friends."

"We're like sisters. They'd do the same."

"That's what's surprising. You're so close, I'd think you'd want to share the burden. Or at least warn them."

"We *are* close," Shay replied, her voice louder. "Just like Michael's close with Beryl's fiancé. And Liz's fiancé. And he's pals with Corey's husband, even though Vance is a dick. They were *fraternity brothers* at Gainesville, for God's sake. Summers, Michael and Elliot both worked for Beryl's father, renovating old hotels. That's the point. We are a tight little group. If one of our guys finds out, all the guys find out."

"I guess that makes sense."

"Does that mean I get an *A?*" she snapped.

"I thought that part was obvious. How many times have you heard me talk about Michael and his buddies? Maybe *you* need to lie in the hammock and get some rest."

That quick, the tears were gone.

"No reason to get mad."

"I'm not mad, just tired. We can talk tomorrow, but tonight? I don't feel like repeating myself." Abruptly, Shay was her alpha-female self, sliding into the car, impatient and eager to get going.

She was also lying again. Why?

I thought about it as Shay drove away. I didn't doubt she was protecting her bridesmaids. The video might contain shots of them that were equally graphic. But it was also possible that something else happened that night on Saint Arc, and the camera had captured it.

Shay hadn't lied about being intimate with a stranger. For a young bride, what could be worse? So it had to be something she considered even more incriminating. A crime . . . an accident . . . what?

The pressure was getting to her. There'd been an edge of hysteria in her voice. Telling. The girl didn't rattle easily.

It worried me. On another level, it also disappointed me — my small, selfish reaction to the girl being human instead of the caricature I had created. I admired Shay Money, so I'd constructed that caricature to mirror my own conceits.

The girl wasn't exaggerating when she spoke of her toughness. Shanay Lucinda Money grew up motherless, servant to an abusive seven-foot, three-hundred-pound father who brokered dogfights and smuggled cocaine. Once, when Shay's ninth-grade boyfriend misspoke, Dexter Money had stripped the boy naked, then forced his daughter to watch while he spanked the kid raw. The boy was so intimidated, he never told the cops.

At sixteen, Shay single-handedly extracted herself from Dexter's influence, moved out, moved on, and changed lives. She got her GED while working a full-time job, then continued studying her butt off until she was offered academic scholarships at the University of Florida. The troubled girl with the redneck accent gradually vanished, along with her name. Shanay Lucinda became Shay — just Shay.

The reinvented Shay knew what she wanted, and where to find it. Even with the scholarships, she had to work nights, but she still found time to seek out the wealthy and the well-educated. She wangled invitations to their parties, then stayed quietly in the background, listening and remembering, until she'd learned the social niceties.

Shay once said to me, "People who inherit wealth tend to inherit beauty. You ever notice that? But they seem less hung up on looks when it comes to choosing a mate. That's not as true of people who pile up their own fortune — you know, guys who want trophy brides. Why, do you think?"

The question was touching: Shay has a buxom, Southern, pheromone sensuality, but she's not a great beauty, and the question implied that a man who'd inherited wealth would be more likely to find her attractive.

I'd told her I was a biologist, not a social scientist. That was Tomlinson's field. Even so, I was impressed by her gift for observation, and her unsentimental approach to mapping a future. Shay was soon an accepted associate of that interesting caste known as Old Money. Once married to Michael Jonquil, she would become a full-fledged member.

I saw less and less of her, but she stayed in touch.

Through the generosity of her new friends, Shay had spent two weeks skiing the Alps. She'd spent a jet-set summer attending parties in Italy, France, and Switzerland. During her travels, she established a reputation as a first-rate organizer, and it leap-frogged her several rungs up the corporate ladder when she went job-hunting.

The redneck girl with cheek had been transformed, but her core toughness remained. Or so I believed. I had never seen Shay lose control. Never saw her concede to weakness, nor look back in fear. Never saw her cry — until tonight.

A tenet of biology is that trauma catalyzes change. It's true on a cellular level. It's true on an emotional level. Something traumatic had happened that night on Saint Arc. What?

As I walked the boardwalk to my lab, I slipped my hand into the briefcase and confirmed the video was there. No . . . I did it because my first instinct was to borrow a Minicam, lock myself in a room, and watch the tape from beginning to end. It contained information. Maybe an answer.

What had the lens captured? Why was the tough girl so frightened?

The cassette was tiny, half the size of my palm. It was unsettling how easily the lives of four complex women had been harvested, digitized, and trivialized on a few ounces of recyclable plastic.

Put this videotape in the wrong hands, and touch *play?* Their futures would be erased.

4

Tomlinson was in the lab, barefooted, wearing a baseball uniform, jersey unbuttoned, hair braided Willie Nelson style. He was talking on the VHF radio when I pushed the screen door open, and he paused to wag a warning finger. *Quiet.*

He'd been as irreverent and optimistic as ever, but was also dealing with a loss of personal confidence, so I attempted humor. "Sorry. I thought this was the men's room."

I closed the door, crossed the breezeway to my quarters, and went inside, switching on lights. I use yellow bulbs near windows because mosquitoes have primitive eyes that don't recognize the color yellow. The little bastards do not fly toward light they cannot see.

Mosquitoes come with the location. I live in what is known as a "fish house" — two small houses built over water on stilts, under a single tin roof. In the early 1900s, fish were stored in one house, fishermen in the other. I now own the property — outdoor shower, rain cistern, and wobbly boardwalks included. Shay was right. I like the place. It's become part of who I am.

Dinkin's Bay Marina, three hundred yards down the mangrove shore, is a neighbor. Another is Tomlinson, whose sailboat, *No Más,* is moored equidistant from the docks, although he behaves as if he owns my property, too — irritating, at times.

Tonight, though, it was okay. He'd been at the propane stove earlier — I could smell fried fish — and he is one of the few self-anointed gourmets who doesn't overcook seafood. Just as uncommon, he cleans up after himself.

I walked beneath ceiling fans to the galley, where I found a platter of snapper, fresh lime, and mango slices. I squeezed lime on the fillets until they glistened, I squeezed lime on the mango, then went through the day's mail as I ate.

There was a manila envelope from a medical lab in Tampa. It contained copies of an MRI brain scan my neurologist had ordered because of headaches that had become more than occasional. I assumed they were caused by a head injury. The doctor wasn't convinced, so I spent half an hour in a tube that bonged and clanked while electron magnets scanned.

The neurologist had already called with the results, so I only stared at the envelope for a moment before I pushed it aside. Then I stacked bills atop it, separating envelopes that were addressed by hand.

There was a letter from an Iowa attorney that I knew would be distressing — it concerned my daughter, and visitation rights. Two other letters from women were of mild interest. A fourth letter, from a man, was of uncommon interest. I studied the labored handwriting. The return address read, *Merlin T. Starkey.*

Merlin Starkey had been a cop in the Everglades south of Sanibel. Years ago, he'd investigated the boat explosion that killed my parents, back when I was a kid. Officially, it was ruled an accident of "undetermined cause," but Starkey and I both knew better. For years, I blamed it on a faulty fuel valve installed by my crazy uncle.

Wrong, Starkey informed me awhile back. He knew who did it, he'd told me — but he wouldn't share the name until after his own death.

I had read Starkey's obituary in last week's newspaper. Even so, to see the man's shaky handwriting days after he, too, had gone to

52

ground was unexpected, and I was momentarily flummoxed.

Merlin Starkey was an old-time Southern cop: Stetson hat, boots, string bow tie with ingratiating manners that masked a nasty disposition. He'd bait punks with his slow, dumb drawl — "You tellin' the truth, young captain?" — professional enough to baton the big city out of them without leaving a bruise. But the man kept his word.

Here was proof, the letter he'd promised. Inside was the name of the person responsible for the deaths of my mother and father . . . the person who'd murdered them, or so Starkey had insinuated.

I am not sentimental. Even as a child I was impatient with the ceremonies of childhood. By the time I was nineteen, I'd logged too many miles to abide unnecessary baggage. But I have a sustained interest in learning the truth. Not a driving interest, but an interest. As a biologist, assembling puzzles is what I do.

Finally, here was a puzzle's last piece.

Who did it?

So why did I now find myself reluctant to open Starkey's letter?

Strange.

I held the envelope between thumb and index finger, as if it were evidence, then held it to the light. It was inexpensive paper, taped at the back, stationery folded inside, no writing visible. I shook it, sniffed it, and nearly smiled. It smelled of horse stalls. Distinctive. Starkey had used Copenhagen snuff until the end.

He'd written my name and *Sanibel Island, FLA* with a fountain pen. But my address was squeezed between in blue ballpoint, a woman's hand — the old man had sealed the envelope, but didn't know my address, so a nurse or maybe an attorney's secretary had added it later.

What did these additional fragments matter? I was stalling. Why?

Did I fear the truth? Or treachery? The same crazed uncle I'd blamed for the explosion was guilty of swindling Starkey, and Starkey had nursed a grudge for fifty years. Maybe duping me, a nephew, was a way of finally getting even. What if the note was blank? Or Starkey had named an innocent person?

Or . . . did I fear something else?

Enough.

I placed Starkey's letter on the counter by the stove with the rest of the mail. I'd waited a lifetime to learn the truth. I could wait another hour . . . *if* there was truth to be learned.

There were more pressing matters. I opened the letter from the Iowa attorney I'd hired — distressing, as expected, and out of my control. So I turned my attention to things I could control. I'd promised Shay that her video would be safe. My past was past. Her future was bright. Maybe brilliant.

I washed the platter, then carried the brief-case to my sleeping quarters and pushed the bed aside. Beneath was a recent addition: ship's carpentry. By turning two flush-set brass locks, I could remove a section of flooring and access a locker that was roomy, dry, and difficult to find.

From the locker, I took a fireproof box, swung it onto the bed, and unlocked it. Inside, I hid the evidence of Shay Money's secret weekend among mementos of my own secret life: notebooks, counterfeit passports, emergency euros, emeralds, and Mayan jade from the jungles of Central America.

There was also a gold locket engraved with a smiling full moon. I held the locket for a moment before sealing the box away.

At the laboratory door, I called, "Permission to enter?"

Once again, Tomlinson raised an impa-tient finger. He turned from the radio's mic and said, "You're not gonna believe this one.

Something very weird's happening out there tonight."

I asked, "Weird on the Tomlinson scale, or by amateur standards?" as I placed my briefcase on the dissecting table, and crossed the room to a row of saltwater aquaria. The aquaria were glowing rectangles inhabited by fish, squid, octopi, and predatory shells that I'd collected from local waters. There were also a couple of new specialty tanks.

"That's what I'm trying to find out. There's a lady in distress. But I lost contact."

"Why am I not surprised? I bet she's beautiful, too. So hail the lady again."

"I just did. I'm giving it a few seconds."

I'd stopped to inspect the new aquarium systems. They were unconventional. One contained poisonous shrimp. The other, venomous jellyfish. Both were projects recently contracted. The research was interesting. My new employer, less so. It was a State Department intelligence agency that had offered me a fat, full-time contract to work as a "preemptory specialist." My task was to anticipate ways the bad guys might attack the U.S. economy through tourism and saltwater food products.

The offer was not unexpected. A man named Kal Wilson had asked me to say yes if the agency came knocking. When a former president of the U.S. asks a favor from his deathbed, how can you refuse?

So I'd signed the contract. Tomorrow morning, three supervisors were coming to inspect my work, and to discuss my PATEE — Personnel Attitude and Task Efficiency Evaluation.

I dreaded it. There was a lot of paperwork to finish before they arrived at 10 a.m.

"How was the trip?" Tomlinson was looking at the briefcase, eyebrows raised. He'd been in the lab four nights earlier when Shay asked me to fly to Saint Arc. Fly to Saint Lucia, actually, and then take the ferry four miles to Saint Arc.

I told him, "Smoother than I'd hoped. They're pros. But instead of helping her, I think I only dug the hole deeper."

"You mean *we* dug the hole deeper." He was shaking his head, instantly mad at himself. "A Zen master's supposed to have balls, man. Lately, I couldn't find mine with a magnifying glass and a hammer."

I said, "Huh?" After a moment, I said, "Oh."

Tomlinson had tried to resist. He had warned Shay about deception and negative energy. I'd warned her that negotiating with an extortionist was like asking a cannibal to change the menu. Yet, she'd won us both over.

"Shay's persuasive."

"No. Shay's a steamroller. She didn't give us time to think it through. Start her marriage with a lie? It put me in such a karmic spin, I've already started the grunt research because I know the kimchi's gonna hit the fan." I followed his gaze to the office computer where he'd stacked articles on the desk. "Did she finally tell you why she's being blackmailed?"

I nodded. "The basics. But it's up to her to decide —"

"I'm not asking. I figured it out on my own. Caribbean islands aren't exactly free with their crime stats, but I mixed Google with some of my old psychic-viewing techniques. Take a look."

I went to the desk. For all his recreational excesses, chemical and otherwise, Tomlinson is an academic at heart. The research was methodical. He'd compiled stats and articles on Caribbean crime, along with figures from the wedding industry — average costs, median costs — all unrelated data until I picked up the yellow legal pad where he'd made notes.

Tomlinson's handwriting is an eloquent dance of loops and swirls — Spenserian script, he calls it. He credits it to his former life as a shipping clerk in eighteenth-century London.

I read:

On the Island of Saint Joan of Arc, in the Caribbean, where crime against tourists is seldom prosecuted, someone may have created a niche industry by targeting women for blackmail.

Statistically, victims are U.S. citizens, eighteen to sixty, women traveling alone or with other women . . .

Preferred targets are engaged to be married, and on holiday during the chaotic weeks prior to their wedding. These women are easy prey because: 1.) They are emotional wrecks. 2.) They have access to bank accounts that can be emptied quickly. 3.) Their wedding day adds the fear of public humiliation to the risk of personal humiliation . . .

Women in this demographic are viewed as raw product by the industry — not unlike harp seals in the fur industry. Entrapment using corrupt police, drugs, sex, hidden cameras, staged events, and phony arrests are likely methods.

I looked away from the legal pad. Tomlinson was adjusting the squelch on the radio.

"How'd you come up with the connection between blackmail and wedding bank accounts?"

The best guess he and I had mustered was that Shay had pissed off some government official, and I was traveling to Saint Arc to pay off the cops.

He said, "Intuitive reasoning. It's no secret I haven't been at peak strength, but my paranormal powers aren't completely on the fritz. So I gave it a shot."

"It's shrewd. Maybe brilliant."

"No kidding?"

"No kidding."

He appeared pleased and surprised. I could also tell that he was very stoned. "Well, the data provided indicators. Behavioral patterns can be predicted even if statistical interactions are vague. A statistical etching appeared, but I let Universal Mind fill the blanks. Universal Mind is all-knowing energy that —" He drifted. His focus shifted. "Are you stroking my ego? Or do you really think I'm right?"

Tomlinson had suffered a loss of confidence in the last few months. It happens.

"I think you nailed it. Shay's a perfect candidate. It's possible they started tracking her the day she made reservations." I was reviewing the figures. "These numbers are accurate? It's insane what people spend on weddings."

"Spoken like a determined bachelor — outrage mixed with secret relief. I agree, even though, prorated, my own wedding cost about a hundred bucks a week. Unless you tally the pounds of flesh taken by that Japanese succubus I married —"

I stopped him before he could get going. "You were telling me how you made the connection."

"Oh . . . yeah. The concept just came to me, man. The vision flowed into my consciousness the way things used to before I lost my cosmic rhythm. So maybe I'm getting my chops back. Or it could've been a lucky guess. Hey — Saint Arc isn't far from Venezuela. South America is your old stomping grounds. You have lots of special contacts. Why not have one of your spook pals check out the island, see if I'm right?"

I said, "I'm not sure if my special contacts talk to me anymore," referring to my recent change of employers.

Tomlinson considered that for a few seconds. "Ironic, huh? Your contacts in the jungle dried up at the same time my contacts in the cosmos took a powder. I can tell you exactly when it happened, too."

I shrugged. *Tell me.*

"It was when, after all those years of dealing with guilt — *wham* — we were both set free. Pardoned. You know what I'm talking about."

I nodded. Yes, I knew.

"But it's not like I thought it would be. Free to live like so-called average citizens? Safe little nine-to-five lives? That's a statistical trap, man, not freedom. Let me remind you that the average American citizen has one testicle, one breast, a three-inch clitoris, and watches football every fourteen days. I wasn't born to be average . . ."

Tomlinson stopped and looked at the radio, then changed subjects. "That's her. *Listen.*"

A woman's voice was calling, "Hello? Are you there? I'm trying to contact the man . . ." But then her voice faded.

He made a face, frustrated. "Damn, she keeps switching channels, so I get nothing but skip or bleed, then she's gone before I can catch her."

He pressed the transmit button. "This is base station Sanibel Biological Supply. I read you. Say again, please."

After a few seconds, he hailed her once more. I realized he was staring, interested in my reaction, as he said into the microphone, "I'm attempting recontact with the vessel

62

that reported sharks attacking the beach. I say again: The vessel reporting sharks attacking the beach, are you standing by, channel sixty-eight?"

I echoed, "Sharks attacking the beach?"

His expression replied: *See? I told you. Weird.*

Tomlinson wears baseball uniforms almost as often as he wears sarongs, but he'd actually played a game earlier, I realized. His pinstriped pants were stained orange from sliding, one thigh a strawberry blotch of blood. As we waited for the woman to respond, he mouthed the words, *I pitched today.*

I was interested. "You win?"

He shook his head. *No fucking defense.*

I smiled. "It should be on tombstones. Every pitcher's epitaph."

Aloud, he shot back, "Not just pitchers, man. Position players, too. It's the universal condition."

I shrugged, looking at his leg. "Steal a base?"

He tried to make me lip-read, but I didn't understand.

"Something bit me."

"What?"

He squinted at the radio, getting impatient. Why didn't the woman respond? He tried hailing her again, then waited through a long silence before answering my question. "About four nights ago, I got bit by something. An insect, maybe."

"Are you sure . . . ?" There was too much blood for an insect bite.

"Maybe. I didn't feel it at first. Then it started to burn . . . then yesterday morning, *wow.* My nervous system fired up. I felt like I had my lips on a moonshine still when lightning zapped it."

"An insect did that?"

"No . . . it doesn't compute. So maybe it was a snake. Or a vampire bat . . . something that injects high octane. I was in the lab when it happened, so who knows with all the far-out creepy crawlers you've been dealing with lately."

"It couldn't have been four nights ago. Shay was here. A Sunday."

"Then it was Monday . . . no, Tuesday, the night before you left for Saint Arc."

Zero time perception. Yes, the man was stoned.

I said, "That was night before last, not four days ago."

"*Exactly.* You had a date with the lady biologist, so I stopped by the lab to use the computer. I got nailed in here or on the porch. The hammock, possibly, where I paused to smoke a joint. I wish to hell I knew what bit me. I've felt like a million bucks ever since."

"You liked it?"

"*Incredible.* Like a pint of carburetor cleaner got pumped through my cerebral cortex. Now all my neuroreceptors feel real sparkly."

I was eyeing one of the new tanks, a low-turbulence Kreisel aquarium. It contained miniature jellyfish shipped to me in polyp stage from Australia. *Carukia.* The sea jellies were lucent parachutes, quarter-sized, with four retractable tentacles armed with a neurotoxin more potent than cobra venom. The stingers injected minuscule amounts, but could still be deadly.

It was a dangerous association to investigate, but I had to ask.

"When you were alone in the lab, did you follow safety procedures? Never lean over the tanks without safety glasses . . . or reach into the water without rubber gloves —"

"Have you confused me with Wally Cleaver? Of course I didn't follow the rules. But even drunk, on acid, I know better than to stick my ass into an aquarium full of fucking jellyfish. How stupid do you think I —"

There was the clack of a mic key, then a woman's voice came from the radio. Tomlinson turned up the volume.

"Hey, it's her again!"

"Someone hears me? Thank God! We have a rental boat, and I'm not sure how to work the radio. Is this the channel people talk on?"

Tomlinson grunted, frustrated again. The woman didn't release the microphone key when she was done transmitting. It was pointless to respond until she did. We could hear a child shouting in the background, then we heard a scream, then more clicking.

I asked, "Where are they?"

"I don't know. I got her first transmission as you came up the steps. She said something about sharks. It *sounded* like she said sharks were attacking the beach. But that can't be right. She's not faking — she's scared. It's tarpon season. The oceangoing meat-eaters have come shallow to feed. I'm afraid some midnight swimmer got whacked."

Walking toward the phone, I said, "I'll call the Coast Guard just in case," as Tomlinson tried again. "Sanibel Bio to the rental boat on channel sixty-eight. Listen to me! Press the button to talk. *Release* the button to listen. Tell me your name and location. Over."

The woman was already transmitting before he finished. ". . . I'll say it a third time! My name's Lynn. My daughters and I are camped on an island. We're on North Captiva, about a mile from the southern point. It's really dark because there's no moon, but we have flashlights. We're seeing what we think are sharks. Did you hear that? *Sharks.* Big sharks swimming with the waves right up on the beach. It's like they're trying to get to our tents. Everyone I talk to thinks I'm joking but damn it, *I am not joking!* Sometimes the sharks make it halfway. Then the water pulls them back. But they keep trying. It's like on TV when sharks chase seals. We're afraid to go near our tent!"

I told Tomlinson, "Those are *not* sharks."

He nodded as he lifted the mic. "I copy, Lynn. I'm here. Stay with me. I've got a question. How big are they? How big are the fish you think are sharks? Over."

"Big. Three or four times bigger than the porpoises we saw at Sea World. That's what I'm telling you! They're great white sharks, we think. Just like on TV. But they're black . . ."

In the background, a girl shrieked as the woman added, "My God, now *two* of them are out of the water! They're almost on the beach by our tents, slapping their tails. *Why*

67

are they doing this?"

I finished dialing the phone as Tomlinson tried to calm the woman. "You're not in danger. Trust me on this, Lynn. Listen to what I'm about to tell you . . ."

Then I couldn't hear him because I was moving fast out the door, across the breezeway, talking on the phone as I stuffed medical supplies and towels into a backpack. I called the Coast Guard. Next, I called Pete Hull, of Mote Marine Lab near Sarasota. Called him at home because it was the fastest way to get in touch with a leading cetacean expert, his wife, Kim.

When I was packed, Tomlinson was waiting for me on the dock next to my flats skiff — an open boat designed for running fast and dry in shallow water. He, too, had assembled supplies.

"Beer?" he asked, offering me a bottle. He had a cooler aboard, a backpack, and a couple of shovels.

"Not now — when we're under way. Do you believe her story?"

He nodded, already drinking my beer. "She's consistent. They're bigger than dolphins. They're black, not gray. Lynn counted more than a dozen with her flashlight while I talked her through it."

I said, "They're whales, not sharks." I was

picturing pilot whales or false killers, sleek as dolphins, the size of my boat, with teeth. Rare.

He was nodding, distressed. "Yep. They're killing themselves. Two are already ashore. The others are trying to follow — a mass stranding just getting started."

He was referring to a little-understood behavior, sometimes associated with disease, or underwater noise pollution. Whales ground themselves and die together, sometimes in pairs, sometimes by the hundreds.

"Doc? Strandings are a chain reaction — whales react to distress calls from an injured whale. That's the theory."

I said, "That's one theory." I was idling away from the dock, more interested in navigation than conversation. Wind was gusting out of the stars on this black night. Visibility was poor.

"That would explain the radio contact. If we can save the sick whale, we might save the others."

"You lost me."

"I should've understood right away. Lynn and her daughters are from Canada. She doesn't know anything about the sea, but she has a radio. Get it? That's why the whales came to her. They used Lynn to contact me. It's classic third-party transferal communication."

"You're telling me the whales knew you'd be in the lab, monitoring channel sixty-eight . . . ?"

"You're being too linear. Universal Mind is connective. Whales are tuned in, man. They sense kindred beings who can help. If you embrace the destination, Universal Mind provides the pathway. I won't be the only healer they contact — watch. Other enlightened souls will arrive."

Over the years, I've heard so many ridiculous claims about the psychic and intellectual powers of dolphins and the family *Cetacea* that my response has been pared to a single word. I use a flat monotone to discourage discussion.

"Interesting," I said.

"Isn't it?" Tomlinson was scratching at the bite on his thigh, excited. "Maybe I am getting the old mojo back."

I attempted diplomacy. "I was never convinced you lost it. But don't expect too much, okay?"

I added the warning because whale strandings seldom have happy endings.

5

Thursday, June 20th

I throttled onto plane, bow fixed on an elevated darkness that marked the entrance of Dinkin's Bay. We angled into the channel, skirting oyster bars and pilings as I picked up markers to open water.

It was 1 a.m. Looking at my watch reminded me of all the work I had to do before tomorrow's meeting . . . so I made a personal decision to stop checking my damn watch and concentrate on driving the boat.

Houses on the point were dark — all but the cottage owned by my cousin, Ransom, next to Ralph Woodring's old Cracker house. Dock lights were on. I could see Ralph and Ransom moving on a flat vacancy of shadow that I knew was a loading platform.

Ralph owns the Bait Box on Periwinkle. The two had been in his trawl boat, netting shrimp.

Like it was no big deal, Tomlinson said, "Did Ransom tell you she's flying to Seattle with me on Sunday? I'm doing a Zen retreat for the Starbucks people, plus America's got a gig there. I play tambourine when they do 'A Horse with No Name.' It could be a new start for us, Ransom and me —"

I cut him off, saying, "I don't want to hear about it," then slowed as we neared Ralph's dock, so I could yell out our destination. Ransom hollered a response, but I waved her off, saying I'd make contact later by radio.

Tomlinson said, "Your cousin could do a lot worse than me."

I said, "Agreed. But you're not going to put me in the middle again."

As we pulled away, I glanced over my shoulder. In the mangrove distance, the marina was a cluster of lights. To the east, the yellow windows of my lab were a solitary constellation, set apart by distance and a darkened space.

I turned toward the cut through the western shoal. It's a propeller track no wider than a ditch. I lowered the bow, and allowed bottom pressure to funnel us into the trough, engine kicking a rooster tail until we were in deeper water. Tomlinson gripped the rail in silence.

Boats communicate efficiency through the

hull. I experimented with trim until I felt the illusion that speed and buoyancy increased in the same silken instant. But the wind was northeast and a heavy chop slammed us. My skiff is among the smoothest and driest ever built — a twenty-one-foot Maverick. Even so, the bay was miserable.

I had to raise my voice to be heard. "I'm heading for the gulf. It's a couple of miles extra, but calmer."

Tomlinson replied, "Rough water's trouble — beer gets foamy, and I could chip a tooth. But is it *faster?* Getting to those whales is all I care about."

I said, "Then hold on," and turned so we were running with the wind.

Ahead was the bridge Shay and I had crossed an hour earlier. It was a strange juxtaposition. In a car, even while discussing blackmail, the world seemed safer for the linkage of asphalt. Not in a boat. Beneath the bridge, in darkness, even as cars passed overhead, stars illustrated the emptiness of space. The safe world ended on the horizon where navigation markers blinked.

When we rounded Lighthouse Point, I found calm water outside the shoal, and asked Tomlinson to break out the MUMs night-vision system because it was so damn dark. It is not a gadget found in boating catalogs. The monocular is fourth-generation technology, a present to me from military pals who specialized in coming ashore quietly after long night swims. It is waterproof to sixty feet, and worn on a headband like a surgical optic. Slip it on, hit the switch, and the blackest night becomes high noon as if seen through a Heineken bottle. A starless sky turns fiery with meteors and stars.

As I removed my glasses and got the monocular locked and focused, Tomlinson muttered, "I love wearing the green-eye. All the fun of van Gogh skies and no risk of losing an ear. Or doing something really stupid."

The green-eye. His pet name for the thing.

I told him, "It's yours on the trip back," as I nudged the tach up to 4200 rpm.

In eerie jade light, we flew along the beach as Sanibel slept, past condos, hotels, and sea grape estates. The sky was animated with meteors that were invisible to the few insomniacs roaming the tide line. They turned toward the sound of our engine, unaware that I could see them clearly — probably wondering why a small boat was gulfside on a night so empty.

Half mile off North Captiva Island, we spotted whales. Spotted the spume from their blowholes first because the spray was backlit by a campfire on the beach. The fire turned each geyser into a mist of sparks that liquefied upon descent. The whales appeared as areas of unsettled darkness, but their skin glowed like wet clay.

As I slowed to approach the beach, Tomlinson surprised me, saying, "Doc, I forgot to ask. Did you see your mail?"

"What?"

"Your mail — I couldn't help noticing the return address on that envelope. I just now remembered —"

"Later. I don't want to miss this. This is a pretty spectacular scene, if you haven't noticed."

"But I'm curious. I know you've been waiting to find out."

I said patiently, "I saw the envelope. I didn't open it."

"Seriously?"

"A few hours isn't going to change anything." I pointed as a whale spouted. "Isn't this more important?"

Tomlinson gave me a brotherly nudge. "A very kendo attitude, man. Death has everyone's number — but we don't have to answer when the bastard dials. Spiritually, you just keep getting hipper. The whales know it. When we hit the water, watch how they react. Then follow my lead."

I said, "Hold on. These whales have teeth the size of my fist, and they aren't your friends. I haven't read of any attacks on people, but —"

"Don't worry, we're simpatico."

"No doubt. But I called experts for a reason. There are written protocols when it comes to strandings."

"But the whales aren't talking to your experts."

"Maybe not. But *we* are."

Tomlinson mumbled a reply as I turned into the sea. When I gave the word, he dropped anchor and began feeding out scope. Even with the engine idling, I could hear the sonar chirps and clicks of whales communicating.

"They're all around. At least a dozen."

I told him, "More. Twenty . . . maybe thirty." Through the green-eye, I could see whales hobbyhorsing close to the boat, and pods of whales a quarter mile offshore. Their heads were streamlined, not bulbous, so they were false killer whales. They were moving toward the beach where people surrounded two animals that lay stranded inside a sandbar. One fluke tail moved oddly, like a broken windup toy. The other whale rocked motionless in the waves.

I was getting a stern anchor ready as Tomlinson said, "You gotta believe me, man. I've been channeling for the last half hour."

"Channeling."

"*Communicating*. They're panicked from the distress calls. They rush to help, but they can't help. There's an emotional meltdown. They freak, then charge the beach. That's why I have to do this."

"Do what?"

He was stripping off his shirt and baseball socks. "What I was called to do. Universal Mind's calling the shots, not me. I'm just a conduit. I have no control."

"No argument here. But wait until we get the boat secured before you go talk to the fish, okay? We're still in fifteen feet of water."

Instead of replying, Tomlinson rolled off the boat, wearing only his baseball pants. He submerged, then surprised me by coming up on the other side, already explaining as he combed water from his hair. "They want us here. Not just me — you, too. That envelope popped into my mind for a reason. You'll see."

I realized I didn't know which envelope he was talking about. The letter from Merlin Starkey, or the results of my brain scan?

"Come on, doctor. We've got to hurry — Whoa!"

I ducked away as a whale surfaced, showering the boat with spray. Tomlinson reached to touch the animal as two more whales broached in tandem.

"How's that for a welcome? Believe me now?"

"No."

"You will. Follow me!"

I expected Tomlinson to turn toward shore. Instead, he began swimming toward open sea. What the hell was he doing? I yelled his name. Yelled it again and ordered him back — "We've got another anchor to set!" — but he kept going.

"I know you hear me! Tomlinson? Tomlinson! You . . . *hippie flake.*"

Now there were four whales alongside him. He wasn't a good swimmer, but his long arms milled the water steadily as he climbed waves seaward. The animals used their fluke tails, maneuvering to stay close.

I watched for several seconds, surprised, and thinking, *I'll be damned. They really are following him.* But then I realized the linkage was fanciful, not rational. A more likely explanation was that the pursuit instinct is common in sea creatures, mammals included. The whales weren't following him, they were shadowing him. I had to stop the man. I got busy.

Going after him in the boat was risky. He was sandwiched between animals that weighed a ton or more. If the engine spooked them, he'd be crushed.

Instead, I threw the engine into reverse, swinging shoreward on the bow anchor, as I pulled off shirt and shoes. When the boat was positioned, I dropped the second anchor, then slid over the side, still wearing the waterproof monocular. Tomlinson hadn't gotten far, only about fifty yards. He'd be easy to catch as long as I could see him.

I bulled my way through the surf line, doing the lifeguard's crawl stroke. Whenever I lost visual contact, I stopped and sculled on roller-coaster waves until I spotted him floundering among whales, then I set off again.

Soon, I was close enough to grab one of his ankles and yank him to a stop. I felt like smacking him. I might have been tempted, if he hadn't been so pleased with himself.

He was laughing. "Isn't this incredible! They're following me!"

I yelled back, "Why not? They're bored shitless. How can they resist watching a crazy man drown?"

"But you're *a witness*. The whales and I are communicating."

"Great. Tell your buddies that King Neptune can't play anymore. Then do me a favor and —" A whale startled me, spouting so close that I was rocked by displaced water, and I could smell the protein soup of its breath. I whirled to look, and saw the whale's dorsal in the green fluorescence of the night-vision monocular. For an instant, as I crested a wave, I thought I saw other fins, too. The fins appeared to be angling toward us.

I continued to stare through the green-eye, waiting for another wave to lift me as I spoke slowly. "Do us both a favor. Let's swim to shore and ask the experts how we can help with the stranding —" I stopped.

Yes . . . there were more dorsal fins — two fins vectoring from the north, cutting green wakes. They were triangular fins, three feet high — as large as whale dorsals . . . but the fins weren't rounded at the tips. I am not an expert on whales. But I could identify these fins expertly.

It was tarpon season, as Tomlinson had said. The oceangoing meat eaters had come shallow to feed.

Sharks.

I grabbed Tomlinson's shoulder, turned him, and said, "Out there. *Hammerheads.* Two, and they're coming this way. Twelve- or thirteen-footers, maybe a thousand pounds. Get your knees up, pull your arms in tight."

"You're shitting me."

"No. But they'll shit both of us if they're feeding."

"Tell me you're joking."

He knew from my tone I wasn't.

"How close?" He thrashed the water, straining to get a look.

I grabbed him again. "Quit splashing. Arms in tight, like you're a chunk of wood. They're thirty yards out, closing fast."

"You can see them?" His voice was shaking.

Yes, I could see them. Each time I crested a wave, the dorsal fins were closer. Their zigzag trajectory was a froth of green. They had locked on to their targets. Us.

"You're sure?"

"I'm sure."

"But sharks don't feed on people! You always say that."

"They were attracted by the whales' distress calls. We're not people out here. We're the smallest mammals on the menu."

"Damn, Doc! I was just starting to get my groove back!"

I said, "Maybe they'll just bump us and move on."

"*Bump* us. I'll piss my damn pants dry. Hey, wait —" He managed to laugh. "— my pants . . . I'm wearing Yankee pinstripes. Unless the bastards eat their own, I'm sharkproof."

I replied, "Just to use that line, we've got to make it back." I took a few strokes to consolidate our profile . . . but it was too late. "Don't move. They're here."

I threw my hands out to fend off as two submarine shapes surfaced within reach, both dorsals higher than my head. Their skin was an armor-work of denticles. I banged one with my fist, kicked at the other. They brushed past with feline indifference, throwing a wake. The sharks arched away, then submerged. Their sensors had identified us. Meat.

"Where'd they go? You see 'em?"

"No," I said. A few seconds later, though, I said, *"Yes."*

The hammerheads were circling back.

The only weapon I had was a folding knife, single blade. I fished the knife out of my pocket and opened it, aware on some internal level of a chemical burn moving through my circulatory system. It was as familiar as the roaring in my ears. It signaled an adrenal overload that keys the fight-or-flight instinct. In some, it also keys rage.

Knife out, I began to sidestroke toward the sharks, charging them as they charged me. Irrational — rage often is.

Suddenly and inexplicably calm, Tomlinson called, "It's okay, I've been warning the whales. I'm *ready*. If it gives them time to run, I don't mind sacrificing myself."

Over my shoulder, I hollered, "Send a message for me. If your whales run instead of attack, they deserve to die," venting anxiety by voicing what I expected of myself because the hammerheads were on us again.

I could see their fins sculpting the weight of the waves. I could see their eyes set apart on stalks as flexible as glider wings. The hammerheads looked like alien spacecrafts tipped with bright black lights. Their dragon tails made a keening sound as they ruddered water.

One of the sharks submerged. I realized that it would probably hit me first. Maybe the second shark would cruise past and take Tomlinson. It was an observation — objective, unemotional, like the sea, like sharks. If it happened, it *happened*.

Knife extended, I lunged forward and downward toward the shark. The night-vision monocular was waterproof, but not designed to focus underwater. Black water became green. There were vague images beneath me, like moons adrift. There were glowing shapes the size of boats. Shapes moved, creating swirling contrails. I used the knife to stab and stab again, but connected with nothing.

Then the sea exploded.

Twice, the sea exploded.

I got my head above water, confused because the sky was exploding, too. I watched a whale arc across the stars, jaws locked on to the midsection of a hammerhead shark. The animals cartwheeled, then crashed back to sea. The shock wave was seismic.

To my right, there was a depth charge percussion of similar magnitude. The whales had nailed the second shark.

Tomlinson was beside me as twin shock waves lifted us. "Holy mother of God! Did you *feel* that?"

"Yeah."

"Did you see that?"

"Yes."

Adrenaline was draining from my system. I felt weak, nauseous. I lay back and allowed the buoyancy of saltwater to support me, aware that whales were now moving away, pointing out to sea.

"Let's get back to the boat. I could use a beer."

"Oh, yeah."

On the ride back to Dinkin's Bay, Tomlinson couldn't stop repeating himself: "You told the whales to attack, and they *attacked*. You doubt you have mojo? Doc — they got your message!"

6

Half an hour later, as Tomlinson climbed aboard his sailboat, I said to him, "Use your psychic powers and tell me who turned off the lights in the lab."

It was 4 a.m., still dark, but the marina's boat basin was streaked with reflections of mast lights and Japanese lanterns strung for Dinkin's Bay's weekly party.

The party was tonight, I realized. Friday — June 21st, the summer solstice.

The cruisers, trawlers, and sailboats were buttoned up tight, air conditioners laboring on this black June morning as owners slept.

"You're sure you left the lights on?"

I remembered glancing over my shoulder as we crossed the bay, my windows distinctive because of the yellow bulbs.

"I'm sure. And if the power goes off, I've got a propane generator. It's automatic."

Once again, my eyes scanned the mangrove shoreline, from the marina to my lab. The windows were the same flat gray as the lab's tin roof.

"Maybe Shay changed her mind and came back. Or it could be the lady biologist you're dating. You said she had some interesting quirks. There's the explanation, Doc. That's not darkness, it's an invitation. Personally, a dark window is something I've never been able to resist."

I said, "You're probably right," willing to agree because Tomlinson was eager for me to be gone. I knew the signs.

On the return trip, he'd decompressed by swallowing something he didn't want me to see — a pill? A sliver of mushroom? He confided that he had an ounce of sinsemilla, a potent, seedless variety of marijuana, and I broke an old rule and gave him permission to light up. He smoked the joint and finished the six-pack — a bizarre-looking, stringy-haired Cyclops as he focused the night-vision monocular, crooning, "Ooohh . . ." and "Ahhhhhh . . ." watching meteors blaze.

"Want a hit?" he asked several times, cupping the joint. "This shit's so strong, you won't have another headache until your next incarnation — then only if some quack grabs you by the head with forceps."

The drugs were beginning to do their work.

Gradually, his focus rotated inward, attuned to some gathering cerebral momentum that he hid outwardly with sly jokes and articulate sentences. But now he wanted to enjoy the drug-crest in private. Either that or he needed a booster. Because my disapproval would cause unease, he wanted to be alone. Or he would wander beachside — somewhere near the Mucky Duck or Jensen's — and seek the sanction of bleary-eyed kindred.

Another sign he wanted me gone was that he refused to let me look at the bite he kept scratching. Or discuss it — even when I told him he could lose his leg if he'd been bitten by something with venom that caused necrosis. A brown recluse spider, for instance.

His decision. I didn't argue. I was exhausted, hungry, and I still had work to do before my new supervisors arrived to evaluate my work. So I was going. But not yet.

I had stowed the night-vision monocular, but took it out as Tomlinson said, "We could've bought the farm tonight, *compadre.*"

He'd repeated that over and over, too, choosing a different cliché each time — kick the bucket, hit the high trail, pushin' up daisies, like shit-through-a-goose. Maybe the homey idioms mitigated the terror of what had almost happened.

Focusing the monocular, I replied, "We're born lucky — maybe they wouldn't have attacked. We'll never know."

I was looking through the green-eye at my stilt house a hundred yards away. Supported by pilings, braced like a railroad bridge, the place looked like a nineteenth-century woodcut.

"Everything hunky-dory? Or maybe there are a couple of fins circling?"

He chuckled as he said it, but wasn't joking. A few minutes earlier, idling toward *No Más,* he'd startled me by breaking into my thoughts, saying, "Sharks are your totem. Predators attract."

At the same instant, I was brooding over two previous encounters with aggressive sharks, both recent. As a biologist, I knew they were statistical anomalies. But why were the statistics suddenly askew? Fact was, I'd had more close calls in the last few years than an entire lifetime at sea.

Same was true of predators of a different sort.

I'd replied, "I thought opposites attracted. But there I go again being linear, bringing

89

up the laws of physics."

"Physics applies," he countered. "*Quantum* physics. There's a theory that whatever we envision becomes reality. I think those hammerheads zeroed in on a distress call. But it wasn't the whales who were calling."

"Ahhh. So they were coming to rescue me."

"In a way. Maybe. You weren't exactly turning cartwheels when you got the news from your neurologist."

I replied, "No, but it could've been worse." Which was true. I'd been diagnosed with cerebral vasculitis, an unusual disorder with numerous possible causes. A life spent banging around the tropics had probably contributed. The disease can be treated with corticosteroids, which may delay the inevitable. Sooner or later, most of us will listen to a physician speak the name of our killer.

I told Tomlinson, "Have I seemed upset? Truth is, I like the certainty of knowing."

"Then your distress signals are job-related. You've been restless as a cat since cutting your old ties. Free to hole up and live a safe little life? Definitely not you, man. Sharks are totemic. They recognize your scent."

Now he was joking about it, hoping I'd react. But the concept of animal totems was something I didn't want to explore. Not now.

"No sharks circling," I said as I slid the monocular into its case. Then I added in a voice loud enough to be heard across the water, "I thought I left the lights on, but I was wrong. You ever do something stupid like that?"

"Damn," he said, recoiling. "What's the deal? I'm not deaf."

He put his hands over his ears as I said even louder, "I'm not going straight home. I have things to do at the marina."

He looked at me like I was nuts. "Never raise your voice to a man who may or may not have recently eaten peyote. *Jesus Christ!* Especially out of the fucking blue. It's like getting hit in the temple with ice balls."

He was suspicious when I waved him closer, but I spoke softly. "We're being watched."

Someone was inside my stilt house, standing at the kitchen window. A man, not a woman.

I came through the living room, switching on lights that didn't work, swearing aloud as if I didn't know someone was in the house. Whoever it was had found the breaker panel in the utility closet, and offed the master switch. Had to be, or the generator would be running.

Maybe that's where the man was hiding.

Or men — in the utility closet.

I had a brilliant little Triad LED flashlight in my pocket, but didn't use it because I was wearing the green-eye. As long as the power was off, I had the advantage. No way my visitors could know.

In my hand, I had a chunk of axe handle, wrapped with manila cord. My friend, Matthiessen, gave it to me years ago, nicely weighted for dispatching fish. I would've preferred to be carrying a handgun — the SIG Sauer, or the little Colt .380 — but they were in the hidden floor compartment beneath my bed.

I hadn't used the fishbilly in a long time. I was eager to use it now.

My house had been ransacked. Books, drawers, clothes were scattered. Maybe he'd done the same in the lab — I hadn't looked yet. Just the thought of it made my stomach turn, but I had to check the main house first. It was because of the smell.

Kerosene.

It had spilled somewhere. A lot of it. When you live in a house built of yellow pine — pine so dense with resin you can't drive a nail — the smell of flammable liquids registers like an alarm. That's why I'd rushed up the stairs instead of taking it slow, using my night vision to surprise the guy. I'd followed my nose, moving incrementally faster as the smell grew stronger.

The petroleum stink had brought me here, to the kitchen, where the pilot light of my propane stove glittered like a sparkler. Not much risk of an explosion, but dangerous. On the counter was a kerosene can on its side, top off, near a heap of towels. The pine floor was stained black.

I had to shove the reading chair out of the way to get into the kitchen where I stood for a moment, alert. There was a rustling sound, then a metallic clack. The lights came on, compressors started, ceiling fans began to rotate overhead. My telephone answering machine came on, too, its message light blinking rapid-fire. Lots and lots of messages — unusual.

I focused on the utility closet as a man stepped out, holding a gun. Not one of mine — a shiny little derringer, so small that maybe it was a lighter instead.

"You're him, right? Ford. The one the girls call 'Doc.'"

I'd taken off the monocular and was adjusting my glasses, looking at a man, late twenties, short, with bulked-up chest and forearms. He was wearing sweatpants and a crew-neck T, but expensive. A guy who spent time in malls, and in front of the mirror.

It was Corey's husband. I'd seen photos.

He'd been a firefighter, I remembered, before he was canned for misconduct. Something about making a scene, losing his temper. One steroid drama too many. But I was blanking on his name. Last name was Varigono, but his first name was . . . Vince? Lance?

I said, "That's right, Ford. The one who's going to introduce you to the cops in a few minutes, then testify in court before they put you in jail for ten years."

"No way. Even if you suspected, you wouldn't call the cops. Shay told us about you." He was trying to be cool, but his face was twitching as he crossed the room toward the stove. "You never call the cops, ever, because you can't. It's because of what you do. Some kind of illegal shit — Shay never figured it out."

A strange time for personal revelation, but there it was: My travels created suspicion. *The mysterious biologist,* Shay often called me, as if kidding. But she'd meant it. I was expert at evasion, so she'd turned to outsiders to discuss it, a natural reaction. So why did I feel surprised — and betrayed?

Whatever she'd told the guy about me, though, had scared him. I could see it in his face, the way he moved. This was the cocktail party brawler? Yell "boo," he'd make a puddle on the floor. But he was also crazy enough to break into my house, trash the place, then wait with a gun because he couldn't find the video.

The video — there could be no other reason he was here.

And he was right. I had not called the police.

"What's the problem . . . *Vance?*"

"Drop that fucking club for starters."

"No, not until we talk."

"How 'bout I shoot you in the knee? Maybe then you'll take me serious." He extended the derringer, aiming.

I held my hand out, *stop,* and turned sideways — not the brave image I wanted to maintain, but the response is involuntary when someone points a gun near your nuts.

I said, "You don't want to shoot me, Vance. *I* don't want you to shoot me. That's serious jail time, and you've got a wife to think about. So let's discuss —"

"Don't mention that bitch! She's done nothing but lie since she got back from that goddamn island. It's her fault I have to do this." He stepped closer. "And you're helping them, motherfucker! Corey and those whores she calls her friends. You screwed

95

with the wrong dude, man! Shay says you've been into some shit? Well, I've been into *real shit,* so you'd better listen!"

Now he was pointing the gun at my chest, leaning toward me, his expression crazed — but crazy as portrayed by TV mobsters: eyes wide, not glazed, screaming his lines not because he'd snapped, but because he was scared.

I knew it then — he wouldn't shoot. Not if I gave him a way out. The phony berserker is a bullying technique. It's used to dodge fights, and intimidate those naïve enough to fall for the act. Vance had the act down. He was a coward, and he wanted out. But who told him that I'd helped Shay? How much did he know?

"Give me the video, or I'll splatter you all over the wall. I mean it! I want to see who my wife was fucking."

I said, "Video? I don't even own a TV, pal."

"Don't play dumb. I *know* it's here. Shay-shay didn't tell you?" He had a nervous, staccato laugh. "The girls got another e-mail tonight. Their island boyfriend kept a copy, and now he wants the rest of his money. If I've got to pay the puke, I should at least be able to see if Corey got her money's worth."

I stared at Varigono for long seconds, the

smell of kerosene strong around me, aware of the stove's pilot light, concerned about what this jerk had destroyed next door. Finally, I turned my back to him, saying, "The only thing I'll give you is five minutes to get out. Your wife is Shay's friend — that's the only reason."

As Varigono hollered for me to stop, I tossed the axe handle aside, walking toward the door, hoping I was right about him, but tense, now hearing real craziness in his voice at the mention of Corey, thinking maybe, just maybe, he *could* do it.

"Why are you covering for them, man? You're a guy, you can't understand? She's my wife! It's my right! Hey . . . hey! I'm talking to you, motherfucker!"

I was walking out the screen door, ignoring him until I heard the ignition *pop* of the propane stove. That made me stop. I turned.

Oh no . . .

Along with the derringer, Varigono was now holding a torch made from papers he'd twisted into a cone. I watched it blaze when he held it to the burner, the expression on his face changing from crazed to triumphant.

"Yeah . . . that's better. So *finally,* I got your attention. Shay told me that about you, too — how much you like this old shack and your little pet fishes. That you're a fucking weirdo with your microscopes and books."

Shay, I was learning, did not always speak in glowing terms about her godfather.

Vance said, "You know the difference between arson and an accident? Don't worry, 'cause I do." He used the gun to indicate the mess he'd created. "You and me got into a fight, and this place is a fire trap. That's what the investigators will decide."

I said, "Your word against mine? They canned you for a reason. You don't think they'll check the files?"

"I'll risk it." He extended the torch, threatening to light towels next to the stove. "I'd rather burn the place down than let you and your weirdo buddies sit around and watch Corey naked, fucking some stranger. I know it's here someplace. So, last chance. Where!"

Enough. I walked toward him, an unconscious reaction. "Vance, the only person your wife fucked was herself when she married you." The adrenal chill was pumping. Why the hell had I dropped the axe handle?

He held torch flames to the towels. "I'll *do* it."

"Then do it."

"I'll shoot you, motherfucker!" He leveled the tiny pistol at my chest.

"Go ahead."

He tried. Got the hammer back as I locked my hands on his wrist, lifting and twisting. The derringer made a concise firecracker *whap* near my ear, putting a round through the roof. I pivoted with good leverage, and stripped the gun from his fingers, then dislocated his elbow with a come-along that dropped him to his knees as he made a sharp, thin whistling scream.

He dropped the torch, too. I watched blue flames sprint across the wooden floor — pine resin instantly aromatic because of the heat. Panic. Kerosene isn't explosive, but yellow pine is. My brain projected an image: flames colored by lab chemicals; firemen hosing charred ruins. Vance deserved to burn with the house — justice. My first instinct was to get to my floor safe and rescue my valuables.

It took three long steps to get to the bedroom. In that brief span, the panic passed. I reassessed. The fire was spreading, but it hadn't yet bitten into wood. There was still time.

Seconds later, I was back with blankets from my closet and a fire extinguisher. The blankets worked. Snuffed out the flames before they got to the wood. Lucky — lucky because I'd stopped the fire, and also because I didn't have to use the fire extinguishers. They leave a powdery mess, and I already had enough chaos to deal with.

Now my phone was ringing, too. Not yet 5 a.m. and someone was calling? Not Tomlinson. If he was coherent, he was aboard *No Más,* watching for me to signal him with the flashlight. I ignored the phone as Vance Varigono sat on the floor, sobbing non sequiturs that begged for understanding but not the police. Now he was a victim of circumstances filled with remorse — another act.

I knelt, pocketed the derringer, and did a quick pat down. Wallet, cell phone, keys. I pocketed the cell phone, too, before I put my lips near his ear and began to whisper. It surprised him, and his eyes widened. I mentioned his wife. I referred to Shay. The last thing I said was, "Vance, I want the subject to disappear. If it doesn't? *You will.*"

It jolted him. He nodded, not risking eye contact. The man was getting to his feet as I hurried next door to the lab.

It wasn't too bad. Varigono had riffled my desk, emptied a file case, but the aquariums were untouched, and the sea life within looked healthy. The power hadn't been off long enough to do damage. Aquarium aerators create ozone, and I took several big breaths, letting good air dilute the adrenal burn. Then I swung the office chair around and dumped my body into it, exhausted.

I had a pounding headache. With eyes closed, a schematic of the back of my brain strobed with each beat of my heart. I sat, taking slow, deep breaths. The pain eased as tension faded.

It didn't last.

The VHF radio was still on, and a familiar voice came over, hailing me. It was Jeth Nicholes, Dinkin's Bay fishing guide and a close friend. He'd tried telephoning me, he said. So had my cousin, Ransom. Using the illegal base station in his garage was a last resort before driving to the marina.

"There's been an accident, Da-da-Doc. Nothing too serious, but you mind calling me on the land line?"

It *was* serious, though, I knew. These days, Jeth seldom stutters.

Shay Money was in the emergency room, Jeth told me, maybe already in surgery. Around 3 a.m., she'd skidded off the road and hit a tree, racing to keep up with the ambulance that was taking her friend Corey Varigono to the hospital.

Corey was in critical condition, he said. Drug overdose.

Shay's condition was unknown.

...was in surgical isolation, I'd said.
Stop moving—
She'd only laughed, I couldn't—

7

Shay used her finger to signal me closer, and whispered in a voice hoarse from sleep, "The black hole's trying to drag me back — you believe me now? It won't let me be something I'm not."

I touched my lips to a part of her temple not covered by surgical bandage and replied, "You're giving up so easy? Now you're even acting like a rich girl. You've got the curse thing backward, sister."

She smiled . . . winced at the pain, then pointed to her water. It was next to the hospital bed beneath monitors. I held the glass while she used the flexible straw, only a curtain separating us from the woman asleep in the next bed. Just us, but we kept our voices low.

Michael and his mother had exited as I entered, like changing shift. Shay's future mother-in-law . . . *maybe.* As we passed, the fiancé stared through me, not a nod, but the mother locked eyes and scowled. Heavy, rectangular brow. Her son had inherited the elongated earlobes. No way to know if she scowled for a reason, or if she was one of those angry people whose face had devolved into a warning to the world.

But Shay dismissed them quickly, whispering, "Understand now why Mrs. Jonquil drives me bonkers?" before demanding a report on Corey. As I answered, Shay's eyes were intense, alert for lies. Reassuring. Even after slamming her convertible into a palm tree, her brain was sharp.

"Doctors haven't downgraded Corey's condition, so she's hanging in there," I said.

"That's all you know?"

"That's all."

"How's her family doing?"

"I've never met them, so I can't say. The waiting room's full. Your friend Beryl's here. Liz, too."

"Did they . . . say anything to you?"

I caught the hesitation. "I don't think they saw me."

"What about Vance?"

I replied, "Vance," in a flat tone, not ready to tell her we'd met.

"Corey's husband. That jerk. When I found her, the side of her face was all swollen, and her eye was turning black. I told the

EMTs and the cops about him. That son of a bitch."

I put my hand on her wrist. "The nurse said I'd have to leave if you get upset."

"Okay, okay. But I show up at three a.m., his truck's gone, and she's nearly dead. I'll bet right now he's out making sure he has an alibi so he can pretend like nothing happened."

A girl who knew how small-time criminals operated. Yes, her brain was functioning fine after a very close call.

Along with scalp lacerations and facial bruises, Shay had a closed head injury — medicalspeak for an injury that could be minor or could make her a vegetable. She'd been unconscious for at least a couple of minutes, so there were more tests to be done. But there were no obvious signs of brain trauma.

So I made her sip some water and calm down before telling me what had happened.

Around 2:30 a.m., Shay had checked her cell and found a hysterical message from Corey. After trying Corey's phone, she drove to the Varigono home, where she'd discovered her friend unconscious on the couch. EMT response was fast, but Corey stopped breathing just before the ambulance arrived.

No wonder the mood was grim in the ICU waiting room.

"I took CPR, but, Christ, I couldn't tell if I was helping her or not. She vomited a couple of times. It was awful! Doc?" Shay turned her head slightly — painful. "We promised we'd be straight with each other, so you've got to tell me. Is Corey dead?"

Her face was swollen, raw in spots from the air bag. Skin around her eyes was pale purple, edged with magenta. Not too bad. "Raccoon eyes" is another medical term, but the girl was going to be okay.

I replied, "Corey's alive. That's the truth. You did everything you could to help her. That's all a friend can do."

"I did something else." Shay touched a finger to her lips, whispering. "Corey left a note, and I took it. It's in my purse. No one's read it but me. Take a look."

It was to her parents.

Papi and Mami
I am so tired and afraid all the time and I've done something I know will never go away. You were wonderful and I never wanted to make you ashamed. I am so sorry and tired of being afraid. Forgive me . . .

It was written on paper torn from a spiral

106

notebook. Written in a rush by a woman desperate for relief.

In the world's most dissimilar languages, pet words for mother and father are touchingly similar. The Chinese say *baba* and *mama*. In Arabic, they are *ami* and *omi*. When conquistadors invaded, Aztec children ran screaming for *apå* and *amå*.

The first two words we learn as infants echo humanity's first words. They are the sound of primal bleating; a child's plea for help. Those two words are hardwired in the womb, and we carry them with us to the grave. It is known, from voice recorders recovered at crash sites, that *mama* is often the last word a pilot speaks.

Corey had called for help, but silently, as proud people sometimes do.

I folded the note as Shay said, "Was I wrong to take it? A suicide attempt . . . all I could think about was how bad it would look on her record. She's given up on the acting thing, but the design department loves her at Chico's. Without the note, they can't prove it wasn't accidental, can they?"

I said, "You did the right thing," as I returned the note to her purse. "She needs help and protection but, yeah, I think Corey will thank you —" Then I said, "Hey," watching her yawn. "Enough for now. I'll come back this afternoon."

"But I don't want you to go. I'm not sleepy."

Yes, she was. The nurse had also told me she'd been given a painkiller. But the girl reached and took my hand, something else on her mind.

"I've been a good friend to everyone but you, Doc. I needed to say that. And apologize."

"I've got no complaints."

"But I haven't been straight. Even now. The real reason I missed Corey's call was because I was at the computer. There was an e-mail waiting when I got home. He wants more money. The full quarter million. He knows my wedding's a week from Sunday. If he doesn't get the money by Friday, he'll . . . he'll . . ." The girl closed her eyes and touched fingers to her head. "He's going to put the video on the Internet. That's what Corey meant, the part about her parents being ashamed."

"I see." I gave it some time, as if surprised by the news, then said, "But maybe he did us a favor."

Her expression read, *You got to be kidding.*

"Think about it. At least he showed his hand — better now than later. And he gave us time, seven days. We have space to deal with it."

"But I don't have the money, Doc. And . . . there's something else. My bridesmaids got the same e-mail. They knew from the beginning. The four of us chipped in to pay the hundred and nine thousand."

I sat back in mock disbelief. "Dex didn't leave a fat insurance policy?"

"All that man left me was a couple of guns, a junker Cadillac, and some real bad memories. Dumb, I knew you didn't believe me. But it was the only thing I could think of." She squeezed my fingers, her grip childlike. "I lied to you, pal."

I smiled. "So what? Compartmentalization — the smart way to handle it. I would've done the same."

Again, she squeezed.

"If I was smart, I wouldn't be in this mess — I think Michael knows. Vance stole Corey's password and read the e-mail before she did. Michael hasn't mentioned it, but Vance told him something. I can feel it, the way he looks at me now. There's not going to be a wedding."

"Did he tell you it's off?"

"While I'm in a hospital bed? No, he'll wait."

"What about his mother? Would he have told her?"

"Uh-uh. If he had, the only reason she'd come to the hospital is to spit on me. Mrs. Jonquil's French, not Swiss, *and* a serious Catholic. The woman wouldn't be here if she knew."

"Were there files attached to the e-mail?"

She moved her eyes. *No.*

"How was it worded?"

"What I just told you. He wants the rest of the money."

"Can you remember specifics?"

"I should, I read the damn thing a dozen times before I trashed it. It was kinda like the first one, the way he tried to be clever. It went, 'Some vacation memories are priceless, so your vacation video is a bargain. Either pay the rest of the money, or . . .' No, that's not right." She thought for a moment. "No, he said, 'Pay the *balance* or you'll be sinning with your new boyfriends on the Internet —' It went like that."

I said, "Sinning. That's a strange way to put it."

"Yeah, he's nasty clever. Called me a slut — that was in the subject line. And he said 'porn sites,' not Internet. But he didn't attach any more video files."

Like before — it wasn't just about the money. The blackmailer got a charge out of humiliating victims.

110

"Is there a chance Michael or his pals can retrieve the earlier files if they go hunting through your computers?"

"No. We trashed everything. Then I found a special software that we all used to make sure it stays gone."

"That includes his latest e-mail?"

She nodded.

"What about the other girls?"

"They got rid of it while we were still talking on the phone. But poor Corey, she didn't know that Vance had already snooped."

I said, "In that case, Michael doesn't really *know* anything."

"Of course he does . . . or soon will. He'll find out the girls and I are being blackmailed about something bad enough we already paid a chunk of the quarter million. That and whatever else Vance slapped out of Corey before she OD'd. He'll know about the video. There's no getting around it."

I looked into her eyes for a long second before saying, "Video? I don't know what you're talking about. What video?"

Shay stared back, her expression blank. *Huh?*

I said it again, deadpan. "*What* video?"

She continued to stare. "You're serious."

"Very."

She tried to sit, but I placed my hands on

her shoulders until she was lying back.

"But they'll *know.*"

"They don't know anything. Michael and his fraternity pals never saw what's on that cassette. Neither did you. Neither did your bridesmaids. I have it. No one's going to get it. So, as of now, it doesn't exist."

"But Vance read the e-mail —"

"An e-mail doesn't prove anything. Some freak in the Caribbean is hounding you about a film he doesn't have, and about a night that never happened."

The girl took a deep breath and settled back, thinking about it. "My God, I'd give anything if it was true. But . . . but how do I explain why we paid all that money? Michael can check my bank —" She stopped, her voice turning inward. Her expression changed. "Wait . . . we have separate accounts. Same with Beryl, Liz, and their guys. We all chipped in, so we didn't have to dig into our wedding accounts. They *can't* check. But what about Vance and Corey —"

"Vance is a loser and liar. They had a fight last night. I'm sure it wasn't their first. He's jealous, pathological, so he made up a bunch of crap as an excuse for hitting his wife. You got involved after hearing Corey's phone message."

"Doc . . . I don't know. Will it work?"

I leaned and kissed the same bare space on her temple. "Maybe, maybe not. Either way, it'll buy us some time — as long as nothing else happened on Saint Arc. Something worse."

"What the hell could be worse?"

"You tell me. An accident? If someone got hurt, and the camera caught it?"

"No. What we did was bad enough."

I looked at her, letting her know this was serious. "Is that the truth?"

"Yes."

"Okay. Then that's the way we'll play it. There is no video. Got it? The party, the swimming pool, the three locals, it never happened. Keep telling yourself that. I'll send Beryl and Liz in so you can tell them —"

"No," she interrupted, already ahead of me, "it's better if I call their cell phones. If the three of us are in here alone, the guys will think we cooked up a story."

I smiled. "Okay. Call them. Then go to sleep. Spend the next few days getting healthy."

"But what happens next Friday? It's the night of our rehearsal dinner. If we don't pay the money —"

"Friday's a week away. A lot can happen in seven days." I turned, my hand on the edge of the privacy screen. "Maybe I'll fly down to Saint Lucia, take the ferry to Saint Arc, and try to reason with the guy."

"Try to . . . *reason* with him?" Shay said the words slowly, testing them for euphemism.

"Why not? The island has a reef system . . . and there's a species of sea jelly I'm interested in. It's rare — a dark blue medusa, so dark it's black. I can do research."

"Research." Her tone was the same.

"I'll need help on this end. We can stay in touch by e-mail. And someone has to look after the lab — Ransom's going to Seattle with Tomlinson. He's teaching at a retreat."

"Just like that, you're ready to go."

"Why not? It's not like you to quit. Remember the night we saved your chocolate Lab?"

The reaction was instant. She smiled, and I had her attention again.

"He was such a sweetie. Davey Dog. Daddy's pit bulls got him, but we pulled him through. I see what you're saying. He never gave up."

"That's better. You're a tough woman, sister. Smart. The poor bastard on Saint Arc has no idea who he's dealing with."

The smile broadened. Then it faded as her eyes began to tear. She found a tissue and used it, studying me. "My dear, sweet mysterious biologist. I wish to hell now I hadn't asked Bill Woodward to give . . ." Her voice caught. ". . . to give the doctors hell if they don't take good care of Corey. I should've put you in charge."

"Don't worry," I said. "If he mentions it at the wedding, I'll pretend not to know."

Beryl Woodward was in the parking lot arguing with her fiancé when I walked outside into the sodium glare of security lights.

I didn't make the association right away. I'd been awake for twenty-four hours. I hadn't worked out or gone for a run, and my swim with the whales wasn't exactly therapeutic. Birds were testing darkness with an experimental twittering that inflamed nerve endings in the back of my brain. But because her silhouette was unmistakably female, the woman registered on an instinctual level that never tires. Unconsciously, I noted height, hair, heft of bosom as I walked.

It was a coincidence my old Chevy pickup was parked a few cars away from where Beryl and her fiancé stood. They were nose to nose, voices hypercharged but so low I was on them before sentence fragments revealed what was going on.

". . . October wedding? Why the hell should

I? You go off for a girl's weekend, then I find out . . ."

". . . you believe Vance? You accuse me?"

"Something happened on that island, god-damn it . . ."

". . . hold it! You get *caught* making out with one of my best girlfriends. But now I'm the one who can't . . ."

"You have changed! You've been acting so freaking weird . . ."

". . . I had fun! That's a big change, I agree."

By the time I realized it was Beryl, she'd recognized me, so it was too late to do a polite about-face. But I slowed my pace and made a show of concentrating mightily on something in my hand. Truck keys. I had nothing else. When their voices went silent, I filled the silence by whistling a tune that didn't resemble the Buffett song playing in my head.

I pretended not to hear her fiancé whisper, ". . . and I've had enough of your Ice Queen bullshit."

I pretended not to hear Beryl reply for my benefit, in a voice almost cheery, "Under-standable. That's fine, Elliot. I'll give you a call later from work. Okay? *Okay?*"

Elliot snapped, "Okay!" as a Corvette beeped and taillights flashed. He slammed the door and revved the engine. Because I didn't want to get run over, I waited until Elliot was accelerating toward the exit before continuing to my truck.

Beryl watched me approach. She leaned to take a remote key from her purse, eyes momentarily holding mine. Behind her, a convertible beeped and blinked, a Volvo, maybe. The engine started remotely. She could leave anytime she wanted.

"Dr. Ford? I'm sorry you had to hear that."

I said, "Hear . . . what?" Then I noted the way her head lifted and tilted, so I amended, "Which is bullshit, and we both know it. Don't apologize. I'm sorry you recognized me."

"Oh?"

"Yeah. It was just getting good."

"Is that supposed to be funny?"

"An attempt. It's also the truth. You never eavesdrop?"

"Of course. But I at least try to be discreet."

I pointed. "That's my truck. It's not like I was sneaking up."

She said, "Ah, a truck . . . so I see," looking at my old Chevy, emphasizing her distaste by making an effort to hide it. "I guess people don't go into marine biology to get rich."

"No. But when I start to get bitter, I remind myself how much I've saved on psychiatrists and expensive women. It keeps me grounded."

Along with the keys, Beryl had taken a pack of gum from her purse. She held a piece between her teeth for an instant, letting me see it, then began to chew. "You must be a guy's guy — you'd have to be to drive a vehicle like that. So let me ask you a guy's question. Do you think Elliot believed me?"

"Can't say. I didn't hear enough."

"Hmmm. That's not very helpful."

"Were you lying to him?"

"If I was, it wouldn't be the first time. But it's the first time Elliot didn't pretend to believe me. I've never seen him so pissed off. And his questions —" She grimaced. "Was my lover older, younger, bigger, better-looking, was he better in bed? What is it with you men? You're a scientist. At what age does a human male mature emotionally?"

I shrugged. "You'll have to ask a human male a lot older than me. Sorry."

Beryl raised her eyebrows, shielding a smile, then held out the pack of gum. I took a piece. Cinnamon.

I said, "You didn't tell him what really happened on Saint Arc."

"If I answer, does that mean we're confidants?"

"We're confidants whether you answer or not."

"Okay. No, of course I didn't tell him. Nothing incriminating, anyway. Why would I? Now it's your turn. Did you hear what I said about Elliot and a friend of mine? Any of it?"

"Not as much as I wanted. But enough."

"Hear any names?"

"Nope."

"True?"

"True."

I let her consider that, returning her stare before adding, "Don't worry. I'm not going to ask who the friend was."

"She's still a friend. No need for the past tense. Elliot, on the other hand . . . well, maybe he's right. I'm different since the island. Everything that's happened has been so . . . shitty. Quite an awakening. But maybe some good will come of it yet. I just talked to Shay on the cell. She told me about the conversation you two had."

I waited.

"It's a good thing Elliot didn't recognize you, Dr. Ford. Our guys think we made a pact with the devil, trusting you, not them. They can't decide if you're part of the drug mob, or a secret government assassin."

I laughed, letting her know how ridiculous it was. "Shay has an imagination. She actually says things like that about me?"

Beryl replied, "Oh, she's said a lot about you — more than you realize. Yes, that girl can get carried away."

Was that a veiled cut? Shay, I suspected, was the girlfriend she'd caught with Elliot.

I let it go.

"No matter what your fiancé thinks of me, trust shouldn't be an issue. You have nothing to hide. Same with Shay and the other girls. Right?"

"Ah," Beryl said, "the official story. I haven't gotten used to it yet. The video doesn't exist. The night on Saint Arc never happened. But you have the tape, Dr. Ford. You saw what went on in the swimming pool."

"Wrong. If the tape was in my hands — and it isn't — I wouldn't watch it. And I didn't."

"Oh, please." I received the tilted withdrawal, like a horse shying.

I put my hands out, palms up. *Honest.*

"You admit you enjoy eavesdropping."

"That's right. But there are lines I won't cross."

"You don't strike me as the Boy Scout type, sorry."

"I'm not. My lines have lots of curves and angles. What about yours?"

The woman had a gift for draping sarcasm in encouragement. Or vice versa. "I don't discuss my boundaries in public. But I can tell you this — I'm trusting you, damn it — I'm way too curious to have that kind of willpower. Especially after seeing some of the clips from that tape — *my God*. I would've watched. I'd pretend like I hadn't, but I would've watched from beginning to end."

"Because you're in it? Or because you're not?"

"Make up any answer that pleases you. That night's sort of foggy and dreamy, and maybe I want it to stay that way. I still don't understand why we did what we did — I'm referring to the party we didn't have, by the way. On the night that never happened. Elliot would've been shocked."

"You're a quick study."

"Really? Then why did it take me so long to figure out that I've wasted the last two years of my life?" The woman checked her watch. "I don't suppose you're hungry?"

I had spoken to Beryl Woodward maybe a dozen times since Shay finished her master's degree. She'd struck me as a one-dimensional mall diva. Too much money, a daddy's-girl ego, and too attractive for life ever to require that she risk an encounter with reality.

Not now. But Beryl had never invited me to breakfast before.

She'd told Elliot she would call from work, so I asked, "Isn't your boss expecting you?"

"I manage the spa at Naples-on-the-Bay Racquet Club. I'm the boss — which means I work twelve to fourteen hours a day. I'll write myself a note."

Ten minutes later, we were drinking coffee at First Watch on U.S. 41, six lanes of asphalt jammed with commuters hurrying into this new summer day.

8

Vance had used Merlin Starkey's letter as a torch . . . Starkey's letter along with unopened bills, and the envelope containing my lab results.

I found the remains on the kitchen floor a couple of minutes after walking into the house, hurrying to clean up the mess before my 10 a.m. meeting.

The front of the envelope was the color of burned toast, my name and address unreadable. The back had flamed through. Hold a match to tissue paper, results would be similar.

I opened the envelope to find out how much of the letter had survived. The paper began to crumble. A flake came off in my hand, and I saw the date. It was written in pen by Starkey.

I tried again, even though I knew it shouldn't be rushed. A larger flake broke off. I read, *"Howdy, Marion. If you're reading this, I reckon it means I'm dead, which is a dis-appointment to me, being outlived by the kin of that snake Tucker Gatrell . . ."*

The paper that remained was as delicate as ash. Was there a process to restore stationery after it had burned? Had to be. Somewhere at a museum, or some forensics lab, there was an expert who knew how to do it. Now was not the time to experiment.

9:35 a.m.

I had twenty-five minutes to clean up Varigono's mess, finish a ream of unfinished paperwork, shower, and change. The place stunk of kerosene and smoke, and I hadn't even touched the lab yet — which was okay, because I'd left it in pretty good shape. But the house was a disaster.

Impossible.

Well . . . maybe the team flying in from D.C. would be late — the weather had been terrible up there, stormy and cold even though it was June.

No, they were early.

I was placing the letter inside a Ziploc bag when I heard a decisive *ding-ding-ding.* Then a woman's voice called, "Dr. Marion Ford? Do we have the right place?"

I went out to the deck, pulling the wooden door closed behind me. I would usher them straight to the lab, and spare myself ex-

124

plaining why someone had tried to torch my house. Two men and a woman stood near the brass ship's bell, looking up from the lower platform. Efficient, professional, humorless. Exactly what I'd expected.

My new employer was one of the best-known U.S. intelligence agencies. The organization recruited heavily from the Ivy Leagues. These three had the look. They'd put in their time, had moved up the corporate ladder, and they were dressed for business. Briefcases and suits. I was wearing khaki shorts and a blue chambray shirt with the sleeves rolled to my forearms.

I was buttoning one of the sleeves as I called, "Welcome to Sanibel. Ready to de-ice?" I smiled, trying to set the tone for what awaited them.

Pointless to try. I had no idea . . .

As I held the screen door open, the woman, whose name was Margaret Holderness, stepped into the lab, then stopped, forcing the two men behind her to stop.

"My God," I heard her say, "is that a cadaver?"

What?

I slipped past them and took a look. Tomlinson was lying on the steel dissecting table, eyes closed, hands folded on his chest, wearing nothing but one of his idiotic sarongs. Black silk with red-and-yellow surfboards. No underwear, as usual — obvious.

I told the woman, "It's not a cadaver, but he'd make a good one," attempting the same nervous smile, which she didn't notice because it was impossible to look anywhere but at the dissecting table.

I crossed the room, calling, "Tomlinson? Hey! Time to wake up," which was overly generous. The man was passed out, not asleep judging from the empty rum bottle at his elbow. Nicaraguan rum, Flor de Caña.

As I removed the bottle, I said, "At least he has good taste. If you ever get a chance, try this rum. Really excellent," playing it cool like this sort of thing happened all the time here in the subtropics, so why not relax, enjoy it?

"Tomlinson . . . *Tomlinson.*" He stirred when I shook him, then sat up, wide-eyed as if he didn't know where he was — which he didn't. It took a few seconds.

"Doc?" His eyes found the Flor de Caña bottle as he focused. "Ummm . . . looks like I caught the red-eye to Rummyville, huh? Demon sugar cane. Yep —" He smacked his lips; made a face. "— *Awwg.* Molasses mouth. What time is it?"

"Time for you to be going."

126

"Huh?"

"Time to be going *now.*"

"Okay. Okay!" He swung his feet to the floor, yawning, rubbing his face. "I would've bunked in your house, but the place smells like fucking kerosene, man. *Whew.* So if you don't want me sleeping in the lab, maybe consider hiring a cleaning lady, because there are other places I can —" He stopped, aware I had visitors. His eyes studied the three people wearing suits before he said to me, "Are you buying insurance? Or getting sued?"

I said, "These are clients. I'm showing them around the lab. We're going to discuss new projects — if you don't mind."

I could tell he hadn't heard about Shay or Corey, because he slipped seamlessly into his Harmless Hippie persona. He nodded to my supervisors, adding a friendly salute. "You folks are in for a treat. Don't let this guy's nerdy side fool you. Get a few drinks in him, he actually has a sense of humor —"

I dug my fingers into his elbow to shut him up. "Too bad you can't stick around —" I glanced at his sarong, then looked away fast. "— but you're in a hurry to get to your boat. Right?"

Confused, Tomlinson studied the sarong until he understood. "Geezus," he whispered. "Piss hard-on. Always happens when you need it least."

I looked at the ceiling . . . looked at my shoes . . . looked at the window as he took a moment to regroup.

Finally, Tomlinson said, "Yes . . . well! I'm damn lucky you folks showed up when you did. Just in the nick of time, apparently, so thanks from both of us. Excuse me while I step outside and write my name on the Saltwater Hall of Fame . . ." He winced. "Or I could hit the head at a public facility. Yes . . . that might be the prudent thing to do under the circumstances."

I used the elbow to give Tomlinson a push toward the door. Feet slapping, he walked barefooted across the room, smiling at Holderness, no rush, apologizing but not really embarrassed, saying, "Sorry . . . sorry. But, hey — what are ya gonna do?"

The woman waited until he was gone to ask, "Does that person work for you?"

Her tone said she disapproved, but her expression suggested she was interested.

"No, he's a colleague — a social scientist. Hard to believe, I know. Harvard doctorate, and he's published some brilliant stuff. But he's . . . eccentric." I didn't bother with the nervous smile.

One of the men tried to help out. "I was

stationed in Malaysia, then at the embassy in Singapore, so I've seen it myself. After a year or two in the tropics, even the best-educated professionals change. The Brits have a term for it — gone Borneo? Something like that. Life slows down; details don't matter so much."

Ms. Holderness — my ranking supervisor, I realized — regained her composure by returning to task. "Well, let's hope it's not contagious. Details are *very* important. So are contractual obligations — isn't that right, Dr. Ford?"

She placed her briefcase on the desk and opened it. "Shall we begin, gentlemen?"

Two hours later, I watched from the deck as Holderness and the men filed down the boardwalk, into the mangroves toward the road. When they were gone, I returned to the lab, carrying the folder containing my job-performance evaluation. I hurried for a reason. There was a lot to do.

I needed sleep, needed to work out, but I also had less than seven days to get to Saint Arc, track down the blackmailer, and persuade him that it was unwise to target Shay and friends. I had to book a flight, get my gear ready, and telephone old contacts. I'd told Tomlinson the truth: I wasn't sure if I could still count on past resources to help.

Time to find out.

As I entered the lab, I folded my performance evaluation, then spun it Frisbee-like toward the trash basket, playing a Walter Mitty game — *Make this, I'll have nothing but good luck.*

The thing caromed off the rim onto the floor. I retrieved the papers, then slammed them it into the basket — a flash of anger that was out of character. But I'd just gutted my way through a morning of bureaucratic bullshit. Venting was okay.

Personnel Attitude and Task Efficiency Evaluation. PATEE. A ridiculous acronym. But I'd asked for it. I'd signed their damn contract. Now I felt like a hawk who was being pecked to death by hens.

Ford . . . you fool, you silly fool. Why the hell weren't you satisfied with what you had?

It is a question that all risk takers ask themselves sooner or later. Dumbasses, however, ask the same question, so the association was not uplifting.

Me, the dumbass.

The agency's PATEE packet contained standardized questions: *Does subject respond positively to criticism? Is subject team-oriented? Does subject maintain a safe, efficient work space?*

As expected, I had not received high marks. But there was no way in hell I was going to review the thing as the gang from D.C. had advised me to do.

Why bother? I read to learn, not to be instructed. Furthermore, it was written in a foreign language. The language was Biz-Speak, a form of oral semaphore. Instead of signal flags, it substitutes phrases that register on the brain as symbols, not words.

Biz-Speak is useful in a culture that seeks standardization because it spares members the need to think as individuals. Biz-Speak also minimizes the risk of offending fellow members individually — imperative in a corporate world where political correctness has become a tool. Companies are easier to manage when "group" or "department" is the smallest unit of measure, not a person.

I'd just finished a two-hour immersion course. Holderness had used Biz-Speak to relay her dissatisfaction without once looking me in the eye, or saying a single true thing.

My "core competencies" were "below the curve," which suggested I might benefit from a personal "repurposing," or perhaps an "offline skills transfer." But that would require increased "face time" and "boots-on-the-ground" attention from

131

Ms. Holderness herself.

When she told me that, I smiled. Yes, the woman had fallen for Tomlinson's carefree hippie act. She was creating a reason to return to Sanibel.

Her underlings wrote notes. I did, too. They approved of my conscientiousness and let me know it — but only because they didn't see what I was writing.

Bottom line . . . on the radar . . . try it on . . . at the end of day . . . empowerment, multitasking, warm-and-fuzzies, synergistic . . . ping (to explore), the Ten-K Perspective (overview), deep-dive (verb — to explore a problem in depth).

Despite my poor evaluation, Holderness backpedaled when I suggested we terminate our contract.

"Don't be overly sensitive, Dr. Ford. Your actual work product is superb."

I replied, "Well then, *that's* the bottom line, isn't it?" moving to the door to show them out.

End of meeting.

From my office desk, I called and got an update on Corey Varigono. Her condition had been changed from critical condition to serious but stable. She was going to make it.

Shay sounded better, too, although we

didn't talk long. Tomlinson had paid her a visit. Now Ransom was with her — stopped on her way to town. My cousin has an earthy stability, and a no-bullshit approach to life. It was good they were together, and I was tempted to ask Ransom to let Tomlinson ravage Seattle on his own for a few days. But Shay was going to be okay, and Ransom would be back in time for the rehearsal dinner Friday night.

After I hung up, I turned my attention to the cell phone and derringer I'd taken from Vance Varigono. For the first time, I took a close look.

The derringer wasn't a lighter. It was a stainless steel over-and-under that opened like a double-barreled shotgun. He'd loaded the thing with .38 caliber hollow-points — man-stoppers engineered for maximum damage. The quasi soldier-of-fortune types buy them at gun shows.

Damn.

Varigono could have killed me if he'd pulled the trigger. A small entry hole but a grapefruit-sized exit wound. It made my stomach knot to replay the encounter, but I did it, taking note of mistakes that I didn't want to repeat. I'd underestimated him, then played it way too close. The steroid freak had a big mouth but shaky hands. Surprising the gun hadn't discharged accidentally. Hollow-points are indifferent. They would have displaced the same amount of flesh.

I removed the cartridges, pushed the gun aside, and opened his phone.

Vance had been in a talkative mood between the hours of 1 a.m. and 3 a.m. I checked the *recent calls* menu and saw that he'd dialed eight different numbers, including Michael and Elliot, whose names were logged on speed dial. There was also a number I knew well. Mine. He'd tried several times — probably confirming I wasn't home.

The calls were local except for an international number with the prefix 4-1-0. I checked the computer: Switzerland.

The time log indicated that Vance had gotten nothing but voice recorders until he tried Beryl's fiancé. Someone had answered, presumably Elliot, but the conversation was brief, only three minutes.

It explained how Elliot knew what he knew. Michael Jonquil, too. But three minutes wasn't enough time for Vance to go into detail about what he'd found on his wife's computer.

Would he tell them the rest? Of course. I'd scared him, but Vance was a type, and his type recovered fast. If the cops found him, though, it might be a couple of days before Vance had free time to spend with his fraternity brothers. Detectives would question him about Corey's bruises and her overdose. How would he explain where he was between the hours of 3 a.m. and 5 a.m.? He couldn't use me as an alibi, so he would lie. Good cops always know. Could be that Vance was sitting in jail right now, nursing his dislocated elbow.

I toggled back a few days into the call log and found the four-digit code he used to retrieve voice mail. I called and used it.

All messages erased.

From my office-supply cabinet, I selected a fresh spiral notebook, reporter-sized. I can tally the number of trips I've taken by the number of similar notebooks stacked in my file drawers, or hidden away. Each trip gets its own, no matter how sparse the notes.

I retuned to the desk and wrote *Medusa* on the cover. Medusa is the free-swimming, predatory phase of animals in the phylum cnidarians. Medusa — the rare jellyfish found off Saint Arc. Research would be my excuse for returning to the island.

I sat for a few minutes making notes about yesterday's trip to Saint Arc. After leaving the Bank of Aruba, I had followed the blackmailer's bagman to a bar called the Green Turtle, then to a parking lot where he got into a Fiat. I had noted the license-plate number on a business card. I found the card, copied the number into the notebook, then flipped to a back page where I copied numbers from Vance's phone.

When I was done, I thought for a moment, then slipped the phone into my pocket, power on. It might be interesting to monitor the man's calls.

Vance had come way too close to killing me not to pay attention.

9

Gear for my trip to Saint Arc was on the bed: two semiautomatic pistols, ammunition, a dive knife, Rocket fins, two masks, a compact spear gun, black watch cap, military face paint, handheld VHF radio with built-in GPS, two false passports, a satellite phone, Triad flashlight, infrared Golight, an envelope containing $10,000 in euros . . .

I had the hidden floor locker open. The collection grew as I moved between the bedroom, the lab, and my boat.

My boat . . . that's what I needed. Saint Arc was only a few miles from Saint Lucia. I wanted to book a room on Saint Lucia and use a boat to slip on and off Saint Arc. It would be cleaner that way. But I didn't want to rent some tourist junker from an island marina. You can't check a twenty-one-foot Maverick at the luggage counter, and I was going to have a tough-enough time getting firearms on a commercial airliner, then past the Saint Arc customs officers. They weren't well-trained, they weren't methodical, but they weren't idiots, either.

Weapons and a decent boat . . .

I have operated in parts of the world where I had neither, but it was rare. I could usually rely on my contacts to provide equipment. I needed their help now. So why was I putting off making the calls?

From the fireproof box, I took a weathered address book. Blue cover; alphabet tabs broken off. Most entries in pencil — pencil because it can be erased, but also because ink bleeds if soaked in a jungle storm.

As I leafed through the pages, I found my attention wandering to the videocassette, which I'd placed on the bed while packing. I had already checked it for serial numbers and identifying marks — nothing to distinguish it from millions of other Panasonic DVD tapes. But now, when I looked at it, Beryl Woodward came into my head. Her face, the auburn hair, her aloofness and heat. Her voice, too.

Especially after seeing some of the clips from that tape — my God. I would've watched. I'd pretended like I hadn't, but I would've watched from beginning to end.

I could hear her saying it, words clipped by wealth and the careful genetics of her caste.

The inflection when she said, *I would've watched.* The stage innocence of her inflection on *my God.*

It wasn't a tease. The subject had changed her breathing. But why tell me? Was she granting permission? Or was she suggesting something . . . ?

Buzz.

I jumped, startled. My pocket was vibrating. It took a long, weird second to remember I was carrying Vance's phone. I took it and checked caller ID without answering.

The brain converts thought waves into electrical energy, Tomlinson often tells me. Like-minded people communicate without saying a word. *On the same wavelength* is the cliché that proves how common it is.

At times, I secretly believe him. Like now. The name "Beryl" was flashing on the tiny screen.

Vance had Beryl Woodward logged in his phone book. But why was she calling him? At breakfast, she'd told me how much she distrusted the guy.

I waited for the vibration to stop, feeling ridiculous because I was so tempted to answer. I didn't.

Instead, I gave it an ungentlemanly-like

minute, then punched in the four-digit code to find out if Beryl had left a message.

She didn't.

I had a list of my old contacts in front of me while I used the office phone. The satellite phone was on the desk, too, but it didn't work. Deactivated, said a computer-generated voice.

Fitting. I'd been deactivated, too.

The list included deep-cover spooks, and State Department suits of the clandestine variety. They can be found in embassies worldwide — Fifth Floor men, they are sometimes called, because it's the traditional office space. When career staffers use the phrase "He's a Fifth Floor guy," they sometimes give it a chiding, insider's twist because it's a way of voicing disapproval without risking transfer.

The names included men I'd known and trusted for years.

I dialed Donald Piao Cheng, now one of the top execs in U.S. Customs. Donald couldn't disguise his surprise, or his discomfort, when he recognized my voice. He said he couldn't talk, but would call me back. Instinct told me he wouldn't.

It took several tries, but I finally located Harry Bernstein, a Texan who spoke Spanish with a drawl so Southern he sounded like one of the Beverly Hillbillies in a badly dubbed movie. We weren't friends, but we'd worked together in Central America. I wondered if Harry's Spanish had improved.

I didn't find out. Harry refused to take my call.

I tried a couple more names before skipping to the end of the list. There were two men I felt sure would help . . . or at least explain why they couldn't.

General Juan Rivera was an old adversary who'd become a friend. He played baseball, wore a Castro beard, and maintained homes (and wives) at several jungle camps in Central America. The man had power and he could pull a lot of strings, as he'd proven to me more than once.

Living in the jungle, though, makes communication unreliable, so I didn't expect Rivera to answer his phone. He didn't. I left a message telling him it was urgent, and that I would also send an e-mail.

Next on the list was Bernie Yager, an elite member of the U.S. intelligence community whose specialty was electronic warfare. He lived in desert, not jungle — Scottsdale, Arizona.

Bernie would answer if he was at home.

He would be eager to help.

I was half right.

"Marion, oh, Marion," Yager said in a tone that was scolding but also sad. "Why did you wait to contact me? You need advice, you don't call. Such a big decision, you don't call. So name one person who is better qualified than Bernie. You can't. *Now* you call."

I asked, "Does that mean we can't talk?"

"For you? A friend I would stick an arm into fire up to *here* for. Of course we can talk. But we can't *talk*. Understand what I'm saying? You, of all people, understand how the rules work in our world."

"I don't remember any rules. It's one of the reasons I left."

Yager's voice changed. "Don't lecture me about rules, Marion. When barbarians crash the gate, they bring the rules with them. Adapt or die. Apologize and die. Same thing. So maybe I'm not so happy to talk all of a sudden. The Marion Ford I know wouldn't say such a thing."

In fifteen years, the man had never spoken to me that way.

I said, "Sorry, Bernie. I was off-base."

There was a long silence before he replied. "There you go again. Apologizing. So say a few words because Bernie's starting to wonder who I'm really talking to."

I smiled. It wasn't an insult. I pictured the tough little man in the office of his adobe complex, scrambler phone on speaker now. The phone was linked to a computer system that he'd assembled lovingly. He was probably studying the monitor, comparing vocal prints, old and fresh, all seismic renderings of my voice.

Not unexpected. Bernie is legendary in the small, secret community of Electronic Warfare Information Operations. It was Bernie who invaded and compromised computer communications between Managua and Havana. It was Bernie who consistently intercepted communications between the Taliban and terrorist cells worldwide.

The man works obsessively. He'd lost his parents in a Nazi concentration camp and considered Islamists the Nazis of a new century. No wonder he'd bristled at my crack about rules. No wonder he was now confirming I was who I claimed to be.

I helped him out, saying, "It's me, Bernie. Promise. I was a friend of your sister, remember? Eve was a good and decent lady, but sometimes things don't turn out the way we plan."

Yager came on the phone again, sounding friendlier but still wary. "The world is a crazy place, Marion. These are dangerous times."

"All times are dangerous times. Especially for women like Eve. Trust the wrong man; make one bad choice at the wrong time, the wrong place. The same thing's happening to some female friends of mine, Bernie. I'm trying to help them."

"Drugs?"

"No, but it could ruin their lives. They could end up just as dead."

I heard the man sigh. "Okay, okay. Tell me about it. But it's not the same, you know. Maybe I can help. But I can't really *help*. Understand?"

I said, "No. This time, I don't understand." With the man's electronic surveillance capabilities, locating an extortionist on a small island would not have been difficult.

"Don't make this harder than it is, Marion! You quit. You're not one of us anymore. That makes you poison; part of the outside world. I'll listen to your problem. As a friend, I'll suggest this, discourage that. But I can't *help*. So go ahead and tell me before I have a coronary — that's how upset this is making me!"

So I told him, but only alluded to the information I needed from Saint Arc.

When I'd finished, he asked a question or

two before saying, "What I think you should do is contact a man I'm not going to mention. You know the name. Talk to him, make things right again. *Then* you talk to me."

He meant Hal Harrington. In my old job, Harrington was as close as I came to having a supervisor. He was a U.S. State Department intelligence consultant, and much, much more. Harrington was confidant and adviser to the military elite as well as senators and, sometimes, presidents. Hal had been a friend, he'd been an adversary. Now, I wasn't sure where we stood.

I replied, "Bernie, I'm going to tell you something I can barely admit to myself. I did call him. More than three weeks ago."

"You said your friends went on their vacation less than two weeks ago."

"That's right." I sat through a long silence before I added, "I called the man before my friends needed help. I called twice and left messages."

"Why? Just to chat? What are you telling me here?"

"No. Because . . . it's not the way I thought it would be. The outside world, you nailed it. That's the way it feels — outside of things. Not that I'm willing to go back and do what I was doing. A modified version, that's what I wanted to discuss with the man. But maybe it's too late."

"You haven't heard from him?"

"Nope. Almost a month it's been."

Sounding more distant, Bernie told me, "Then there's your answer."

10

An electronic clatter awoke me at a little after 4 p.m. Vance's phone. It was on the nightstand with my glasses.

Caller ID flashed *Beryl . . . Beryl . . . Beryl.* A determined woman.

I gave her time to leave a message, then checked. None from Beryl, but four I'd missed during my short run and swim. One from Michael, two from Elliot, all brief: *Call me!*

The fourth was longer. A woman's voice, furtive, talking as if she feared being overheard. "Hey, it's me. I just heard about your wife. My God, it's terrible and all, but they say she's gonna be okay. So maybe we can actually, like, spend some time together, you know? Call me at the club."

Georgia accent. Valley Girl rhythms. *Club* was a nightclub. The word becomes a proper noun when referring to a country club, spoken with affected emphasis. So she was a waitress, a hostess, a stripper, or a regular at a favorite bar. A woman Vance knew well enough that her name should have been logged in caller ID. But it wasn't.

Vance, who was desperately jealous of his wife, had a girlfriend on the side. An opportunist. She was looking forward to the free time Corey's near-suicide provided them.

As I wrote the number in the *Medusa* notebook, the phone next to my bookshelf began to ring. It's an old black desk model with buttons. No caller ID — same as the cheap answering machine. But because I recognized the woman's voice when she began her message, I rushed to answer.

It was Beryl. She couldn't get Vance, so she was calling me.

I answered, "Beryl?"

She said, "Why the surprise? You knew it was me, or you wouldn't have picked up. Eavesdropped on any good conversations lately, Dr. Ford?"

I replied, "Nope. But not because I haven't tried," pleased with the secret honesty. She caught it.

"I *believe* you. I think you're one of those people who ducks the truth by telling the truth. The innocent-looking type. You know the kind I mean? When actually they're hell-raisers."

"This morning you accused me of being a drug mobster. Now I'm an innocent type? I feel like I let you down."

"What I said was, 'drug lord or government assassin.'" Beryl listened a beat, as if I might reply. When I didn't, she added, "And I don't know you well enough to be disappointed. Shay gave me your number. Hope you don't mind."

I didn't.

Beryl had just left the hospital, she said. Corey was conscious and doing better. Corey's mother and father also were doing better. Their attorney had delayed questioning by the police.

"They called their lawyer after talking to Shay. She — the lawyer — had a private talk with Corey. The overdose was *accidental.* Corey knows how important that is. Her parents are really relieved, but they're also very pissed off at Vance — as in pushing for prosecution."

Shay was doing well, too, Beryl added. She would be released soon, possibly tomorrow.

I said, "Smart girl, your pal, Shay. Savvy and tough."

Beryl became more businesslike. "From what Shay tells me, she's got a very savvy godfather, too. I hope it's true, because she told me something surprising. It was something you could've told me at breakfast, but didn't. I thought we were supposed to be confidants, Dr. Ford."

"Drop the prefix," I said. "Maybe it'll help me open up."

"Okay . . . *Ford.* I just found out you plan to pay a visit to our favorite island. That you're going there to try and solve our little problem. You know — the thing that doesn't exist, and the night that never happened?"

I replied, "I have to be in the area anyway, so why not?"

"Oh, *please.*"

"It happens to be true. I'm working on a project that has to do with jellyfish. There's a rare species found in that section of the Caribbean, so I have to go anyway. Not very interesting, but it's what I do."

"True?" Her signature question, I realized.

I echoed, "True."

"Then you *are* going."

"Yes — but not for fun. When I'm not holed up working, reading journals and making notes, I'll use the free time to talk to authorities and ask a few questions. I doubt if there's much I can do."

"When are you leaving?"

"Tomorrow. Sunday at the latest."

Beryl asked, "Do you want company?" She

said it so coolly, it took a second to register.

"What?"

"You heard me. I can help. I know details you don't. Who, what, when, where — it'll save a lot of time. And I am motivated."

"You sound mad, not motivated."

"I'm both. You said Shay-shay's tough? Have you ever asked her about me?"

"No. Should I?"

"I'll leave that up to you. Maybe she'll tell you the truth." That hint of animus again — Beryl and Shay weren't as buddy-buddy as I'd believed.

I said, "I'd rather hear it from you."

"Okay. I'll skip the personal history and give you the short version: I don't like being manipulated, and I won't tolerate being bullied. I'm not some naïve airhead. I'm a big girl, reasonably intelligent, and I'm good at getting what I want. Can't we at least talk about it over drinks?"

Whew.

Tempting, but I couldn't.

I said, "Sorry, Beryl. The problem is —"

"I know, I know, you always travel alone. Shay told me you'd say that. But know what else she said? She said your marina has a party every Friday night. And if I really wanted to convince you, I should show up whether you invited me or not, and have an honest talk.

151

Shay says you're big on honesty."

When I started to speak, the woman interrupted again. "Tonight's Friday. Maybe I'll be at the party, maybe I won't. But I'll tell you this, Ford — I don't need your permission to go to Saint Arc. If I decide to go, *I'm going.*"

"But, Beryl —"

She hung up.

I wandered around the lab, too wired to sleep, too much on my mind to work. Tried different scenarios that included an auburn-haired female who left a wake of staring men when exiting a room, and whom the bad guys already knew.

Beryl was right. I travel alone. How could I explain carrying weapons and night-vision gear to a woman who'd grown up in a privileged, protected world?

No way.

To get my mind off it, I went to the computer, sat, and researched techniques for restoring charred paper. Found an article in the *Journal of Forensic Sciences* that was useful, and e-mailed the two experts it quoted, and a third expert who was mentioned in the footnotes.

A handwritten letter of personal interest

was damaged by fire before I had a chance to read it. I have no interest in restoration, but I would like to know the letter's contents. Would you be willing to advise me on methods of data recovery . . . ?

Next, I compiled background material on Saint Arc.

Officially named Saint Joan of Arc, this tiny island in the Eastern Caribbean chain is eight miles long and four miles wide, and a member of the French Commonwealth. The island is one of four French overseas departments in the Caribbean. The others are Martinique, French Guiana, and Guadeloupe — all former French colonies.

Because of this, Saint Arc is governed by French law and its citizens are legally French citizens, although France seldom interferes with the local government.

First inhabitants were Arawak who mixed with escaped slaves called Maroons (derived from the Spanish, Cimarron, meaning "untamed" or "wild"). Later, pirates used the island as a base. Saint Arc remained unsettled by Europeans, and was a lawless stronghold until the mid-1700s, when a French weapons manufacturer began purchasing bird guano, used in the making of gunpowder.

In the 1770s, when England took control of nearby Saint Lucia, Loyalists fleeing the American Revolution were commonly awarded land grants by the crown as a reward. The growing population of Loyalists soon spilled over onto nearby Saint Arc. Today, tourists are often surprised to discover that a large percentage of native islanders are white . . .

Escaped slaves, pirates, gunpowder. On an island with that kind of history, blackmail would be considered a benign enterprise.

I went for a short run, stopped at the beach at the end of Tarpon Bay Road, and swam two laps around the NO WAKE buoys before returning to the computer. I still had to book a flight.

I could fly Air Jamaica out of Miami, switch planes in Montego Bay, and be on Saint Arc by early tomorrow afternoon, depending on whether I took a boat or a private plane from nearby Saint Lucia. Or there was an Avianca flight that stopped in Bogotá, but got in two hours later . . .

But how the hell could I take the weapons I needed on a commercial flight?

I'd figure out something, I decided, or buy what I needed locally — which meant taking another five thousand euros from the floor safe.

Because Jamaican airports are a nightmare, I booked a commuter flight to Miami, then a first-class seat on Avianca departing 12:35 a.m.

I'd have to be on the road early, so I finished packing, then cleaned up the mess left by Vance Varigono. As I did, I thought about Shay and her attempt to apologize for not asking me to give her away at the wedding. I hadn't considered it a slight until Michael mentioned it.

Now, though, it made sense. There were reasons enough for a success-oriented woman like Shay to keep her distance. My occupation had to be guessed at, though never openly. To Shay's friends, I was kindly, bookish, and weird.

But Shay was savvy enough to assemble the truth about me even without the help of concrete details. No wonder she'd asked another man to give her away. No wonder she'd never introduced me to her prospective in-laws. To finesse that without alienating anyone took a hell of a lot of thought and effort. I admired her unsentimental approach.

Hadn't I constructed the woman's caricature to reflect my own conceits?

It didn't cause me to doubt her loyalty. I

was the man she came running to when she needed help.

An hour before sunset . . .

Through the window, I could see the encampment of buildings that was Dinkin's Bay Marina. Fishing guides were in for the day, hunkered together at the picnic tables outside the Red Pelican Gift Shop. Probably eating fried conch sandwiches and debating where to fish the next morning.

The Friday night party was taking shape, too. Mack, the owner, was lugging a tub of beer to the docks. Three new lady live-aboards — Jane, Deanne, and Heidi — were his cheerful, smiling overseers. Guys in Jensen Marina's beach band, the Trouble Starters, were testing speakers, and it looked like Danny Morgan and Jim Morris were sitting in.

Big night — the summer solstice. A few people would be wearing Druid robes; almost everyone would be behaving like heathens. A good night for Beryl to crash the party, except for one thing — the woman I'd been dating would be at the party, too.

Well . . . sort of dating: Kathleen Rhodes, Ph.D. A fellow marine biologist and a former love interest who seemed determined to make me her current love interest.

Through the window, I could see the pretty trawler Kathleen called home. The *Darwin C.* White hull, green trim. It was moored at the deep-water docks between a soggy old Chris Craft, *Tiger Lily,* and Coach Mike's thirty-eight-foot-long Sea Ray, *Playmaker.* The trawler had been at the marina only a few weeks, so still caught the eye.

I'd met Kathleen a couple of years back when she was a research biologist at Mote Marine. We'd had a relationship so intensely physical that the emotional component never caught up. There were always sparks of one kind or another. It made it easier for both of us when she announced she was leaving Florida to cruise the coast of Mexico. Her farewell letter to me was touching but also uncomfortably honest. It was in the fireproof box along with other important papers.

Seeing the *Darwin C.* brought back memories of the nights I'd spent aboard. It brought back the shape and scent of the woman; the qualities of her intellect; and her lucid, scientist's view of life. But having the boat moored so close to home also made me jumpy.

Kathleen had arrived unannounced. There are marinas on the islands that are better equipped and easier to access, but she'd chosen Dinkin's Bay. No accident. Why?

My marina neighbors include a tight little group of women who aren't shy with their opinions, especially about female outsiders. The ladies had taken me aside at parties; they'd stood on tiptoes to whisper advice in my ear.

Kathleen had reached *The Age,* they told me. The woman was single, childless, and ready to nest. It didn't matter how many college degrees Dr. Rhodes had, they said. Didn't matter that she was bright, independent, and financially set. Maternal drive is a powerful force. It was controlling her behavior and her scruples.

I chided them gently for trivializing their own sex, saying, "You talk like she's under a primitive spell." But the lady live-aboards only blinked at me, shaking their heads. How could I be so damn naïve?

"Primitive spell" described the transformation perfectly, they said.

No wonder I was jumpy.

I'd taken Kathleen to dinner a couple of times. Went to a concert at Big Arts. But the line that allows old lovers to meet comfortably as friends is a dangerous border. Sex is the only basic human function that can complicate the hell out of a human life.

So I was taking it slow — too slow for Kathleen, although she hadn't said it.

She would, though. Maybe tonight, if Beryl showed up. Two powerhouse women at one small marina. How smart was that?

Hmm.

But Kathleen had no claim. And Beryl hadn't signaled a romantic interest, and probably wouldn't. So . . .

I went outside and did pull-ups. Did descending sets 15-14-13-12 . . . Did them until I couldn't do any more. Then I showered, changed into clean khaki shorts, and selected a black guayabera shirt recently purchased in Panama.

Before leaving, I checked myself in the mirror.

So let the two ladies meet. See what happens . . .

Because of the party, cars lined the shell lane that is the terminus of Tarpon Bay Road, but only a black Mercedes was occupied. Two people, front seat. Female with beehive hair on the passenger side.

I spotted the car while checking for Beryl's Volvo convertible, but I would've noticed anyway. Beryl's car was parked near the gate. She'd already joined the party. Why hadn't the couple in the Mercedes?

I kept an eye on them as I exited the boardwalk, aware I was being watched through tinted glass.

The driver's door opened. A man got out: basketball-tall, early thirties, wire-rimmed glasses, blond hair styled to appear thicker. It was Shay's fiancé, Michael Jonquil.

"Dr. Ford? Have a minute?" As he closed the door, I got a peek at the passenger — his mother.

I replied, "Of course," but glanced at my watch to let him know I was in a hurry. I don't like surprises. Michael could have asked Shay for my number. Why hadn't he called?

"It won't take long. Do you mind sitting in the car?"

"Why? It's a nice evening."

"My mother would like to speak with you."

"No problem." I turned and smiled at her silhouette: heavy forehead, small chin. "She can roll down the window."

"I'm afraid that won't do."

I said, "How about my lab? That's private."

Jonquil said, "So I've heard," meaning something, I didn't know what. "But she prefers the car."

I looked at my watch again. "Well, life's full of little disappointments. I'll give you my number, we can arrange a meeting. But if it concerns Shay and it's important, I guess I could —"

Jonquil gave a private shake of the head, and silenced me with his eyes. He faced the Mercedes, shrugged — *I tried* — then told me, "I'll be right back."

I waited as he leaned into the car and spoke to his mother. I got another quick look at the woman: dark dress, hands on lap, black hair that framed the familiar scowl.

"Sorry about that," Jonquil said as returned. He sounded relieved, not disappointed. "Mind if we talk? Confidentially, I mean."

"Confidential as in exclude Shay? Sorry, can't agree to that."

"Good for you. Isn't it irritating how many people say yes automatically? No idea what they're being asked to keep secret, but it doesn't matter because their word's meaningless." He'd put his hand on my shoulder and turned me so we were walking with our backs to the Mercedes — a politician's device. "Listen to what I have to say, then decide. Okay?"

I answered, "Okay," aware of his mild accent when pronouncing *W*s and *O*s. A man who'd spent his summers in Europe speaking French-Swiss.

I listened to Jonquil say how shocking it

was, Corey's overdose. And what a close call for Shay. He regretted not getting to know me better, and looked forward to the two of us hanging out. When he sensed my impatience, he got serious.

"Truth is, I'm glad you didn't talk to Mother. It's good for her not to get her way occasionally."

I said, "If it's only occasionally, you're mother has lived an unusual life."

"You couldn't be more right. She comes from old money, she and her six sisters. Royal bloodlines — I suspect you know what that means in Europe. On the paternal side, her grandfather was an international industrialist. My own father was a brilliant man, Dr. Ford. I wish you could've met him. But the fortune that he . . . well, let's say the *success* my father enjoyed doesn't compare to mother's family. My aunts are strong women. They didn't approve of my father. Some of mother's family still don't, even though it's been two years since he died."

I said, "Then your engagement to Shay must be quite a shock. Does your mother know Shay's background?"

"The investigators she hired gave a full report. A father who was a convicted felon. A mother who, as you know, was a . . ." He hesitated, then left the sentence unfinished.

"So of course Mother doesn't approve. But I think she's come to admire Shay in her own way.

"Shay's a leader, and a hell of a good organizer. Mother can't intimidate Shay — you have no idea how rare that is. But Mother also realizes that politics is a damn tough business. I need a strong wife. So, in a way, she does approve of the marriage. Or did — before the girls had their weekend on Saint Arc." He let that settle. "Do you care to guess what Mother wants to discuss?"

I said, "I'm a biologist. We're not supposed to guess — it's in the handbook they gave us at biologist school."

He chuckled. "Shay-shay never mentioned you had a sense of humor. But *seriously* —" He cleared his throat. "Mother's heard rumors about what the girls did down there. She knows you flew to Saint Arc to make some kind of deal with a man who's blackmailing them."

I stopped walking and turned to face Jonquil. "Who would tell her something so ridiculous?"

"It wasn't me. But Vance Varigono is a fraternity brother of mine. So I know it's true."

I smiled; shook my head and waited.

Jonquil maintained eye contact. Pale blue

eyes larger because of his glasses, and half a head taller, so I had to look up.

"You're going to deny everything?"

"I didn't know I was on the witness stand. Along with my great sense of humor, Shay also forgot to tell you I'm not known for my patience. No more questions until you get your facts straight — okay, Michael?"

"Patience? It was never mentioned. But I heard about the dangerous temper."

"Dangerous? Me? That's funny; not something I often hear — I look through a microscope for a living. Maybe a rumor like that will improve my image."

Jonquil said, "You have no image, Dr. Ford." Seeing my reaction, he added quickly, "Mother doesn't hire local hacks when she needs a private investigator. She uses a London agency with contacts at Interpol, and probably organizations they'd never admit. Your name was red-flagged because almost no information was available. What was the term . . . ? *A significant pattern of chronological gaps*. Yes, it was highlighted. The investigator used an interesting phrase. He said you were like a ghost in front of a mirror."

I replied, "Selling marine specimens to schools isn't a high-profile occupation. That's why I like it. It's not because I have something to hide."

Jonquil was shaking his head. "You may look like a college professor, but I'm willing to bet you deal in more than microscopes and fish. Haven't you wondered why Shay didn't ask you to give her away at the wedding? It's because she feels there's a potential for embarrassment — violence, too. You scare her."

"Shay would never say that about me."

Jonquil's amused expression read, *Didn't she?* But he replied, "She didn't have to. You caught Vance in your house this morning. He told me about it. You scared the shit out him — and not because you almost broke his arm. When the police took him in, they didn't scare him as much as you did. I'm not condemning you; I admire you for it. Dr. Ford, what you don't understand is, I don't want Mother to find out the truth about Saint Arc. I want the whole goddamn problem to go away. I'm offering to help."

The profanity sounded out of character. So did his earnest manner.

I said, "The only problem you have is your pal Vance. He has a personality disorder. He invents stories to justify his behavior. Tell your mother that."

"He's a liar, sure. Vance lies so often that it's easy for someone who knows him to spot the truth. His wife *did* get an e-mail demanding more money. The videotape's real. Shay won't discuss it, and I wouldn't allow Mother to question her because of the accident. But Mother will. That's why I'm asking you to level with me."

His mother — why did he keep referring to his mother? There are people so poisonous that prolonged exposure ensures contamination; their unhappiness is shared by osmosis. She was that type, apparently.

I said, "I have leveled with you. Now you should stand up like a big boy and tell your mother to mind her own business. Doesn't it bother Shay that she's the only one with balls in your relationship?"

The man's eyes glowed, his nostrils widened. He had a temper, too. Before he got it under control, he said, "If you're not smart enough to read between the lines, I'll make it easy. I don't care about what's on the tape. The girls went away for the weekend and had fun. Good! What's the term? Sport-fucking? Shay spent a night with some island jock she'll never see again. Who cares? I'm not an insecure man. Apparently you can't relate. I spent summers living in France, so I don't have all the American hang-ups about monogamous sex."

I said, "Shouldn't the German army get credit for that?"

For an instant, I thought he was going to take a swing at me. "This isn't a joke, god-damn it! I don't want my mother to find out the truth because she'll sabotage the wed-ding. I love Shay. I want to protect her. If there are men on Saint Arc who are black-mailing her? Personally —" Jonquil's voice dropped. "I think they should be dealt with privately. I think they should be . . . put away."

"Put away?" I said it slowly, gauging his reaction. "Jailed, you mean."

"No. I mean put away — *permanently*. My family's done business in the Caribbean for years. There's no justice on an island like Saint Arc unless you buy it. I'm willing to buy it. I'll pay the right man to do whatever needs to be done. Or to arrange it — I don't care how."

I glanced at the Mercedes, forty yards away. I looked toward the marina. Lots of empty cars on the shell lane; a few people on the other side of the gate, but none close enough to hear.

I said, "Michael, you watch too many movies."

He leaned closer, his pale eyes focused. "I am totally serious. I have the money. A hundred thousand dollars. A hundred and a half? What's the going rate? I don't want that video hanging over our heads after we're married. I'm running for the Florida House, for Christ's sake!"

Suddenly, I understood. I had warned Shay about what the video could do to the man's political career. But he seemed unconcerned what it could do to Shay's career.

I knew what he was suggesting. But I had to ask, "Why are you telling me this?"

"Because I want you to convince Shay she can trust me with the truth —"

"I see!" My tone said *bullshit*.

"— and because I think you're the man for the job. You're the closest thing Shay has to family. You can be trusted. And she's talked about you enough that we both understand you're not in a . . . a conventional line of work."

I laughed, my tone now saying, *I can't believe this.*

"I'll pay you a hundred and fifty thousand cash, plus expenses. Plus whatever else you need. We have a corporate jet. We're vested in a company that owns part of a marina and resort on Saint Lucia — that's only a few miles from Saint Arc. Fly in, take care of business, fly out.

"Ford —" He reached to put his hand on my shoulder. *"I'll go with you.* Some son of a bitch is hurting the woman I'm going to marry. I would do anything to protect her."

I rolled my shoulder to free myself of his hand. "As a wedding present, I'll pretend we never had this conversation. I'm a marine biologist. That's all. My research takes me to a lot of places, including the Eastern Caribbean. It's a coincidence. Give Vance credit — he used what I do to make up one hell of a story."

"Damn it, Ford, at least consider my offer!"

I shook my head. "Your mother's waiting."

11

As Jonquil and his mother pulled away in the Mercedes, I was thinking, *Private jet?* It was exactly what I needed. There were a couple of private airstrips on Saint Lucia, and at least one on Saint Arc.

But I couldn't risk accepting the guy's offer. Professionals only deal with professionals. Michael Jonquil was a rich kid, adult-phase. He was believable. Maybe he had a good heart. Maybe he really wanted to protect Shay — and his career, too, of course.

But it was also possible he was baiting me. If I agreed to go after the blackmailer, it proved the blackmailer and the video existed. A backdoor way of confirming his fiancé had been unfaithful.

If I'd gotten into the Mercedes, would his mother have made the same offer? I gave it some thought — hide a tape recorder under the seat and hope I jumped at the money. Why else insist I get in the car?

The woman was a puppeteer. If the offer was her idea, I'd find out soon enough.

I ducked through mangroves to get around the marina gate. Mack locks the thing every Friday at closing time. It's become ceremony. The gate keeps the outside world out, while sealing visitors and live-aboards in. The sense of security it creates encourages excess in all forms.

After the last twenty-four hours, fun and excess seemed well-deserved. But I also reminded myself that locking locals and visitors into a space with narrow docks and unlimited beer could be volatile.

Kathleen would be there. Beryl, too. Tricky. The same was true of the marina's parties. They were a tradition, but no two were the same. Each had its own pace and mood.

I knew from experience the marina's parties could be dangerous. They had ended marriages and partnerships, engagements, too, but they had also prompted spur-of-the-moment weddings. The party had hosted receptions, and *many* conceptions, although the number was impossible to track. It had brought together people who would be friends for life, and a few who would remain lifelong enemies because of drunken arguments and an occasional fistfight.

Years ago, Mack gave the party a name:

171

Dinkin's Bay Pig Roast and Beer Cotillion. But it's been shortened to Perbcot as a spoof on Epcot, the Orlando tourist attraction. "I took the kiddies to Perbcot" is island code that explains disappearing for the weekend without risking details.

I decided to enjoy myself but stay on my toes.

I stopped at the marina office, said hello to Mack and Eleanor, and dropped a fifty-dollar bill into the donation bucket. Then I took a quart of beer from the cooler and carried it outside to the bait tanks, where I listened to the guides trade stories.

Snook were thick off the beach in knee-deep water. Tarpon were schooling inside Captiva Pass near the fish house once owned by Judge Lemar Flowers. Judge Flowers had been a friend of my uncle Tucker Gatrell, and hearing the name reminded me of the scorched letter back at the lab.

From the little I remembered, my mother was nothing like the angry woman in the back of the Mercedes. She was an amateur naturalist; one of the earliest advocates of a Save the Everglades movement. Long ago, I'd found her name on a little brass plaque near Flamingo, headquarters of Everglades National Park.

I was pleased when the guides switched

the topic to the whale stranding of the night before.

"Killer whales," Captain Nels told us, "only two of them dead. But there were hundreds for a while. I had a shelling charter this morning and talked to a woman who was camped on the beach. She saw the whole thing. And stink? Oh, man! It'll be awhile before I take clients back there."

Dozens of whales had tried to beach themselves, Nels had been told, but then suddenly turned en masse and headed out to sea.

"You think somethin' could'a scared them, Doc?" Nels asked. "Maybe some of them big sharks come down from Boca Grande. That's what *I* think. Other day, Mark Futch saw a hammerhead long as his boat."

I sipped my beer and said, "I guess it's possible."

Tomlinson observed, "It's a mystery why a straight arrow like you, Doc, is always knee-deep in women trouble," frowning as if concerned, but actually enjoying himself. "I'm starting to think they don't love you for your intellect."

I said, "As if you're an expert."

"Shallow-up, Amigo. I'm giving you a compliment, for Christ's sake. Only trying to help."

"Umm-huh. Like a hangman giving advice about knots."

We were standing by the canoe rack, looking across the water at the *Darwin C.* with its green trim and green Bimini canvas. Beryl Woodward and Kathleen Rhodes were sitting in captain's chairs on the fly bridge, sipping drinks, leaning close the way women do when they've just met but already have things in common.

"Here's an idea — how about I page you from the marina so it goes over the PA? I'll say a U-Haul has just arrived, big enough so you can finally get your shit together. It'll give you an excuse to skedaddle. You've never noticed how much nicer women are when they know you're leaving?"

I said, "Funny. You're a regular Dr. Laura."

I had told Tomlinson I was flying out of Miami in the morning and Beryl wanted to go.

"Have you talked to her since she got to the marina?" he asked. He meant Beryl.

"Nope."

"Have you told Kathleen you're leaving for a week?"

"When have I had a chance? I've been standing here listening to you jabber for the last twenty minutes."

Tomlinson was grinning, not bothering to hide it. "You're screwed, amigo. The only difference between cliff diving and your love life is there's no ambulance parked near the rocks." Now he was laughing — cheerful despite a hangover, and not even stoned. "If it wasn't for you, I'd be convinced reincarnation is all about perfecting my role as the island's village idiot. Thanks for sharing the load. That's friendship."

I took the quart of beer and poured the last of it over ice in a plastic cup. "I didn't ask Kathleen to tie up at the marina. And Beryl's not here because she's interested in me. I already told you what she wants."

I hadn't use the word "revenge," but Tomlinson had figured it out.

"You're kidding yourself. Women don't come to marinas to guzzle beer and sit on expensive boats. Only men are that simpleminded. Women come to marinas to meet the simpleminded men who own the boats — or for more serious reasons. Kathleen's here because she's serious. Maybe you should go face the music before those two women bond. You're really S-O-L if that happens."

Tomlinson turned to look at a sleek Sea Ray idling into the basin. "Hey — you said you aren't happy about flying commercial?

If your old contacts can't help, maybe your new contacts can." He waved his hand toward the Sea Ray. Coach Mike Westhoff was standing at the controls of the *Playmaker* with two men I recognized beside him: Dave Lageschulte and Eddie DeAntoni.

Tomlinson said, "Lags told me he and the guys are opening a new Hooters on Martinique — that's close to Saint Arc. He's been flying back and forth in the Gulfstream. Didn't you say there's a private airstrip there?"

I nodded. "Saint Lucia, too." I didn't want to fly directly to Saint Arc. Didn't want the attention.

"Talk to Lags, man."

Lageschulte and "the guys" were high school buddies from tiny Waverly, Iowa, who had founded a chain of sports bars. They'd done okay for farmboys.

I said, "Gulf Stream as in Gulfstream jet?"

"Yep. Five hundred knots, range four thousand miles, and a galley stocked with beer and chicken wings. A couple weeks back, the guys invited me along on a trip to Waterloo. We played pinochle, then hit some Amish auctions."

"You're kidding. Farm auctions?"

"The scene was incredible. Talk about

drama. Lags had to outbid four or five bowed-neck Hawkeyes for a crosscut saw with a painting on it."

I looked at Tomlinson, who was focused on the Sea Ray while combing a shaky hand through his hair. He'd been doing a lot of that lately — hanging with rock stars, business stars, jock stars, traveling, holding court among people who admired his writing, or his skills as a Zen roshi, or who felt set free by his Happy Hippie persona.

I hadn't heard about the trip with Lags, but wasn't surprised. Tomlinson was spending less and less time at the marina. There were long periods when we didn't talk. Maybe he traveled to mask his bouts of self-doubt — there's a fine line between traveling and running away. Or maybe it was because he'd achieved rock-star status of his own. His book *One Fathom Above Sea Level* had a growing cult following. Fans considered a trip to Dinkin's Bay a form of pilgrimage. Because of that, the marina was no longer a refuge for Tomlinson.

"It's flattering," he had told me months ago. "But I worry that I disappoint people who love what I wrote. I can't live up to my own words. I admit it. Words turn paper into stone — I'm not stone."

Now, though, watching Coach Mike dock

the Sea Ray, Tomlinson sounded right at home giving me travel advice.

"Flying commercial sucks. If you need a last-minute flight, talk to Lags, and don't forget about Eddie. He's a pilot. You could rent your own plane. You can afford it — why not?"

Eddie was a nephew of the late Frank DeAntoni, a man I had admired, but didn't get to know nearly well enough before he was murdered. Eddie had called Mack in March, asking if there was space to moor his customized go-fast boat. Eddie had won a chunk of a New Jersey lottery and was interested in Dinkin's Bay because Frank had talked about the fun people, including a guy named Ford, and some Tinkerbelle weirdo, Tomlinson. Before fate — or maybe mobster friends — made him rich, Eddie had been a commercial pilot.

"Fly to the islands with Lags or Eddie," I said. "That's not a bad idea."

"Skip Lyshon's here, too — you said you needed a boat? Skip's got boats everywhere." He paused. "Doc, ol' buddy, you've got your thinking cap on backward lately. Are you sure you don't want me to come along? I'll cancel the Zen retreat. That's a serious offer. Please?"

A dozen times, he'd offered. Truth was, I

didn't want Tomlinson along. He would attract too much attention on Saint Arc, where ganja hustlers were on every street corner.

I was nodding my head, letting him know how helpful he was. "I *saw* Skip. You're right — I have plenty of contacts. Why didn't I think of it?"

"You're on autopilot. We're all on autopilot until something gooses us out of our routines. Last night — those sharks? We both died, you know. Best thing that could've happened to us."

"We . . . died?"

"Yep. I'm certain of it. Hammerheads got us."

I was smiling — funny the way the man said whatever came into his head when he was preoccupied. Like right now, watching Lags step onto the dock as Eddie lifted a box of something — fruit? — waiting to unload.

I said, "Died metaphorically, you mean."

"No — but what's the difference? We're just as dead. That makes four times for me and at least twice for you — plus, you've got another big one already scheduled. Trust me, we both already have weeds growing through our ribs. This marina's full of ghosts."

He often said that.

"If you're a ghost, why are you still scratching that bite on your leg? And why is my beer empty?"

"Death doesn't explain everything. But it's a perfect excuse for almost anything. Hey —" Tomlinson's energy level jumped a notch, and he began walking toward the Sea Ray, grinning as he signaled me to follow. "I just realized what's in that box — mangoes! Coach Mike went to Saint James City to load up. Pine Island mangoes are the best on earth, Dr. Ford. So why're we standing here making small talk?"

As if I were invisible — ghostlike — Beryl said to Kathleen Rhodes, "I thought I hated mangoes. The ones I've tried — from supermarkets, you know? Those were like turpentine. Stringy, too, with this fibrous junk that sticks in your teeth. So you'd think that's the way all mangoes taste, but there's no comparison."

Beryl spooned another slice into her mouth and closed her eyes. "Ummm. My God, these are ambrosia." Then leaned back and smiled, showing Kathleen her perfect teeth, but also giving me her good profile, nose . . . chin . . . pert little breasts beneath a white blouse with creases. The white blouse darkened Beryl's amber hair.

I started to say, "There are dozens of varieties —" but Kathleen raised her voice to cover mine, interrupting as she'd done several times already, only now it was to correct me.

"Actually, there are sixty-nine species of mangoes, and a thousand varieties. They originated in India, but I've eaten them all over the world. Every varietal is different — like wine."

She added, "You can tell a lot by the shapes. The elongated mangoes —" the picnic table was draped with banana leaves; halved mangoes everywhere "— are from Indonesia. The round ones are East Indian stock. But some of the best cultivars were developed right here in Florida." Kathleen favored me with a glance before asking, "Isn't that right, Doc?"

She'd timed it so I had a mouthful, but I managed to say, "Pine Island . . . lots of types. My favorite —"

"*My* favorite is the Num Doc Mai from Vietnam. They taste like a blend of grapes and peaches. These Hadens? A wonderful custard apple flavor. I spent two years cruising Mexico, Central America, Cuba. Mangoes became a sort of hobby. Beryl? If Doc does decide to drag you along to Saint Arc, you have to try this wonderful liquor they make. Distilled from guess what?"

Beryl was right with her. "Distilled from *mangoes?*" She said it with a breathless edge that I hoped was sarcasm. Nothing I could do about it — the women had obviously discussed the trip. But the night would only get chiller if the two became buddies.

Kathleen's jaw tightened for a moment — yes, Beryl was being sarcastic. But then Kathleen laughed, done with it. Done with Beryl, too, because now she addressed the table — Eddie, Lags, me on one side, Coach Mike with the women on the other. "Why don't we have our own little mango tasting? A blind test. We sample five or six different types, and keep score on paper."

Eddie was mashing slices of fruit into a paste — no idea why — but stopped to ask, "We don't gotta wear blindfolds, do we? I'm not into that blindfolded crap. I come to have fun, not get weird."

Earlier, when I'd asked Eddie to fly me to Saint Lucia, or to the private landing strip on Saint Arc, I'd received the same suspicious, tough-guy reaction. "Is Shay going? Or what's-her-name, the pretty one — Beryl?" he'd asked.

When I told him no, they were staying in Florida, he made a face — *Are you nuts?* — and said, "Why the hell would I fly some guy, just the two of us alone, way down there where they got beaches, and girls don't wear no tops? Did you fall and hit your head or somethin'?"

If I hadn't liked Eddie's uncle so much, I probably wouldn't have invested the time it had taken to like Eddie. And I did like him, but the man took some getting used to.

Not so with women. Women adored the guy; couldn't get enough of his bad-boy attitude and his dimples. Kathleen was clearly charmed; let me see how taken she was with this good-looking Italian guy with his broken nose, his New Jersey accent, his gladiator body, and his lottery fortune.

She said, "No, Eddie, you don't have to wear a blindfold, but like they say, don't knock it. What I mean is, we score each mango without knowing the name. Coach Westhoff?" Kathleen ran her fingers over Mike's hand. "Would you mind helping Beryl with her score sheet if she gets confused?"

Mike raised his eyebrows and shrugged, too smart to answer.

Beryl Woodward had confident, faded-denim eyes that now became double-barreled. She knew how to handle it, saying, "It's true, Mike. I can be such a ditz at times. Do you mind? I don't have Kathy's experience when it comes to scoring."

Dr. Rhodes didn't flinch. "Actually, it's Kath*leen,* dear," she said, turning to smile at Beryl — a chance to show off her own perfect teeth while giving us a look at her profile: nose . . . chin . . . blond hair silver over a navy blue tank top that strained with the weight of her breasts, skin freckled tan in a valley of cleavage.

Eddie banged my knee beneath the table — an adolescent guy-thing to do when women spar — but I was looking at Kathleen's breasts, thinking my own adolescent thoughts about the boundary that separates former lovers. A woman's breasts are fraternal twins — distinct entities in their secret space that respond independently of the other. Kathleen's had once been my private playground, the focus of many sweaty intimacies. Now they were as foreign as the moon — and the odds of physical contact were just as remote.

You are always alone, Doc. No matter who you're with, you're alone inside that thick head of yours . . .

Kathleen had written that two years ago — or something close — in the letter I'd kept. She was right — tonight, anyway.

Beneath the table, a foot brushed my leg.

I turned and gave Eddie a look of distaste. *Hey.*

Eddie, now stirring the mango paste into his beer, stared back and said, "What's your fuckin' problem, Ace? Never seen someone make a beer Slurpee before?"

The foot touched my leg again. I looked across the table. It was Beryl, signaling me with her blue-jean eyes.

Let's get out of here.

A little after midnight, Shay called from the hospital, chatty in a way that told me she wanted information without revealing that she wanted it. I'd been at the computer doing research. I didn't have to get up to answer the phone.

Shay said, "They wake my butt up every twenty minutes to make sure my brain's still functioning, so I figured I'd check in. Ask you how the party went."

I thought: *She's calling because she knows Michael and his mother came to the marina. Or because of Beryl.*

I replied, "Party went fine. Good band, some great mangoes. Jeth and Janet brought their baby boy. He's a cutie." I played dense — stubborn after several beers, but also reacting to Shay's gambit.

I listened to an update on Corey — she'd

had a setback, but nothing serious. Something about electrolytes. Police had taken Vance in for questioning, then released him. Corey wouldn't admit that Vance had hit her, but community services had stepped in, anyway. Her parents, too. Thumb bruises on a woman's biceps tell a story. Corey's family was getting a restraining order.

I said, "That's good news," looking at Vance's phone on the microscope table. He'd gotten so many calls, I'd switched it off. Later, when I had time, I would copy the numbers. The phone was with my boat keys — next to Beryl's purse.

As Shay continued talking, I stood, put Vance's phone in a drawer, and closed it.

Shay told me, "A restraining order isn't all *I'd* do if Michael hit me. But I don't have to worry about that, thank God. He's a good man, Doc — that's why I'm worried. I'm scared I'm going to lose him over . . . over, you know, what I did. After the wedding — if *there is* a wedding — I hope you and Michael get a chance to spend time together."

Was she fishing to get a response? Maybe. But she was also afraid — no finessing that. It was time to stop playing dense and reassure the girl. I told her Michael and I had talked. Nothing confidential, so he could fill in the details. I didn't mention Michael's offer, but said, "The man's determined to marry you. He made that clear."

"Really?"

"Yes."

"You *swear*?"

"Yes."

"But what about Saint Arc? He knows that I did something shitty when I was there. But how much does he know?"

I said, "Calm down, take a slow breath. You're hyperventilating. I mean it — a *slow* breath." I covered the phone and turned an ear to the lab's north window. Through the screen, I could hear the shower running and a woman's muffled singing.

I uncovered the phone and asked Shay, "Are you okay?"

She was crying again — only the second or third time since I'd known her. "*No.* I feel so goddamn helpless! Ida is doing everything she can to screw it up, that bitch! She's always hated me."

I said, "Michael's mother."

"*Yes.* Ida hires detectives when she wants information. She's determined to dig up more dirt — not the first time, either. That's why you have to tell me, Doc. How much does Michael know about the video?"

I said, "What video?" with the familiar emphasis, then added, "He asked about a video. I told him it was a story Vance invented. You know, to give him an excuse for hitting his wife."

"Did he believe you?"

"Why wouldn't he? Vance is a pathological liar. Your friends know it."

Shay made a helpless, groaning sound. "Some nice circle of friends, huh? A wife beater. Two of us in the hospital after we fucked around like sorority girls, then flipped out. And Ida, the Grand Dame of Blame, stirring the pot."

I said gently, "Take it easy, Shay. The blame's not all yours. I'll print out some stuff I researched and bring it to the hospital in the morning. I was right when I said you were targeted by pros."

"That's what *I* think. Those lowlifes!"

I had returned to the computer. On the screen was an article about a party drug known as "Icebreaker."

Now was not the time to tell Shay.

I listened to her say, "Know what those pretty boys deserve? What Dexter Money would've done. Daddy would've tracked them down and shot the sons of bitches dead. You know who feels the same way? Beryl. We talked about it — we're going into attack mode. She's so pissed off about what Vance did, she's been trying to get him on the phone to unload. He won't answer, of course. She didn't tell you tonight?"

Through the window, I heard the shower stop, along with a woman's muted humming. I said, "No. Beryl didn't mention it."

"Beryl was at the party, wasn't she?"

"Yes."

"I bet she was all over Eddie now that her engagement's off. I told her I liked him a lot, so it's practically guaranteed she'll hit on him."

An interesting friendship, these two women had.

I said, "Maybe they talked, I'm not sure. Eddie said to give you a hug." He'd also said some things I wasn't going to repeat to an engaged woman — Eddie had a thing for Shay, too.

"I don't blame Beryl, it's just the way she is. Probably because of what happened."

"What's that mean?"

There was a silence — Shay getting calmer as her brain began to put things together. "I . . . I got the impression she was going to take you aside and have an honest talk. I told her it was the best way — you're big on honesty."

Cupping the phone, I said, "Beryl mentioned it. Thanks."

"But she didn't tell you anything . . . personal? She said she would. I told her you should know where she stands. Beryl and I feel the same when it comes to the three pretty boys. All bullies, period, and guys who victimize women. If the cops don't do their jobs, hey, what's the alternative?"

"Beneath those beautiful faces, you both have hearts of steel."

"Don't make jokes. It's the way a woman has to be. With me, you understand because you met Daddy. With Beryl, though, it's because of something that happened when she was thirteen. It took her a long time to recover — that's the reason she started college late. But if she didn't tell you what happened —"

I interrupted, "Actually, she brought it up. She said you'd tell me if I asked."

"*I'd* tell you?"

"Yes, that maybe you'd give me her background. So I'm asking."

I listened carefully — also hearing a woman's bare feet on the deck outside — as Shay said, "Well, it was on the national news, so it's not like some deep, dark secret. Think back — it was a long time ago. Fifteen, sixteen years — you might remember. Beryl was abducted from her bedroom. Some man, they never caught him — this was in Colorado. He kept her for three days. A couple of Boy Scouts found her wandering in a state park near Boulder. That's why her family moved to Florida."

I was thinking, *Woodward . . . Colorado . . . schoolgirl missing,* picturing the headlines, but possibly confusing her abduction with others. One missing child is a tragedy. Hundreds of missing children, year after year, is a statistic.

I said, "No wonder she left it up to you to tell me," turning to get a glimpse of the woman through the east window, wearing a towel like a sarong, using another to dry her hair.

"Thing is, she doesn't mind talking about it. She doesn't get into the details, of course. But generally, how the legal system should deal with men who do that kind of sick crap. That's why Beryl's the way she is."

"Tough, you mean."

"Yeah, tough. But also . . . well, she's different —" Shay lowered her voice. "When it comes to men, I mean. I don't know how Elliot put up with it for as long as he did. I don't know if I told you, but Elliot and I were close friends."

I said, "Were?"

"It's a long story. Beryl has a problem with jealousy. The woman's like a sister, Doc, but you're family, too, which is the only reason

I'm telling you this —"

I interrupted, "Let's talk in the morning, okay?" as Beryl came through the door, still toweling her hair, but already talking, saying, "That's an amazing shower. It's like washing in a thunderstorm. It *is* rainwater, isn't it? Nothing else leaves your hair so soft —" She stopped, seeing I was on the phone.

I held up a finger — *Done in a minute* — as Shay whispered, "My God, she's there. Why didn't you tell me?"

I said, "Glad to hear you're better. I'll give you a call in the morning."

"Jesus, just you and Beryl alone?" Shay was still whispering, but talking fast. "Doc, *listen* to me. If she hasn't done it already, she'll try to get you into bed. It's what Beryl does after breaking up with a guy. Don't do it. Trust me — there's a *reason.* I'll tell you later. When she's like this, she'll say anything to get what she wants."

Looking into Beryl's blue-jean eyes as she walked toward me, the room suddenly warmer, I said into the phone, "Follow the doctor's orders, that's good advice."

I hung up.

12

Beryl said, "That was Shay-shay? I told you she'd call. Did she warn you to stay away from me?"

The woman continued drying her hair, then gave her head a shake, creating a loose amber curtain that framed her face.

"Shay said you two are like sisters. And she told me what happened when you were thirteen. I hope that's okay."

"*Hmm* . . . Interesting."

"You said I should ask."

"That's right. I did." Beryl turned a tan shoulder to me, towel knotted above her breasts, inner thigh visible as she stepped toward an aquarium, skin whiter where shadows angled upward. "Did she tell you all the nasty details?"

"She said you never discuss the details. I didn't ask, but she said it, anyway. Shay had an abusive father — I met the guy. He was about as nasty as they come. She was explaining that you two had a lot in common. It helped me understand why you want to return to Saint Arc."

"I wish she'd given me time to tell you myself."

I was tempted to tell Beryl she'd had ample opportunity. Instead, I said, "Don't blame Shay. I pressed for information."

"Do you think I'm some kind of freak now? A lot of people do. That I'm damaged goods, some kind of psychological cripple. Rescued by Boy Scouts, so I must be some helpless twit. That's what they think. Men, especially. But some women, too."

I said, "You're talking about Shay."

Beryl said, "Maybe." She was staring at the venomous sea jellies that oscillated in the aquarium's cool light. They were translucent prisms, living wafers of light. "We *are* like sisters in some ways. Territorial. Shay's always had a thing for you. A physical thing, so she'd be defensive." Beryl turned to me, eyes hoping for a reaction.

"If she told you that, she was kidding."

"You didn't know? No . . . I can see you didn't. Shay says you're sort of dense that way. When we first met, she had a bad case of Doc Ford — tried all the little tricks, but you never took the bait. Michael's still jealous as hell of you. Funny — I didn't believe

194

her when she told me you never figured out that she was interested."

"Maybe she had a crush. I would've noticed if it was anything serious."

"It was a lot more than a crush. That's why she asked my father to give her away at the wedding, not you. One of the reasons. She said it'd be too strange. You know, because she still has sexual feelings for you."

Apparently there were many reasons.

"Shay will say anything to make sure that you and I . . . that we don't become more than friends."

I said, "Anything?" In my mind, I was replaying Shay's warning. *She'll say anything to get what she wants.*

"Well, almost anything. I love her. She's one hard-ass girl. But she won't be happy if she finds out what we did tonight."

I said, "Why? We didn't do anything wrong. You told me about Saint Arc. I made notes. We looked up some things on the Internet. Nothing wrong with that."

"You know what I mean. It was innocent, but she'd still be jealous."

I knew what she meant.

We'd been out in my skiff. No wind tonight, and the bay was a bioluminescent soup, bright as emerald paint when disturbed. Beryl had stripped to bra and panties and jumped overboard — "Like jumping into a cloud of fireflies!" she told me when she surfaced. "A billion stars explode. You've got to try it."

That's why she was showering when Shay called. That's why I was wearing nothing but running shorts and sandals.

Beryl touched a finger to the aquarium, tracing the path of a sea jelly as it descended. "I shouldn't talk that way about Shay. You two are close. But she should be more understanding about your feelings and mine. After two years with Elliot — Mister Perfect — it's nice to be with a guy like you."

I said, "I'm anything but perfect. The rumors are true."

"Are they?"

"That I'm not perfect? Yes."

She smiled, watching the sea jellies. "It wasn't a cut. It was a compliment. I like it here, Ford. Everything neat and orderly. It has a nice smell — sort of like living in a tree house." She turned. "And I like you. A lot."

I said, "You're welcome here anytime."

"True?"

"Yes."

"But you're not going to change your mind about me going to Saint Arc."

"No."

There was a towel next to the computer. I

196

put it over my shoulder as I tapped the monitor, eager to change the subject. "I found this while you were outside. It's about party drugs."

She smiled. "I've heard of them." Said it as if I was the naïve one, not her.

"Well, maybe there's one you haven't heard of. A friend told me about an amphetamine derivative that's popular at resorts in Jamaica."

"The tall hippie-looking guy?"

"That's him. Guys slip it into girls' drinks. Or they soak marijuana in it. The medical abbreviation is MDA — methylenedioxyamphetamine. It could explain your behavior that night."

"They drugged us? I kind of suspected it. More than just the grass, I mean." Beryl crossed the room and put her hand on my bicep, pivoting behind me so she could see the screen. I could feel the heat of her fingertips. I watched her breathing change as she read, chest moving beneath the towel.

"Unlike most stimulants, MDA does not increase motor activity. It suppresses it in a remarkable way. Inhibitions normally present in group situations are reduced (although it can have an opposite effect on a small percentage of users, causing paranoia).

"In group MDA experiences, people typi-

cally want to explore mutual touching and the pleasures of physical closeness. Even a group of strangers may feel very loving toward one another. They describe a 'warm glow' that radiates gradually into the penis or clitoris, but the experience is not always explicitly sexual because MDA tends to decrease the desire for orgasm.

"Some subjects, however, feel it heightens the sexual experience because pleasurable sensations do not end abruptly with orgasm . . ."

After several seconds, Beryl said, "My God, that describes exactly the way I felt. Sort of dreamy and unreal. I loved *everybody*. And the part about people in groups, the way they behave . . ." She hesitated. "Did you tell Shay about this?"

"I'll print it out. I may drop it at the hospital tomorrow — or you can give it to her. We need to make sure she's strong enough."

Beryl read the article again. "Those damn little manipulators. I suspected, but it's so obvious now. You know what's most humiliating? That night in the swimming pool, with this guy — a *stranger*. A sort of weaselly kid, really. For the first time, I . . . I —" She turned away, then shook her head and made a growling sound. "— I'm too mad to talk about it."

198

"No need."

She said it again. "They drugged us."

"I think it's probable."

"It would explain a lot. In the pool, it was never like that with Elliot. It was always routine with him, more like exercise. Never really . . . exciting. And all because of some damn drug?" Now she sounded unconvinced. Or disappointed.

I said, "My friend, the hippie-looking guy, he says a drug can't give you anything you didn't bring to the party. You felt what you felt."

"But they used me — all four of us. Like those sick blow-up dolls they sell at sex shops. If that was all they did, it wouldn't bother me so much. But now they're making a small fortune off us, too, while they ruin our lives. Ford? They're not going to get away this. I won't let them get away with it. You have to let me help."

Her hand was on my shoulder now. I put my hand on hers — comforting, but also to free myself. "You already have. Get dressed while I shower. It's late."

As I opened the screen door, Beryl stopped me, saying, "Can I ask you something? The video — where is it?"

Before I could answer, she added, "What I'm thinking is, it would be smart to watch it — for information. You'll know what the guys look like instead of just descriptions. And personally? I'd like to find out if we really were drugged, or just drunk and high. I'll know from the way we act."

I said, "Even if you were serious, I don't have a TV."

"If it's a cassette tape, won't it play through a video camera? I have a little Sony in the car that we use at the resort. It plugs into a computer monitor."

I looked at her until she added, "I *am* serious. I'm willing to watch. We're both adults, for God's sake, and if we can learn something, isn't it kind of adolescent not to have a look?"

Her breathing had changed again. Mine, too, as I watched her combing fingers through wet hair, head back, neck exposed. Blue eyes brighter now as her skin flushed.

Instead of asking, *Without permission from the other girls?*, I heard myself reply, "Maybe. Think it over while I shower —" But then I stopped when I heard a distinctive *bong-bong-bong* chiming in the next room.

A phone was ringing. My government-issue satellite phone. Someone had reactivated it.

When I answered, a male voice said, "Don't talk, just listen. I'm doing this for a dear,

200

departed lady, not for you." He sounded like a robot that had inhaled helium because the voice was digitally scrambled.

It was Bernie Yager. By referring to his sister, Eve, he sent a message that also confirmed his identity.

The computerized voice said, "There's a place nearby that's safer. Go now. Order a drink. Five minutes."

He hung up.

I stood for a moment, looking dumbly at the phone. Did he mean the 7-Eleven on Tarpon Bay Road? I'd used the pay phone there before. No . . .

Order a drink.

No . . . he meant Sanibel Grille. It was closer than the 7-Eleven, only a couple hundred yards from the marina entrance. The bar was open until 1 a.m. The year before, I'd called him from there. Bernie would've saved the number.

I pulled on a shirt, traded sandals for boat shoes, then poked my head into the lab. Beryl smiled from the computer desk until I told her, "I've got to go — but I won't be long. Fifteen minutes. Twenty-five at the most."

Her smile faded. "You're kidding."

"It's a business emergency — sort of."

She stood, reknotting the towel. "Was it

201

Shay? I bet it was Shay —"

"No. It's business. That's the truth. Twenty minutes — I promise. I've got to go."

I heard Beryl say, "Marine biologist. *Right,*" as I went down the steps.

Exactly four minutes later, I was reaching for the door at Sanibel Grille when Matt, the owner, came out with the portable phone, and said, "So you are here. It's some guy asking for you."

I took the phone to a private spot on the balcony before putting it to my ear. "Bernie?"

"No. Just listen."

It was Bernie. His real voice now.

I listened to him say, "The trouble your friends are having can be traced to a health resort on the island you mentioned. The Hooded Orchid Retreat and Spa. Got that? Don't answer."

He repeated the name twice, before adding, "Take a lot of money 'cause it's expensive. Exclusive, too — the place is booked way in advance. Which is why someone took the liberty of pulling some strings and holding a reservation. If you think it's the right move, check-in's Tuesday morning. You're booked through Sunday. But don't be surprised if they're a little confused because of a glitch in their computer system."

I could guess what that meant, but I said, "I can't wait until Tuesday —"

"Then work it out for yourself. Or cancel. Understand what I'm telling you — Dr. North?"

One of my bogus passports identifies me as Marion W. North. The middle initial had once been significant. It defined my operative boundaries. The *W* stood for *world,* as in World License.

I said, "I understand," and noticed car lights on the marina's shell road. A Volvo convertible.

"This place, I don't even want to guess what they pretend to heal. It's couples only. So you've got to take a girlfriend. You've also got to take a dinner jacket, 'cause it's fancy."

I said slowly, "A *girlfriend,*" watching the car. It was at the four-way stop now, brights on, no turn signal even though it turned left, tires kicking shell, then squealing as they hit asphalt.

Bernie said, "Yes, a girlfriend or a wife — unless you changed teams all of a sudden, 'cause it's gotta be you and a partner. No singles without special permission. One more thing, Dr. North — the instrument that was deactivated. Get rid of it. The thing has ears — understand?"

The satellite phone. It was a passive monitor. Not that anyone could've heard much, locked away in the floor. Still . . .

As I watched Beryl speed away in her Volvo, top down, I said, "Thanks. I'll let you know how it goes."

Bernie was already gone.

A beautiful predator . . .

That's what I was thinking — about sea jellies, not about Beryl, although maybe it applied. Same for Kathleen Rhodes and Shay. A secret predaceous creature lives within us all — *A voice that whispers,* Shay described it. Women mask it more expertly than men because fifty thousand years of misogyny have encoded patience.

I called Beryl's cell. No answer. I didn't leave a message. While waiting to try again, I was looking at the jellyfish where the woman's finger had streaked the aquarium glass.

Interesting creatures, jellyfish. These were tiny animals — the size of a quarter. Uncomplicated. No brain, no heart, no hearing. Simplex nervous systems that responded to light and odor. Pursue. Attack. Feed. Reproduce.

Tentacles trolled beneath them, lures to fish or zooplankton. Passive but not benign.

Each was coated with an arsenal of micro-scopic projectiles. Hair triggers, *cnidocils*. They fired darts attached to coiled thread. Harpoon cannon, a human equivalent, were slow in comparison and not as deadly.

After penetration, each nematocyst in-jected its ordnance of poison. Feeding be-came a leisurely process.

In Australia, these tiny jellies and their basketball-sized relative, box jellyfish, had killed dozens of people. They were feared, like crocodiles. Yet their corporeal form was an illusion. Their bodies were ninety-eight percent saltwater, two percent living cells.

That morning, I'd written in my lab jour-nal:

Jellyfish are as close as evolution has come to producing intelligence unconstrained by tissue.

Predatory drifters . . . delicate as flower blossoms. Jellyfish were killers without con-science.

I was raising *Carukia* as an experiment in bioterrorism. If I could raise lethal sea jellies in a Florida lab, terrorists could, too. Differ-ence was, I wasn't going to sneak them into vacation ecosystems at South Beach, Key West, Fort Lauderdale, and Sarasota. They spawned by the millions.

Poisonous shrimp — another project. They were housed in a plastic drum attached to hoses, filters, and pumps. The drum was kept locked. A viewing window had been installed.

Inside were several hundred shrimp, feet fanning water for steerage. They were the same variety served in restaurants, but these had been raised on toxic feed. I made the stuff from fish that contained a poisonous dinoflagellate, ciguatera.

Ciguatera is commonly found in reef fish, and in the predators that eat them. That's why you don't see barracuda on a restaurant menu.

Shrimp were unfazed by the toxin, but their flesh absorbed it like sponges. Half a dozen, eaten even after being shelled, boiled, or fried, would paralyze a healthy man. Maybe kill him.

Shrimp served in chain restaurants are commonly raised in Central American ponds. Ciguatera poisoning is associated with eating fish, never shrimp. If the Red Lobster crowd started dropping in the streets, there would be panic and economic calamity before the Centers for Disease Control figured it out.

Margaret Holderness and her underlings had been impressed.

Anticipate tactics — that was my task. An enemy loses more than a battle if he finds you waiting at his ambush spot.

It's something I'm good at.

Before signing the new contract, I'd operated on the dark side of the fence, a phrase used by State Department types. Marine biology was a cover, not an assignment. Now, ironically, it was my research that was classified.

At first, I welcomed the change. I no longer had to switch passports after border crossings. Didn't have to ship weaponry to prearranged destinations. Didn't have to blend in, studying local sea life while also tracking assigned targets.

Sometimes, people just disappear.

I was good at that, too.

I was working regular hours, staying home instead of jetting off on fictional research trips. I ate, slept, and socialized like a normal American professional. And . . . the lifestyle was suffocating me.

I had been unmasked by the truth, and I was growing impatient with the lie I'd been living.

I turned from the aquarium and dialed Beryl's number again. No answer.

This time, I left a message. "There's a health spa on the island we discussed that might have something to do with your problem. The Hooded Orchid. I may book a room. Your family's in the spa business — find out what you can about the place, and give me a call."

Beryl didn't call that night. The next morning, I left a similar message before leaving to catch my plane.

13

Shortly after landing at a private airstrip on Saint Lucia, two hundred miles off the South American coast, I rented a boat and made the short water crossing to Saint Arc.

Now I was working my way down a rain-forest mountainside toward the rental house where Shay and her bridesmaids had stayed. Occasionally, I got a glimpse of the place through trees alive with orchids and canoe-sized leaves.

Shay had picked it as the ideal spot for a women's getaway. As I got closer, I understood the appeal.

It was a Tahitian-style house on stilts, built of tropical wood so rich with natural oils it glowed amber in the lavender afternoon light. The house sat among coconut palms, overlooking a lagoon on its own little cusp of beach. A wicked beach for topless sunbathing, Shay had described it.

There were people on the beach now. Four stretched out on towels. Women, probably, but I was too far away to be sure.

Palms and a rock ridge screened the house from a longer beach and a resort hotel a quarter mile away — a busy place with umbrellas and Jet Skis. Here, though, the house and lagoon were quiet, a private island on a larger island. It looked idyllic, safe. An inviting rental — also an alluring trap for blackmail.

I spent another five minutes descending the hillside, the forest floor spongy underfoot as parrots and macaws quarreled in a tree canopy that filtered sunlight, so it was a little like being underwater — darker, cooler, until I stepped into a clearing a hundred yards above the beach.

Yes . . . women. All topless; two of them nude. Seen from above, their bodies mimicked the curvature of wind sculptures; skin dark against white sand that edged the lagoon. I'd studied the nautical charts. The lagoon formed the upper basin of a canyon that descended to the sea bottom several hundred feet below. Water was Jell-O blue in the shallows, then dropped vertically in black shafts of light.

I stood for a moment, feeling uneasy and

ridiculous — a reluctant voyeur unaccustomed to imposing on the privacy of women. I hadn't known the house was occupied.

I ducked into the forest, moving quietly downward. Soon, I was close enough to see the swimming pool behind the house. The pool was kidney-shaped with an adjoining Jacuzzi built into a stone deck. There was patio furniture, a grill, and a bar. The area was unscreened, but hedged by bougainvilleas in pale yellow bloom. Hedges gave the illusion of privacy, but they were trimmed low, so my view was unobstructed.

It had to be close — the place where a cameraman had set up equipment and filmed Shay, Beryl, Liz, and Corey with the islanders. If the girls were random victims, there wouldn't be much to find. But if the rental house was designed for blackmail, there would be a fixed place for filming.

I found it. The camera blind was so well-camouflaged with netting and branches that I nearly passed it. The netting covered a structure built of bamboo and lumber, open on all sides, and roofed with palm thatching. Like a hunter's blind.

The entrance was a slit in the netting. I found a stick, broke it, then used it as a probe to check for booby traps. I tossed the stick away, then stepped through the opening.

It was a cozy little place: two folding chairs; an Igloo cooler beneath a table where there was an ashtray, and a plastic box — the kind you burp to seal. Inside were a couple of French magazines, a crumpled blue pack of Gauloise cigarettes, and several mini-cassettes, unopened. Panasonic DVM-60s — like the one used to film the girls.

I picked up a magazine. *Paris Match,* logo in red.

On the cover was an attractive middle-aged woman, looking good in a two-piece swimsuit, hands combing her hair back as she exited the water — a candid shot.

I don't speak French, but I understand a little. The headlines were easily translated; the woman's name was familiar to anyone who follows world events via shortwave radio. I do.

The woman was Senegal Firth, a candidate for British Parliament, favored to win until she withdrew one month prior to the election. Controversial. I didn't remember details.

I checked the date of the magazine. Seven months old. Ms. Firth had been vacationing on Saint Arc when the photo was taken. It was an unflattering shot of a photogenic woman: late forties, interesting eyes, brown hair, very fit in a navy blue two-piece that clung.

I flipped inside. More candid swimsuit photos. I read enough to understand that Ms. Firth was outraged by the breach of privacy and was threatening to sue.

Sniper photographers were welcome, apparently, on Saint Arc.

The other magazine, also French, was for orchid aficionados.

An odd combination.

The front of the blind looked down onto the pool, only fifty yards away, but it was insulated from the property by a sheer ledge that dropped a hundred feet onto lichen gray rocks. The ledge rimmed the mountain, so it was a quarter mile or more to the house on foot.

As I closed the magazine, two women who'd been on the beach came into view, very tall, bony, towels over their shoulders. They were so close, I could hear bits of conversation — American women, middle-aged, Midwestern accents.

As one of them leaned to step out of her bikini bottoms, I felt a creeping revulsion. I reached to drop a curtain that covered the viewing window. This cozy little camera blind was a nasty little place. Violence can be done in silence. I'd come to gather intel and evidence, not to ogle unsuspecting women. Let the ladies swim in private.

I opened the cooler — several champagne bottles inside, two empty, all of them warm. A thread of spider's silk angled from the table to the window frame. It takes a spider several hours to construct a web, but this lone thread was older — no spider in sight.

No one here today. That might soon change. Women were renting the house, and tomorrow was Sunday. I remembered Shay telling me there was nothing going on at the nearby resort the night the men showed up — a Sunday night.

I got busy.

I pulled on surgical gloves. One by one, I opened the videocassettes and used a pocket knife to cut the magnetic tape where it bridged the rollers. If the camera's computer didn't flash an alert — *media error* — the cassette spools would turn, the tape would not.

I left two cassettes intact, securing them separately in plastic bags. If the day came when I needed fingerprints, they might be useful. I also bagged several cigarette butts — DNA. A roach butt went into another baggie. If it had been infused with a synthetic drug, forensics labs could identify it.

From a waist pack, I removed one of two tiny digital recorders I'd brought, then a remote microphone the size of a pencil eraser. The recorder was voice-activated. It had enough memory to record twelve hours of conversation.

After several frustrating minutes, I figured out how to reduce microphone sensitivity — I wanted conversation, not twelve hours of birds chirping. I tested it, sealed it in its case, and hid the recorder under moss along the inside wall. I'd just found a spot to clip the microphone when I heard leaves rustling . . . the crack of a branch . . . another . . . then a muffled male voice, very close.

Visitors.

I knelt and parted the netting: two men coming from the north, where the road angled close to the forest. White guys, early twenties, with tangled black hair. Each carried a backpack. One also carried a tripod; the other lugged a bag of ice.

They were twenty yards away, facing the blind's entrance, making it impossible to leave the way I'd entered. Instead, I took a last look at the microphone, then burrowed under the netting at the south wall and crawled on my belly into some ferns.

I gave it several seconds, then turned and faced the camera blind, pulling leaves closer for cover. I also unholstered the palm-sized Colt .380 clipped inside the back of my pants.

I confirmed there was a round in the breach, then held the pistol ready as I waited.

I couldn't see the men as they entered the blind, but I could hear them whispering in patois French. I caught a few words, but understood little. I heard the ice chest open; heard the measured, metallic sounds of a tripod being set up.

Fifteen minutes later, they were joined by a third man. After that, they whispered in English — islander English, which was only slightly easier to understand than French, and almost impossible to hear.

I was getting them on tape, but I didn't want to wait. I decided to risk it. I left my soft spot in the ferns, crawled to the blind, and put my ear against the netting. There was the flicking sound of a lighter lighting a joint, and the clink of a bottle.

I found a hole in the webbing wide enough for one eye, and took a look. The third man wore a red bandanna tied pirate style, blond dreadlocks spilling out from beneath. Open white shirt with cuffs, hairless chest, skin tanned butterscotch. Shay's guy in the video. He stood smoking a cigarette while the others shared the joint and drank beer, in no hurry. The impression was they were done for the day even though there was no camera mounted on the tripod.

They'd rolled up the canvas curtain and were watching the women. I couldn't see the pool, but I knew what the men were seeing from their whispered jokes and laughter. I could read their facial expressions — distaste; pained locker-room grimaces at the sight of forty-year-old women swimming naked. They traded clinical assessments. Made cruel and graphic comparisons. But they watched, anyway.

Pointless cruelty invites a violent response.

I had the pistol in my right hand. I slipped it under the netting, then touched the gun sights experimentally to each man's head, one by one — an adolescent demonstration that a professional wouldn't do. Stupid. This was personal business, not an assignment. I couldn't go running to the U.S. Consulate in Grenada if local law enforcement came after me. But it was so damn tempting.

The three continued to joke about the women as I lowered the Colt and turned my eye away from the netting. Listening was bad enough without seeing their facial theatrics.

It was another ten minutes before they tired of the subject and said something useful.

I heard, "Mon, do you really 'spect me to

screw them women tomorrow night? Put our hands on them ol' ladies? I goan have to drink myself blind first."

Translation: *I'll have to drink myself blind first.*

In the same dialect, the man with the pirate bandanna — Bandanna Man — whispered, "Then you better start drinkin' 'cause those ladies are the golden egg, what you're seein' down there. Them women are rich."

"Okay, man, okay. I'll *do* it, but I ain't likin' it." Laughter.

The third man's accent was more French than islander. "Then what we sittin' here for? We'll be seeing them too soon as 'tis. Burnin' up all our drinkin' time tonight don't make no sense. Dirk?"

"Yeah, man."

"Wolfie's comin' with the camera tomorrow. That right? You tell that pompous fool be on time. We meet him at the Green Turtle, six o'clock. You hear me?"

"Yeah, man, doan worry. It takes a bottle of rum before I go blind *and* deaf."

They were laughing as they left, one by one — a standard security precaution that told me they'd done this before. I crawled to the edge of the camera blind and got a good look at them sneaking away through the rain forest toward the road.

Beryl and Shay had given me descriptions of the men who'd lured them into the swimming pool. Two looked European, possibly Dutch, jet-setter Shay had told me, but they were locals with French–West Indies accents. She'd also described the butterscotch islander with blond dreadlocks, but I would've recognized him, anyway. Shay's partner.

These were the guys. They'd be back tomorrow night.

So would I.

I gave it five minutes, then took another look inside the camera blind. It was now supplied for tomorrow night's filming. Snacks, Red Stripe beer wedged around a block of ice, the tripod, and a sleeve of three new videocassettes. Would Wolfie, the cameraman, notice broken cellophane wrappers?

My guess: Wolfie was the bagman I'd followed from the Bank of Aruba to the waterfront bar they'd mentioned, the Green Turtle. If true, Wolfie was fifteen years older, a big, round man, wore expensive Italian sunglasses, and drove a nice car — a man competent with money and cameras. Wolfie might be a pompous fool, but he wasn't the one who'd lugged all this gear up the mountain.

Wolfie was the man in charge. Maybe the blackmailer. If he wasn't, he was better connected than the other three.

Below the blind, a third and fourth woman had joined the others. Two wore gauzy beach kaftans. One had pulled on a man-sized T-shirt, *Michigan,* in blue and gold. Moneyed ladies on vacation — but their faces didn't have the glossy angularity I associate with face-lifts and wealth. They looked cheerful, full of fun, as they made a pitcher of margaritas and kibitzed about where they would go for dinner.

Four old friends, comfortable with themselves and their age, their flaws — my read. They didn't deserve the ambush that awaited.

I popped the cellophane and disabled the new cassettes. If the cameraman noticed, so be it. If he carried fresh cassettes, there was nothing I could do.

I confirmed the recorder was working, then slipped through the opening into rain forest. I scouted around until I found a good viewing platform of my own: a rock ledge to the south. If I sat on the ledge, the camera blind's viewing window was uphill, to my right. The swimming pool was downhill to my left.

From my pocket, I took a roll of special reflective tape. Hit it with a regular flashlight, it resembled green ribbon. Use infrared light, though, in combination with night-vision optics, it glittered. Because I might have to find this ledge at night, I tied a couple of pieces on nearby foliage, then used four-inch lengths to mark an escape route.

I chose a trail that ran along a rock ridge. At a couple of spots, the ridge dropped off fifty or sixty feet onto rocks below — okay for a man wearing night vision; dangerous for a man who wasn't.

At the narrowest section, I thought about stringing a trip wire. Wrap it with the special tape — I would see it. Anyone chasing me would not. But if an innocent hiker came tromping along this path . . . ?

Couldn't do it.

I continued walking . . . then froze as parrots flushed from trees to my left, screaming an alert. I stood there for a long minute, searching the shadows. Something, or someone, had spooked the birds.

I pocketed the marking tape, and slipped the Colt from the back of my pants. Slowly, I started uphill toward a grove of traveler's palms where the parrots had been. The leaves of the palms fanned out like a green wall . . . but the wall was moving — something in there.

I had the little semiautomatic palmed, not showing it but ready, when two iguanas came snaking out — miniature dragons, skin iridescent green, reptilian tongues probing. They were the size of small dogs.

I watched, focusing on the green wall. Iguanas eat birds' eggs, and sometimes birds. Parrots would flush at their approach and scream an alert.

So why did I suddenly feel as if the jungle had eyes? That I was being watched?

Ridiculous. A cliché from cowboy movies; folklore from childhood. I don't believe in such things.

I holstered the pistol and moved on.

14

The woman who'd been wearing the Michigan shirt, but was now in a sundress, tropical yellow with spaghetti straps that showed her thick tan shoulders, asked me, "Is it dangerous to swim in the lagoon? Sharks, I mean. That's what the girls and I were wondering. We're from the snow belt —" She shrugged, grinning to let me know it might be silly. "— and this is our first trip to the islands."

I told her, "Most resorts, you don't have to worry about sharks until you're out of the water. Probably the same on Saint Arc."

Big smile. "Like the Jimmy Buffett song? 'Fins.'" She was intrigued, not concerned.

"Who knows the islands better?" I smiled, joking but not joking. Letting her think about it as I opened the plastic case I carry as a portable lab. It contained collecting jars, chemicals for testing water, a plastic slurp-tube for catching sea jellies and small reef fish — the dutiful biologist at work.

I had anchored my rental boat in the shallows — a cheap tri-hull with an antique Evinrude that would do until tomorrow when I took possession of a loaner — a seventeen-foot Maverick with a one-fifty Yamaha. It was as fast and stable as my boat, just smaller.

Tomlinson had been right about new contacts. I'd hitched a ride with Lags in his Gulfstream jet — no problem with customs at the private airport — and my friend Skip Lyshon arranged for a demo boat from the Hewes/Pathfinder dealer on Saint Lucia.

I had decided not to phone Beryl again — even though it meant I couldn't check in to the couples retreat that, according to Bernie, was somehow associated with the blackmailer. If Beryl agreed to join me, there would be too many questions to dodge.

That was okay. I was playing it by ear, letting the situation pull me along until I sensed the right opening. Locate a trap and, sooner or later, the trapper will appear.

I had found the trap. I still had six days — plenty of time to lay low and let events play out until the blackmailer revealed himself. Trouble was, this smiling woman in the yellow sundress was his prey. Her three friends, too — I waved at them now as they walked from the house, and stopped when they spotted me on the beach.

The temptation was to tell them what to expect tomorrow night, but I couldn't. If they contacted police, the blackmailer would know. He'd shut down the operation for a week or two, then be right back at it. Worse, it would put him on alert and make it tougher for me to locate his stash of videos. If he'd kept a copy of Shay's tape, he probably had them all. That's what I was after — the collection. If it didn't work out, negotiating a private deal was a last option.

I couldn't tell the ladies, but I could at least plant a warning. So I had changed into jogging shorts, then waded with mask and fins to the beach, as if getting ready to dive into the lagoon. Then I'd futzed around with the portable lab until the woman struck up a conversation.

The woman glanced at her friends now and waved them closer, still smiling at my joke about land sharks. She extended her hand. "My name's Madeleine. But everyone calls me Mattie."

I said, "Marion — or Doc," doing first names only — common at resorts — even though we'd been talking for several minutes.

I already knew that Mattie was the mother of two college-aged children. Because she didn't mention a husband, I assumed she was divorced, not widowed. She wasn't exactly retired, because managing the family business took a lot of time. "Managing" was said in a way that suggested stocks, properties, and liquid assets. Wealthy — golden eggs, the guy with the pirate bandanna had called them.

Mattie was on Saint Arc because two of her best friends were getting married. This was their private girls-only celebration before the October wedding.

A familiar scenario.

She was looking at her friends now as she said, "See the two tall gals? Those are the twins. Never been married before, never came close, and we're so darn happy for them. At *our age,* I mean. We thought it was never gonna happen, then *boom,* they met the two nicest guys you could ever want. Can you guess what I'm about to tell you?"

"The twins met twins?"

Mattie had an easygoing familiarity not uncommon with large women. She nudged me with her shoulder, lowering her voice as her friends approached. "Yep. Identical twins, just like the gals. Farmers. Big spreads in upstate New York, and they've never been married, either. You've never seen four happier kids in your life."

I smiled. *Kids* — talking about those tall, bony women in their forties, but it fit because of their suntan glow and their vacation faces.

"We're all Smithies. We've been through hell together."

I said, "Smithies?"

"Smith College. Northampton, Mass. Our class colors are yellow and blue —" In a louder voice, she called, "Haven't we been through hell together, gals?" The women were laughing as they joined us, all dressed for dinner in the tropics, bright scarves and sandals, frozen margaritas in their hands as they gave me the eye — *Who was this big stranger with Mattie?*

Twins in blue dresses; Mattie and Carol wore yellow — Carol, another large woman, but not outgoing. Unlike Mattie, hers was the articulate syntax of Long Island wealth. She was suspicious, too. Good for her.

After a while, Carol asked me, "Why would a marine biologist come to a resort to do research?"

I told her, "I'm not staying on Saint Arc. I've got a place over there." I looked beyond the lagoon toward Saint Lucia, four miles away. Green volcanic peaks, half a mile high, on an emerald canvas. "This lagoon looked interesting from the air, so I decided to take a look."

Carol was unconvinced. "Then we shouldn't keep you . . . *Doc,* did you say? Doctor of what? And where did you get your Ph.D.?"

I told her, adding, "My name's North. Marion North," aware that Carol's attitude had alerted the others: four women with money, but *smart.* Had to be. Unless a sex change increases the human IQ by twenty points, there's no possible way I would have ever been accepted at Smith College.

Because I wanted to keep it friendly, I turned to Mattie and asked, "Do you ladies like seafood?"

"Are you kidding? We love it. But . . . we already have dinner plans tonight —" She glanced at Carol, their leader. "Don't we, girls?"

I said, "That's not what I meant. If you're still around when I finish my dive, maybe I'll bring you a present. Something for tomorrow night."

"A gift from the sea," said Carol with an edge. "How nice."

The lagoon was a sand basin that sloped toward a precipice at the canyon's rim. I snorkeled to the edge of the drop-off, jackknifed, and descended, kicking leisurely with my old Rocket fins.

Staghorn shadows on white sand . . . cone shells burrowing — venomous hunters. Reef fish. Prismatic scales: yellow, blue, chrome. There were parrotfish . . . sergeant majors . . . snappers . . . barracudas dark on the rim of visibility, horizontal observers like rungs on a ladder . . . medusa jellies dragging rain-squall tentacles.

I'd brought the spear gun, but continued downward along the canyon wall. Ledges . . . brain corals . . . mouth of a cave?

I surfaced, took several breaths, then dived again.

Yes, a cave. It was wider than my shoulders; a natural opening in the wall. I looked to the surface thirty feet above — barracuda over me now — then peeked into the cave. Expected a moray eel . . . instead, saw a forest of antennas.

Spiny lobsters.

I surfaced, traded spear gun for gloves and a net bag, and returned to the ledge.

A couple of minutes later, the bag was alive with kicking, creaking lobsters.

The women were scattered among hammocks and porch rockers as I approached the house. Lost in books, fresh drinks, conversation. Carol was saying to Mattie,

". . . but why waste time with another tourist when we can meet people who actually live here —" then stopped when she noticed me.

Instead of pretending I hadn't heard, I said, "I agree. Getting to know the locals is the best part of travel." I held up the bag. "Let me introduce you to some locals."

Mattie and the twins surrounded me as I spread the lobsters out on a banana leaf. Six biggies, no eggs — I'd checked.

"Where are their claws?" one of the twins asked.

"New England lobster are a different species. I like these better. Melted butter, fresh limes, sea salt. Tomorrow night, you could build a fire on the beach and steam them."

Mattie said, "How does that sound, Carol? Do it like the islanders do it."

I said, "You should — but stay smart. Trust the wrong islanders, you're in big trouble. It could be fatal."

Carol placed her book on the chair as she stood. "I hope you're not talking about the wonderful people who live here."

I let her see that I was confused before saying, "Oh, you thought I was talking about . . . ? No, I meant the lagoon. Not everything's safe to eat. I saw cone shells — their sting's venomous. Probably wouldn't kill you, but it would put you in the hospital. Certain fish — barracuda, some reef fish — can be toxic." I thought about it as I rebagged the lobster. "On the other hand, maybe I accidentally made a good point. Resorts attract con men. Crooks hustle tourists. They slip drugs into women's drinks. It's rare — like a black jellyfish I saw in the lagoon. But the poisonous ones are around."

Carol didn't soften. "It must be nice to be so well-traveled that you can pass judgment on people you've never met."

I smiled as I replied, "If I sound overly critical, it's probably because I'm overly sober," thinking the woman would loosen up and offer me a margarita. She didn't.

As I left, Mattie walked me to the beach and said, "Doc, you have to come back tomorrow night and have lobster. We'll build a fire."

I said, "Maybe. I'd have to boat back to Saint Lucia after dark — pretty scary. Think it would be safe?"

The woman sent a signal with her eyes as she said, "Not necessarily," having fun with the double meaning. "We have plenty of room — and we also have two bottles of rum and half a bottle of tequila to drink before we leave on Tuesday. And, uh —" She lowered her voice. "— even Carol agreed

231

that what happens on this island stays on the island. We're here to have fun. Three days from now, we'll be back where everyone knows us."

What I wanted to do was take the woman by the shoulders, look her in the eyes, and unload the truth. Share a couple of the nasty jokes from the camera blind so she knew the kind of men she'd be dealing with.

Instead, I said, "Don't hold dinner — but don't be surprised if I show up, either. It might be late. Okay?"

The possibility of my showing up might make it less likely that she and the others would follow the blackmailer's script.

"Just bang on the door," Mattie told me. "Or come around back to the pool if you hear music. We'll be here."

15

That night, I watched Mattie and Carol from my hidden spot above the beach house. They had their backs to the bar when the guy with the pirate bandanna — Bandanna Man — slipped the drug into the pitcher of margaritas. Something poured from an envelope. Powder. He crumpled the envelope, jammed it into his shorts, and hit the blender button as Carol turned.

"Bob Marley okay with you? Or something better for dancing?" Mattie was flipping through CDs while Carol did the talking, already sounding eager to please these three young guys wearing baggies and open shirts as they shared a cigar-sized joint in the glow of tiki torches and blue pool lights.

"Or maybe Marley's too commercial. Whatever you say — in the States that's all we hear, commercial garbage. But we're not typical tourists, okay? Traditional reggae, steel drums — I love it. But what are islanders really *into*?"

Now the guys were sharing private smiles, too — funny, this straight-looking woman already drunk, trying to sound hip before she'd even tasted the special margaritas. Embarrassed, maybe, by the cornstalk twins who didn't want to dance, who didn't want to invite strangers to the pool, so they'd split, leaving these two wide-bodied ladies on their own.

"Carol? *Carol.* What's wrong with Bob Marley? We don't have to dance. I don't even feel like dancing." Mattie made a show of yawning, a CD in her hand. "In fact, it's getting late. And these fellas probably have better things to do."

Bandanna Man's face reacted: Christ, now *she's* scared. The evening would be a bust if he didn't act fast, so he held up the blender and said, "Man, there ain't nothin' better than hanging with pretty ladies. Why you want us to go 'way now? It's not yet eight-thirty."

Flashing Mattie a look, Carol said, "We *don't* want you to leave."

Ritchie was Bandanna Man with his dreadlocks and pirate scarf . . . his pals were Dutch and Peter Lorre — that's the way I thought of them even though I'd heard their names. Shay had said two looked European, possibly Dutch. What the hell did that mean? I finally saw it in Dirk, the biggest of the three: square jaw, square shoulders, square blond sideburns. A few years back, an Alabama high school girl disappeared on Aruba after partying with locals. He resembled one of the suspects — *Dutch.*

Clovis was Peter Lorre because he looked like the old-time actor from the Bogart films. Same slumped shoulders and protuberant eyes. He struck poses and moved like a weasel. Smooth, quiet, black hair slicked back with busy hands.

Clovis struck a pose now — mock deference — when Ritchie said, "What these ladies need is a drink. Why are you gentlemen standing there when you should be lookin' after refreshments for our new friends?"

He began filling plastic beer cups from the blender, saying, "Bob Marley — nothin' *ever* wrong with listenin' to brother Bob. But you serious about not wantin' the same junk music every tourist wants?"

"Yes! I told you, we're not tourists, we're *travelers.* We didn't come to buy trinkets and get a tan."

"No 'Yellow Bird'? No 'Jamaica Farewell'?" Big grin.

"My God," Carol said, "spare me! Mattie and I study cultures. It must be horrible for you, putting up with a bunch of idiotic tourists, the same music, the same questions day after day. Ritchie, don't let the age difference throw you. We're open to new experiences."

"Age? Carol darlin', age don't mean nothing. It's a woman's soul what matters."

"That's so sweet; like poetry — and it's so true! Mattie, isn't that wonderful?"

Now Mattie flashed Carol a look, but Carol didn't catch it because Ritchie was handing them margaritas as he danced past.

Carol took a sip, then another before saying, "Here . . . this is exactly what I'm talking about. A *real* margarita, not that awful Kool-Aid crap they serve in the States. Fresh lime and damn good tequila." She touched the rim with her finger. "Real sea salt."

Resigned, Mattie took a long gulp, looking at the door. She said, "Yeah, sea salt," as if thinking about the lobster they hadn't cooked, and maybe about a marine biologist who'd failed to arrive.

Then the music started. Marley and the Wailers, *Jammin'*. I couldn't hear them clearly anymore.

Wolfie, the bagman, was also the cameraman.

From my platform on the rock, through an opening in the ferns, I watched him move through the forest toward the blind, a canvas bag on his shoulder. Huge, round, stocky man with an oversized round head, wearing the Italian sunglasses even though it was dark — a man committed to fashion. Beside him, walking at heel, was a dog. Well-trained but alert — Doberman and pit bull mix, it looked like — tall as a greyhound, all muscle beneath brown brindle hide.

Geezus.

Shay's father had been in the dogfight business and raised pit bulls. They were as nasty as Dexter Money. My uncle Tucker had owned one, too, a surly animal named Gator. But Wolfie had obviously spent a lot of time or money training his dog — a man who worked alone and needed protection.

I got ready to retreat when I saw the dog, my hand on the little Colt pistol. But then I got a whiff of the cigarillo Wolfie was smoking and relaxed a little. Wind was out of the west, blowing my scent away from the dog. Because of the ferns, and because I was wearing dark pants, a black T-shirt, and an old Navy watch cap, it was unlikely they'd see me. Stay quiet, remain hidden, and the dog would be as unaware as Wolfie that I was doing countersurveillance.

Even so, I felt uneasy. It was one big damn dog.

Sunset on the island was at 6:30 p.m., and the two had arrived shortly afterward. Now it was nearly nine, and Wolfie still hadn't shot anything worth a damn.

I had. That morning, I'd bought a palm-sized Kodak plus a mini shotgun mic, so I could film and record from a distance. The camera shot HDV, and it had infrared mode for filming at night.

I didn't need a tripod. I'd packed a military-grade spotlight with an infrared cap — a Golight. Cap off, you could see the beam from miles away. Cap on, you couldn't see the beam from a foot away — unless you were wearing night-vision optics.

I was. The green-eye monocular over my right eye.

It was almost funny. Countersurveillance occasionally is. Wolfie was in the spotlight and didn't know it. The infrared Golight lit up the blind like a stage, and my camera captured it all. No reaction from behind the camera blind, either, where the dog was.

I got close-ups of Wolfie's face as he focused his camera. I did slow zoom-outs to show the viewing window and camouflaged blind . . . then panned to the swimming pool where Bandanna Man, Dutch, and Clovis were working the tourist ladies.

No cuts — if you cut from scene to scene, it's useless in court. Same's true of digital memory. Too easily manipulated. That's why I was using videotape.

I got a close-up of Ritchie looking sneaky as he opened the envelope, then poured powder into the blender, making margaritas. Kept shooting as he poured drinks and handed them to the ladies. Got close-ups of the ladies drinking, then did another slow zoom-out and panned to Wolfie in the camera blind. He was standing beside the camera, not shooting, but the shotgun mic recorded him saying in French, *"Finally!"*

The earbud I was wearing amplified it nicely. Good sound — until Carol turned the music loud.

Because I thought Wolfie might bail when the twins left, I'd burned through four tapes, getting it all down while I had the chance. The brides-to-be weren't coming back — it'd taken the twins a long time to find their New York farmers. They were devoted ladies; no interest in a last fling.

But blackmail targets didn't have to be prospective brides, because Wolfie hadn't given up. Humiliation is a broad-spectrum weapon. In lieu of husbands, grown children could be leveraged. Or careers. Mattie was a mother; Carol owned her own business.

Finally!

Wolfie said it again.

He was right. Down by the swimming pool, it was starting to happen.

I got a shot of Wolfie putting an eye to his camera as he began to film Mattie and Carol dancing with Ritchie and Dutch. They'd finished their drinks and were working on seconds. Good dancers for big women, loosening up fast, feeling tequila along with the unexpected rush of the drug.

"Mattie? Mattie!" Carol was laughing, talking loud enough to hear without the shotgun mic. "Do you know what this terrible young man just suggested? He wants to . . ."

I couldn't hear the rest. But Ritchie was taking off his shirt as they danced, big grin, doing a slow striptease.

I paused long enough to load a fresh cassette into the Kodak . . . and felt a familiar surge of revulsion. It was unlikely the stuff I was shooting would get to court — but, if I worked it right, the video could cost tiny Saint Arc millions in tourism if this blacklist story was leaked to news agencies or hit the Internet.

Make the Saint Arc power structure aware of the tape, and the island's money people would do my work for me. Local authorities would react with shock and indignation before arresting the blackmailer, then crucifying him publicly. Reassure the tourists — the island's economy came first.

There was another angle I could work, too. The island was a member of the French Commonwealth. According to my research, it was one of only four French overseas departments in the Caribbean. People born on the island were French citizens, entitled to French passports. France seldom interfered with the local government, but her laws could be applied — if I twisted enough arms.

The video of Shay and her friends could damage their lives for years to come. The video I was shooting could put their extortionist in jail for a lifetime.

Blackmail the blackmailer. He was ruthless, but no dummy. He would either cooperate eagerly, or eagerly try to have me killed. Either approach would be time-consuming. Shay would have her wedding.

Yet, I was reluctant to continue shooting as Dutch, who'd stripped his shirt off, began goading Mattie to dance, taking her in his arms and turning her in slow circles as Carol shrieked, "My God, I wish I had a camera. This man could make poor ol' Lucy

Hunt smile. No, wait! I take that back — no one can know about this!" as she laughed and danced with Bandanna Man, then reached to touch his face. "Ritchie? You are the sweetest, dearest young man I've ever met. I mean that. I think you're just . . . a beautiful person."

I was remembering what I'd read about the drug called Icebreaker.

It is common in group MDA experiences for people to explore mutual touching and the pleasures of physical closeness. Participants may feel very loving toward one another. They describe a "warm glow" that radiates gradually . . .

I told myself it wasn't my concern. Mattie and Carol were adults. I was here to gather evidence, not make moral judgments.

I put the camera to my eye and touched *record*.

Carol was feeling it now, drunk but more than that, judging from the way she lifted her arms, sleepy-eyed, cooperating as Ritchie began unbuttoning her dress, his hands pausing on her breasts as she arched her back in invitation . . .

But Dutch wasn't getting the same cooperation from Mattie at the other end of the pool, where he'd danced her into the shadows. I heard Mattie yell, "Hey, that's enough, damn it. Please quit!" She pushed his hands away as he tried to slide the straps of the yellow dress off her shoulders.

. . . for a small percentage of users the drug has the opposite effect, causing paranoia . . .

I remembered reading that, too.

Mattie was having a bad reaction, but Dutch wouldn't stop. He was forcing it, holding the woman close, kissing her neck as she tried to fight him off — "Get your hands off me. *I'm serious.*" — and now Peter Lorre was there, too, sandwiching her from behind as she tried to wrestle free until the spaghetti straps broke, both men grinning as they peeled the yellow dress to her ankles . . . then began to laugh at her oversized white panties and bra.

"Hey . . . hey!" Carol had finally noticed. "What are you doing over there? Stop that!" She turned, holding her unbuttoned dress together, speaking to the sweetest man she'd ever met. "Ritchie — look what they're doing! Are your friends drunk? Make them stop. Please."

Bandanna Man's grin turned nasty. "You

on our island, why should we be the ones got to leave? Most old women, they'd love a chance to party with me and my boys." When she started to reply, he cupped his hand behind her neck, laughing.

I'd already stowed the camera and Golight in my backpack. I was moving downhill when Carol screamed.

16

Someone was following me as I jogged down the trail. Who? *How?*

I stopped, listened. The reflective tape I'd tied to the bushes was only visible through night-vision optics, infrared switched on. Because I was wearing the green-eye, strips of tape glowed like road signs as I turned to look uphill.

I heard a faint, rhythmic crashing of brush in the distance. A man running through ferns? No, not a man . . . but *something.*
Wait . . .

A beam of light was now scanning the tree canopy, but there was something odd about the light.

Experimentally, I killed the night-vision monocular and the beam vanished . . . vanished into a night hollowed by tree shadow and stars. I flipped the power switch and the monocular glowed green — and the light beam reappeared, sweeping along the ridge above me.

Someone was up there with an infrared spotlight. I wasn't the only one wearing night vision.

Wolfie?

No, the light was farther up the mountain, to the east of the camera blind. Whoever it was had found my trail, but continued to pan back and forth over a single section as if they'd spotted something of interest.

Then I saw it . . . two coal-red eyes dolphining in rhythm to the crashing noise that was closer now, coming fast.

A dog.

Wolfie's pit bull was after me. Had he sent it after me, or had the dog reacted to the noise of me descending the trail? No way of knowing. But some unknown person was up there using an infrared spotlight to follow the animal as it charged downhill, scenting my trail.

Shit.

I turned and ran. For the first minute or so, I ripped the reflective ribbon from bushes as I rumbled past, but then it came into my mind the dog was using its nose to follow me, not its eyes. Canines have better night vision than primates. With the green-eye, though, my night vision was a hundred times better than the dog's. Unless the person with the infrared spotlight was after me, the tape wasn't worth slowing for.

I was on the narrowest section of trail — the spot where I'd thought about stringing a trip wire. Why the hell hadn't I? The path was only a couple of feet wide, rain forest to my left, darkness to my right, where a gravel incline descended a hundred feet onto more rocks. Through the monocular, the rocks resembled miniature volcanoes.

On the next turn, I slipped . . . caught a bush as my feet swung from beneath me over the precipice. As I hung there, heart pounding, I could hear the hard, scrabbling sound of the pit bull's paws clawing for purchase.

I also heard a distant scream — Carol? No . . . Mattie.

I panicked. Came damn close to risking the fall onto the rocks rather than waste more time or face the pit bull. Instead, I got my feet on the ground, checked the trail behind . . . and could hear the dog coming, growling now, aware the quarry was near even though it couldn't see me.

I couldn't outrun the damn thing, there were no low limbs to grab, and the panic in me was turning into fury. In my left hand was the Golight, power off. I removed the infrared filter and put it in my backpack.

The lens — the size of a paperback book — would blast a white, blinding beam when I hit the switch. In my right hand was the little Colt semiautomatic.

Facing the trail, I squatted, focused the monocular, and waited for the dog to appear.

Come on, you bastard . . .

It did, running hard, eyes glowing, teeth bared. I could see the animal clearly in the eerie green world of night vision . . . but the dog couldn't see me, I realized, as long as I remained statue still.

Come on . . .

I was going to kill it. Didn't want to use the gun and alert Ritchie and the others, or some distant cop. What I wanted to do was break the animal's damn neck — all the fear in me now converted into anger — but that was irrational, so, yes, I would use the gun. Try to drop the dog with one shot, which meant I couldn't shoot until the animal was almost on me.

I thumbed back the gun's hammer, feeling the weapon's metallic density as I leveled the sights. Could hear the pit bull's harsh breathing now, its eyes a dull dead yellow as it closed in . . . twenty yards . . . ten . . . shoulder muscles rippling horselike.

The dog still hadn't seen me as I touched

my index finger to the trigger . . . but suddenly the animal sensed a change in polarity; maybe sensed that the quarry had turned killer, because it abruptly slowed to a trot, pointed ears alert, growl deepening.

Five yards away, the dog stopped. *Now* it could see me. The dog pivoted one ear toward me, then the other, nose up, sniffing, as it gathered sensory data. It took a step toward me . . . then jumped away, as if dodging a striking snake.

I waited and watched, gun ready . . . then slowly lowered the gun, surprised, as the pit bull dropped to its belly and began crawling toward me, no longer growling but making a whining sound of submission as its stub of a tail thumped the ground.

What had Tomlinson said about sharks sensing their kindred?

I reached out a tentative left hand. It took a few seconds for the dog to find my hand with its nose. Then it lifted its head into my palm — a beta animal requesting acceptance.

My nerve endings were on overload as I scratched the loose skin on the dog's neck, then turned and looked uphill. No sign of the infrared light now. Who was up there?

I stood. Looked at the dog, then stomped my foot, hissing, "Get out of here!"

The pit bull turned and ran.

As I exited the trail onto the beach near the house, I was looking at the wall of forest to my right where the camera blind was hidden. Next time — if there was a next time — I'd rig a rope so I could rappel down the rock wall instead of taking the long way around.

I glanced at my watch as I ran toward the house. Nearly ten minutes since Carol's first scream. Too long . . . but not long enough for Ritchie, Dutch, and Clovis to finish what they'd started. The place was brightly lit, windows showing the undersides of palms, casting shadows on white sand, so I hugged the forest wall.

I expected the men to be in the pool area, where Bob Marley music was still wailing, or inside the house.

Wrong.

They were outside, standing behind a maintenance shed at the rear of the property. If I hadn't spotted them from a distance, I wouldn't have slowed in time and they would've heard me coming.

I lifted the night-vision monocular from my eye because I wanted to see the night as the three men saw it. Dark of the moon. Mountain black against a black sky. No palm shadows on white sand, and I could barely make out the shape of the shed. No hint the men were there.

I glanced behind me, worried that I was backlit by the house. Nope. Rain forest, waxy black beneath stars. They couldn't see me, and I couldn't see them . . . until I pulled the monocular into place, hit the power switch, and it became dusky green daylight again.

There they were . . .

The three of them were huddled together, whispering. Clothed now, too, and smoking another cigar-sized joint. Dutch had his back to me as Ritchie turned to Clovis, gesturing with his hands — pissed off about something, maybe — because Clovis and Dutch were nodding the way kids do when they're being scolded.

And Ritchie was . . . holding a towel to his nose?

Yes. A white towel splotched with black. The man was bleeding.

What the hell had happened in the last ten minutes?

I moved closer, sliding along the forest rim, ready to freeze or duck into the shadows if they noticed me. I was also aware that Wolfie could still be in the blind, looking down on the house from the ridge. I'd been unable to see the maintenance shed from my rock platform. Could he?

I stopped, removed my backpack. Considered using the infrared beam to locate the camera blind . . . but decided, no, someone else was up there in the jungle equipped with night vision.

Instead, I hid the backpack behind a tree, checked to make sure the Colt was secure in its holster, then got down on hands and knees and continued toward the men.

When I was close enough, I heard Dutch whispering, with his accent, arguing with Ritchie. I dropped to my belly, crawled a few feet closer, and listened.

". . . So why you want to risk something like that when you know they're gonna tell the law?" Dutch asked.

"Of course they're gonna tell the Babylon. That's what I'm *saying.* We need go back and take care of them old women before they start flapping their gums. They got no phone, they've got no car. What's that tell you? Tells you they ain't gonna risk leaving this house tonight."

"Take care of 'em. What you mean is —"

"*Whatever it takes,* that's what I mean, man." There was a sustained orange glow — the man with dreadlocks inhaling on the joint.

"And what're we gonna do with the bodies?

I got to remind you that bodies don't sink so easy. And that stink. I don't want no more blood on my hands, man. Let the women go, that's my advice on this subject."

"Let them *go*? They go back to the States, what's gonna keep them from gettin' on TV and telling what happened here? Wolfie didn't get nothing on the camera that's gonna keep them quiet," Ritchie said. "How's the Widow gonna react to that news?"

"The Widow — fuck the Widow."

"Man, you're crazy to use that talk about her. You're beggin' for something bad to happen to you. Watch!"

"You sound like some damn ignorant child. Why you bring that crazy woman into this?"

"Because she's paying us, that's one reason. Plus, I'm telling you, the Widow's got magic ways to find out things. She'll know even if Wolfie don't tell her, that's why."

The Widow — a name spoken with reverence. I'd spent enough time in Cuba and the Caribbean to know that locals take the power of magic seriously, and even the best educated practice forms of santeria or obeah, a complex mix of Catholicism and an ancient African religion.

I thought about it as Ritchie said to Dutch, "You don't believe she's a vitchy woman?

Man, you're gonna believe she's a witch by the time she's done fuckin' you over, man!"

"Don't be talking that stupid shit, Ritchie, there's no such thing as *that*. That's the old ways, not modern times. You're just mad 'cause one of them twin bitches hit you. Clovis? What do you think? You want to go in there and help this crazy man kill a bunch of old women?"

Clovis wasn't taking sides. "Those women aren't so old, man. Those two cornstalk women, they scare the shit out of me. Done fucked up Ritchie's nose pretty good, I'd say. But it would be fun, so I'm not sayin'."

I smiled from the shadows — that's what had happened while I was coming down the hill. The twins had returned. There'd been a confrontation, and Ritchie had gotten his nose busted. Perfect.

But Ritchie wasn't done with it. He'd been humiliated, he wanted revenge, but his partners weren't jumping into line. Murder? That was a long-term commitment, and they were smart enough to know it. Which really pissed off Ritchie.

"Then you boys run away. I'm going into that house and do what needs be done. Faster you get outta my sight, the sooner I can do a man's work. Dutch, you got a knife on you, that much I know."

"You're not using my knife, man."

"You better listen to me, Dutch." The two men stood nose to nose. "I can take that knife if I want. You know it's true."

Dutch hesitated, then said, "Take the fucking knife, man. But I'm wiping it clean first. Then give me and Clovis twenty minutes to get to the Green Turtle so we got alibis. I don't want to hear nothing more about this shit."

Ritchie reached and took the knife. "I ain't giving you shit, man. A minute from now, you'll hear those tall bitches screaming. That makes you an accessory. So you better run, boy."

As Ritchie turned toward the house, though, the other two were walking fast to keep up with him, not running away. He was the leader, Shay had told me. Now they were following him into murder.

I *was* running as I drew the Colt.

They couldn't see me, but I could see them . . . could see the three men marching toward the house single file, Dutch at the rear, taller, heavier than the others. Could see Ritchie in tank top and baggy shorts, blond curls beneath the pirate scarf, still using the towel to dab at his nose. Glint of knife blade . . . Clovis took a folding knife from his pocket, too, and snapped it open, then handed it to Dutch, who hesitated before he took it. Clovis with his weasel ways, playing both sides, letting others do the dirty work. But he was *into* this.

They never saw me coming.

At the last second, though, Dutch heard me. I was running full speed when he turned. I saw his eyes: a mix of confusion and surprise. The expression was still on his face when I dropped my shoulder and hit him in the spine, kidney-high, from behind.

"What the fuck!"

The impact was jarring, but I rolled, came up onto my feet, then used the gun butt to club Ritchie on the side of the head. Too stunned to react, he collapsed backward onto the sand. I stood over him for a moment before I stepped on his right wrist until he let go of the knife.

As I picked it up, he said, "Who . . . who the hell are you, man?"

I was breathing hard, already moving toward Dutch. "Leave the women alone. Understand?"

To my left, Clovis was backing away, saying, "I've got nothing to do with what they was planning, mister, you can believe me on that . . ." Then, his voice changed as my head swiveled toward him; sounded like he was scared shitless, saying, "Ritchie . . . Jesus Christ, you see that? He's . . . he's only got one eye, man," talking about the glow from the monocular.

When I got to Dutch, he was moaning, saying he thought his back was broken, and asking, "What the hell happened? Am I dreaming this?" sounding like he was going into shock. I'd hurt him.

I picked up the second knife, tried to fold it closed, but couldn't find the lock, so I held both knives in my left hand as I holstered the Colt.

Clovis was still looking at me, backing away, whispering, "This here person ain't no *man,* man. You see? He's got one eye in the middle of his damn head . . . it's *glowing.* Just like the old people say - got an eye that glows like a cat."

He turned to Dutch, yelling to make sure I heard. "You see what you done, saying those nasty things about the Widow? It wasn't us that did it . . . it was you that talked bad about that good lady."

Islanders believed it.

I nudged Dutch with my foot as I said to Clovis and Ritchie, "Get this guy on his feet, and don't come back. *Move.*"

I didn't stomp my foot like with the pit bull, but the reaction was similar.

17

Carol said to me, "Our hero. Just in the nick of time," being sarcastic as Mattie led me into the kitchen of the beach house where one of the twins was boiling water for tea as the other held a bag of ice to Carol's cheek, which was swollen, already turning purple.

The twin making tea gave Mattie a pointed look and said, "Why would you bring another stranger into this house after what just happened?"

Mattie was a sobbing, shaky wreck, still paranoid from the drug they'd slipped into the margaritas. It had taken me several minutes to talk my way into the house. Now this.

Mattie said, "We need help, that's why. Carol should go to the hospital. And we've got to tell the police —"

"No hospital!" Carol snapped. "No police! We are getting off this fucking island tomorrow and no one — *no one* — is ever going to mention what happened tonight again."

The twin holding the ice began stroking the woman's hair, calming her. Carol was wearing a bathrobe now, her yellow dress nearby on the tile floor. It was ripped and missing buttons.

I said, "Mattie's right. I've got a boat. I can take all of you to Saint Lucia — it's only a few miles. You'll be safe, and the place I'm staying will know a good doctor."

Carol yelled, "No," as the twin making tea focused on me, sounding like an attorney as she asked, "Safe from what? Mattie, what did you tell this man?"

Mattie said, "Nothing. He's only trying to help, can't you see that?"

The twin was staring at me. "Answer my question — safe from what? Our friend slipped getting out of the pool and hit her face. So why would you think we're in some kind of danger?"

I said, "Because I passed three guys when I was coming up the road. They looked suspicious, like they were in a hurry to get away."

"Did you speak to them?"

I took too long to respond. "No."

"If they looked suspicious, and you were concerned about our safety, why didn't you at least speak to them?"

I pointed to the dress. "Because I hadn't seen that yet. Or Carol's face."

Carol said, "He didn't speak to them because he's a coward. Now he wants to play the hero, but what he really wants to do is get in Mattie's pants. I knew it the first moment I saw him. For all we know, he's one of them."

Mattie began to cry harder, disconsolate as I squeezed her shoulder and said, "You're wrong. I should've said something to the men, I agree, but there's nothing I can do about it now. What I *can* do is find a doctor and bring him here. But I think Saint Lucia is a better idea. Saint Lucia isn't corrupt like Saint Arc. You'd be safe, and it's not far. We'll come back for your things tomorrow. My boat's anchored just around the point."

Maybe both twins were attorneys, because the one holding ice to Carol's face asked, "Why did you park your boat on the other side of the point if you came to visit us?"

I was crossing the room to the sink, where dishes were piled, including the blender Ritchie had used — a few inches of margarita left. I opened the lid and sniffed as I said, "If you had company when I got here, I was going to walk to the resort and have a drink. I didn't want to anchor twice."

I sniffed the blender again and made a

face. "Did one of you make this?"

The twins could converse without speaking. Their eyes met, as if confirming something. "Why do you ask?"

"It smells odd."

"You warned us earlier, didn't you, about resorts where the drinks are drugged?"

I said, "That's right, I did."

"What a *coincidence.* And why do you have sand all over your clothes? Those scratches on your face and the back of your hands — they weren't there yesterday. It looks to me like you've been sneaking around in the bushes. Now I suppose you want to take the blender, so you can test it in your little portable lab?" More sarcasm.

I knew what the answer would be before I replied. "As a matter of fact, I'd like a sample. Half-a-test-tube full, that's all."

The twins locked eyes, discussing it in silence, before they stopped what they were doing, then came around the counter to face me, standing side by side. "We've decided it's time for you to leave, Dr. North — or whatever your name is. If you want to argue the point or continue your silly little act, you should know we began studying the martial arts when we were in grade school . . . *and* we both played field hockey at Smith. You won't be the first man we've tossed out of a room."

Mattie had recovered enough to say, "I'm sorry, Doc. But I think you'd better go," looking at me, a nice woman with sad, aching eyes.

I squeezed Mattie's arm, gave her a wink, and said, "Don't be sorry. You're safe now, in good hands. That's all that matters."

I shouldered my backpack as I started for the door, but then stopped, unzipped the bag, and tossed the two knives I'd taken from the men onto a chair. I'd already inspected them — cheap, no inscriptions on the blades.

I said, "Keep these, just in case there's trouble."

The twins were escorting me, only a step behind. "Where'd those come from?"

I said, "The three guys I passed coming on the trail? They dropped them."

"They *dropped* them. Just like that, huh?"

I said, "That's right. Like I told you, they were in a hurry. I don't think they'll be back."

The twins' eyes moved from the scratches on my hands to my face, and then they exchanged looks again with a new awareness — *reappraisal time.* "You took these knives from them, *that's* what happened." I smiled and said, "I hope your grooms realize how damn lucky they are. It's like tonight — sometimes luck's just on your side."

I got to Saint Lucia around eleven and walked into my luxury suite with its infinity pool, ceiling fans, a room with only three walls open to the sea, to find that someone had slipped an envelope under the door.

Dr. M. North
Personal

Expensive stationery embossed with the initials JHM on the seal. Heavy, masculine hand with a slight tremor, suggesting age. I opened the envelope.

Dr. North, I am having a nightcap on the upper terrace of the Jade Club. I've had staff organize a midnight tea if you're interested. I realize I'm being presumptuous in advance of an introduction, but it concerns a matter of mutual interest, I believe, and of grave importance.
Cordially,
Col. James H. Montbard RM (ret.) GBE DMC FIEC

Written with British syntax and formality, as were the postnominal letters associated with the British Honours System. I had never heard of the man, but understood it was from Sir James Montbard, recipient of the Knight Grande Cross, the Distinguished Military Cross, a retired colonel in the British Royal Marines, and an International Fellow of the Explorers Club.

Impressive. But how did he know I was here?

It was only my second night at Jade Mountain, a lodge and nature preserve consisting of six hundred acres of rain forest and beach on the southwestern shore of Saint Lucia. I'd chosen Jade Mountain because it is among the most private and exclusive resorts in the Caribbean, and because it was built into a mountainside with a clear view of Saint Arc, a few miles to the west, and Anse Chastanet Bay below, where I'd moored the Maverick.

Because I was doing countersurveillance, it would've been easier to stay near the beach house on Saint Arc. But that would put me under the control of the local government. It would have invited interaction with authorities and suspicion from the locals. If you seek anonymity, hide yourself among the very poor or the very wealthy.

Jade Mountain attracted the famous and rich, but of an unusual variety. The lodge had no air-conditioning, no glassed windows or screens. Suites were open on the seaward side, no walls or shutters, so it was like living outdoors in a luxury cliff dwelling — rare woods, custom tiles — jungle all around. The place was brilliantly designed. Rooms were breezy, each with its own infinity pool, water cool as the deep mountain spring that fed them. The staff was unobtrusive; privacy guaranteed.

But I hadn't been at the place long enough to meet anyone — and I didn't want to meet anyone. The previous evening, I'd had dinner alone at the beach restaurant at Anse Chastanet — jerked pork with lime rice, mango chutney, and some very good pepper sauce. In the morning, I'd gone for a long swim, ordered fresh fruit and coffee brought to the room, then went looking for a place to send e-mails.

The only Internet access was at the reception cottage, a quarter-way up the mountain. I wrote to Shay and Beryl, asking questions I should have asked earlier: Aside from investing in the resort on Saint Lucia, did Michael's family have other business connections in the Eastern Caribbean? Saint Arc — had Shay discovered it on her own, or had someone recommended it? What was Ida Jonquil's maiden name?

Aside from the woman at reception, and my waiter, I hadn't spoken to anyone else.

That's why it made no sense there was something so gravely important that a distinguished man like Sir Colonel James Montbard would track me here . . . if Sir James was who he claimed to be.

Standing on an open terrace, looking down at the Caribbean Sea four hundred feet below, Sir James told me, "In my opinion, Saint Lucia is the most beautiful island in the British Commonwealth — apart from England herself, of course."

I said, "Of course," sipping the Singapore Sling he'd ordered, looking at silhouettes of mountains across the bay where a few lights glimmered: beach huts, cooking fires, sailboats at anchor.

"Saint Lucia was undiscovered for decades," he said, "like a beautiful mistress — but only because it was so wonderfully camouflaged by her association with the French. Napoleon's wife, Josephine, was born here, you know. All the French names: Soufriére, Castries, Moule á Chique. And those famous peaks you're staring at: the Pitons — Gros Piton and Petit Piton. 'Tip of a bull's horn,' it means. Naturally, travelers assumed this island was French, so they avoided Saint Lucia like the plague. Under-standable, in my opinion."

I said, "Some would agree," before asking, "Why are they famous?," meaning the twin volcanic peaks, weathered rock, and jungle that rose from the sea like pyramids, towers half a mile high.

"I could give you the standard line about landmarks for sailors," Sir James said, "but, truth is, they're famous because they're the most sexually suggestive rock formations in the Caribbean. Have a look now, let your eyes blur for a moment. Then tell me what you see."

I did it, and laughed. "X-rated. I under-stand now."

"They've found petroglyphs on those mountains more than a thousand years old. Are you interested in archaeology, Dr. North?"

"I have a traveler's interest."

"Traveler, eh?" His reply had an unusual inflection, as if inspecting the comment for double meaning. "I'm a traveler myself . . ." He waited several beats before continuing. ". . . and an International Fellow of the Ex-plorers Club, I'm proud to say. Archaeology is a passion of mine. Inherited it from my grandfather. Amateur or professional, you must do serious field work to be voted in as a Fellow. I've published a few things on the pre-Colombian sites in the Caribbean and Meso-America that I'd like to think contributed to the literature."

We talked for a few minutes about the Caribs, the Arawak, the stone pyramids of Tikal in Guatemala — he'd worked at a dig there — before he got back to the subject of the famous peaks and sexuality.

"The Pitons have always been associated with fertility rites and magic — first the Arawak, then escaped slaves with their obeah and voodoo. Now it's every mix of race and religion because Anse Chastanet is a favorite honeymoon destination.

"My God," he continued, "you didn't hear the sounds coming out of the forest this morning?" The man chuckled and cupped a hand over his pipe as he relit it. "Positively obscene — and delightful. One couple awakes, sees those peaks, and they become amorous. Their sounds arouse the couple in the next cottage, and then the next — there are no windows or shutters, of course, to buffer the sounds — so the entire rain forest is echoing before long with the most primitive noises you can imagine. They yip and roar like gorillas. Even to an old campaigner like me, it occasionally gets the blood stirring."

I said, "You don't strike me as old." A half truth. Sitting across the table, wearing pleated slacks, a sea-cotton shirt, and shooting jacket with a recoil patch and epaulets, Montbard was the 1940s prototype of the retired English gentleman. He was balding, not tall, and had the brown, tight-skinned face of a Brit who'd spent decades in the tropics.

On closer inspection, though, I noted the thick forearms and hands, the crease of scar tissue beneath his left eye, the way slacks bunched around his waist while the jacket strained at the shoulders. The man was in great shape.

Something else I noticed: the way the jacket's inseams were tailored loose beneath the arms — room for a shoulder holster? — and, on his left hand, a gold ring engraved with a symbol that was difficult to make out because he wore the engraving palm-side down. Also because the ring was weathered. I finally got a look: a skull and crossbones raised within a pyramid — an esoteric Masonic symbol that I'd seen only a few times in my life.

"But I am old," Montbard insisted. "The howling of young honeymooners reminds me of the truth. My first and last wife, Victoria, God rest her soul, would agree. My quarters are just down the mountain, so there's no escaping it. Family property, you know, deeded to us during the colonial uprising — the American Revolution, you'd call it."

I said, "I'm surprised someone hasn't made a recording and sold it on the Internet — 'Sunrise at Anse Chastanet,'" letting the sentence hang there so I could gauge the man's reaction. I'd decided his invitation probably had something to do with black-mail.

We were halfway through our first drink and were still making small talk. Montbard had the focused, easygoing manner of an executive used to assessing applicants after only a few minutes of polite conversation. I expected to be dismissed at any moment, which convinced me he was the man he claimed to be.

That's the only reason I stayed there listening to a seventy-some-year-old Brit lecture me on the history of an island that, so far, I didn't find as interesting as Colombia or Nicaragua, countries to the northwest.

Sir James said, "Ah . . . here we go," as two women came onto the terrace, carrying trays. "I'm a bit of a night owl, I'm afraid. Keep odd hours — an old habit from my days with the regiment. Hope you don't find a midnight tiff too shocking."

I began to get interested. Because he was so immaculately dressed — slacks, white shirt with cuffs, shooting jacket — I said, "Sandhurst?"

The terrace was open on three sides, with ceiling fans and wicker tables. He laughed as he led me to a table. "That obvious, is it? Yes, I was born to the boots and bear. Grandfather was a major general in the Great War when your lads helped us run the Huns out of Argonne. Father learned a bit of Japanese in Malaya, then served in Suez after the French mucked up the bloody business. Between wars, our family have always come back to Saint Lucia." He reached for a plate of biscuits. "Scone?"

The table was now covered with a tea service, a silver tureen, and heated serving dishes. There were cheeses, salted cod, fresh mangoes, tamarinds, local pineapple, and sugar bananas. Within easy reach were bottles of Harper's bourbon and Pinch-bottle Haig & Haig, a siphon of soda, ice in a bucket, a flagon of spring water, and two pint glasses thick as crystal. Montbard had also ordered poached snapper, some kind of curry dish, and roasted marrow bones — something I'd never tried. The marrow bones were served wrapped in napkins, with caviar spoons.

"Like those, do you? I have Chef bribe the local butchers. When good marrow bones come along, he snaps them up. I believe that fine food and drink are a form of art."

I raised my caviar spoon in acknowledgment. "You live here, at Jade Mountain?"

"No! I'm the resort's closest neighbor and a friend of the man who designed the place — a Russian who also happens to be a brilliant architect. His name's Nick, but I call him the Mad Russian. A joke of ours.

"The food here's wonderful, of course, but Nick doesn't mind if I have my own chef send over the occasional delicacy. I live there —" He nodded toward lights on the dark hillside overlooking the sea. "Perhaps you noticed the place?"

I had: a mansion of rock and gray wood, yellow *flamboyant* trees in bloom, staff cottages with green tiled roofs, and steps winding down to a dock where a trawler was moored. I commented on the view he must have, and the long descent to the water.

He was proud of it. "There are precisely three hundred and eighty-one steps from my dock to the terrace of the main house — the equivalent of climbing twenty flights of stairs. Believe me, I've counted them enough times to know.

"Keeps a man fit, climbing up and down

these mountains. When I hear visitors whining about all the steps, I'm tempted to ask them how much they paid for the exercise equipment in their homes. Every day but Monday, I do the hillside six times, quick march pace, then swim from my dock to the beach at Anse Chastanet." He patted his flat stomach. "Daily PT is absolutely crucial, that's my personal belief."

I said, "Spoken like an officer in the Royal Marines. You didn't mention where *you* served, Sir James."

The man gave me a sly look as he poured more whiskey. "Didn't I? I thought I had — the memory starts to slip a bit when you reach seventy. Bloody boring, I should think, listening to me ramble on about my days in harness. And we have more important matters to discuss." He leaned to open a canvas shoulder bag he'd brought. "It's time we got down to brass tacks. Very rude of me to invite you here at this hour, Dr. North, and not tell you the reason."

The sly look narrowed as he took a stack of glossy photos from the bag and placed them on the table.

He asked, "Recognize that man?," his eyes bright above his whiskey tumbler as he drank. "Quite a rough-looking character — when he's not clomping around our beaches, pretending to be a biologist."

The photos were of me.

18

The photographs were taken on Saturday, my first day on the island, as I explored the hillside above the beach house on Saint Arc.

There was a shot of me as I knelt to pick up a stick, then another of me probing the entrance of the camera blind, checking for booby traps.

I paused long enough to ask Montbard, "How did you get these?"

He was no longer the warm and cheery host. "Keep going. We'll discuss details later."

The next photo was taken from outside the camera blind, looking in through the viewing window. I was holding up *Paris Match,* the issue with the attractive female politician on the cover. My face was only partially visible.

In the last two photos, I was looking downward from the viewing window, then I was reaching to drop the curtain — the twins had appeared, I remembered, and I was allowing them their privacy.

"Interesting," I said. "Were they taken with some kind of remote-control camera?"

"Not exactly. I have an interest in what's going on on that nasty little island. You were being shadowed."

"I'm a relatively observant man. I didn't see anyone shadowing me."

Sir James said, "That's what you may expect to see when I'm shadowing you. But you're right, in a way. These photographs were taken by cameras equipped with motion detectors. I was higher up the mountain. I followed you as you marked your trail."

I remembered parrots flushing from a stand of travelers palms.

I was about to say *I suspected* . . . as Montbard said, "Now you're about to tell me you suspected someone was there all along." He smiled, but there was no humor in his face. "They always do — once I confront them. You asked about my years with the Royal Marines? For part of the time, I was attached to Defence Intelligence and Security in Bedfordshire. PSYOPS. So I've had a bit of experience at the game."

PSYOPS — psychological warfare operations.

I asked, "What about tonight? Did you have a quiet evening at home, watching for my boat to return? Or did you follow me again?" I was thinking about the infrared light I'd seen.

His severe expression faded. "Let's put our cards on the table, shall we, Dr. North? It's obvious that we're both aware what's going on at Saint Arc. A very shrewd operator is using the place as a filmset for blackmail — and not just that pretty little beach house. It's quite a sophisticated operation. If you don't mind, I'll save the particulars for later.

"Saint Arc, along with Jamaica and Aruba, is the only island in the Caribbean corrupt enough to allow that sort of business. I have a personal interest in seeing the bastards hang, and I am quietly assembling their gallows. Forgive me for being frank, but what I don't need is some amateur Yank mucking up all my work by tipping off the buggers in advance — or by calling in the authorities."

He reached for the bottle of bourbon and freshened his drink before adding, "I've seen enough to know you're not working for the opposition. I therefore take it you have a personal interest in the matter — someone has hired you, perhaps, to investigate."

With some people, the smart thing to do is

keep your cards close to the chest until you have an idea what's in their hand. Not this guy, though. I told him, "No. My goddaughter is a victim. She's supposed to be married on Sunday. The blackmailers gave her until Friday to pay the balance on a quarter-million dollars."

"The balance?"

"Yes. She made a deal to pay them a little over a hundred thousand, but they reneged the day after she transferred the money."

"Really." He appeared to find the information useful. "Well, I can empathize with the fact that you and your goddaughter are in a bit of a tight situation. Tomorrow's Monday — only four days to deal with the problem. That's all the more reason for me to worry you're going to ruin all my work by rushing matters. Let's be frank: Are you some bumbling amateur, Dr. North?"

I said, "I'll answer that question honestly, if you'll answer a question honestly for me. Are *you* the blackmailer, Sir James?"

I was reassured by his nodding look of approval. "Very smart. I would have followed the same chain of reasoning. Problem is, I checked with a few friends — State Department types; immigration people. They had some difficulty coming up with background information on you. North is such a common surname. According to your passport, the middle initial is W. If I knew your middle name, I might be more inclined to speak freely."

"You found out all that about me?"

"Does that offend you? Perhaps you have something to hide."

Montbard had avoided eye contact in the comfortable way people do when they are busy eating and drinking, but now his eyes locked onto mine. Instinct told me he already knew the answer or he wouldn't have asked the question.

I said, "My middle name doesn't begin with a W."

"A mistake on your passport?"

I shrugged as he stared at me. "Everything's computerized. If someone hits the wrong letter on a keyboard, it's better to live with the mistake than deal with all the bureaucracy getting it changed."

After several moments, he said, "I think that answers my question."

"But you haven't answered mine. Are you the blackmailer?"

"Understood. Why don't you come 'round to the house for tea in the morning. Nine-ish? I'd like to introduce you to someone who, I think, will answer that question for me."

He snapped his fingers to get the waiter's attention, then pointed at me — *Another drink here.*

"Singapore Sling, Dr. North? Got the recipe from the barman at Raffles personally." He looked up from his glass, studying my face. "Or may I start calling you by your real name . . . Dr. Ford?"

19

Monday, June 24th

Sir James Montbard's estate was named Bluestone, maybe because of the slate blue rock used to build the main house. The place was fully staffed — armed guard at the gate, gardeners, maids in bright plaid skirts sweeping around the veranda's rock pillars — so I was momentarily flustered when the photogenic woman on the cover of *Paris Match* opened the door.

I didn't recognize her at first, but that's who it was.

"Welcome to Bluestone, Dr. Ford. I was expecting you."

I'd assumed a maid would answer, not this attractive fortyish female wearing crisp morning clothing, white blouse and jodhpurs, brown hair tied back from her face, just a touch of lipstick. Looked dressed for a morning ride.

The woman's hair was lighter, she had aged a year, but those weren't the reasons I didn't recognize her right away. There are a few rare people whom the camera lens sees more clearly than the human eye. Perhaps it has to do with bone construction, the angles of cheek, chin, and nose. Whatever the reason, the lens loves them. They photograph differently than they appear in person. I've read that some of the classic film stars were examples: Bogart, Hepburn, Gable.

Here was another. It wasn't until the woman thrust out a firm hand and said, "I'm Senegal, a pal of Hooker's. So nice of you to come," that I realized I was speaking to Senegal Firth, former candidate for British Parliament, who'd been featured in the magazine: the unflattering shots of a photogenic woman with interesting eyes, who looked good in her revealing swimsuit.

The pictures had been taken while she was vacationing on Saint Arc, according to the article, and she had threatened to sue the magazine.

I said, "Hooker?" to cover my surprise.

"Oh, sorry. That's what chums call Sir James. His middle name is Hooks — from the maternal side." She smiled. "You're embarrassed because you didn't recognize me. Don't be. I'm flattered. Couldn't be happier, actually. Hooker told me you'd seen the horrible photos the magazine published. I never really appreciated the value of privacy until I ran for public office. Now I revel in my anonymity. Tea?"

I followed her through a great hall, past a billiard room, then a library where walls were covered by framed, antique maps. The room smelled of books, pipe tobacco, the nutty musk of pecky cypress. When I stopped, Firth said, "Go ahead, have a walk around. Sir James is mad for this sort of thing."

There were charts of the Caribbean, the early Americas, and ornate world maps with notations in Latin. I slid glasses to my forehead and said, "The plaque says this map was drawn in 1507."

"That's right. The Waldseemuller map." There was a smile in her voice. "It's not the original, of course. Notice something unusual about it?"

"Yes. It shows the western coast of South America, and the Baja Peninsula. Hudson Bay, too. All fairly accurate. I'm trying to remember my fifth-grade history —"

"Excellent catch, Dr. Ford. You're thinking of Magellan. He didn't reach the Pacific Coast until decades later, and he never really explored it. And explorer Henry Hudson didn't arrive in the Americas until a hundred years later."

I said, "So the map couldn't have been made in 1507."

"But it was — it's been well documented. The maps on that wall represent some of history's great mysteries. That's what Sir James claims, anyway. The Stuttgart Map, for instance, is from the sixteenth century. It shows Antarctica in incredible detail — two hundred and fifty years before western explorers had laid eyes on it. Not only that, it's the Antarctic as it would appear without ice. I checked for myself. It's true."

I compared the map to the world globe that sat beside a leather reading chair. She was right about the accuracy. The map was dated 1535.

"How can that be?"

The woman shrugged.

The library's shelves were stacked from floor to ceiling, and there was a glass display case containing jade carvings similar to those I'd seen during my years in Central America. There were a dozen wedge-shaped amulets — owl motifs, archaeologists had told me — with *V*s carved into the necks, representing beaks. In a corner, mounted on a pedestal, was a piece of what looked to be a stone wheel. Carved into it were what might have been pre-Colombian glyphs. Part of a

Mayan calendar, possibly.

"Mind if I take a look at that?"

"Not at all. But I warn you, if you ask James about it, he'll bore you to tears with the details and his pet theories about world history. Same with the maps."

I crossed the room and leaned to look. A chunk of gray stone . . . a fifteen-degree section of a stone circle. I was puzzling over the glyphs as the woman said, "His grandfather, General Henry Montbard, found that years ago. James claims it's ancient — probably Mayan or Olmec. Sir James's father didn't catch the bug, but personality traits skip a generation, don't they? Archaeology is in his blood."

Only one of the glyphs had the Asian-flavored, geometrical complexity I associate with Mayan writing. Looked like a rooster, with a cross on its breast. Tomlinson would have remembered the name of the glyph and what it symbolized — he'd been with me in Guatemala and Masagua a few years back, tracking artifact smugglers.

The other glyphs, however — if they were glyphs — were simple, open-ended rectangles and *V*s similar to those on the owl pendants. Some had dots drilled in the center. Because I thought Tomlinson might recognize them, I took out a pocket notebook and copied them.

Along the stone's broken edge was a fragment of a glyph. I copied that, too.

As I sketched, I said to the woman, "Sir James is a man with eclectic interests."

"Oh, just wait until you get to know him better. He's more like a precocious boy who wants to learn everything about *every*thing. A regular wizard when it comes to history. Warfare, too, I suspect, but he only hints at that."

"I hope I'm half as active when I'm his age."

Her tone wry, Firth said, "Funny thing about Hooker — only men comment on his age. Women never seem to notice . . . or care."

She motioned with her hand, and I followed her through a sitting room — antique furniture, dark wood, coat of arms above the fireplace — to a terrace that faced the sea. A tunnel created by sea grape trees led to a croquet court, an orchid house, a manicured garden filled with roses and ornamentals, then to the bluff overlooking the bay. Three hundred and eighty-one stone steps to the dock, Sir James had told me.

A wrought-iron table had been set for breakfast: sliced fruit, silver serving dishes, rashers of bacon, poached eggs, kippers;

frangipani blossoms afloat in a bowl.

The woman said, "Hooker rallied long enough this morning to tell me you two had a great chat last night. Turns out you have a mutual friend or two. He said I should treat you like one of his colleagues — which I take to mean you're mysterious, you're obsessive, you're a gentleman, and you drink gin tonics or whiskey neat."

I said, "I think you're confusing me with another sort of colleague," amused because it was the kind of thing Shay would say.

It was true that Montbard and I had mutual friends, probably more than either of us would ever know. Despite our age difference, there was a sufficient overlap in our careers to create ties.

With British PSYOPS, the man had spent time in Borneo, Hong Kong, and also Belize, where he'd worked with the Gurkha contingent stationed there.

"Got my first look at Tikal while T-D-Y," he'd told me. "Brilliant pyramids, simply brilliant. My little Gurkha friends scampered up and down them like they were nothing."

In the Falklands, he'd helped get *Radio Atlantic del Sur* operational. In Iraq, he'd been involved in a psy-war night operation that had used "the voice of Allah" to frighten several hundred sleeping Iraqis into surrendering — an operation I'd heard about. Sir James enjoyed telling the story, because it allowed him to segue into stories about digs he'd worked on in Egypt, Cyprus, and the Syrian Desert.

Yes, he was a traveler. I didn't doubt he had long service with the British military. I also suspected he had worked for MI6, the U.K.'s equivalent of our CIA. Possibly still did. Saint Lucia was only a few hundred miles from intelligence-gathering hot spots in South America. And even though Sir James was in his seventies, he was sharp, tough, and so physically fit that, for me, he'd already become one of those people that I file away in memory for inspiration later.

A man in a white tunic and white slacks appeared at the table — member of the staff. He nodded first to me, then the woman, and said, "Mornin', sir. Mornin', Miz Senny," without making eye contact as he pulled out the lady's chair.

I answered, "Good morning. Nice day, huh?"

The man replied, "Aw'right, aw'right," turning toward the kitchen to bring our tea.

Senegal Firth was explaining why Sir James

probably wouldn't join us for breakfast, but would come around later for a Bloody Mary in the library. "He sleeps in on Mondays. Always has, for as long as I've known him."

"What's special about Mondays?"

"He didn't tell you about his workout routine? I'm surprised. He's very proud of himself. Six days a week, he does swimming, jumping jacks, and stretches, then marches up and down those terrible steps an incredible number of times. I'm not exaggerating, Dr. Ford, when I say my legs are absolutely on fire after just one trip from the beach to the house. But Hooker does it every morning of his life, when he's in residence . . . *except* for Mondays."

I asked again, "Why Mondays?" because her emphasis invited the question.

Firth had a nice laugh: eyes closed, nodding her head, white teeth showing as she touched a hand to her lips.

"Because Hooker's a man of precise habits. He doesn't take exercise on Mondays because Sunday night is 'grog night.' It's something that goes back to the regimental mess when he was in K.L. It's the only night of the week he allows himself to drink to excess. And he does! The old dear gets happily, song-singing pissed on whiskey. So he sleeps in Monday mornings, steels himself with a Bloody Mary, then spends the day in his smoking jacket working in the garden — he's crackers about gardening and plants, particularly orchids. But come Tuesday, bright and early, his regimen of discipline and exercise starts all over again.

"I've known him since I was a little girl, and I adore him," she continued. "More important, I'd trust him with my life. My father was an artillery officer stationed at Ouakam Military Base in Dakar, Senegal — this was back when Senegal was still a French colony. Hooker and father met there, and they became chums —" She chuckled, buttering a piece of toast. "— despite Hooker's bias against all things French. Or maybe it was because of it."

I said, "You're French?"

"My namesake's African because I was born there. But I lived in France until I couldn't stand it anymore — nothing against the country, I love France. Family problems, I'm afraid."

Her father was a difficult man, she explained. She was the youngest of six children, and never got along with the man.

"When I was seventeen, I moved to London and worked as an au pair. Hooker became a sort of Dutch uncle. He and his late wife were great advocates of mine. By that time, my father was aide to the mayor of Champagne. Father had a live-in mistress, yet he refused to divorce my mother, or pay child support. So I brought suit against him. I was at university by then. It took years, but I finally won the case."

I said, "You sued your own father?" and immediately regretted my tone.

Firth had been uncharacteristically outgoing for a Brit, but now her eyes changed. It was like two chestnut windows slamming closed.

"Dr. Ford, I've spent my political life fighting for the rights of children, and for people who've been disenfranchised by traditions that should have been abandoned back in the days when floggings were outlawed.

"As an aide to a member of Parliament, I helped write the Parental Rights and Obligations Act. I personally championed the Prostitution of Minors Act, which provides penal measures for child predators. Yet you find it surprising that as a university student I was willing to fight for the rights of my brothers and sisters?"

I said, "I apologize, Ms. Firth. I spoke without thinking."

Her shield remained in place. "No, Dr. Ford, your reaction was instinctive — and very typical of men. Fortunately, not all men are typical."

We sat facing the sea. I was fumbling for a response when, thankfully, a voice from behind us said, "Already on the subject of male domination and politics, are we? Dear girl, will you do me the greatest of favors and please delay the discussion until staff brings me my medicine?"

It was Sir James, crossing the terrace in slippers and a silk bathrobe, with a towel around his neck. The towel, I realized, was packed with ice. He gave us both a sharp look. "I would have bet the treasury that you two would either trust each other or hate each other at first sniff. Appears I was right."

The woman said, "I have no idea what you're talking about, James."

"Really? Then why the flushed face?" He looked at me. "Senegal turns the color of a pale rose whenever she's excited —"

"Hooker!"

"I was about to say, when you're excited *and upset,* if you'd only let me finish. At any rate, I strongly advise that you two postpone further sniffing until we've discussed our mutual problem. Afterward, we can talk about —" He abandoned the sentence, and smiled as our server approached, carrying a drink on a tray. "Oh, God bless you for this,

Rafick. Hair of the dog — exactly what the doctor ordered."

Two Bloody Marys later, Sir James dropped his napkin on the table and picked up his pipe. "All righty, then! Dr. Ford, I suggest you tell Senny what you're doing on Saint Lucia. Hear him out, dear girl, then you can decide whether to hate him and send him away, or to trust him and let him help with our little problem."

20

Senegal Firth's little problem had nothing to do with the photos published in a French magazine. Her problem was that a hidden camera had filmed her during an "injudicious evening" inside the mountain villa she'd rented while vacationing alone on Saint Arc less than a year ago.

The blackmailer had contacted her a month before the elections and threatened to send a copy of the video to her husband, another to the London *Times,* and also to post it on Internet pornography sites if she didn't pay four million pounds into a Bank of Aruba account.

"It's the same blackmailer who went after your goddaughter," Sir James said. "Same modus operandi. I'm assembling a list of victims. Senny certainly was not the first, and your goddaughter will not be the last. That's why we have to nail the buggers to the wall and cut their heads off."

The woman said, *"Hooker,"* with an expression of distaste. "No need to be gruesome, is there?"

Montbard said, "There's every reason to be gruesome. We are dealing with people who are absolutely ruthless. Ford? Tell her what would've happened to those four American women last night if you hadn't come along."

I said, "Honestly? I think the women would've scared the guys off without my help. They were a tough bunch."

"Frighten three men who were armed with knives? *Please.*"

Senegal looked sickened, asking, "Men with knives?" as Montbard said, "Bullocks. I saw what happened with my own eyes. If you won't tell her, I will."

He did, minus a few details I hadn't shared with him last night on Jade Mountain as he'd sipped his third whiskey, and I'd switched from Singapore Slings to the local Piton Beer over ice.

When he was done, Firth said, "They would've murdered the women? You're serious."

I weighed the probabilities before saying, "Were they capable of murder? That's tough to say. Murder's the sort of thing that's easy to talk about, but very few people can actually do."

"Do you really believe that?"

I looked at Sir James to see his reaction — it would tell me a lot about him. I realized he was looking at me for the same reason. "Dr. Ford clearly has some knowledge of the subject —" The man cleared his throat. "— the academic sort, of course. The military has done studies. In the second war, fewer than twenty percent of our boys could bring themselves to pull the trigger even when under attack. One percent of our pilots accounted for forty percent of enemy planes shot down. It's a rare bird who can truly do the deed. But some people seem born to it."

I looked at Senegal. "Maybe they were. From what I overheard, it wouldn't be the first time. I think it would've depended on how the women reacted. Sexual predators in a pack behave differently than a predator operating alone."

"That's true," she said, interested, but also evaluating my words — she was the expert, not me. She'd helped draft laws on the subject.

"Packs target the weak. If the women had tried to humor them, we might be reading about a multiple homicide in tomorrow's paper. But if they'd fought back, I think the men would've found an excuse to run. There was nothing to gain financially. It was all ego."

Firth said, "Three men. Unusual," as if processing new information. "Could you describe the men if you had to?"

"I can describe them whether I have to or not. But Sir James has photos. You haven't seen them?"

"Yes. But the photos aren't very clear. They're . . . not lifelike. Would you mind?"

I noticed Sir James watching the woman as I described the men. When I was done, I also noticed him inhale and sigh when Senegal said, "There are some vague similarities. But nothing really rings a bell."

Was she lying?

I said, "Then let's compare notes. The night you were secretly videoed — how would you describe the man?"

Firth's chin lifted as she took a butter knife into her hand and began drumming the tip on her place mat. "Unfortunately, I can't answer that question with any certainty. That's one of the hurdles Sir James and I have been dealing with."

"I don't understand."

Looking pained, Montbard interceded, "Senegal was going through a very rough patch in her marriage. You'd been married to Harold for how long?"

In a flat voice, the woman answered, "Fourteen years."

"Fourteen years, right. She was just putting together her campaign team when Senny discovered her husband was . . ." He turned to the woman. "Do you mind if I share the story, dear? I think we can trust Dr. Ford. It's important that he have all the data, but if you'd rather I not —"

Firth didn't look up from her teacup. "Go ahead. Doesn't bother me in the least now."

Clearly, it did.

Montbard and I exchanged looks before he continued, "Turned out, her husband was having an affair with one of her old college chums. It was a terrible shock, as you can imagine. I was the one who advised her to take a couple of weeks off and fly to the Caribbean." He looked at the woman. "A bit of punk advice, that. Sorry, love."

Firth said, "I make no apologies for the decisions I've made in my life. What I deeply regret is putting myself in a position where I have no control — and that's what happened.

"I cannot describe the man I was with with any clarity, Dr. Ford. I was hurt and angry and alone. He knocked on the door, asking for directions. I invited him in. It was after sunset, but it wasn't late. We started chatting. He spoke French, which made the situation feel safer for some reason. I hesitated when he offered to make drinks, and he must have sensed what I was thinking, because he laughed and told me I was being silly. I don't know why in the world I didn't order him out of the house then! But I didn't. That's the last thing I remember clearly. I was an idiot. My marriage had ended long before I vacationed on Saint Arc. But I still feel like an idiot."

I said, "You aren't. You were targeted. Sir James is right — they're expert at what they do. They demanded a quarter million dollars from my goddaughter. She doesn't have that kind of money personally. But she's successful enough, she can pay it off in installments, and that's what they're now demanding. I think they research their targets carefully. What about you? Four million pounds is, what? About eight million U.S.?"

Firth nodded. "I couldn't possibly come up with that much money — not in a month, not in a year, not in twenty years."

"Then the blackmailer didn't really expect you to pay. He timed it to sabotage your campaign. Why?"

Firth gave me a look that seemed to say, *Smart.* But I wasn't asking anything she hadn't already thought about.

"Either to sabotage my career, or to guarantee a hold over me if I was elected. As I think you are now aware, I'm passionate about certain social issues — the right to privacy; child pornography; punishing people who break those laws.

"Good laws cross boundaries. Even a freshman MP could affect the economy of a corrupt island such as Saint Arc. I think the blackmailers saw an opportunity to secure influence over my career, and took it. They never expected me to pay the money."

Further proof, she said, was that they didn't carry out their threat to make the video public when she refused to pay or negotiate.

"The last e-mail I received was —" She turned to Montbard. "— three months ago?"

He nodded.

"And it's been three months of absolute hell. It was impossible to push out of my mind. The constant fear. The sense of impending doom. And I was too embarrassed to go to Scotland Yard or even share the problem with a therapist. I am not a dramatic person, Dr. Ford, but I feel it's accurate to say I was on the verge of a complete emotional breakdown. Dealing with a

divorce, withdrawing from the election —"
Her voice began to waver.

Montbard took over. "Senny hadn't contacted me for months, and I began to wonder if something was wrong. So I called and
called until she rang me back. That was . . .
about three weeks ago, right, dear?" The
man reached and patted Firth's hand af-
fectionately. "She didn't realize that, thanks
to my previous line of work, I was qualified
to help with her problem. No one would, I
suppose. Best thing about it is, I conned this
beautiful creature into abandoning London
and spending the summer at Bluestone while
I track the bastards."

Firth had regained her composure. "I feel
anything but wonderful. Their last e-mail
gave the impression they were holding my
video as a trump card in the event I stood
for election again. That's why I feel like such
a damn fool. I ruined my career, the chance
to do real service, because of one incredibly
stupid decision made in a moment of . . ."
I watched her face turn pale rose, just as
Montbard had described it. ". . . during a
moment of emotional instability. I would do
anything to make it right again."

I sat forward in my chair to stress a point.
"Ms. Firth, the camera was set up, ready
to go, before the man who seduced you ar-

rived. The drinks he fed you were drugged. Same with my goddaughter, same with the women last night. You have nothing to feel guilty about."

"Drugged? I suspected that. I felt so strange . . . rather giddy and dreamy and . . ."

"Amorous?" I used Montbard's word.

The woman looked away. "Hardly that."

"You didn't feel unusually affectionate? Or at least behave with an unusual feeling of . . . let's say, willingness."

"I told you how I felt — strange, and not at all myself. That's all I remember. Excuse me, please, gentlemen." She stood.

I said, "I'm sorry. I was only trying to discuss the drug they may have used."

"Not a problem. I'll be back," she said, placing her napkin on the table. "Please wait, won't you? Just need to freshen up a bit."

Over coffee, I explained what I'd learned about the party drug, MDA, and the effects of similar amphetamine-based chemicals.

The woman and the Englishman listened attentively, but Montbard became interested when I asked, "Have you heard of something locals call Icebreaker?"

"A potion? I haven't heard of that one, but the locals use all sorts of potions. They don't talk about it openly, but obeah dominates the culture. I began a personal study, actually, years before I started getting into this blackmail business."

"Why?"

"Because it's a powerful historical force. The knowledge is useful to me now because I believe the blackmailer uses obeah to control the organization.

"I've been able to identify the men you dealt with last night — Richard Bonaparte, Dirk Van Susterin, Clovis Desmond. I have photos of the fourth man, too, Deepak Wulfelund, originally from Suriname. He does the camerawork at the beach cottage, and —" Montbard glanced at the woman. "— presumably, at the rental villa, too."

Deepak Wulfelund. *Wolfie.*

"Three of the four are employed by one of the major landholders on Saint Arc, a woman who's considered an obeah *gajé* — a sort of fortune-teller, priestess, and witch all rolled into one. Her name's Isabelle Toussaint. Madame Toussaint has a tremendous amount of power. Money, too. Some people on Saint Arc believe she's the Maji Blanc — a sort of she-devil in obeah folklore."

I said, "Do they call her the Widow?" I hadn't told him about what I'd overheard.

"Sometimes, yes. I'm impressed you know.

Years ago, she married one of the wealthiest man in the Caribbean, but he died in an accident. Left her a bundle. More often, though, she's referred to as the 'White Lady' because of the double meaning — it's considered bad luck to speak the Maji Blanc's name, you see.

"It's all an act, of course. Toussaint plays the role, I'm sure, to keep the locals in line. The more I find out about her, the more I'm convinced she's utterly ruthless. Her late husband, for instance — he was thirty years older than she. A few days after the wedding, he supposedly got drunk and stumbled off a cliff. And Madame Toussaint is . . . well, let's just say she's not the marrying type." He smiled as he lit his pipe, sending a message about the woman's sexuality.

"You're convinced she's the blackmailer?"

"Yes. I think it's possible she's involved with every profitable criminal activity that takes place on the island. Surprised?"

I was. From the beginning, I'd operated under the assumption it was a man. It was difficult to shift gears now and imagine a female extortionist — especially one who made it a point to humiliate her victims.

"I say again, the power this woman has over her followers can hardly be exaggerated. Are you a religious man, Ford?"

"No."

"Nor am I. So I have no pious illusions of superiority when I discuss obeah. In fact, in many ways, I think it's a more sensible religion than the major religions. They all use fear, one way or another, to keep believers in line. But obeah is proactive. You don't simply kneel down and pray for your heart's desire, you go out and *get it* by making a potion or paying someone like the *gajé* to provide you with a lucky fetish.

"Traditional religions tend to be wishy-washy when it comes to dealing with one's enemies. Turn the other cheek, that sort of nonsense. Not obeah. It encourages believers to take the offensive. A properly done curse can banish an enemy, or even kill him.

"Obeah isn't about the afterlife. It deals with the here and now. If a believer gets out of line? There are creatures who come out at night and punish — vampire witches and flesh-eating spirits. No waiting for Judgment Day."

"Adults really believe that?"

Montbard signaled impatience by striking another match. "Are you telling me you have no secret superstitions? Aren't we all absolutely certain that what we believe is right and real? It's true of all faiths. I think it's true of people like you and me, as well. Science is your religion. Archaeology, history — tradition, too, I suppose — are mine."

I shrugged — *Valid point* — remembering Ritchie telling Dirk the Widow would punish him for his disrespect.

"Obeah isn't fantasy-based. It's as real as blood and bones. I think you'd have a better understanding if you had a chat with Lucien St. John, a man who was employed by my family for years. He was my source for much of what I've just told you. Lucien is in his nineties now and doesn't mind talking about it. Only fair that we share intelligence assets."

Turning to Senegal, Sir James said, "Last night, Dr. Ford told me that his sources have linked the blackmailer with that spa we were discussing, the one on Saint Arc. The place called the Orchid — so exclusive the waiting list is months. But Ford must have friends in high places, because he somehow finagled a reservation, starting tomorrow. Quite a coincidence, eh, Senny?"

Over drinks at Jade Mountain, Montbard had been poker-faced when I mentioned the spa, but now he was being facetious. I said, "You already knew about it?"

The man was nodding. "Quite. The spa includes the ruins of a monastery that I've been interested in for years because of its archaeological importance. The place is ancient. Built by French Carthusian monks — an order that dates back to the eleventh century. The maternal branch of Toussaint's family has done business in the islands even longer than my own. That's how she came to own the place."

Toussaint owned many other properties on the island, Montbard told me, including the beach cottage that Shay had rented, and the mountain villa where they'd entrapped Senegal. The woman used corporate fronts, he said, but he'd finally tracked the titles to her.

"Privately, Madame Toussaint oversees her holdings as ruthlessly as a dictator. Publicly, she's rarely seen. She raises orchids — has an international reputation in the field — and one of her companies markets a line of boutique beauty concoctions. She also fancies herself a jet-set hostess, even though she seldom attends her own parties. Didn't you tell me that, Senny? I suppose some people crave any association with power."

Senegal said, "I heard it from a member of parliament who's been to the spa — a particularly unsavory member, by the way. Part of the woman's mystique, I guess. Makes people want to meet her all the more. A year ago, she upped her stock with that

crowd when she bought the Midnight Star
— among the world's most famous star sap-
phires. Had it set as a necklace."

I said, "An obeah priestess who hosts parties?"

Montbard said, "Oh, she would never
admit she practices obeah, just as she would
never admit she promotes the rumor she's
the Maji Blanc. Most islanders won't even
acknowledge that obeah exists. Secrecy is
one of the religion's tenets.

"I met the old girl only twice — at an embassy function in Kingston, then again two
years ago when I asked permission to spend
a day or two photographing the monastery
ruins. She looks like a bit of a flake — rouge
and lipstick, turbans and kaftans, that sort
of business. Her overall appearance is . . .
memorable. And her breath! My God."

"She refused?"

"Screamed like a crazy woman. Ran me off
the place. Ever since, I've wanted an excuse
to slip back there. Now Senegal has provided me an excellent reason. But it's not an
easy nut to crack. The woman's château and
the staff quarters adjoin the spa grounds,
which includes the monastery. The property
sits atop a peak similar to our smallest piton,
and she controls the only road. Security is
better than you might expect."

"Sounds remote."

"Everything on these bloody islands is remote unless you travel by water."

"Does she ever leave?"

"She keeps an apartment in Paris, I've been told. Goes there for two months in the autumn for an international orchid competition. Otherwise, she stays on her mountain."

I said, "It's my experience that the reclusive types keep their valuables close at hand. They're pathological about it in some cases."

Montbard caught the inference. He turned to address Senegal. "Give us the female perspective. If you had to hide illegal videotapes potentially worth millions of pounds — or the Midnight Star — would you choose a trusted bank and lock everything away in a safe-deposit box?"

Firth said, "Of course not. That's not a female insight, it's simply prudent. A safe-deposit box can be searched or sealed if authorities get interested. I'd want my best jewelry close at hand so I could use it when needed, and also to keep an eye on it. The same would be true with anything else of great value. A first-rate safe, possibly . . . or some secret cubbyhole that only I knew about."

"Ford?"

"I agree. Someplace secure, but easily accessible."

"*Exactly.* There you have it. I think the videos are up there. Toussaint uses a form of psychological warfare to scare off intruders — obeah spells and legends, that sort of thing. Locals are terrified of the place. They believe she uses those flesh-eating monsters I mentioned to patrol the area."

"That wouldn't stop you."

"Oh, but flesh monsters *did* stop me — because it's true, in a way. I tried to reconnoiter the place a few nights ago, and her monsters damn near got me. I was just telling Senny about it, wasn't I, dear?"

Firth had recovered her aloofness along with her poise. The woman enjoyed my reaction when she replied. "Yes, a terrifying story. Dodged yet another bullet, Hooker did. That's why I'm so relieved you'll be with him tonight, Dr. Ford — when he goes back."

Irritated, Montbard snapped, "Senny!" as I asked, "When he goes back where?"

"Maybe I was presuming too much, old sweat," Sir James said. "But I thought I was on safe ground since we're working together now." He caught Firth's eye. "That is *our* decision, isn't it?"

The woman responded with a cool nod.

"Good. I took it for granted you'd be willing to pop over and have a look around the monastery. We can take your boat or mine — doesn't matter. There's a lot to do if you plan on checking into the retreat tomorrow: establish a communication channel, locate escape routes — the regular drill. Breaching security in a place like that is a bit of a load for one man. For the two of us, though, it should be easy sledding."

I said, "I'm not even positive I have a reservation . . . and I was told it was couples only, unless I get special permission — which is unlikely."

Montbard reached and tapped his teacup against Firth's empty coffee cup. "Not a problem. The three of us are on the same team now. Right, Senny, dear?"

21

At sunset, Sir James and I were sitting in my skiff off Piton Lolo, Saint Arc's leeward peak, looking up at the monastery and attached lodge — a stony geometric surrounded by rain forest, a quarter mile above the sea. Isabelle Toussaint's estate was a spattering of white, hidden by trees.

"Do you see how that cloud appears to cling to the top of the peak?" he asked.

Gray cumulus had drifted into the mountain, then flattened as if pinned to the apex. The leeward edge of the cloud angled skyward, sculpted by thermals.

He continued, "Most peaks in the area are arid desert, but this one catches clouds for some reason. That's why the rain forest is so dense. There are species of plants and orchids up there still not cataloged by science, or so I've heard. Fascinating spot. Always wanted to have a look around."

I got the impression that, sooner or later,

Montbard would've found some excuse to explore the place, to hell with the hazards.

By dark, I was sure of it. We were working our way up the incline, halfway through the forest, when we came to a chain-link fence. Spaced along the fence every few hundred yards were signs in Creole and English.

DANGER!

KEEP OUT!

There were also obeah fetishes, feathers and bone — another form of warning.

It was 7:40 p.m.

Montbard touched his walking stick to the fence, then used the back of his hand — it wasn't electrified. "I didn't have a problem getting over the other night," he said, voice low, "but that was the opposite side of the peak where there's a footpath. Never hurts to double-check."

I was leaning against a tree, pissing, as he added, "I wasn't joking about nearly being eaten, by the way."

I said, "You mentioned the dogs."

"Hounds, I'd call them. Real monsters. They were nipping at my bloody heels as I vaulted the fence — a damned narrow squeak. I ripped a good pair of trousers. Found out later the woman's staff keeps Brazilian mastiffs. Do you know the breed?"

I said, "No, but if they're anything like the

313

dog that chased me last night, I think we can deal with it."

"I wish I could pretend they're the same, but these are very different animals, indeed."

Brazilian mastiffs, he said, were a mix of bull mastiffs, bloodhounds, and South American jaguar hounds. They had the size and strength to lock on to a steer's nose and drag it to the ground.

"I did a bit of research afterward, and was almost sorry I did. Adult males stand seven feet tall on their hind legs — only weigh eight stone, but pure muscle, with the temperament of snakes. At pedigree shows, the beasts are disqualified if they don't try to attack the blasted judge."

I was calculating in my head. "A little over a hundred pounds?"

"That's right. There aren't many of them in the world — good thing, too."

I zipped and turned. "Then why are we doing this? I don't want to have to kill a dog for doing its job. I also don't want to be mauled."

Sir James said, "We should be all right. Last time I tried this, it was three in the morning. Since then, I've pieced together the retreat's schedule. It's strictly forbidden for guests to exit the monastery walls after

314

eleven. And someone who should know told me the forest is dangerous only after midnight. In other words —" He held his Rolex to his eye. "— we have a window of three to four hours before they lock the doors and loose the dogs."

The man was facing the fence, standing on tiptoes and using the walking stick to lower his backpack as I asked, "The person you spoke with — I assume he works at the retreat."

"No. Too risky, don't you think, tipping your hand by chatting up the hired help?"

"Was it Lucien?" Montbard had introduced me to the old man that afternoon. We'd listened to him talk about obeah.

"No. Lucien hasn't been to the monastery in years. You heard him — he's terrified of the place. The man who gave me the information —" Montbard paused, hands on the top of the fence. "— is a beggar. Talked to him last week. One of those poor chaps I see too often on Saint Arc. No legs, missing an eye, so he scoots around on a mechanic's dolly. From the looks of him, he doesn't have many days left. Too bad. Very nice chap, but broken, of course."

Montbard climbed the fence, dropped to the other side, then continued, whispering.

"The fellow made extra money poaching

315

orchids near the monastery, but stayed too late one night. Dogs caught him. Of course, he claimed that obeah devils attacked him — there's cachet in that. But we're having none of that nonsense. It's all about timing, you see?"

I asked, "Did the man hunt orchids on weekends?" Today was Monday, four days until Shay's deadline.

"What in blazes does it matter?"

"Weekend schedules and weekday schedules vary. Maybe they let the dogs out earlier on weekdays."

"Didn't think to ask — and it's too late now. I heard the poor sot was taken off to the hospital. But we can't expect to have every *t* crossed and every *i* dotted in our trade, now can we?" Montbard shouldered his backpack, then retrieved his walking stick. "*Right.* Over you go, Ford. You're the new La'Ja'bless, according to Lucien. The hounds won't bother a fellow demon."

Lah-zjay-*blass,* the old man had pronounced it. He'd said the word with a reverence that was becoming familiar, and softly as if he were afraid the trees would overhear.

"The creature, he attack three mens jes last night over to Saint Arc," Lucien had told us, delighted to have news to share with visitors. "The creature, he hurt one fella purty bad. It because that fella were disrespectful, and speak a profanity regarding the spirits. But all them men's lucky, in my opinion, 'cause the La'Ja'bless got the power to do much worse than break a fella's ribs."

I didn't make the connection until I noticed Sir James looking at me, waiting to confirm the significance with a slight smile.

"Three local men, Lucien?"

"That right. Boy who bring me my coffee, he tol' me this mornin'. He down to the wharf and hear the fishermens talkin'. The La'Ja'bless, he quick to punish. But that fella very fortunate he only in hospital, not the grave."

The La'Ja'bless was a night creature that could assume different forms. Sometimes he was a wolf or a cat — "If those things cross the road in front of you at night, it the creature, an' you smart to run, man!"

More often, though, the La'Ja'bless was half man, half horse . . . or a faceless man dressed in black.

"Las' night, the creature be a man — all black but for the eye in the center part his head. It a green eye that burn like fire, the fishermens sayin'. That fella in hospital? He never be disrespectful again, that much I know!"

We had stood in the shade of a tamarind tree, listening to Lucien tell his stories while chickens scratched in a neighbor's garden. There was a scarecrow made of sticks and a calabash gourd, a faded red scarf over its face, like a bandit.

Lucien, I discovered, was father of the subdued man who'd served our breakfast, Rafick. It was Rafick who drove us to the old man's cottage on the outskirts of Soufrier and encouraged him to talk freely in front of Senegal, a woman, and me, a stranger.

Before Sir James asked the first question, though, Rafick was gone — a true believer who'd done his duty, but who wanted no part in discussing obeah.

Senegal appeared surprised that I jotted key words in my notebook as the old man talked.

Gajé: Practitioner of witchcraft

Zanbi (Zombie?): Creature who rises from grave to do evil

Dragon Tooth: Volcano

Anansi Noir: Black spider whose supernatural power is equal to a snake's

Bolonm: Tiny person, born from a chicken's egg, who eats flesh

Maji Noir: Male spirit who roams the

night, preying on women walking alone

Maji Blanc: Female spirit who appears as a beautiful woman dressed in white and has sex with men who are asleep or drunk. Uses her fingernails on their backs and genitals as her calling card

Flirting, Lucien had said to Senegal, "You would make a mos' lovely Maji Blanc. Not a evil spirit, a'course, but the pleasuring type. Why you not allow this gen'lman buy you a pretty white dress, 'stead of wearin' them pants?"

Senegal let him see she was flattered, even though the subject made her uncomfortable. "I'd rather have a white dress from you, Lucien. I'll come back and model it."

"Oh my, I like that! The Maji Blanc visit me several times when I were a young man. What you think my wife do when she see them scratches? She take garlic and rub it. Garlic *burn* when you been scratched by the Maji Blanc, tha's how you know it was a spirit woman."

The old man tilted his head skyward and laughed, showing freckles on his cinnamon skin, and eyes that were milky blue. "I tell you true now — sometimes the garlic don't burn so bad, but I yell like fire, anyway!"

He stopped laughing when Montbard asked about the monastery on Piton Lolo.

"That a dragon tooth long 'go. It stick out the ocean so high it snag clouds. That why it a dark place where the wind got a chill, and it have washerwoman rain all the time. It a fine spot for orchids, but it bad for peoples.

"In back times, it were a godly place for monks. But them monks all die sudden of fever. By the time they found, the birds been feedin' and carried they spirits away. Left nothing but they robes.

"The robes still up there to this day! I tell you 'cause I know it true. One night, I seen it with me own eyes, them empty robes comin' down the mountain, candles for faces. Trottin' alongside was a wild pack of *mal vú chien*. Them animals glowed, so I knew they was demons . . . on fire with *bawé yo*."

I wrote in my notebook:

Mal vú chien: Demon dogs; hounds from hell

"Any wonder the islanders stay away from the monastery?" Sir James had said as we drove away. "Madame Toussaint takes pains to ensure her privacy."

He wasn't talking only about the mythical dogs. According to Lucien, worse things awaited people who ventured onto the mountain at night.

"Some say the real Maji Blanc live up there now," Lucien had told us, "but I seen that Madame Toussaint. She were wearin' black, not white. I think she *invented* that tale, make peoples think she become beautiful at midnight. But I feel she a vitch, you ask my opinion. *Obayifo,* or a *sukkoy-uan,* that what we old people calls her."

A vitch, the old man explained, had the power to quit their bodics and travel great distances in the night, and could be identified by a foul odor and a phosphorescent light visible in the hair, armpits, and anus. A thirsty vitch sucked the sap and juices from crops, but their rcal power came from human victims.

My notebook:

Sukkoy-uan or obayifo: Vampire witch
who drinks blood to stay young

22

Sir James whispered, "Males on one side, females on the other. Senegal will be very pleased by that. I think you make her nervous, Ford."

I said, "She doesn't strike me as the nervous type."

"Not just you, old boy, don't take it personally. It applies to most men, which is why I'm surprised she was lured into this fix. Interesting, your theory about victims being drugged. Do those people look as if they've been drugged to you?"

We were positioned in a clearing looking down on the monastery, where there was a quadrangle with miniature spires at the four corners, tile-roofed buildings within, and a cemetery on the seaward side. Torches added medieval light.

Within the walls, eleven people sat on mats, facing a fire, meditating or doing yoga, men on one side, women on the other. A few wore monks' robes with hoods and rope belts. Others wore jogging suits or leotards, or white surgical scrubs as baggy as robes. Japanese flute and the sound of chanting drifted upward on incense.

I whispered, "You mean drugged with MDA?"

"The love potion you mentioned. Whatever it was they slipped Senny."

I said, "No. I think they'd have the robes off by now, hugging, talking loud, laughing — something."

Sir James said, "Quite," and pressed binoculars to his eyes again. After several seconds, he said, "Why eleven? Five men, six women. If they accept only couples, shouldn't it be an even number?"

I had called the Hooded Orchid earlier and confirmed that Marion W. North and friend did have reservations starting tomorrow. In Montbard's mind, for some reason, that made me an expert.

I said, "They make exceptions, I guess. Or maybe the couples were given a choice: do meditation here, or hang out at the pool bar next door."

Montbard swung the binoculars toward the lodge. "That makes sense. Looks a bit more interesting over there among the heathens — often the case in my travels. Folks are chatting, not chanting, at least. More like a cocktail party than this dreary business."

He was looking to the west, where the retreat's modern facilities were layered into the mountain with elevated walkways, subdued lighting, a four-lane lap pool and dip pools glowing blue beneath the rental suites. There were three white vans in the tiny parking lot, only a couple of cars.

Sir James had told me the road up the mountain was a private one-lane, with two security checkpoints on the hour drive to the top. The maximum number of guests was less than thirty, and most arrived via helicopter from Saint Lucia's Hewanorra Airport. Because of repeat clientele, there was no need for the lodge to advertise. Judging from the scarcity of articles, it also did not offer journalists a free stay in exchange for stories.

Montbard did find a piece on international spas in a magazine that mentioned the place. He'd shared the clip.

HOODED ORCHID
RETREAT AND SPA,
SAINT JOAN OF ARC ISLAND,
EASTERN CARIBBEAN

Called simply the "Orchid" by its devotees, and named for a rare wild orchid that grows on the island, this spa claims to offer "rare elixirs" made from local fruits and herbs, as well as purifying ceremonies that slow the aging process and rechannel libido.

Incorporating the ruins of a French Cistercian monastery, spa operators make up for limited amenities by maintaining the monastic spirit. The operation caters to "betrothed or wedded couples." Even so, guests are assigned separate quarters and are expected to remain celibate during their stay, while following a strict schedule that includes exercise, meditation, and "purification."

Here, sex is considered toxic, and sin is taboo — but money still counts for something at this cultish retreat. Despite a three-star rating, the Orchid is a favorite dry-out spot for bad-boy rockers, royalty, and Hollywood film stars, whether they are "betrothed" or arrive alone. But don't rush to make plane reservations. "We are not actively seeking new clientele," a spa spokesperson said.

Along with the article, Sir James had made a detailed map of the area by printing a satellite photo onto sketch paper, then labeling it. He'd also created a rough diagram of the monastery's layout.

He took out the diagram now and compared what he saw with what he'd drawn.

"Not bad for guesswork," he told me as I looked over his shoulder. "Got most of it right."

I said, "There was no data available?"

"Very little. But I suspected the design was similar to a template created by the Knights Templar. The Templars were warrior monks. They returned from the Crusades with drawings of Solomon's Temple. See here —" He touched a finger to the diagram. "— here's the portico that borders the courtyard, then the second courtyard where those dreary people are chanting. The roofed walkway . . . the cloister. The doors leading off the portico are dormitories where the monks slept. It's all joined by arcades and passageways."

I said, "Passageways?"

"When Mother Church was burning her critics at the stake, underground tunnels were a sensible addition. You've spent time in Central America. Supposedly, they're a fixture in the old churches there."

A tunnel dug during the Inquisition had once saved my life. I said, "I've heard rumors. How do you know all this?"

He began to toy with the Masonic ring on his right hand: skull and crossbones; squares and dividers. "I belong to a sort of fraternity that studies the subject. If I told you how many years the group's been collecting information, you wouldn't believe me."

I said, "You're a Freemason. I noticed your ring last night."

"I'm surprised you made the connection. Very few associate the Masons with this symbol." He held the ring toward me even though it was too dark to decipher detail. "The Knights Templar were the original pirates of the Caribbean. Their ships flew the skull and bones long before Hollywood got the idea. When we get back to Saint Lucia, I'll give you an article to read."

He hesitated before asking carefully, "You mentioned that you're a traveling man. Are you?"

Strange question. I said, "Of course."

The man suspected I was confused, but he wanted to confirm it. "You're here for the sake of the widow's son? You came from the east, traveling west."

Stranger questions. I realized I was being tested. I had the feeling that I would've become the man's instant confidant if I had provided the correct responses. But there could be no faking it.

It was like a shield rising into place when I replied, "No, I came from Florida, to the north. My uncle was a Freemason. A man named Tucker Gatrell. He had a ring similar to yours."

"Tucker Gatrell — the name's curiously familiar. Did he spend time in the Caribbean?"

"He was a tropical bum."

Sir James said, "Yes, familiar," interested, but it was time to move on. End of test.

The old Englishman had picked up his thread about the monastery's layout. I listened, but was getting impatient. It was 8:30 p.m. We still had a lot to do. There was no guarantee they'd wait until midnight to let the guard dogs out on this moonless Monday night.

"See those ruins beyond the courtyard wall?" Montbard whispered. "They might be the remains of a convent, or a distillery. Monasteries from the period often made herbal liquors as a source of income. Benedictine — a good example. Chartreuse and soda — Senny's favorite. Secret recipes hundreds of years old. But what I'm looking for is a smallish stone structure that was called the Misericord. It's where punishment was doled out to the monks. I picture it a chamber built of slabs — Stonehenge but without spaces. A secure place, if you get my meaning."

Secure. I understood. A place to keep valuables.

"Let's look for it."

"Capital idea, Ford, but first things first." He slipped the blueprint into his backpack, then unrolled the map and used a red penlight as a pointer.

"It's nearly twenty-one-hundred hours. I suggest the first thing we do is mark our escape routes with your infrared tape. If they set the dogs on us, we want the fastest route to the fence. It's tempting to string a couple of trip wires along the way. Dogs might see them, but it could also save our bacon. What do you think?"

I said, "Your story about the beggar on the mechanic's dolly has made me a believer."

"Good." He was into his backpack again, confirming he'd brought wire. "Now . . . if we are pursued by guards, my feeling is we should lay a trail that first takes us *up* the mountain, because they'll expect just the opposite. How do you feel about that? Think you can manage a few hundred yards uphill, triple time, without getting knackered?"

Was that a subtle barb? During the hike, I'd stopped a couple of times to catch my breath. Sir James had waited with exaggerated patience, breathing normally as he checked his watch and tapped his walking stick on the ground. With his tweed walking cap, trousers, dark shirt, and shooting jacket, he looked like a butterfly collector who'd lost his way — except for the night-vision goggles that were now pushed up on his forehead, and the Walther PPK semiautomatic pistol I'd gotten a glimpse of beneath his jacket, left armpit, in a shoulder holster, butt out.

It was hard to believe the man was over seventy. He was aggressive, focused, and in better shape than I — and I'd been jogging and swimming twice a day, six days a week, since spring. But mountains are the curse of a Florida flatlander. Even in the tropics, it takes awhile to acclimate.

I replied, "My endurance improves when I'm being chased. Always loop uphill when escaping down a mountain — I agree. I'll *try* to keep up."

"That's the spirit. One more thing —" He fitted his night-vision goggles into place. I did the same as he pointed toward the cemetery on the seaward side of the monastery. "— during your stay, if you do manage to grab the videotapes, we should have an emergency jettison spot. Prearranged.

A place you can get rid of them quick, and collect later. What do you think? Might be a spot over there that's just the ticket."

He used an infrared flashlight to indicate an area near the cemetery where the cliff wall dropped several hundred yards to the sea below. Earlier, we'd sat looking up at the same cliff from my boat.

"Those people seem involved with their chanting — or whatever it is they call that nonsense. I don't think they'd notice if we popped down for a quick look-see — but we'll need a bit of billy goat in us to negotiate that ledge." Montbard had been kneeling, but now stood as he tucked his map away. "You don't have an aversion to heights, do you, Ford?"

"Not at all," I said, lying. "I live in a house that's built on stilts."

"Excellent, then you're an old hand. Off we go!"

By 9:15 p.m., we had our three escape trails marked. We headed for the cliff.

To get to the cemetery unseen, we had to inch our way along a ledge that was half the width of my shoulders, and several hundred feet above a rock field that inclined briefly before dropping into the sea. Sir James wasn't joking about billy goats — it was a path used by feral goats that lived on the island.

I dug fingers into the igneous rim above us, nose pressed close to the cliff so I wouldn't be blinded by falling gravel, and also because I was scared shitless. I had looked down only once. Rocks were vague spires in the blackness; sparks of starlight communicated the movement of waves far below.

The Englishman went first. He seemed oblivious to the danger; so unconcerned that halfway along the ledge he'd stopped and fished the penlight from his pocket, then shined it for an instant on a clump of bushes topped with dark flowers.

"Here're some rare beauties for you," he'd whispered. "It's a flowering sage — Divinorium, possibly. Ancient; very rare. Love to have this in the garden. Maybe we'll come back for it when we put this business to bed."

When I only grunted in reply, the man had actually turned sideways on the ledge. "Are you all right, old man? Need a minute to regroup?"

I'd hissed, "I'm fine. Keep moving!"

I don't have an irrational fear of heights, but I do have a healthy fear of falling. It's an atavistic fear that, for me, was intensified a few years back when I was thrown from a helicopter just before it crashed. All the horrors of the unknown were condensed into those microseconds of free fall. By the time we reached the cemetery and I'd belly-crawled onto firm ground, I was soaked with sweat.

No way in hell was I going back the way we'd come — not unless it was more secure — so the first thing I did was rig a rope handhold. I tied a hundred feet of braided anchor line around the base of a tree, then dropped the coil over the ledge so I could use it to traverse the goat path on our return. The tree jutted from the lip of the cliff, roots exposed, but felt solid enough to hold my weight.

When Montbard misread my intent, I was too embarrassed to set him straight.

"Damn smart of you," he whispered. "Establish a secure base for rappelling. Bring more rope when you check in tomorrow. A few hundred feet and a couple of proper bowlines should do it. Hide the rope in your kit. Spa staff will be none the wiser."

I said, "That's what I plan to do," as my heart began to slow.

We found a good place to drop the video-tapes. I would need a waterproof bag and a buoy, but it was okay. There was a spot on the leeward edge of the cliff where monks had sculpted a Gaelic cross out of rock. There were prayer benches shielded by bushes . . . an iron safety railing . . . nothing below but sea.

Montbard was fascinated by the cross. Same with the headstones in the cemetery. He lingered, using the infrared light to reveal details, until I said, "This isn't an Explorers Club outing, okay?"

It got him moving. "Sorry, sorry. I really must come back and give the place a thorough going-over." He grunted, frustrated. "You're right, of course. Back to business. Here — come have a look." He knelt, picked up a rock the size of a grapefruit, and walked to the lip of the precipice. I followed on hands and knees.

"Listen." The Englishman reached out and dropped the rock. A blast of warm sea air nearly blew my watch cap off when I peeked over the edge. It was like looking down into a wind tunnel. The rock melted into darkness without striking the cliff face. The roaring updraft muted the splash.

"Bloody perfect, eh? Now all we must do is find out where the old girl keeps her valuables. Any thoughts about how to manage it?"

I said, "Maybe. It would be nice to confirm she has the tapes ... but with only three more days —"

"There's a difference between rushing and acting on sound data. I think it's time to act. What's your idea?"

"How hot are you prepared to go?"

"Go hot or go cold —" His voice communicated a nasty appreciation. "— it's been awhile since I've heard those terms. I find it heartening. I'm fully willing to go hot — rob Madame Toussaint at gunpoint, or persuade a member of her staff to tell us what we need to know. But I would prefer not to give my neighbors more fodder for gossip unless absolutely required."

More fodder? I was smiling. "Then we take the soft approach. Get the woman to show us where the tapes are hidden without knowing we're interested. Last night, the guy they call 'Wolfie,' the guy who runs the camera —"

"Wulfelund," Montbard said, "he's originally from Suriname."

"Right. Last night, he shot a few tapes — nothing incriminating, but maybe she expects the tapes to be delivered anyway. Hide a couple of your motion-sensing cameras in the right place —"

"Cameras, right — which I didn't happen to bring," the man interrupted, not impressed. "It's an idea. Perhaps we're putting the cart before the horse. Let's give it some thought, then discuss it later, after we're finished with our little look-see —"

"I'm not done," I said. "Even without your cameras, I think we can get the woman to show us where she keeps the tapes."

"How, pray tell?"

"We create an emergency. Convince her she's in danger of losing the tapes — cops are coming with a search warrant, the threat of a robbery, a fire. We watch her reaction."

Montbard said, "Without her knowing she's being watched."

I said, "That's why I suggested the cameras. A couple of nights ago, I thought my house was on fire. It was a false alarm, but my first instinct was to run straight to where I keep my valuables — things I won't risk keeping in a bank."

Sir James said, *"Humph,"* thinking about it. "Yes . . . interesting." A few seconds later, he said, "Ford? I think the idea has merit. A variation on one of the psy-war stunts we pulled in the Falklands, but original in its way. Madame Toussaint unknowingly reveals where the tapes are hidden. You nick the lot of them later, after you've checked into the spa."

"It could work."

"Yes," he said, warming to the idea. "It just might. After you and Senny check in, we'll make radio contact at assigned times. When you've got the tapes, I can be standing by in the boat, waiting for your drop. Very tidy operation if things go our way. Nothing to find if authorities search you as you leave the spa."

"Tidy," I agreed, aware that no black-bag operation — a theft, a kidnapping, an assassination — ever goes as planned.

I began to back away from the precipice, but Sir James remained where he was, the toes of his boots extended slightly over the rim of the cliff, hands on hips, breathing deeply as if the warm upward thermal contained helium, and made him immune to gravity. "You ever do any jumps, Ford?"

It took me a moment to realize he was talking about parachuting. "Seven. Six with a static line, once without."

"Ran short of time at camp, did you? By God, I love the sound of silk! This is a peach of a spot for a base jump. I'd try it now if I had one packed and ready. Steady updraft; straight drop. I'd steer the chute seaward, cut loose at three meters, then an easy swim to shore." He turned. "Wait 'til you're my age — you'll understand. The only real death we suffer is the things left undone!"

I made a hushing motion with my hand — *Get down. Quiet.*

"Oh," he said, unaware. "Got carried away for a moment."

I crawled toward the cemetery until I felt it was safe to stand.

23

James Montbard was an exceptional man, no question. In less than twenty-four hours, he'd impressed me as much as anyone I'd ever met. How was it possible that we'd been in the same shadowy trade yet I'd never heard of him?

Or maybe I had . . .

False names and passports are standard in the field. Great Britain has produced many dark stars on Her Majesty's Secret Service. Montbard had all the necessary qualities, along with certain quirks that I associate with the trade's best. He was obsessive, focused, and detached when violence was discussed. He was adrenaline-driven, devoutly disciplined, and, when off-duty, he redirected his gifts into a public persona that was affable and unremarkable. Hobbies provided a vent — archaeology, in his case. For others, it was stamp collecting, model planes, astronomy, crossword puzzles, Scrabble.

As Senegal had said, the man was mad for history. She'd also warned me not to ask about the stone artifact I'd seen in the library — so I did, of course, during our boat trip to Saint Arc.

"Yes, the stone is Mayan or Olmec," he began. "The Yaxkin glyph is unmistakable. But my grandfather didn't find it in Central America. He found it there." He pointed to the volcanic peaks of Saint Arc. "Surprised?"

I was. We were more than a thousand miles from the Mayan ruins of Central America.

"Where?"

Montbard had smiled. "In the monastery. One day, Dr. Ford, when this business is behind us, I'll tell you the source of the other glyphs on that artifact. You won't be surprised, you'll be shocked. My grandfather was convinced there was trade between these islands — Europe and Africa, too — long before Columbus. Wouldn't it be lovely to prove it?"

An hour later, the man was still talking about archaeology, and what he called his theory of "relentless human motion." Man is genetically driven to wander — that was the premise.

"Senegal showed you the maps in my library. Most of history's so-called inexplicable mysteries are hoaxes. Those maps are not.

"Spare me the ridiculous fairy stories of quasi-archaeologists. Peru wasn't a landing strip for extraterrestrials, Quetzalcoatl wasn't Jesus in disguise. Inca stones depicting men fighting dinosaurs are fakes, for God's sake, and — speaking of God — if He actually did impart supernatural powers to the Ark of the Covenant, or the chalice that caught Christ's blood, or to the four nails that held Christ on the cross, why did He hide the damn things where no one can find them?"

Archaeology, Montbard told me, was the study of human movement using stationary materials. He had no interest in fairy tales.

Yes, the man had all the obsessive quirks — a righteous certainty, too — that I associate with the best in our business. We had exchanged enough information to know we had mutual acquaintances in the trade — names weren't used, of course. I suspected that Bernie Yager was among them. Had Bernie told the man I was coming?

I thought about it as we returned along the goat path toward the cemetery — something to take my mind off falling. It was easier now because of the rope, but I was still sweat-soaked by the time we arrived at the rock base where we'd started — a clear view down onto the monastery where the eleven men and women had concluded their chanting and were now walking single file toward what may have been stone dormitories on opposite sides of the quadrangle. Men went one way; women the other.

"The article was right about that celibacy business," Montbard whispered, binoculars to his eyes. "Senny will be relieved, I dare say."

He'd made the inference more than once, so I decided to ask, "No interest in men?"

"Occasionally. If she wasn't open about it, I wouldn't compromise the girl by telling you. Something to do with her bastard of a father and her ex-husband who wasn't . . . well, let's just say he wasn't attentive. But maybe a few nights here will set her right. Magic elixirs, secret herbs. Who knows? You and Senegal have chemistry — oppositional, true. But that's how many passionate relationships begin. I would heartily approve, by the way."

When I didn't respond, he added, "Reticent — I understand. But don't dismiss the girl. She's magnificent in her way. Brilliant and true as steel. She'll relax a bit when I confirm you two will be in separate quarters."

Senegal Firth would be relieved — so would I. The woman was attractive, productive, and independent, but she was also carrying emotional baggage that I had no interest in shouldering. We all acquire scars over the years, but adults who wince at the thought of intimacy — particularly sexual intimacy — are a bad risk even to those of us who are rescuers by nature. I've learned to keep my distance.

Montbard was still looking through the binoculars. "What a blasted waste — some damned attractive women in that group."

I realized he was back on the subject of celibacy.

"And those surgical scrubs some are wearing; more like night dresses, wouldn't you say? Revealing enough to test any man . . . and all of a type, like uniforms. Why would management forbid conjugal relations yet issue that sort of attire?"

I said, "Forbidden fruit?"

Sounding distracted, he said, "Suppose so. Makes more sense than magic potions." Then his tone freshened. "Have a look, Ford. The one with the angelic hair . . . auburn, I think. Scandinavian features — isn't she an American film actress? Yes . . . yes, I think she is. By God, she's exquisite."

I took the binoculars, beginning to suspect

that the man's list of hobbies included beautiful women. I removed my glasses, touched my finger to the zoom focus . . .

The woman he was describing was the last of six women and men walking single file along a path toward the monastery's inland cloister. The remaining five people filed toward the cloister on the opposite side of the quadrangle. Dormitories weren't segregated by sex, apparently. They walked at a ceremonial pace, heads down like monks — all but the woman Montbard had described. She was alert, eyes moving, taking in the surroundings.

When I saw her face, I pulled the binoculars away for several seconds, looked again, and said without thinking, "What the hell's *she* doing here . . . ?"

"A film actress — I was right!" Sir James whispered, enjoying himself. "Thought so. Don't tell me her name — it's right on the tip of my tongue."

I said, "If you insist," relieved he was giving me time to collect myself. Should I trust him? Should I wait?

I had to trust him, but I'd tell him later. The woman was Beryl Woodward.

24

Isabelle Toussaint was holding court on the pool terrace, hosting a cocktail party for guests. A rare appearance at one of her own parties.

"Lovely stroke of luck, eh, Ford?"

I was so preoccupied, thinking about Beryl, that Sir James had to repeat himself before I replied, "Sure, lucky. But let's keep a little in reserve for later."

We had traversed the face of the bluff above the lodge, then moved downhill to a fence that screened the terrace, pool, and dining room. The lighted pool was a rectangle of black tile. The dining room, visible through open French doors, was done in bamboo and dark wood, with traditional plaid curtains — common in the islands.

"I may have misplaced the actress's name," Sir James whispered, "but I can identify the woman you're looking at beyond doubt. That's the Maji Blanc herself. Dressed for the part . . . and wearing her famous necklace, too. As a gentleman, I will only point out that her famous sapphire isn't the sole reason she's memorable."

My glasses were pushed up on my head, and I was looking through the binoculars. Silently, I filled in the blank . . . *She's memorable because there's so much of her to remember.* Something like that.

I was still thinking about Beryl — how the hell had she gotten into this place? I'd told her I might be staying at the Orchid, but there was no way for her to know I'd be registered under a different name. I hadn't been near a computer to check if she or Shay had replied to my e-mails, true, but . . .

"You do see the woman, old boy. Or have you dozed off?"

I refocused the binoculars, and forced myself to concentrate.

Madame Toussaint was a linebacker-sized woman. Sunken cheeks blushed with rouge, a heart-shaped mouth made girlish with lipstick, and wide, dark eyes that moved with tactical precision from guest to guest, even while engaged in conversation.

She was dressed in white robes with a white gabled hood trimmed in scarlet. The robe was the white of a hospital hallway, not the silken white of gowns issued to female guests. The hood was a starched rectangle that framed her face — a monastic touch that attempted stylishness with a shoulder veil that was knotted as if it were a ponytail. The Midnight Star, worn high on her neck, was a blue sapphire the size of a robin's egg. No risk of exposed cleavage. A convent nun with Madonna affectations — that was the impression.

I asked Montbard, "Are you sure Isabelle Toussaint's a woman?" The conical breasts and eyelashes were unavoidable, but I had also noted the masculine larynx and slim hips.

"I don't presume anything I'm not willing to confirm personally," Montbard said, taking the binoculars. "My curiosity has limits. I'd sooner risk the Himalayas."

I said, "Understood. Even so, she — or he — is damn popular with the guests."

Two dozen men and women dressed for cocktail hour in the tropics had formed a loose line, drinks in hand. They mingled with an aloof, A-list poise as they awaited their turn to speak with Toussaint, who was sitting between male attendants near the pool. The cheery indifference of some guests reminded me of fans waiting to meet an oddball celebrity — an amusing story they could share with friends. Others, though, wore the congenial masks that signal uneasiness or hostility.

More blackmail victims?

Toussaint handled the attention with a less careful indifference. She affected regal gestures that seemed an intentional parody. She nodded and smiled when introduced, holding out her hand to be kissed. It was an old familiar role, yet Toussaint made it clear she rarely interacted with clients. They knew it. Some didn't want to miss the opportunity. Others seemed resigned.

Montbard whispered, "I told you she looked a bit daft, but don't be misled. Do you recognize any of those people?"

"More actors? I don't go to many movies."

"Nor do I. But I read the London *Times*. One of the men is a South African industrialist said to be among the wealthiest men in the world. The svelte women in the red dress? She's the wife of a former French president. Rumors aplenty about her!

"There's a lot of power and wealth down there, Ford. Toussaint's no fool. She's earned a certain European vogue — orchids; her herbal lotions, now the Midnight Star. The woman's also a legendary bitch. For some reason, artistic types find sexually ambiguous snobs alluring.

"I dare say most of those people fancy themselves artists of one sort or another. I'm referring to their flamboyant attire. Who else would come to a place such as this?"

Flamboyant? Compared to Sir James, the staff was dressed flamboyantly in their white shirts, white slacks, and plaid headpieces, carrying trays of drinks and hors d'oeuvres, serving with fixed, Third World smiles on their faces.

I took the binoculars and studied the guests more carefully. I saw horn-rimmed glasses and John Lennon glasses, a few wild scarves, and . . . a Nehru jacket? Yes — a Nehru jacket. A man with spiked hair wore his shirttails outside his slacks despite a beige blazer. Ages from late twenties into the sixties or seventies. People with money, but not obsessively health-oriented. Several smoked cigarettes. They drank red wine and martinis — not the sickening sweet punches most tropical resorts serve — while patiently waiting to get what I realized was the house specialty. The drink was a mix of fruits, vegetable greens, and something else — flower petals? — liquefied in a blender. It took the bartender several minutes to produce a champagne-sized glassful, so the drinks were served sparingly. Guests put aside everything else, though, when the specialty drink was offered.

Artistic sensibilities — Montbard was probably right about the guests. Now, though, I was paying more attention to the staff. There was something familiar about two employees near the kitchen entrance at the rear of the dining room.

I continued to use the binoculars as I listened to Sir James say, "Rumors that Madame Toussaint practices obeah adds to her mystique. Same's true of her ambiguous sexuality. I've heard that she was once a man. I've also heard that her personal kit includes the complete assortment — male and female. Some orchids are that way, you know."

I said, "You lost me."

"There are species of orchids that are sexually self-sufficient. Quite literally, the flower's blossom twists and turns until it fertilizes itself. What would Freud make of Madame Toussaint's fascination for orchids? Care to speculate? Why . . . the old girl *looks* like an orchid in that hooded white gown."

He added, "Is it any wonder that locals fear the Maji Blanc sneaking into their bed at night? . . . or into their dreams? By God, Ford, just the thought of that woman in my bed has earned me a stiff whiskey!"

The man was still enjoying himself.
I wasn't.

Beyond the pool was a forested incline where the fence turned sharply uphill. The area between was landscaped with birds of paradise, Japanese bamboo, sections of medieval rock wall. White Christmas lights spiraled through the forest canopy — a fairyland effect — while hidden LEDs panned from tree to tree, spotlighting orchids that were framed on wood, like paintings.

Montbard, standing ahead of me, said, "It appears the electrical system is computer controlled. The low-voltage system, anyway. Emergency lights, fire alarms, and surveillance cameras all linked. I don't see any sign of a generator, so it may be battery backup only. Just a guess. I'm not an expert, of course."

He'd seen all that from this distance? I said, "Of course," not sure what to believe.

"Not many cameras either, have you noticed? I think the old girl has more faith in her reputation as a witch when it comes to protecting her precious orchids from poachers. Amazing collection. I've seen varieties I'd love to have in my orchid house. For instance, that dark-petaled beauty near the fire pit? She developed it herself — highly coveted, especially by Japanese collectors."

An unattended fire smoldered in a nearby commons area — maybe there'd been a ceremony before the cocktail party. My eyes shifted to the fire's smoke, noting the direction of the wind, as Montbard said, "She named the spa after that orchid. Or vice versa. I believe it's a variety of *Masdevallia.* If I had the chance, I'd nick it in a flash. Next visit, eh?"

The tiny LED lights shifted among dozens of blooms. The black orchid was spotlighted for fifteen seconds before the next orchid was illuminated. Hundreds more orchids decorated the patio and open dining room.

The dining room — I had the binoculars zoomed tight on the place, watching the two staff members who stood shoulder to shoulder, talking intensely, gulping drinks, while their colleagues hustled trays. The men wore the white uniform, but they weren't waiters. They held a more elevated position. Guests approached them occasionally and exchanged greetings. Mostly female guests, I noticed.

The way they moved, their attitude, suggested it was Ritchie, Shay's fashion model islander, and Clovis, the slick Peter Lorre look-alike. But the one I thought was Ritchie wasn't wearing his signature bandanna, and

Clovis looked bigger, fitter than I remembered.

It wasn't until the men moved into the light that I realized I was mistaken.

I touched Montbard's shoulder, and handed him the binoculars. "Do those two remind you of anyone?"

"*Hmm.* Yes . . . I see the similarities. Late twenties . . . rather nasty-looking young chaps. Same cocksure swagger. On some islands, those types are referred to as beach boys. Gigolos in many cases, not all."

"How's Senegal going to react if the man who seduced her works here?" I was thinking about Beryl — the same could happen to her.

"We've already discussed it. I told her to pretend as if she's never seen the man before in her life. I'd be very surprised if he didn't do the same. If spa management, or an employee, behave in any other way, it's the same as admitting they're the blackmailers. It won't happen."

I wasn't so sure. I still hadn't told Montbard that his exquisite actress wasn't an actress. Not a professional actress, anyway. It was unlikely Beryl would pretend she didn't recognize Ritchie and Clovis if they worked here.

Like the Englishman, I wore a battered

old Rolex — a basic Submariner, stainless steel, no date — that I'd been given when I was nineteen. The radium-coated numerals of a Rolex have never been adequate for low light, and I had to put my eye to the crystal: 10:07 p.m.

Getting late. I was about to remind Montbard that it was time to go, when a startling sound descended from the stars — a forlorn howling. A predacious howl, like ice on the spine. The note echoed through the tree canopy, then was absorbed by rain-forest gloom.

"Dogs," I whispered.

"Worse than dogs," Sir James replied, still using the binoculars. "They're bloody young vipers if they're anything like the others."

He was talking about gigolos, I realized. I also realized that Isabelle Toussaint was leaving the party, suddenly in a hurry.

"She's heading home," I told Montbard. "We can follow her, but we have to start down the mountain no later than ten-thirty. That only gives us twenty minutes." When he didn't reply, I added, "Agreed?"

The man was toying with his Freemason's ring again. "You run along, old sweat. I have business to attend to here. Now that the Maji Blanc is leaving, I may take the opportunity to pop down to the lodge and have a look around."

"What?"

"It's not as mad as you think. A well-dressed Englishman is accepted without suspicion at most social functions, no matter the circumstance. Fortunately, we are also dependably forgettable. To the uninitiated, we all sound alike, you know."

"You've got to be kidding."

"No, I've heard it's true."

"I'm not talking about your accent —"

"I know, I know." There was a sly smile in his voice. "Shadow the woman in white. Stay close. You suggested we create an emergency? I have something in mind."

Now he was standing and taking off his shooting jacket. He folded it, put it into his bag, then surprised me by taking out a stiletto, which he fitted behind the shoulder holster that held his Walther PPK.

I said, "You plan on stabbing someone?" as he reached into his bag again. I watched him produce a white dinner jacket, which he slipped into as if standing in front of a mirror.

"I certainly hope not; I had this tailored in Hanoi. Pure silk, you know. Bugger of a job to get stains out. Ford? —" He was straightening the jacket's lapels now. "— would you mind very much staying on post until ten forty-five? A fifteen-minute lead on a Brazilian mastiff is more than enough — even if you are slightly out of training. I'll pull stakes no later than ten fifty-five. Or thereabouts."

I said, "But before we make any decisions, there's something you need to know — the actress isn't an actress."

I told him about Beryl. When I'd finished, he gave the situation some thought before saying, "That gorgeous woman is here posing as your fiancé?"

"I have no idea. I mentioned the place in a phone message, that's all. She's . . . a resourceful woman."

"That may make it a bit sticky for our girl Senegal, don't you think?"

"For all of us. Maybe worse for Beryl if Ritchie and Clovis work here. She wants revenge."

"When you say revenge, you mean —"

"I'm not sure. If she had access to a weapon, violence maybe. Beryl's motivated. She has more reason than most."

"I shouldn't ask any particulars, I gather."

"I appreciate that."

"But do you really think she would —"

"I wouldn't be shocked. She's not as even-tempered as Senegal."

"Really. Part angel, part lioness, eh?" Montbard liked that. "What a splendid creature — you can tell me more about her later. But I think Lady Beryl is actually in less danger here among the enemy, so to speak. Those two cretins won't dare lay a hand on her while she's a guest. And it's all the more reason for me to slip down and mingle."

"No way. I'm not leaving you. Let's drop the stiff-upper-lip stuff, please."

"Don't be silly! This is a perfect opportunity to discover where the old girl keeps her treasures. Stick with Madame Toussaint. Keep your eyes open. If I'm not back at the boat by midnight, it simply means I've taken a different route down the mountain. Return to Saint Lucia without me."

"But where will you —"

"My God, man! This won't be the first time I've grabbed a bit of kip without a roof over my head. I'll take the morning ferry and meet you for breakfast at Jade Mountain. The buffet's excellent. Say, ten-ish? Have a Bloody Mary waiting, won't you?"

I was rubbing my forehead, annoyed.

"Oh . . . a couple of details." He was putting a fountain pen in his pocket, next a lighter. "The moment we split up, night vision is required. I have my little infrared. You have your lovely little Triad flashlight.

No one will be the wiser. Swing the light side to side, it will mean stand fast, something interesting may happen. Circular motion means regroup immediately. Rapid series of dashes means danger approaching, run. Got that?"

He added, "And remember to keep your eye open for the Misericord. A secure little structure where monks were punished — it would fit with Madame Toussaint's psychological profile."

I said, "Someone's compiled a profile?"

"Several dozen pages."

"A professional?"

"I'd like to think so. I already knew a fair bit about Toussaint because of the monastery, but I really went to work on it when Senegal told me about her problem. Ample time to put together a decent profile." Then he added, "You have no idea who I am, do you, old boy?" He said it as if he found me entertaining.

I said, "No . . . but I'm starting to get the picture. James? Hey . . . *Hooker.*"

He was already moving down the hill, straightening his jacket, using fingers to neaten his silver hair. When he got to the fence, I watched him hide his bag behind a tree, then reach for something growing near a low limb. An orchid.

Sir James inserted the flower into his lapel. He patted it in place before scaling the fence.

25

I was straddling a tree limb outside Isabelle Toussaint's château when I heard the man scream. It was the frantic, soprano wail of someone who was falling . . . or being mauled.

Sir James?

Had to be, although it was impossible to identify the voice. It was an unearthly bawling mixed with what resembled the rumble of a distant waterfall.

No . . . not a waterfall. It was the rumble of growling dogs.

Only five minutes earlier I'd been lying belly-down on the stone wall that enclosed the woman's estate, when the power went out. Not just her house — the entire property, lodge and monastery included. A moment later, emergency lights blinked on. Frail blue beams in the darkness. Simultaneously, I heard a warbling siren, like a police car in an old French film. A fire alarm or a burglar alarm.

The Englishman had wasted no time.

I'd been wearing the night-vision monocular, as instructed. From a forested area unexpectedly close to the house, an infrared flashlight painted horizontal streaks on trees. Montbard's signal: Stand fast, something's going to happen.

I no longer doubted the man, but I wasn't in position.

I'd dropped over the wall and jogged toward the rear of the house. The area was landscaped with hedges, like an old English garden. A maze of hedges, literally. Ficus trees cut low, roots like bars, so it was impossible to bust through the hedge when I came to a dead end. I encountered several dead ends. Maddening.

It took a couple tries before I exited into a garden behind the château. The château was built over a wedge of stone ruins that disappeared into the side of the mountain like a storm cellar. There was a terrace, a lily pond, a marble statue of Saint Francis, trees weighted with moss, bromeliads, orchids. One of the trees had limbs low enough to climb, and I did. Pulled myself up as a light came on inside the house. Someone had struck a match to an oil lamp.

It was Isabelle Toussaint. She was a ghostly

figure, carrying the lamp in both hands as she glided through the house. The interior was overfurnished, like a museum storeroom. I could see tapestries and ornate furniture and paintings in heavy frames. There were religious icons on every wall. Crosses . . . a life-sized carving of Christ in agony. It was like watching a series of TV screens as the woman disappeared, then reappeared inside glowing windows and glassed French doors.

The alarm was still warbling. Toussaint looked concerned — turning her head to listen, sniffing the distant wood smoke, touching a hand to her necklace — but in control. Apparently, power outages were common on the mountain. The alarm, though, troubled her.

She had removed her hood. I watched her lean over the lamp to light a thin black cheroot, smoking unself-consciously as she crossed into the kitchen where there were skillets and pots suspended on hooks above a stainless gas stove. Beyond the refrigerator was a narrow staircase — the servant's back steps to the second floor. On the wall next to the staircase was an oversized painting: an infant's white crib in a black room. Bizarre.

The woman poured a glass of wine, sniffed the air once again, testing for fire despite her cigarette. Once again, she touched fingers to the Midnight Star sapphire . . . then turned toward the window, startled, because of a sudden, piercing sound outside. The screaming had begun.

It was a man's voice, shrill . . . vocal cords tearing as terror peaked. After several seconds, the bawling transitioned into a series of ragged shrieks. Terror had become pain.

"Godohgodohgod . . . HELP MEEEEEEE!"

The confusing sound of a waterfall became the snarling, clacking chorus of dogs dragging down prey. I kept telling myself it wasn't Sir James's voice. But it was coming from the forested area where he'd last used the infrared to signal. Who else could it be?

"Noooooo . . . NO!"

When horror is converted into childlike cries, panic becomes transmittable.

You have a gun, James . . . goddamn it, pull your gun!

I felt the panic . . . so did Isabelle Toussaint. I started down the tree, fixated on the source of the screams, but a peripheral part of my brain noted that the woman was also reacting. She was removing her necklace as she hurried toward the back staircase. I saw her lean . . . guessed she was reaching for something out of my view. Then . . . as if on rollers, the middle section of steps opened upward like a hatch.

Toussaint returned for the oil lamp, then crossed again to the hidden compartment. No . . . it wasn't just a compartment, it was a second stairway that descended into a basement.

The château had been built over stone ruins. The ruins apparently extended underground, into the mountainside. I watched the woman disappear down the steps into an unseen chamber. As she pulled the hatch closed, the man's screams were fading into a silence of screaming frogs and rain-forest insects.

I now knew where Toussaint kept her valuables. But it had cost James Montbard dearly. Maybe his life.

I dropped from the tree and ran toward the ficus maze, suddenly furious at myself for not using reflective tape to mark an exit route. A stupid oversight. I didn't have time to waste on more dead ends — I had to find the Englishman.

To my right, a sliding gate opened. Two men with flashlights appeared. The lights scanned the garden terrace I'd just left . . . then swept toward me.

The men didn't see me. But the dogs that followed them into the garden did. I would've known even if I wasn't wearing night vision. The dogs had fluorescent collars, bright as glow sticks. The collars illuminated their jowls and bright, black eyes — two gigantic Brazilian mastiffs.

I ducked into the maze, my speed fueled by fear. Seconds later, the dogs skidded into the hedgerow behind me. I could hear their pounding weight and their salivary growling. Make a wrong turn, hit a dead end, the dogs would be on me. Did it matter? They were going to catch me, anyway.

Ahead were three corridors to choose from, none much wider than my shoulders. I took the opening to the left. There was a sharp right turn, then a sharp left. In the monocular's green light, the hedge walls appeared black, a foot higher than my head. It seemed familiar. But the dogs were closing, tracking me by scent — *hopefully.* After all the wrong turns I'd made earlier, my scent was everywhere. Maybe they'd get confused.

Two more openings appeared. I chose the inner corridor, running as hard as I could until the maze began to narrow. The other dead ends had narrowed in the same way.

Shit.

As I slowed, I reached to pull the Colt from the holster tucked into the back of my pants . . . then made another mistake — I fumbled the gun and dropped it. Had to stop, retrace my steps, then kneel to retrieve it. Too late, and I knew it — the dogs were waiting.

As I knelt, a wolfish rumble vibrated near my ear. Both dogs were somewhere in the shadows, so close I could smell them. Because I'd stopped, they'd stopped — pack mentality — and now they were waiting for me to move. I'd found the gun. Had it in my right hand. I remained motionless for several seconds, then slowly raised my head.

I expected to be nose to nose with the mastiffs . . . but the hedgerow was empty. Where the hell were they?

I stood . . . then fell backward as a dog lunged at me from above. The animal looked demonic with its glowing collar, straining to get over the hedge. It was joined by the second dog. Their growling was a sustained howl punctuated by snapping teeth. Sir James had said that Brazilian mastiffs were seven feet tall on their hind legs. It was not an exaggeration.

I'd gotten lucky. The dogs had followed my scent into a parallel corridor, one of the dead ends I'd hit earlier. The corridor I'd chosen had narrowed, but I could see that it opened just ahead.

I held the gun ready as I backed away, expecting the dogs to claw their way over the hedge. But each time they tried, the top of the hedge separated beneath their weight, and funneled them into a tangle of ficus roots. From the distance, I could hear one of the men whistling for the dogs. Maybe he thought they'd treed an animal. He would be here soon.

I turned. I ran. I found the trail we'd marked with reflective tape — the shortest route down the mountain. I barely slowed when I got to the chain-link fence. Didn't look back until I'd vaulted over.

In an area cloaked by elephant-ear leaves, I stopped. Stayed hidden there until I'd caught my breath in the leaning-rest position — hands on knees, head down. I came close to vomiting. My legs were shaking, and a schematic of the back on my brain pulsed inside my eyes. It wasn't just because of my close call with the dogs. The man's screams were still banging around in my head. Haunting — as was the guilt I felt for leaving James Montbard behind.

I felt sick. Stood there and argued with myself about returning to the spa compound. But what could I do for him now? Couldn't avoid the obvious question: Was it true I couldn't help? Or was I afraid to go back over the fence?

Afraid. Yes, I was afraid — an honest admission. But it was also true that if the screams I'd heard were Sir James, he was beyond my help. Even if he were alive, the compound would be on full alert. An anonymous call to the island police was my best option. Contrive some lie to get an ambulance and a couple of nosy cops to have a look around the spa.

It was quarter after eleven. I still had to cross four miles of open ocean in an eighteen-foot boat. But first I had to get to a pay phone. Or . . . I could try to raise the local water cops on the handheld VHF radio I'd left on the Maverick. That would be faster. No chance of caller ID giving away my location, either.

I started downhill, jogging when I could, walking when the trail narrowed. People who are obsessive by nature are commonly the victims of their own cyclic thought patterns. Their brains function like a compass needle, swinging inevitably back to whatever it is they are trying to put out of their mind. I am obsessive. To muffle the screams ringing in my head, I thought about Senegal Firth. What would I tell her?

The decision wasn't as time-consuming as I wanted it to be. Long ago, in a faraway jungle, a buddy and I dulled our own fears by constructing a series of brave maxims. Maxims are distilled truths, orderly beacons. In our violent world, they reminded us that the existential has an orderly counterpart. One of the maxims we hammered out was this: *When telling the truth is the most difficult choice, it is almost always the right choice.*

I would tell Senegal the truth, but an amended truth to spare her pain. It would be after midnight by the time I got to Saint Lucia. I would hike up the steps to James Montbard's home and bang on the door. Get it over with. She deserved to know.

The boat was hidden in a tidal creek in a tunnel of mangroves. The creek was a hundred yards off a gravel road that circled the mountain, jungle on one side, sea on the other. I'd marked the place by tying reflective tape in the trees.

When I got to the road, I stowed the night-vision monocular and jogged the last quarter mile in darkness. There was no sense of relief that I'd made it off the mountain, and felt no pleasure in the thought of getting in the boat and pointing seaward. Instead, I felt flat and empty, as if the dogs, the screams, the jungle had punctured my spirit and drained me of purpose.

It is remarkable how quickly we recover when good fortune displaces misfortune

— and it always does, sooner or later.

On this night, it was sooner.

When I was close enough to spot the tape, I took out the infrared flashlight, fitted the night-vision harness over my right eye, and flipped the switch. Instantly, shadows were illuminated . . . but there was another source of light, too. An unexpected source.

In the mangrove thicket where the boat was hidden, an infrared light was painting slow circles on the tree canopy. It wasn't my infrared light. It wasn't me who was flashing Montbard's signal to regroup.

I ran toward the boat. Unholstered my pistol just in case, but didn't bother trying to cover the sound of me crashing through the mangroves. Sir James was lighting his pipe when I broke through the trees.

"About time, old boy," he said calmly. "I was beginning to worry dogs had caught more than one trespasser tonight. Poor bastard — up there poaching orchids. You heard?"

"Yes."

"You sound a bit shaken."

"I am. I thought it was you."

"Could've been. Terrible way to go. But you would have heard at least one shot — better by my own bullet than the indignity of being ripped apart by dogs. It was a local

370

boy, barely out of his teens. Nothing I could do."

"A boy?"

"Sadly, yes. Athletic-looking lad; poor family, judging from his rags." For the first time, Montbard sounded like a weary seventy-year-old man.

He had used the VHF radio, he added, and told harbor patrol that a wealthy tourist had been attacked, and might still be alive. There was a better chance they'd respond if they believed it was a tourist.

I untied the boat, started the engine. We were idling into the slow lift and fall of a trade-wind sea before I said, "I don't know about you, but I could use one of your midnight teas."

Montbard tapped his pipe empty before putting it in the pocket of his dinner jacket. "Right you are. A stiff whiskey or two's just the thing."

26

Tuesday, June 25th

The Hooded Orchid was on an early-to-bed, early-to-rise schedule. Senegal and I signed the guest book before noon the next day. She was assigned Room 7, one of two dozen doors spaced along the cloister on the inland side of the monastery. I was in Room 36, a stone cubicle on the seaward side: an iron convent bed, a chair, a tiny bathroom, a pad of Persian carpet, a cross, and an incense burner in the "meditation corner."

Couples were forbidden to "interact," we were reminded — as if putting us in different buildings wasn't reminder enough. Orientation was at 4 p.m.; attendance mandatory. Until then, we were asked to stay in our rooms and rest.

I didn't feel like resting. I unpacked and headed outside.

A few minutes later, I was standing at the

edge of the cliff that had scared me dizzy the night before, imitating a tourist who'd never seen the place. The rope I'd secured to the tree was hidden in the rocks. I had to peek over the safety railing to confirm it was still there.

I also was surprised to confirm that a police boat and two fishing boats were anchored at the base of the cliff. They had a line and a grappling hook attached to something that looked like a chunk of brown sponge. A man's body. No . . . the man-sized body of a teen.

Surf was breaking under the rocks, geysering upward through spume holes. From where I stood, the geysers appeared stationary, like ice sculptures. I knew better. The boats were standing off because of the rocks and whirlpool currents. Not an easy place to retrieve a body — what was left of the body, anyway, after a night crashing among rocks.

I had seen the boats from our helicopter on the flight in, but didn't get a good look. I was seated next to Senegal, but said nothing because we were crammed among four other new spa arrivals. I wouldn't have said anything anyway until I was sure. Now I was.

This was how Isabelle Toussaint's staff dealt with trespassers — convenient, clean, and utterly ruthless. For those with blood on their hands, high cliffs and deep water are efficient disinfectants. It is something that accomplished criminals know.

Extortionists are motivated by greed, but these were killers. Blackmail was a sideline — one of several, I suspected. How many people had gone off that cliff? If Montbard hadn't contacted the harbor patrol, I doubted if the boy's body would've been found.

It was freeing, in ways, watching the grappling hook do its work. It changed the rules. It expanded the limits of my own conduct. I'm not a policeman; was never trained in the protocols of assembling evidence. But I know how to deal with killers. After years in the trade, I am competent.

Freeing, yes. But I was also aware that somewhere a mother was grieving. The teen's family would turn from his coffin with scars they would carry to their own graves. Through association, I was now vested in their loss — I had heard the boy's screams. Only sociopaths and the righteous feel unconstrained by convention. I was suddenly at liberty to take righteous action.

A few days before, I'd tried to make Shay smile, saying her blackmailers had no idea who they were dealing with.

Now it was true.

"Excuse me, sir. The Lookout's off-limits to guests. You need to return to your room."

I turned to see the man I'd mistaken for Ritchie. Similar size; muscles under the white shirt with its Hooded Orchid logo. Otherwise, there was no resemblance on this afternoon of sunlight and low silver clouds. He had shoulder-length black hair, a geometric chin, and spoke articulate English with a French accent. His name tag read: FABRON MMT.

Was Fabio a derivative of Fabron? He looked a little like the guy I'd seen on the cover of romance novels. Maybe he'd picked it out himself, like a vanity license plate.

Standing behind Fabron, like a shadow, was a tiny woman in a blue maid's uniform, her expression blank. She remained disinterested as I smiled, put my arms out, palms up, to let the man know I felt confused and foolish. I also didn't want him to get close enough to spot the rope. "Off-limits? Geez, sorry. Didn't know. Maybe you should put up a sign or something —"

"We don't use signs. Guests are expected to know monastery rules. We expect the rules to be followed."

A smooth, condescending manner — Fabron had something else in common with Ritchie.

I said, "Monastery? I was under the impression my lady friend and I were at a health spa, not a church retreat." A joke — I chuckled. Fabron didn't. The woman's expression remained blank, as if she didn't hear.

"Whatever impression you got, sir, it's wrong. This is a monastery, a sacred part of the spa grounds. That's how we refer to it. Maybe you weren't paying attention at orientation. Occasionally, guests find it's helpful to go through orientation twice."

At the front desk, a woman with a German accent had been just as arrogant — suspicious, too. Same with the attendant who'd shown us to our rooms. From their reactions, I could tell they recognized Senegal, but it had only fueled their rudeness. Maybe people came to a place like this as atonement for personal excesses. If the staff treated guests as subordinates, it was probably encouraged.

Interesting. What were the staff's limits? I was curious.

"Your name's Fabron?"

The man blinked at my stupidity. "Yes. That is why I chose to have it on my name tag."

"What's M-M-T stand for?"

"Male Massage Therapist, sir."

"Back rubs, huh?"

The man reacted, but caught himself. "Ask all the questions you want at orientation. What I'm telling you is the Lookout's off-limits. Must I tell you again?"

Fabron turned, expecting me to follow.

I didn't.

When he glanced back, I touched the safety railing, and pointed at the boats. "Looks like I'm not the only one who missed orientation, huh?"

"Excuse me?"

"There's a body down there — a man. Do you think the spa's gonna give the guy his money back?" I still wore the harmless smile.

Fabron's nostrils widened, but it backed him down a notch. "One of the locals drowned. Too bad, but you know how it is — islanders don't receive swimming lessons. They go out in homemade boats, anyway. They are stupid. Spend time on this island, you will learn it's true."

I looked over the railing again. "If that guy was in a boat, it was an invisible boat. He didn't need swimming lessons, Fabio. What he needed was flying lessons. Do you know who it is?"

"No."

"Then show some respect. You don't know anything about the man."

Behind him, the woman in the maid's uniform smiled.

I squinted at my watch, expecting the man to react. When he didn't, I said, "But thanks, anyway, for the reminder."

"Reminder, sir?" He said it in a flat voice.

"My lady friend and I got to the spa about an hour ago. I don't want to miss orientation — sounds like it might be unhealthy."

I didn't need any more enemies on the island, but I had made one.

I got a glimpse of Beryl late that afternoon as I hurried toward the health spa. The facilities were housed in a modern building of stone and wood, down the mountain from the monastery and Isabelle Toussaint's estate.

Beryl was in the quadrangle with three other women. She wore jeans and a white knit blouse. The others wore the familiar white scrubs that, I realized, were belted at the waists, and more like togas. They were walking single file around the quadrangle — walking meditation, it was called. No talking.

At orientation, we were told that for the first forty-eight hours we could speak only to staff members. Otherwise, conversation wasn't permitted. New guests were referred to as Novitiates — a monastic touch. As Novitiates, we were expected to remain silent or we would be asked to leave. I was tempted to ask if we would be banished by helicopter or pushed off the cliff. By then, I'd told Senegal about watching the boats retrieve the body. As if reading my mind, the woman had nudged an elbow into my ribs to keep me quiet.

After our morning together, I'd begun to appreciate Senegal Firth. She had a cool head and a first-rate intellect. Because of the circumstances, she'd loosened up a little, creating a space for me behind her mask of aloofness. Senegal had also decided to make the best of the situation even though she'd battled against coming to the Orchid.

"As long as we're here," she'd said, "I'll use the time to shed a pound or two and treat myself to whatever it is the spa offers. The staff may be bastards, but they do seem to have a sound approach to fitness. Lots of exercise and simple food. The last few months have been bloody rough, and I've let my health slip a bit."

I liked the woman's attitude and decided to take the same approach. Less food, tougher workouts, harder runs — I could scope out the area while I was jogging. But I had no interest in treatments offered by the spa.

Turned out, though, I had no choice.

At orientation, all new arrivals had been assigned "body analysis" appointments. They were required — as were "purifying treatments." Because I was a little late for my first appointment, I had been jogging across the quadrangle when I noticed the women in white, and I singled out Beryl.

Beryl's chin lifted when our eyes met. She acknowledged me with a stricken shake of the head. I got the impression that something bad had happened . . . a sense of emergency, and she was eager to talk. A moment later, she touched three fingers to her cheek and tapped three times, communicating something else. What?

I touched my face in reply, but I also shrugged — *I don't understand* — then winked. *I'll figure it out.*

As I filled out forms in the spa's waiting room, I gave it some thought. Three . . . Why was the number significant? Beryl, Shay, Corey, and Liz had been seduced by three men. It was three days until Shay's wedding rehearsal . . . The women had only three days to wire more money to the blackmailer's account. As maid of honor, Beryl had three days before she had to return to

380

Florida. It had been three days since I left Sanibel . . .

What else?

That's all I could come up with.

Shay and Beryl had already given me all the details they could about the three men. I didn't need to be reminded we were running out of time. Beryl was smart. Why would she risk communicating something I already knew?

She wouldn't.

Maybe it had something to do with a reply to the e-mail I sent from Jade Mountain. That morning, before Sir James drove Senegal and me to the Saint Lucia airport, I'd stopped at the reception office to check for replies, but the Internet was down. No way to check now.

To hell with the rules. I had to talk to Beryl.

27

A door opened and a woman, mid-thirties, with corded forearms stepped into the spa's waiting room, drying her hands on a towel. White towel, white shorts, white blouse showing a hint of cleavage. An attractive woman who would've been striking if it wasn't for the frown and sterile, professional manner. Her name tag read: NORMA FMT.

"Mr. North? Ready for your body analysis?"

No, but I followed the woman, anyway.

Along with the body analysis, the Orchid required new arrivals to have a sea-salt cleansing treatment, then spend two hours alternating between a sauna and a cold-water dip pool — "sweat lodge rotation," it was called.

As an outsider, I was considered unclean. I couldn't argue the point. I also couldn't talk my way out of the treatments. There could be no interacting with other guests until I'd jumped through their hoops.

Making conversation as I followed the pretty woman down a hallway, I said, "I noticed all the rooms in this building are named for flowers. Orchids, I guess."

"That's right."

"Is that confusing for newcomers?"

"Everything's confusing for Novitiates. That's why we number the guest rooms. Keep it one-two-three simple for you people."

"Us people, huh? Like we're kinda dumb. I don't blame you. I bet you get some weirdos in here occasionally."

"*Occasionally.*"

"Anyone ever ask what F-M-T stands for?"

The woman's reaction was unexpected, but it revealed how fast news traveled. "You already asked Fabron that question. You didn't believe the man? Or are you testing me?"

I said, "*Oh . . . F* as in female. Like in female massage therapist. I get it." Fabron would've also confirmed I wasn't very bright.

He had told the woman more than that.

Norma opened a door to a room that smelled of eucalyptus, steam, and body lotion. There was a massage table, wall speakers mounted flush, and a stainless table stacked with sheets and towels. "Get yourself undressed, Mr. North. You're about to learn there's a lot more to massage therapy than a back rub. We're professionals. Health care–trained, like doctors."

Her condescending manner was consistent with the rest of the staff, but it was still irritating. What were Norma's limits?

"Like physicians, you mean?"

"That's right."

"No kidding? I'm surprised."

"Novitiates usually are."

I said, "It's not because of that. It's because I read an article — some medical journal, maybe. You can get a massage certificate in two weeks, some places. Or you can get a certificate over the Internet, watching videos. Even where it's regulated, it only takes a little more than a month."

The woman knew it was true. I smiled at her reaction before adding, "How'd you like a doctor with a month of medical school try to take out your appendix?"

She was arranging towels to show my opinion didn't warrant attention. "If you got something against massage, mister, why come to a place like this?"

"Because I like back rubs."

Norma's eyes became slits — two dark

creatures peering out. Like Fabron, she had boundaries that were seldom tested.

"You've got a hostile streak in you, Mr. North. A sure sign of poison in your system. Lots of built-up toxins and free radicals."

I said, "That sounds unhealthy. I've never been a fan of radicals, particularly when they're free."

"You're one for jokes, but I know what I'm saying. Herbal tonics are the best way to flush those toxins, so why not have yourself a drink before I start?"

There was a carafe of tea-colored liquid on the counter, iced, and garnished with a sprig of blue flowers. Looked like the same flowers I'd seen the previous night. Montbard had said the flowers were rare.

I said, "No thanks, bottled water's fine. I prefer to flush my toxins in private," pushing the boundaries, but what the hell.

The woman's frown communicated irritation, but also suspicion. "It makes no sense. You've no respect for what we do — massage purifying the body — so why pay all that money to stay here?"

I shrugged, opening a bottle of water.

"You're not wondering why I'm even bothering to care? I see a lot of clients in this room. Asking why they're wasting their money isn't something I usually do."

"I already told you, Norma — I enjoy back rubs."

Still frowning, the woman gestured toward the table. "Slip out of those clothes and lie on your stomach. I've got another appointment soon."

My list of enemies at the Orchid was growing.

Norma was wrong. I don't have a problem with massage. I have a problem with members of the massage industry who promote pseudoscience and quackery-for-profit.

Some "therapists" make claims so outlandish they would be funny — if they weren't dangerous. They claim to massage away lymphatic toxins, alter body polarity, restore positive energy, correct meridian imbalances, heal through therapeutic touch, treat disease with reflexology, calm hyperactive pets and children via manipulation or aromatherapy. It is quackery without anatomic or scientific foundation, yet it goes unchallenged even in states that claim to regulate the business. What many dismiss as goofy, new-age fun is actually an intentional con.

There are good universities where students work their butts off studying the science of sports medicine, a respected field that includes therapeutic massage. The fact that these professionals are confused with "massage therapists" is unfair to the discipline and dangerous to the public. The frauds, of course, love it.

I'd told Norma I'd read an article about massage. Truth was, I'd read a lot on the subject because of something unfortunate that happened to a female friend. The reading included a book on "voodoo science" by Dr. Robert L. Parker, professor of physics, University of Maryland. Dr. Parker had isolated seven red flags that signal bogus science. Many of those red flags were obvious in the Orchid's spa literature. I'd thumbed through the stuff in the waiting room.

The spa offered standard massage fare, along with typically murky claims for shiatsu healing, hot-stone chakra balancing, and the "reintegration" of soul and body.

There were also flags of much brighter red.

Aromatherapy: Essential oils balance the patient's biological background while neutralizing toxins such as free radicals and other causes of disease . . .

Lymphatic Massage: Acu-probe safely applied by experts. Causes lymph to flow, and improves detoxifying function of the kidneys . . .

Colon Hydrotherapy: Detoxifying external and internal massage. Warm herbal water is used to gently flush the colon of intestinal stasis . . .

Body/Mind Integration: Patients share innermost thoughts with their therapist during massage, particularly toxic feelings of anxiety, guilt, and negative past-life experiences . . .

Sexual Energy Massage: Using an ancient technique, ching chi is released from the genitals through digital manipulation that rechannels libido and eliminates toxins created by undirected sexual energy . . .

Rechanneling libido was one of the Orchid's few legitimate claims. But rechanneling libido isn't uncommon in the trade — a nasty little secret the massage industry tries to conceal.

A lady friend of mine who adored massages told me about an experience at a ski resort. An expensive hotel with a spa that had a sterling reputation — according to the spa's literature.

My friend scheduled a massage in her room. She requested a male therapist. "Their hands are stronger," she told me. "I've used the same guy in Lauderdale for years. He's great."

It is true there are good, reputable massage technicians. It's true there are fun, reputable spas that monitor the behavior of their staff. Not all promote quackery. But my friend wasn't in Lauderdale, and the man who came into her room carrying towels and a folding table was a stranger.

After half an hour on the table, the hotel's "therapist" started using a technique new to her, concentrating on her inner thighs. The man's intent was obvious, but only in hindsight — gradual sexual persuasion. My friend didn't participate, but she didn't protest. By the end of the hour, she was no longer fully draped, and the man's hands had moved to what the industry refers to as "inappropriate regions of the body."

That's when my friend's husband walked in. No reason he shouldn't. The massage had gone over the allotted time. He was paying for the room — and the massage. It was only a few seconds before they realized the husband was watching, but it was time enough for him to see what the therapist was doing, and to misinterpret his wife's role.

For years, the husband had believed his wife. Massage was therapy. But what he saw transformed years of trust into suspicion.

Accusations, denials, and arguments led to counseling.

When I asked why she didn't protest, she was sincerely puzzled. "I really don't know. I guess I was so out of it I didn't realize. . . . Wait. I don't believe that. Why should I expect you to believe it?

"Massage is . . . intimate. You drift off. You give your body up to the therapist. Of course I knew. I didn't stop him because, well, it felt good, damn it! I felt safe because he was a professional. It just . . . *happened*."

She's a fine person, my friend. She hadn't done anything wrong, but she'd been conditioned to accept an intimate and dangerous environment that real professionals — physicians, chiropractors, sports-medicine specialists — wouldn't tolerate even if it were considered ethical. An hour alone with a naked patient?

It is a bizarre phenomenon — another reason I'd researched the subject.

The massage industry doesn't publish data that hurts business. Newspapers do. Cases of sexual assault and prostitution are public record. An example is the "Tibetan healer," a massage therapist licensed in California, who was expanding his practice to other states when charged with seventeen felonies, including rape and oral copulation with an unconscious person.

Because it's rarely reported, there's no accurate tally of the number of women assaulted after inviting "therapists" into their rooms. For sexual predators, it may be the safest of all covers. Juries aren't sympathetic to women who willingly take off their clothes and invite a male to touch them. Why bother to report a crime that will never be prosecuted? It's a sad capitulation to the dim-witted belief that women invite rape through their behavior.

I found a confidential poll of female massage clients and gave it to my friend to read. A startling percentage responded that on at least one occasion male therapists had touched them "inappropriately." Only a tiny percentage reported the incidents.

"It happens," I told my friend, echoing her own explanation.

Instead of being relieved, though, she became furious.

"What are you telling me? Oh . . . I get it! It's wrong if a man massages a woman, but it's perfectly okay for a woman to massage a man. Give him a hand job, a blow job — whatever! But never the opposite. I've been hammered enough with that goddamn double standard. I'm not going to take it any more — even from you, Doc!"

There wasn't much I could say. She was right.

Sometimes life's weird symmetry gets weirder. The same technique used to seduce my unlucky friend was now being used to entrap me.

I was naked, faceup on the table, draped with a sheet, while Norma stroked the inside of my legs, forcing blood up the thigh into the femoral triangle and genitals.

Spa literature was right. It is an ancient technique. The geishas of Japan study it; the massage prostitutes of Southeast Asia are masters. Squeegee strokes up the inner thigh affect even unwilling men and women for reasons that have more to do with hydrology than sexuality.

The clitoris and penis are the same organ but for the differentia of an X chromosome, a few inches, and thousands of years of sexual taboo. Both have spongelike regions of tissue. In the penis, the tissue is called corpus cavernosum; in the clitoris, it is glans clitoridis.

Male or female, penis or clitoris, the spongy tissue becomes engorged with blood when stimulated — or when blood is manipulated into the region. The primate brain reads the increased pressure as arousal.

The body readies itself.

But my body wasn't reacting as Norma expected. She kept at it, though, applying more oil, cupping the inside of my thigh, using strong fingers to accelerate blood through the saphenous vein, and also to stimulate the sensitive pudendal nerve, a high-voltage link between thigh and genitals.

A couple of times she pretended to slip and her fingers made contact — teasing what Tomlinson refers to as "Zamboni and the Hat Trick Twins." No results.

It wasn't the first time in my life I didn't respond to a woman's touch, but it was the first time I was ever happy about it.

Not that it was easy. Almond-scented oil . . . the woman's knowing hands . . . sound of ocean waves rolling from the stereo . . . waves and the occasional caw and moan of sea birds.

I kept my eyes closed and pretended to be unaware of what the woman's fingers were doing. I concentrated mightily on lofty topics — shark dissections . . . jellyfish . . . befouled water filters — because I was enjoying Norma's frustration a hell of a lot more than I would've enjoyed what Norma was offering.

It helped knowing that this classic massage finesse had been used to hurt a friend. It also helped knowing that I was being filmed. Filmed . . . or, at the very least, watched on a monitor.

There was a miniature camera lens mounted over the massage table, disguised as a sprinkler head. There was another built into a smoke alarm hanging on the wall at the foot of the table. Common little mini-cameras — amateur spy shops sell them.

I'd located the cameras as I got undressed. The discovery wasn't accidental. Recalling my friend's experience had provided link-age to what should have been obvious: Shay, Beryl, and friends had been entrapped by a similar ploy using gradual sexual persua-sion.

My friend's hotel "therapist" had done it for his own amusement . . . or maybe he'd had a hidden camera, too. But Norma was doing it because she worked for a woman who profited by luring wealthy people into this orchid-scented trap.

A health spa with snob appeal on a tropi-cal island — the perfect vehicle for someone like Isabelle Toussaint. I reminded myself of something else: Toussaint enjoyed humiliat-ing her victims.

Of course there would be cameras hid-den in the treatment rooms. In the clois-ters, too. I'd already confirmed there was one in my room — a mini-lens in the clock radio. Someone had searched the place, too; expected — which is why I'd stashed my contraband gear in an overhead gallery bay outside my door.

"You got big, thick muscles, Mr. North, you sure do. And some scars here and there, more than most. That tells me you live a man's life." Norma had switched to the other leg and was lathering her hands with oil. She had also switched her approach.

"I feel bad now, being sharp with you earlier. Man like you deserves to be treated right. So you just . . . you just *let go* for Norma, and Norma will make you feel very fine. Sure you don't want a drink of my herbal tonic?"

I said, "No, but I'm just about ready for a beer. Hey — take it easy."

"Little pain's good for the body, but I'll be real gentle from now on."

Norma cupped her hands around my thigh, and began forcing the blood upward. You can't remain sexually disinterested when someone you find attractive does what she was doing. Physically, Norma was attractive — an abundance of curves in a select few places.

Focusing on sharks and jellyfish was a battle. There was also something oddly arousing about the stereo sounds of those ocean waves with birds crying in the background. Why?

It was a battle I began to lose.

"Well, well . . . I can see you like that. Um-huh. Yes . . . you like that a lot . . .

". . . nowwwwww you're starting to relax. Why . . . yes, you are. I bet you'd find it even more relaxing if I started massaging this part right here —"

There was a delay of a foggy few seconds before I put my hands under the sheet and stopped her.

"Why . . . what's wrong, Mr. North? You're enjoying what I'm doing. That's very obvious."

"Yeah, I am. Feels great."

"Then why stop me?"

"Surprised, I guess. I've never had a doctor do that before."

"Didn't say I was a doctor. Said I was highly trained like one."

"You've had a lot of practice, I'm convinced. But what's the catch? You aren't selling. You're not the type . . . or are you?"

The woman pulled her hands away. "I don't tolerate that kind of talk, mister. Why say something so nasty?"

I sat up. "Because you've got too much

going for you to make a living giving hand jobs to strangers. There has to be another reason."

She was flustered by my reaction. "I'm . . . I'm just trying to make you feel good. You've got knots and ching chi blockages from your feet to your neck. You don't want me to get rid of those things?"

"Sex isn't allowed — that's what they told us at orientation. You're a pretty woman, Norma. Beautiful, in the right gown, the right makeup. I'm attracted — obviously. But who am I supposed to believe?"

People paid to act like drill sergeants seldom receive compliments. I was surprised at how she softened. The woman touched a hand to her hair; her tone became confidential. "You're right, but not all the way right. Novitiates aren't allowed to have relations with their *partners*. It's a way of purifying — so the man and woman can start fresh together after they leave."

I asked, "But it's okay to have sex with someone who's not your partner?"

The woman gave me an odd look, her expression asking, *Are you kidding?* "It's possible that's why some clients come back. It's a spiritual thing, experiencing other human beings. Just another form of therapy, like we're doing right here. Don't think of it as sex."

When she reached to continue, I took her hands in mine, and squeezed them fondly. "It is tempting. You're more than attractive — you're spectacular when you get rid of that frown. But what would I tell my lady friend?"

Norma looked at me like I was crazy. "Man, why do you have to tell the woman anything? What happens in this room stays in this room, I promise you that."

I was tempted to wink at one of the cameras. Instead, I said, "If you were dating a man who didn't tell the truth, how would you feel?"

"Not surprised. I buried one man, got engaged to another, but it didn't last. Neither told the truth."

"I'm sorry to hear that. But I think the lady and I should at least be engaged before I start lying to her. Don't you?"

Instead of bristling, Norma smiled, then chuckled. It was genuine, and she softened even more — a good-looking woman with tropical eyes, sweat beading on her skin where her blouse was open, showing rims of beige bra cupping her breasts.

"You don't want me to go any further? You're serious."

"This time, yeah."

"You must be in love with the woman."

"Will I be breaking a monastery rule if I say no?"

Norma grimaced and gave me a warning look. "It's plain you're in love. You won't do your therapy. I'm done trying to talk you into it, so you're just gonna have to live with those toxins."

Had Norma turned off the cameras?

Maybe. As I got dressed, she faced the wall, cleaning her hands with a fresh towel. Before turning, I noticed that she tried to block my view as she flicked toggle switches near the lights. The sound of ocean waves stopped. Maybe the cameras, too.

"The woman you brought, I saw her picture in a magazine. She's pretty for a woman her age. Has looks, a fine education. You've got good taste, Mr. North. But you have to learn not to talk so free while you're at the monastery."

Yes, the cameras were off.

I said, "The walls have ears?"

"*I've* got ears, just like the rest of the staff. That's what I'm telling you."

Gossip traveled fast here, so I wasn't surprised Norma knew I'd arrived with Senegal. But why would she bother to offer a warning?

"I hope I don't get you in some kind of trouble by refusing that ching chi business —"

She cut me off. "Don't worry your head about me. Worry about yourself. I expect that's a full-time job for a man like you. I heard what went on at the Lookout this morning, when they were fishing the boy out of the water. I heard you told Fabron to mind his own damn business — be best if he showed some respect for the dead. Isn't that what happened?"

I said, "Something like that," recalling the face of the tiny woman in the maid's uniform, picturing her smile.

"How'd Fabron swallow that? That man, he's dangerous."

"Then I'm glad you gave me the massage, not him. He wouldn't have gotten nearly as far."

She chuckled, shaking her head. "You are a piece of work, you know that? Only men ever said no to the treatment weren't really men, if you understand my meaning. But there's something I want you to know — personally, I mean. I was only offering my hands. Nothing else. Never have. That part of me's not for sale. I'm no damn B-girl, like some others. I'm a health-care therapist. I take it seriously, whether you believe it or not."

I said, "I believe you. I'm also starting to believe I was a fool to refuse. Maybe I should've chosen another spa. Next time, I will — and maybe ask you to come along."

The dark eyes became more alert — a woman who rarely dropped her defenses. "Some men toss out lies like chocolates. Others use them as carrots. Which are you?"

I was buckling my belt. "When it comes to getting what I want? Both."

The woman wasn't expecting that. She studied my face for a moment. "You're a funny one. Kind of a smart-ass and stubborn, but that's okay. You're . . . different. I'm surprised the bosses let you in here."

"Bosses?"

"That mean-ass German woman at the desk. And the other one — the one who owns everything you see around here. Maybe you don't know who I mean. The White Lady."

She used it as a proper noun, capitalizing the words with an inflection that mixed respect and fear. White Lady.

I nearly asked, *Are you talking about the Maji Blanc?* Instead, I said, "I don't know who you mean. A friend suggested we come here — a last-minute thing. What's the owner's name?"

"Doesn't matter. She owns the place, that's

all I'm saying. I do my job."

"Sounds as if you don't like her. Tough boss, or a bad tipper?"

Norma said, "If that's a joke, it's not much of a joke. The White Lady's never come in here for a massage. Never will, either." She put it out there, hinting at something, but she wasn't going to let it go much further.

"A spa owner who doesn't get massages? That's not much of an endorsement. She must have something to hide."

Norma shrugged. "I never said that." Done talking about it.

"Well, if she's anything like the woman at the front desk, *I* wouldn't like her. There's not much chance I'll last a week here. This spa business seems like a bunch of silly bullshit, to be honest."

"The wrong person hears you say that, man, you'll be out of here faster than you think."

I smiled at her expression of concern. "You say that as if I should be afraid."

"Maybe you should be afraid. You seem like a nice man — unusual, in my line of work. Could be, you should be real careful about what you say and do around here."

"Friendly advice?"

"That's right."

"I'm flattered, but why?"

"Because of the boy you saw them hauling from the sea this morning. You showed respect. He was my . . ." The woman turned, and began folding towels. ". . . he was my nephew. The damn people who work here, they pretended not to even notice his body floating down there, but you took the time. You showed respect."

I said, "I'm very sorry."

"Me, too. You don't know. He was a fine young man. Had a compass in his head that kept him steady — like you. I wished I'd known him better, but I . . . I didn't get the chance. That boy could have been *something*."

"What was his name?"

"His name was Paul, but —" Norma paused for several seconds as she concentrated on towels. "— but people called him Rafael, so I guess that was his name."

It was a complicated subject, apparently. I decided not to press. "My name's Marion. Friends call me Doc. Okay?"

"You're a real one?"

"No. A nickname."

"Then you watch yourself . . . Doc. There *is* somethin' different about you, and the bosses don't miss much."

"You lost me."

"Senegal Firth — you two don't fit. She

doesn't like men . . . not nice men, anyway. Sometimes that's the only way the cold ones can let go. And I heard you're from Florida. Yesterday, a very pretty woman about my age showed up. She's got a spa business same place you live — Florida. Kind of strange, a pretty woman checking in alone."

"A lot of people live in Florida."

"Maybe so. But the woman asked Miss Bunt — that's the German manager — she asked Miss Bunt if a man named Ford was here. Dr. Marion Ford. And your name's Marion North — right . . . *Doc?*"

As I began to reply, she held up a hand. "All I'm saying is watch yourself. Don't ever go walking outside the monastery walls after midnight. Hear? *Ever.* And take care what you say and do, especially around the staff."

"The White Lady? Or do you mean the Maji Blanc?"

Norma's eyes burrowed into mine. "How'd you find out that name?"

"I can't remember. I always forget who gives me information — probably because of all the toxins in my body."

I saw Norma ready to smile, but not quite there. I reached and squeezed her hand. "The White Lady's no lady, Norma. But you are. Thanks for the advice. What would happen if she knew you'd warned me?"

Norma gave a weary shrug — *Who cares?* — before replying, "I'd lose my job and a place to live. That's all. And I'm going to be leaving soon, anyway."

"Quitting?"

"In a way."

"I didn't know the staff lived on the grounds."

"Not all of us. It's a seniority deal. You come by helicopter, so you wouldn't've seen them, but there're cabins down the mountain, maybe a quarter mile by road. I've got a pretty nice place, set off by itself. I like it. Got it fixed up nice. Getting fired and losing that cabin — that's the worst they could do to me."

Norma was wrong.

28

Beryl told me, "Corey's dead. She died Sunday morning, the day after you left. The doctors aren't sure what happened, an aneurism, maybe."

We were standing in a closet so cramped that my lips were next to her ear. Candlelight bounced shadows around the adjoining room, showing a stone floor and Beryl's bed, where the pillow, the mattress, were still imprinted with her weight.

I whispered, *"Dead?"*

"I know . . . unbelievable. When she was in intensive care, they think one of the procedures maybe caused a blood clot. She was fine, sitting up, talking . . . then she said something about a pain in her head, and closed her eyes. That was it. She never woke up. I'm still in shock. Damn it, I won't let them get away with it."

Beryl didn't sound in shock. She sounded cold, in control — a woman who was experienced at concealing rage. But she didn't bother hiding her impatience with me.

"The party boys are responsible — and whoever took the video. From your phone message, I expected to find them working here. So where are they?"

I shook my head. "I'm not sure. I've seen them, but it wasn't here."

"Then *where?* Why come to this freaky place if it wasn't to deal with those three? I think you're wasting my time."

This was the same woman who'd come into the lab wearing a towel, eyes smoky as the candlelight that now illuminated her nose and eyes in a flickering triangle. Cold voice, cold eyes. Finally, I was meeting the Ice Queen.

I said, "It's more complicated than that."

"Damn right it's more complicated — as of Sunday morning. They killed Corey the same as using a gun. And she didn't do anything — not compared to the rest of us. But they blackmailed her anyway, and she's dead. If we don't pay up by Friday, they'll try to destroy my life, too. And Liz's life. Shay's already such an emotional wreck, I'm worried she might be next."

The first thing Beryl had told me was that Shay's wedding had been postponed for two weeks, then gave me the bad news about

Corey, when I asked, *"Why?"*

The funeral was on Friday — the day of the rehearsal dinner. It had to be the all-time worst week in Shay's life.

I put my hands on Beryl's shoulders and squeezed, trying to reassure her. Trapezius muscles, beneath pale skin, felt like rope left too long in the sun. When my fingers began exploring for knots, she shrugged my hands away, and said, "Those bastards. We have to find them. I'm *going* to find them."

I said, "Take it easy. I'm working on it."

"You've had three days to work on it. We're running out of time."

In more ways than Beryl realized. It was nearly midnight.

An hour earlier, for the benefit of the hidden camera, I'd made a show of getting ready for bed. The only thing I'd brought to read was the article Sir James had given me on the Knights Templar. I took it from my bag, adjusted the reading lamp, and lay on the bed.

The Knights Templar was a fraternity of warrior monks founded in 1118 by André de Montbard and Hugh de Payen. These two knights, along with seven companions, presented themselves to Godfroi de Bouillon, ruler of Jerusalem . . .

I paused to clean my glasses. André de Montbard? If James Montbard was a descendant, how many generations separated the two men? Twenty-five? Thirty? In the U.S., the time span was incomprehensible. In Great Britain, ancestral records and properties might date back even farther.

It was their intention, they told the monarch, to organize an order of able monks to protect pilgrims traveling to Jerusalem — the Knights Templar. Because the Templars took sacred oaths of honesty, chastity, and loyalty, they soon became the trusted guardians of travelers to the Holy Land, and also the world's first international bankers. They accumulated enormous wealth during the Crusades.

By the 1300s, the Templars controlled more wealth and land than most kingdoms, and they had the largest sailing fleet in the world. There is evidence the Templars were already doing trade in the Americas.

When the Templars began to exceed the Vatican's power, Pope Clement V ordered all members arrested. Some were burned at the stake, but most escaped, preserving their order, and their secrets, by founding a new secret fraternity, the Freemasons.

The Templar sailing fleet disappeared, as did their vast treasure holdings, which included artifacts from the Holy Land taken as spoils of war.

Some historians believe they loaded their vessels and sailed west toward the land they had discovered two hundred years before Columbus . . .

No wonder Sir James Montbard, the Freemason and amateur archaeologist, wanted to have a look around the monastery. Lots of linkage. But it had the fantasy flavor of a conspiracy theory. If I ever meet more than three people who can keep a secret, I'll give conspiracy theories serious consideration.

Interesting, but I had things to do.

Before turning out the reading lamp, I took a sleepy look around my room, then tossed a shirt over the clock radio, covering the miniature lens. I spent the next twenty minutes in the dark, expecting spa employees to arrive with an excuse to check the room.

Nothing.

I got dressed, poked my head outside, then took a few things from the pack I'd hidden overhead in the gallery bay. Among them was the little Uniden handheld VHF, which I clipped to my belt. Montbard said he would attempt radio contact at 6 p.m., 9 p.m., and midnight, but I hadn't been able to risk retrieving the VHF until now.

By 11:30, I was working my way through shadows to the opposite cloister, jumpy as hell, spooking at every sound. It was supposed to be safe inside the monastery walls. Even so, I expected dogs to come tumbling out of the darkness.

The three fingers Beryl had flashed earlier — the meaning had popped into my head as I suffered through a sauna treatment, sweating imaginary toxins I hadn't allowed Norma to purge.

"The guest rooms are numbered," Norma had told me. "It's one-two-three simple."

Three.

I was in Room 36, Senegal was in 7. Beryl was telling me her room number — 3. Obvious, in hindsight, as most puzzles are.

Now Beryl and I were huddled in her closet, out of the range of the lens hidden in the smoke alarm — a useless precaution if someone had been monitoring the place when Beryl opened the door wide, saying, *"Doc?"* and I stepped into room.

Any second, I expected to hear pounding at the door.

Yes, nearly midnight, and we were running out of time.

I touched my cheek to Beryl's cheek, and whispered, "You're obsessing on the three guys, but it's more complicated than you think. Trust me, I'll do something if there's an opportunity. I'm more concerned about you. We have to get you off this mountain. Soon. They're already suspicious."

"Who?"

"Everyone, including the woman who owns the place. She's the blackmailer. You don't think she knows who she's blackmailing, for Christ's sake? The staff's scared shitless of her. Think about that."

Beryl was too angry to think about it. "The woman with the bizarre robes, the hood, all the makeup? You've got to be kidding."

"No. I'm convinced."

"*Isabelle?* I've met her four or five times — at least twice at the trade show in Paris. There's nothing scary about Isabelle — unless you're afraid of dyke nuns. Maybe that's your problem."

"Afraid of nuns?"

"You tell me. Afraid of the party boys, I can understand. If you don't have the balls for confrontation, okay. But afraid of a middle-aged woman who dresses like Madonna? I think Shay chose the wrong man for the job.

412

The three who came to the beach cottage that night, they're the blackmailers. If you're afraid of them, just admit it."

I took a breath and released it slowly, letting Beryl know that my patience had its limits. Some people strike out at anyone and everything when they're angry. Beryl was in attack mode.

"I wasted an entire day walking around this nuthouse with people in robes. Now you tell me a woman who grows orchids and markets face cream is the one who took the video. Do you really think Isabelle sent those sick e-mails? That she gets her rocks off by filming people screwing? *Please.*"

"You haven't done the research, Beryl. I have."

"*Research?* My God — you really are just a biologist, aren't you? The rumors about you being a dangerous character — a drug smuggler, a government agent, *whatever* — what a laugh. Shay was feeding us a bunch of bullshit. How could I ... how could anyone've believed that a guy who looks like a science teacher is dangerous?"

"I never asked anyone to believe anything."

"Really? I'm not so sure. Your secret trips, the mysterious men who come to the lab — did you invent those stories? Or did Shay?

413

She's good at making up stories, I know."

I had just checked my watch but now, instead of replying, I looked at it again. 12:18 a.m. Once again, I'd missed the radio appointment with Sir James. Outside, thunder rumbled through the forest canopy. There was a whistle of gusting wind. I listened until I'd confirmed it was the sound of a squall approaching, not the distant howling of dogs.

I said, "We can talk about your best friend, Shay, another time. Let's concentrate on you. You can't spend another night here. It's too dangerous. I know a man who owns an estate on Saint Lucia. You can stay there until you catch a flight out."

Beryl groaned — *Here we go again.* "I am not leaving this island. If I go anywhere, it'll be to the beach house where we were filmed."

"What are you talking about? It's a rental. You can't just show up."

"You're so full of wisdom, Doc. You're also full of something else. I called and gave the realtor a credit card Sunday after I found out about Corey. I rented the place through Saturday. I'll bet anything those jerks are still hanging out at the resort, like the night they showed up. They're stalkers. I know the type. Pretty girls all alone, they can't resist.

It's what they do."

I said, "Pretty girls?"

"Shay's as mad as I am. I told you the wedding was postponed for three weeks. The Italian guy from the marina, Eddie, may fly her down to join me."

"Eddie?"

"You're the one who told me he's a pilot."

"First you said the wedding was postponed for two weeks. Now you say three weeks. Which is it?"

"I told you three weeks. Your hearing must be going, too."

I was sure she'd said two weeks, but there was no point in arguing. I asked, "What will the pretty girls do if the men who assaulted you show up?"

"That's something I've had a lot of time to think about," Beryl replied in an aloof, impatient way that was becoming familiar. "Make them pay for what they've done — isn't that justice? We'll deal with them. Don't worry."

Eerie, the way she said that. Like it was something she'd been thinking about for years.

The sound track I'd heard in the spa was now being piped into Beryl's room. The lulling percussion of ocean waves . . . the faint yip and moan of seabirds in the background.

Somewhere, someone had hit a switch. I wondered if there were speakers in all the rooms. Speakers can also be microphones.

I waited in the closet while Beryl peeked outside to see if anyone was watching, then she moved around the room and blew out all but one candle. Her white nightgown became translucent when she picked up the candle. As she walked toward me, I wanted to look away but couldn't.

"Hey . . . are you okay? Why don't you answer me?" Beryl stood at the closet entrance, whispering, holding the candle at breast level, a glass of something in her other hand.

I said, "What . . . ? Sorry . . . my mind was on something else."

"I was talking about the white noise from those speakers. I asked if they played it in the spa when you went through that purification business. Beach sounds, crashing waves. Same thing last night, all night long. It was irritating at first . . . but then it got so I liked it. I went to sleep, finally, but I had weird dreams." She sipped from the glass. "Want some? Herbal tea."

"No. How were they weird?"

"The dreams? Don't ask. It's personal. I'll

just say they were . . . unusual."

I said, "Oh," with no idea what she meant. At least she was less combative. I looked at the smoke alarm wired next to the ceiling fan. "I've got to go."

She put the glass on a table and touched her fingers to my chest. "Doc?"

"Beryl?"

"I shouldn't have been so hard on you. I've been furious for the last three days, and I was venting. Sorry. I don't really believe you invented stories. And I don't think you're a coward. It's just that . . . well, I think maybe I expected too much from you."

"Not unusual. I do it all the time — to myself."

She laid a light hand on my arm and patted me the way people do when they are trying to comfort themselves. "You're an intelligent guy, I should respect that. If you think it's not safe, I'll leave. But first, I'll arrange a meeting, and ask Isabelle a few questions. I won't mention we know each other. Maybe start out like I'm asking for advice. 'My girlfriends and I did something foolish, do you have any influence with the local police?' Like that. If she gets tricky, if she lies to me, I'll know."

"Don't do that. Please."

"How else are we going to find out?"

"I told you: I'm convinced. I don't need to find out." There was something about the familiar way she said *Isabelle* that set off an internal alarm, so I asked, "Did you get my e-mail? I sent one to Shay, too."

Beryl shook her head. "Something important?"

"Maybe. Shay's fiancé told me his family had been doing business in the Caribbean for years. He mentioned a marina and resort on Saint Lucia. In the e-mail, I asked if his family had any other holdings in the area."

"I can answer that — yes, they do. Sort of. The reason I know is because my father's involved. You know what he does — buys hotels in trouble, and we turn them into high-end spas. He just locked up a deal on Saint Vincent. Michael's mother and some of his aunts are investors."

I said, "Does Shay know that?"

"There's no reason why she should. I'm not even sure Michael knows. Have you ever met his mother, Ida? Ida doesn't share information, she collects it like ammunition. She'll be the mother-in-law from hell."

"Any chance that Isabelle Toussaint is an investor, too?"

"I doubt that. My father may have consulted her as a sort of courtesy thing. He's

a thorough man, and it's a tight little industry. How do you think I got into the Orchid
without a reservation?"

I was thinking, *incredible*. Unlike Tomlinson, I believe in coincidence. Life is a
series of random intersections that conform to a statistical pattern, so coincidence is inevitable. But when multiple
coincidences create their own pattern, I
become wary.

"When Shay was researching places to
rent, who told her about the beach house?"

"I thought she found it on the Internet. But
I guess —" Beryl put a hand to her mouth
and yawned. "— I guess it's possible she
asked around for advice. Maybe my father,
I don't know. She didn't ask me, because it
was a surprise."

I was looking over the woman's shoulder.
On the far wall, near the meditation corner,
was a familiar painting. A child's crib. White,
like the painting I'd seen in Toussaint's château. Strange.

Beryl yawned again, dozy enough to smile,
and said, "You enjoy this, don't you?"
sounding more like the woman who'd stood
in my lab, wearing a towel. "Helping friends,
I mean — Shay told me that about you. Putting together all the little pieces when someone's life gets broken. True?"

I said, "Sometimes. I don't like clutter."

"I'm the same way, you know. Chaos, I can't stand it. Life should be balanced. Fair . . . but lots of times it's not. So I can relate . . . sort of. You're like some Boy Scout who goes around neatening up a world that's way too messy. That's how we're different. I'm not nearly as respectable as I pretend to be."

Beryl had said something similar in the hospital parking lot, then again when she spoke of her abduction. This time, though, her tone was affectionate and dreamy . . . like the steady flood and thunder of waves from unseen speakers, the volume turned louder now.

The woman moved a step closer, her face and auburn hair golden above the candle, like an old photo. "I can prove it to you, if you want. Do you really have to leave?"

I cupped the flame with my hand, looking up at her as I answered. "Yes. But it's not because I took some kid's oath. If you go to that beach house alone, Beryl, don't expect a Boy Scout to save the pretty girl this time. It might not happen."

"Are you being mean because I criticized Shay?"

"No. I'm being honest. I want you out of here in the morning. The first helicopter leaves at nine. If the helicopter's full, take the ferry. Okay?"

I blew out the candle and left.

29

As I exited Beryl's room, I heard a latch open a few doors down, and I ducked into the shadows of an arched recess in the cloister wall — a space created for religious artifacts, not men my size. I tried to flatten myself as the door opened and an equally large man stepped out. Because of LEDs on the balustrades, there was enough light for me to recognize Fabron.

I relaxed a little, tempted to step out and let him see me. I had my reasons.

I didn't like Fabron. It wasn't just because of his indifference at the cliff that morning. As I left Norma's massage room, I'd found Fabron and another staffer waiting in the hall, eager to punish me with the Orchid's sweat lodge rotation. For two hours, they'd ping-ponged me between a sauna, a steam bath, and a cold-water dip pool, berating me as I transitioned from oven to ice.

Fabron was dangerous, as Norma had

said. He was also a sadist. He and his partner taunted me in the good-natured way sadists do, testing me with insults — my thick glasses, the scars, my farmer's tan — trying their damnedest to get a reaction. It didn't happen.

I rotated from sauna to ice pool, wearing a fixed smile as if enjoying myself, even though I was monitoring a growing fury. But maybe it was therapeutic after Norma's massage. Imaginary or not, I felt like I was on ching chi overload. Thoughts of Beryl, Senegal . . . and Norma, too, all added to the fluttering abdominal tension and genitalic barometrics that define extreme male horniness. It was easier to deal with in the plunge pool where water was a scrotum-numbing fifty degrees.

I endured that circuit for two hours. For two hours I smiled, which only made Fabron madder. So he pushed harder, and the insults got nastier, but never once did he see me flinch. It wasn't until another Novitiate banged on the door that I let Fabron see my distress.

"Does this mean we have to stop?" I asked, frowning for the first time. "Or did the real therapist finally show up?"

Fabron and I locked eyes. In those clarifying seconds the façade crumbled, all the bullshit pretense vanished.

I hoped that Fabron and I would have our day. So did he.

Now here he was.

Fabron was tucking in his shirt as he let the heavy door swing shut, and I heard him say, "Silly bitch." The door didn't close completely. He didn't notice or didn't care. Just kept walking, working at his shirt.

I relaxed, stepped into the light as he hurried toward the quadrangle, and I fought the temptation to whistle him back. But then another man appeared from my right, and I lunged for the shadows again as he called in a loud whisper, "Hey there, Fabron. *Fabron.* How you doing, man?"

It was another staffer. He followed Fabron a few steps . . . called his name again . . . then stopped in front of me, ten yards away. The man looked familiar — a mistake I'd made before. White shirt with logo, white pants, a large round man with an oversized round head, black hair slicked back, wearing sunglasses on this moonless night and smoking a cigarillo that smelled of maple syrup in the dense sea air.

Christ . . . I *did* recognize him. It was the bagman from the bank. The one who'd been in the camera blind shooting video, and owned the dog that almost nailed me above the beach cottage. Sir James had said his name was Deepak Wulfelund — the one they called Wolfie. He was older than Fabron and Ritchie and the others; the one who I suspected had more power. Which meant he was more closely linked with Isabelle Toussaint. So why was I surprised to see him?

Beryl was mad because the party boys weren't at the monastery — which made no sense because she's not a woman easily forgotten. Now here was the fourth, and he was just as likely to recognize her. Wolfie was also the only man on the island who could ID me. The two of us had spent half an hour at the Bank of Aruba, sizing each other up, not bothering to disguise our mutual contempt.

It wasn't a large place. Wolfie would spot me tomorrow or the next day, and tell Toussaint that I'd okayed Shay's money transfer. She'd run me off the island. Or worse. Probably much worse. They might use the dogs, or the cliff . . . or both, as they had with Norma's teenaged nephew.

I couldn't let that happen.

Preemptive strike is the military term. But was it my best option? I had to think this one through. I was no longer authorized to take extreme action. I couldn't go running to the nearest embassy if I got in trouble. There would be no choppers sent to extract me. What were prisons like in the Eastern Caribbean?

But then I thought of Corey's family, and I thought of Corey: an attractive, Cuban-looking girl, warm-eyed, sweet, who could've been an actress if her life hadn't intersected with predatory men. Her husband was one. Deepak Wulfelund was another.

Preemptive action was the right choice.

I touched a hand to the back of my pants and repositioned the little Colt semiautomatic. I don't like using guns. They're loud. They're impersonal. But I would let it play out, and do what I had to do.

I watched Fabron return, smiling and shaking his head. He banged Wolfie's outstretched fist, the way ballplayers sometimes do, saying, "No luck with the ladies tonight? Me neither, man. I've been downed twice, and the bitch in that room slapped me. That's enough." For a moment, I thought Fabron was pointing at me, but he was pointing at the door only a few feet away. How could he not see me?

He didn't.

Fabron said to Wolfie, "Probably a good thing to get some rest after last night, hey, man?" his accent more Caribbean than French now that he was alone with a friend. "These women, Wolfie, they're wearin' me out."

They laughed, voices low.

Wolfie said, "Yeah, man, yeah. Wait 'til you been working for the Widow long as me. I've seen women — you want to talk stories? We get the Canadian ladies, the German ladies, the ones from hick towns back in the States. They get down here so cold, all they want is to get warm and show how hip they are. Hear what I'm sayin'? One day, you and me, we'll get us a case of Piton and talk stories."

Then Wolfie said, suddenly serious, "My man, we've got something important to take care of tonight. That's why I been looking for you. We got another problem — sort of like last night, that kid. Only this time it's a woman. And it's someone we work with. That bother you?"

"Who we talking about?"

"Answer my question. Something like that bother you?"

"No. Nothing bothers me, man. First time for everything, eh? But if she looks okay, you know, got a decent body, we don't want to just waste something like that. That's why I'm asking —"

"Man, you do whatever you want with her. We discussing a woman who did something very stupid. Created a serious situation here, and the Widow, she found out. The Widow has her ways, you know. So she's taking care of business . . . in the way the Maji Blanc takes care of business."

Wolfie meant something by that, I could tell by Fabron's sudden interest — a touch of awe in his voice, asking, "She's taking care of the woman personally — right now? As we stand here?"

"She'll probably get started in ten, maybe fifteen minutes."

A smile came into Wolfie's voice. "You ain't never witnessed the Maji Blanc with your own eyes, have you? You want to watch our Lady come out in her robes — she sortta floats. I've *seen* it — torches burning, big ol' fire. And her skin is so white, man, it glows. Like a fucking movie, I'm telling you."

Fabron chuckled, maybe sounding skeptical, which Wolfie didn't like. "You don't believe in the spirits, man? You witness the Maji Blanc just once, and you'll be wearin' beads and mixin' turpentine with bluestone along with the rest of us. Dirk, he didn't believe — he spoke a profanity toward the Widow, and you see where he is tonight? In hospital. A creature come out of the night, only one eye in his head. The La'Ja'bless, size of a fucking gorilla, and he crushed Dirk's ribs. You're hearing this from me, a man who was *there.* The spirit world's real. Don't you be laughing when discussing these matters."

Fabron said, "Hey, I'm not laughing at that. I'm very respectful to what you're saying. That's why — do you think I could see it with my own eyes?"

Wolfie put a heavy hand on Fabron's shoulder, turning him, and began walking — the wise elder taking charge. "In that case, why'nt we go to the Lookout first, and burn something special? You want a very mellow mood in your head before you see the Maji Blanc. If you still up for it then, I'll ask the Widow can you see this special thing."

I waited until the two men were halfway across the quadrangle before I stepped into the light. I'd give them a minute before following . . . but then I noticed the room number on the door that Fabron had left ajar. Room 7.

You silly bitch.

Senegal.

When I cracked the door, I heard Senegal yell, "Stay away! I'll call the police, damn you. The British Consulate, too. Get out!"

Something metallic banged the wall, and I realized she'd thrown a candleholder.

I gave it a few seconds, knocked politely, then stuck my head in, whispering, "Senny? Senny, it's me." I hoped the familiar nickname would register before she threw something else.

It did.

"Doctor —"

"Quiet. No need to say my name."

"You're not . . . wait . . . I don't —"

I pushed the door wider and held a finger to my lips. *Shhhhh.*

There was the sound of ocean waves in this dimly lit room where there was a lamp broken on the floor and bedsheets were in a heap near an overturned chair. It looked like the aftermath of a fight.

Senegal, in her dressing gown, was a wilted gray shape in the corner, a glass in her hand, ready to throw. She stepped away from the wall when she recognized me, and I touched my lips again.

She moved closer, whispering, "I'm very glad you're here."

I was looking at the ceiling. No smoke alarm, no fire sprinklers. On the chest of drawers, though, was a radio clock like mine. Senegal said nothing as I walked toward the clock as if approaching a snake, then slowly turned it toward the wall.

"Why are you —?"

I shook my head — *quiet* — as I walked around the bed and put my hands on her arms. I expected a response when I pulled her close and put my cheek next to hers. There was none. The woman leaned against my chest, stiff as a mannequin.

"Keep your voice down. There's a miniature camera in the clock. Probably a microphone hidden somewhere, too."

"I suspected."

"It's okay. I don't think they can monitor all the rooms at the same time. Odds are in our favor — especially if they believe I work here. I think the staff visits the guests on a regular basis."

She nodded, her body beginning to tremble as she said in a normal voice, "Of course I know who you are. You work here. It's good to see you again."

The woman caught on fast.

I put my mouth next to her ear. "Senny . . . it's all right now. He's gone."

She nodded again. "Are you very sure?" Her nightgown was damp. Her skin felt too cool.

"Yes. You're safe."

Slowly, as if thawing, her body softened against my chest. She moved her hands to

431

the back of my shoulders, relying on them to support her weight as she melted into me. I felt her shudder, then felt her breath on my neck as she whispered, "How bloody awful to have to pretend to be brave when you're not."

I said, "That's the definition of bravery."

"You're wrong, I'm afraid. It really is a bastard of an act to pull off."

"Whatever you did, it worked. He's not coming back."

"You're certain."

"One way or the other, yes, I'm certain."

The woman pulled away, and stood on her own. "I feel absolutely drained. He almost saw me cry — silly of me to care about something so trivial, but I didn't want to give him satisfaction. And I didn't, by God!"

Senegal was a tough one, already rallying. I was relieved, but had to remind her, "Your voice. Whisper."

"Yes, of course." She looked at the clock radio, then at the mess on the floor. "I was being filmed the entire time . . . with him?"

"Filmed or monitored. Maybe both."

"Then we finally have the bugger. He thought he could seduce me again. When I refused, he tried to force me. I gave him a hell of a whack on the face. If a jury sees the film, off he goes to prison. Fabron — such an absurd name."

I said, "Seduce you again?"

"Yes." The woman moved from the shadows to the bed, and sat in silence for several seconds, neatening her nightgown. I reached into the bathroom, hit the switch, then adjusted the door so a wafer of light reached her. Her sleeve was ripped. Buttons were missing from her gown.

"Did he hurt you?"

"No. This time I fought back. He was the one who came to the villa the night I was filmed. I never thought I'd see him again. But when I showed up for my massage appointment, there he was. Came into the room after I was already undressed and under the sheet — smiling that sickening smile of his.

"He recognized me, of course. Expected to continue where we'd left off. So I've been doing it all day, pretending to be brave. He damn near succeeded during the massage. He . . . knew how to do things with his hands. I nearly gave in, but I didn't. Then about ten minutes ago, he tapped on my door and wanted to give it another try. I'd hoped it was you."

There was a carafe filled with herbal tea and ice on the nightstand. She poured as she whispered, drinking from the glass she'd intended to throw. I shook my head when she offered it to me, then watched her gulp the glass empty.

"I was parched . . . didn't even realize it until this moment. But what I really need is a tumbler of gin. God, what I'd give for a bottle of iced Plymouth." She laughed — yes, a strong woman — then looked toward the light that angled from the bathroom. "Would we be safer there?"

I said, "I'll check." A few seconds later, I said, "It's clear."

She was still thirsty. The glass hid her face as she came toward me. I was saying, "I think it's best if we —" but stopped as she lowered the glass. When Senegal saw my expression, she looked at the floor, as if ashamed, and covered her left cheek with the palm of her hand. "It's not that bad, is it?"

I had to move her hand to look. What I'd mistaken for shadow was a bruise that was beginning to swell, already showing purple hues.

"He hit you."

She nodded, still looking at the floor. When I released her hand, she used it to hide the bruise again.

"More than once?"

"No. Well . . . only hard once. But I told

you, I hit him first. Gave him a hell of a whack. I was surprised no one heard us! And during the massage, I let him go farther than I should — it's only right to admit it. I don't know what got into me. So, in a way, he's not entirely to blame."

It was a struggle to keep my voice low. "That's nonsense. You know it." Now I was beginning to shake.

"I'm only trying to be fair. And there's something else — please understand. I can't bear to have my photo in any more magazines. Or more stories telling lies about my personal life. A woman who whores about in the tropics, that's how they'll portray me. It's precisely what will happen if we complain to management, or the police —"

I said, "You're in charge. I won't say a word," as I sat next her. "Whatever you tell me to do, I'll do. So calm down, it's going to be okay. We need to get some ice on that bruise."

"Thank you. I can't tell you how much I appreciate your understanding —" Senegal flinched when I rested my hand on her shoulder, then turned to look at me. "Your body's shaking. Why?"

I stood and found the ice bucket. "I'm upset," I said, because it was easier than explaining symptoms of rage. "It's not safe here. As a favor, I'd like you to return to Saint Lucia in the morning. There's a woman in Room three, a few doors down. Her name's Beryl. She's leaving on the first helicopter, too."

"You met her here?"

"It's a long story. Do you remember my room number? If there's trouble, go there. The door's unlocked."

I handed her a washcloth packed with ice, and watched her touch it to her face. "I'll have some things to do, so don't worry if I'm not there." I drew the little semiautomatic and tossed it on the bed. "Use this if you need to — and don't forget about Beryl. She's a friend."

I made sure the woman's door locked behind me, and I jogged toward the cliff they called the Lookout.

30

The employee who had created a situation, who had done something stupid, was Norma. As far as I knew, all she'd done was entrust me with the truth. If that was her crime, the truth had a heavy price on this island.

Fabron had the woman over his shoulder, carrying her toward the rim of the cliff that jutted out over the sea. She was rolled into a section of carpet, like a mummy. I didn't realize there was a person inside, at first. Didn't know it was Norma until they passed me, almost to the cliff.

The only reason I happened to spot Fabron was because he and Wolfie weren't where I'd expected to find them, so I'd gone searching. Toussaint's château was the logical second stop. Fabron wanted to see the Maji Blanc in her robes, with torches burning. Wolfie was his eager mentor. So that's the direction I headed.

I was almost to the cemetery when I noticed

a figure in the distance. I had been walking fast, not jogging, sometimes turning full circles without stopping — alert. It was the only reason I saw Fabron before he saw me. Noticed a large shadow coming through the trees. The shadow became a man walking in the slow, staggering way men walk when they're carrying something heavy.

I had knelt behind gravestones and waited. Saw that it was Fabron when he took out a flashlight and shined it around. I saw that he was carrying a roll of something — carpet, maybe — and knew there had to be a person inside because of the weight, and what else bends to conform to a man's shoulder?

Had he killed Wolfie?

I thought about it as he came closer, headed for the cliff. No . . . Fabron was big, but Wolfie was bigger. There was no way the man could carry Wolfie's corpse several hundred yards.

A corpse, that was my assumption. It was a thing — no movement, no cries of protest. But, as Fabron passed, the thing became a person again, dead or alive, because I recognized who it was. When he used the flashlight again, I saw a corded, butternut forearm, and the profile of a woman's face and head flopping puppetlike on Fabron's back.

Norma.

Maybe there was a hidden microphone in the massage room, but why kill her just for confiding in me, a guest? Or maybe it had to do with her job. She'd told me she was quitting soon. But then I reminded myself that Toussaint and her people didn't need much of a reason. The night before, they'd killed Norma's teenage nephew for pilfering orchids . . . or maybe he'd simply come to visit his aunt.

Evil is seldom original. Typically, evil's color is gray. The common criminal is *common.* Most are the spawn of yawning stupidity and the intellectually stunted. But Madame Toussaint was not a common criminal. She inflicted pain for profit. She enjoyed humiliating her victims, and it was unsettling to imagine how Norma had died.

Fabron was a kindred sadist. I could hear him saying, *If the woman's got a decent body, why waste a chance at something like that?* Toussaint would probably name him employee of the month.

Fabron was moving so slowly, I'd have no trouble intercepting him at the cliff. But where was Wolfie?

I was at the Lookout waiting when Fabron came huffing and puffing into the clearing and dumped Norma's body onto the ground.

Despite the carpet shroud, her body made a flesh-and-bone *thump* when it hit.

Still no sign of Wolfie.

Fabron was big and lean, but he was cramping after carrying Norma's body all that way. I watched him shrug and stretch, and roll his head — a massage therapist dealing with his own blockages — close enough that I could hear his breathing, and whispered profanities. I must have sounded like I was right beside him when I spoke. Raised my voice to ask, "Need a back rub, Fabio? Bad timing, killing Norma tonight."

"Huh?" The man whirled around, then used the flashlight to scan the area. Nothing to see in this clearing but the stone cross, the bench, the safety railing . . . and a solitary tree angling from the precipice, over the sea. I hadn't tried to disguise my voice, but the ocean updraft had a hollow resonance. Fabron couldn't pinpoint the source.

"Enjoy the ceremony? Did the Maji Blanc's skin really glow? Maybe she'll pay you a visit. Leave you all scratched and bruised . . . like you left Senegal Firth."

The Frenchman turned again. "Funny game, trying to scare me. I am laughing!" But he didn't laugh. I watched him take three careful steps and use the flashlight to check behind the stone cross. Then he yelled, *"Who are you?"*

"Wolfie told you who I am. The La'Ja'bless, remember? I'm here . . . behind you."

Fabron didn't fall for it. He crouched low, searching with the flashlight, fine-tuning with his ears, but was maybe actually scared, so I called, "I sent Dirk to the hospital. Crushed his ribs. Maybe I'll send you to hell. Why did you kill Norma?"

Fabron yelled, "I didn't!" then took a deep breath, gathering himself as his head vectored slowly toward the solitary tree. He painted the canopy with his flashlight and began to creep toward the edge of the cliff, eyes fixed as he pulled something else from his pocket — a switchblade. He flipped the knife open, calling, *"Where* are you?"

I didn't reply. I was peering through exposed roots on the tree's seaward side where, the night before, I'd tied the hundred feet of braided anchor line. My feet were on a narrow section of the goat path — a ledge not wide enough for my size 13 running shoes, so I had knotted a rough rappelling harness and roped myself in.

Fabron was a curious man. He'd find out where I was — soon, I hoped. I didn't want to spend any more time than I had to clinging to roots several hundred feet above the sea. The rope would hold, but I wasn't sure about the tree. Loose stones and earth had showered down when I lowered myself to the ledge. Felt as if the roots were breaking free — a sickening sensation.

I'd looked down only once. The phosphorescent cresting of waves below resembled the lights of a village seen from a jetliner. If the tree busted free, I would go with it.

"Are you tired of your game? Why don't you answer?" Fabron was closing in, and he no longer sounded rattled. Didn't he believe that a one-eyed creature, the La'Ja'bless, roamed the night?

No . . . he didn't believe, because then he said, "You think you're invisible? You're only invisible to yourself. Maybe you should clean your ugly fucking glasses!" He was standing directly over me now.

I had my left hand on what I hoped was a solid root, my right hand on the rope where it was knotted to the tree. I waited . . . waited even though he was close enough . . . waited several slow seconds, expecting him to poke his head over the roots to peer down.

He didn't. In the silence of whistling wind, the distant percussion of waves below, I became aware of an incongruous sound . . . a faint but rhythmic sawing noise . . .

Shit.

Fabron had discovered the rope and was

cutting it with the switchblade.

In one motion, I vaulted up onto the rock rim using the rope and roots for leverage. Got my upper body onto solid ground, while my legs dangled . . . and there was Fabron on his knees, sawing frantically, his left side to the tree, the flashlight nearby. He turned when he heard me and swung the knife, trying to pin my hand to the tree. When I yanked my hand away, he lunged and tried to stab me again . . . then grinned as I began to slide back over the edge.

Because there was nothing else to grab, I grabbed Fabron's long hair — he wouldn't risk stabbing himself in the head. I yanked and kept yanking until he dropped the knife to pry my left hand free. When he did, I caught his wrist with my right hand, and augered my thumb between tendon and ulnar nerve until my fingers were anchored.

Fabron began sliding with me over the cliff's edge.

The man swore . . . then screamed, as my weight pulled him downward. He scratched and pounded at my fist, trying to free himself. But we continued to slide. For an instant, we were face-to-face — me looking up, Fabron looking down. He had the wild black eyes of an animal unaccustomed to darkness.

"Let go — you're insane. You're hurting me!"

I said, "Like you hurt the English woman?" I had threaded my left arm through a space where a huge root was anchored to rock, but my right hand was still locked on his wrist. I continued pulling him downward.

"What did that bitch tell you? She *asked* for it. She's lying!"

I said, "No. *You* asked for it. And you're dying."

I released the wrist, got a handful of his hair, and gave a final yank. The man shrieked as he tumbled over me. But instead of tumbling clear, he got an arm around my neck, and we both fell . . . fell until the rope jolted taut, humming with the strain of our combined weight.

The impact bounced us away from the cliff, over the water . . . back to the rocks . . . over the water . . . then back again . . . amid a shower of stones and the machine-gun crackle of breaking tree roots. Each time a root ripped free, there was another jolting descent of a few inches as the tree began to fall in slow motion.

Fabron had managed to keep his right arm locked around my neck, but he was slipping. As he slipped, he screamed, "Loop the rope around me. For God's sake, loop the rope around my waist!"

Then, he went silent. He felt my fingers on his right wrist, prying, squeezing, levering. His chest spasmed. He was crying, I realized, as he moaned, "Don't . . . I'm begging you. We're both going to die!"

I told him, "Don't we all?" and popped his hand free.

He fell, and I watched . . . watched as he shrank into a funneling darkness despite his clawing attempts to fly. The last desperate words of grown men, good and bad, are often a child's cry.

"Mamaaaaaaaan."

Fabron's scream lingered, then faded into vacuous silence that was dizzying.

I looked away, then at the tree above. Roots were holding now. No more firecracker popping . . . just the open-sea sound of wind . . . and somewhere, the muted howling of a dog.

Hand over hand, I climbed the rope and pulled myself over the rim. I staggered farther from the ledge than necessary to be safe, then rested on one knee while my head throbbed and my pounding heart began to slow. After a minute or so, I walked to where Fabron had dumped Norma's body.

The carpet was there, but it had been

rolled out flat. Norma was gone.

What the hell . . . ?

Had Fabron dumped her off the cliff without me noticing?

No, impossible.

Or maybe Wolfie had come along and . . .

No, Wolfie would've cut the rope to get rid of me before bothering with a dead woman.

I'd hidden my radio and flashlight in a crevice near the tree. With the flashlight, I returned to the carpet. I found traces of blood, and a balled-up wad of duct tape. Several yards away, I found another wad of tape.

I smiled. Norma was alive. Hurt . . . maybe badly hurt, but still strong enough to free herself and get away.

I called her name, but not loud. I walked toward a wall of trees where chain-link fence bordered the monastery grounds. Found another strip of tape, and called, "Norma? *Norma,*" in a hoarse whisper.

She was gone.

I returned to the Lookout and gathered Fabron's flashlight, his knife, and searched for anything else he might have left behind. As I searched, I imagined the woman out there, hurt, bleeding. Where would an employee of the Orchid go if the boss lady wanted her dead?

Home, probably. Staff housing was down the mountain, not far from the road. Norma had told me her place was set off by itself. But that would mean climbing the fence. What about the dogs?

Maybe there was someone inside the compound Norma could trust. Could be that she was safe, already being taken care of by a friend. I hoped so. I occasionally meet a person I dislike initially, but end up liking intuitively. She was one of those.

A dog howled . . . then another. It came from the elevated darkness beyond the fence. Not far.

Out of habit, I patted the back of my pants even though I knew I'd left my gun with Senegal. I had the radio, though. Maybe Montbard was still in the area . . . even somewhere on the mountain — no telling with him.

I put the radio to my lips . . . then stopped and sniffed the heavy air. I pointed my nose at the stars and sniffed again, testing until I identified a familiar odor: cigar smoke. A combination of maple syrup and tobacco — a cigarillo.

Wolfie.

I crouched, pocketed the radio, flicked open Fabron's switchblade, then looked for an ambush spot. The rope again? No . . . no way in hell was I going back to that cliff. My muscles were twitching — part nerves, part exhaustion. Wolfie wasn't an athlete, didn't have the look of a brawler, but I was running low on fuel. I had to come up with something better. My eyes came to rest on the carpet. Wolfie would expect to find a body there. I gave it some thought — decided he would find a body.

I gathered the discarded duct tape and jammed a ball of it in my pocket — the stuff was still usable — then laid on the carpet. Instead of rolling myself into the center, I pulled a flap of it over me.

A few minutes later, I felt a small glycogen charge as Wolfie came tromping into the clearing. Hunters get the same feeling when they hear the snap of a twig telling them the quarry is approaching. He was swearing and complaining about lazy French playboys, pissed off at Fabron for not dumping Norma's body, his Caribbean accent so thick he was tough to understand. Then I waited through several seconds of silence before he said, "Dumb bitch!" and I pictured him looking at the carpet, thinking he'd have to carry Norma's corpse the final few yards. Lazy.

I felt the weight of his foot on the carpet.

Expected him to give it a kick, and he did.

"Bitch. *Answer* me. You dead under there? You not, you will be."

He was scared. I don't know why I was surprised. Death is communicable, one of the oldest superstitions. It would've been funny — if it wasn't actually happening. But it was.

"Hey . . . you hear me?" He kicked the carpet again. Another long silence, then he began talking to himself. "Ain't nothing to be scared of. If she's dead, she already with the Gran' Bois. She got no reason to do me harm. I got my beads and bones. I'm *protected.* Nothing evil's gonna mess with me."

I heard a rattling noise, like dice — maybe Wolfie was clutching a necklace – but then he began second-guessing himself, whispering, "But where's Fabron if there ain't no danger? The Maji Blanc . . . could be. A damn *anansi noir* could be crawling on the woman's body right now, eating the woman's heart. *Shit.*"

In a louder voice, I heard him say, "Gonna kill that French batty boy." Then he yelled, "Fab-b-b-ron. Fab-RON! Better answer me, you punk-ass! You nothing but a whoring milk bottle with a dick — get back here and do your damn job!"

I had the knife and blinding Triad flash-light ready. Wolfie had to pull the carpet back sooner or later.

It was sooner. Because I'd been under the carpet, the night sky seemed brighter when Wolfie yanked the carpet away. When I moved, the man exhaled a muted scream and stumbled backward, as if Norma's spirit had grabbed him. He jumped again when I rolled to my feet, blinded him with the flashlight, and pointed the knife.

"Seen any good movies lately, Wolfie?"

"Who . . . who the hell are you?" He used his hands to shield his eyes from the light.

"A film critic. What's it matter?"

I lowered the light enough for him to see the knife. He put his hands up automatically, but still couldn't see me. He'd been scared, now he was close to panic. He began moving sideways, trying to get an angle so he could run toward the safety of the monastery. I moved with him, keeping my back to the place.

"You ain't her. There was a woman here, she's supposed to be —"

"Dead? Maybe I am dead."

I pointed the light at the ground, and he squinted at me. "You can't be dead. You're bleedin'."

I touched the scratches on my face and

looked at my fingers. "It's not my blood."

Wolfie stopped trying to slip around me and began backing away. "You're lying."

"Fabron said the same thing."

"Fabron? Did you . . . ?"

I swept the flashlight toward the Lookout. Because Wolfie expected me to say something, I said nothing. Instead, I switched the light off. Let the man deal with darkness now.

"You killed him?"

"No."

"Then what the hell you mean —"

I said, "Rocks killed him when he hit," as I pointed the light at Wolfie and touched the button. His face contorted as if he'd been shocked.

"Man, why you doing this to me! I don't even know you!"

"I know you."

"*How?* Okay, man, you're pissed off about something. Put that knife away, and we talk about it. Discuss what we do next."

I said, "There is no next. Not for you."

"But, man, we've never even met!"

I didn't reply. No way he could recognize me from our morning at the Bank of Aruba.

I started toward him, not sure what I would do. Eighteen times, I'd been precisely where

I was now, close enough to feel a man's last breath on my cheek. But it wasn't like Fabron, who'd done his best to kill me. And I wasn't carrying out orders. This time, the decision was mine.

Wolfie swung his head away. Behind him, the flashlight created a bright corridor of escape. Nothing back there but black forest, black sky, and the distant percussion of barking dogs.

He yelled, "I didn't do nothing, I swear!" Then he ran. I folded the knife and ran after him.

Wolfie had speed for a man his size. Faster than me. For the first minute, I thought I was going to lose him. But he lacked endurance. There was also something else that slowed him — the chain-link fence where it curved in close to the Lookout.

That's where I caught him. By the fence. He'd slowed to a jog, winded, lungs whistling. He reminded me of a wounded rhino as he crashed through brush inside the fence perimeter. He was turning to face me when I lowered my shoulder and cracked him from behind.

Cornered animals fight, and Wolfie did. I leveraged him onto his belly, then got my legs threaded through his, so he couldn't stand. When he tried to elbow me off, I caught his left wrist. I had the tape out and ready, and I used a half nelson to control his arm. I got a couple of wraps with the tape. Then I caught his right wrist.

I was taping his hands together when I heard a rushing, ascending noise that sounded like a mountain river. I swung the flashlight toward the fence just as two Brazilian mastiffs lunged for the top of the chain-link, trying to get at us, their orange eyes burning. Only then did they growl — more of a pack roar, really. It surprised me and scared me so badly that I vaulted off Wolfie. I rolled, and came up holding the switchblade, expecting the dogs to be over the fence.

No . . . the fence was just high enough for them to get their heads and paws over, but they couldn't lift their own weight.

I used the light. There were four dogs, not two. Rabid, slavering — a horror movie shown by a projector's bright beam on a screen that was black, not silver.

I moved the light to Wolfie. He was struggling to get his hands free. I'd used enough tape, so all he could do was look at me and yell, "I know those dogs, man! If I tell them to jump the damn fence, they'll do it! You cut me loose! Hear?"

I was afraid to take my eyes off the mastiffs. "They're your animals?" I had to talk louder to be heard.

"They'll do any damn thing I tell them!"

Wolfie the dog lover. I said, "You'd better hope so." I knelt and used the switchblade to cut his hands free, then touched the point of the knife to the hollow spot under his ear. "Get over that fence."

"What?"

"You heard me. Move."

"Why you doin' this to me? Motherfucker, we never even met!"

I wanted him to know. "A couple weeks ago, you filmed four girls, then blackmailed them. They're friends of mine. One of them's dead because of what you did."

I kept the knife to his neck as he got to his feet. He said, "Because of some damn women? That's why you're doing this?"

"Four girls from Florida. I met you at the bank."

"Man . . . I *remember* you. Those girls, too! But here's what you gotta understand: They come to this island asking for somethin', and the boys just gave 'em what they asked for. And you blame me? All this over some damn split-tails? You're shitting me, man!"

You're shitting me. Tomlinson had said almost the same thing the night hammerheads charged us. I would've rather dealt with

454

sharks than the dogs. But Wolfie chose the dogs — once I convinced him I would use the knife.

From the way he calmed the animals as he climbed to the top of the fence, cooing and calling their names, I thought I'd made a mistake. But then Wolfie made a mistake — he turned his back as he climbed down.

Packs don't have friends.

That's what I was thinking as I ran toward the monastery, sickened by the sounds.

31

When I opened the door to my room, a woman's voice startled me, saying, "Leave the lights off."

I knew who it was.

"I need a safe place. Is it okay?"

I said, "Sure," even though I wasn't sure.

She yawned. It sounded more like a groan. "Thanks. I don't think I've ever been so tired."

I pulled the door closed, eager to be inside, then waited while the woman's shape acquired definition as my eyes adjusted. She was in bed, under the covers. The sound of ocean waves still rumbled from the speakers, but not as loud now. I emptied my pockets on the table, then felt around until I found a towel. Used it to wipe my hands, my face, but what I needed was a shower. I stood at the foot of the bed, and my hand found her ankle.

"Are you okay?"

"I'm fine, just tired," I heard her sniff. "Were you outside smoking a cigar? I can smell it."

I said, "No. I was . . . out wrestling with some old demons. Couldn't sleep."

"You shouldn't be outside. They say it's safe inside the fence, but you didn't hear those dogs? Ten minutes ago, I never heard anything like it. Like the whole pack was fighting over a bone. I was worried that you —"

"It wasn't me." I saw her hand reaching for the reading lamp on the nightstand. "No, leave the light off. I can see fine now."

"Light's okay if the door's closed — I already used the shower. I'm thirsty. I've been thirsty all night."

"Give me a couple of minutes." I didn't need a mirror to know I was a mess. I wanted to stuff my clothes into a bag and throw them in the garbage.

There was a carafe of iced tea on the night-stand. I filled two glasses, but she said she didn't want the herbal stuff, it would make her sleepier.

"That's exactly what I need." I took a sip. It tasted of mint, anise, and sandalwood. I emptied the glass on my way to the bath-room. I exchanged the glass for a bottle of water, then hit the bathroom light. Took one look at myself, and turned the light off fast.

As I returned to the room, the woman said, "You found another bottle of water? Thanks."

I'd gotten it for myself, but handed her the bottle, asking, "The French guy, how bad did he hurt you?"

"How do you know about that?"

"Fabron and I got better acquainted today."

"Fabron, he's a pig. Worse than a pig."

Returning to the bathroom, I was thinking, *If pigs had wings* . . . but didn't say it because I'd have to explain. Later, though, maybe I would. It might put a smile on Norma's pretty face.

When I'd finished showering, I left the bathroom light on. It added pale angles and shadows to the room. I came out drying myself, a towel around my waist.

"What happened? Do you mind talking about it?"

Norma said, "It wasn't Fabron so much. It was that witch, the White Lady. She's a hundred times worse than the others."

She blinked when I switched on the reading lamp. She was sitting up, bottle of water in hand, the bedsheet tucked primly around her neck. In the afternoon, she'd looked like

458

a thirty-year-old in training for the Olympics. Now, though, she was gaunt. Her eyes were dark, oversized, like kids in Ethiopia.

I sat on the bed, and took the glass of tea I'd poured for her. "You're not all right. You need a doctor."

"No, really, I'm better. Mostly, I feel lucky to be alive. She had them tie me to a post. You believe someone would do something so crazy? No . . . first she made me strip, *then* they tied me to a post. Only it wasn't just a post, it was a cross. That's how I lost my clothes. I'll need to borrow some of yours because I have to leave soon."

I leaned to look in her eyes. She didn't appear to be in shock. I said, "You're not going anywhere. But if you don't want to talk about it —"

"I don't mind. I can see you're tired, though."

"Don't worry about me."

Polite houseguests are deferential. This was a polite woman. I had to reassure her again before she settled back and began to tell me what happened. It took her awhile because she was processing it all for the first time.

"I heard rumors of her putting demons in people, doing her magic. Some things even worse. But my God almighty, I never imagined how crazy she really is. She made them tape my hands and my mouth. I felt like I was going to suffocate. You think something like that, having tape over your mouth, is no big deal, but *man.* Things go through your head. They could drown me, throw me off the cliff . . . bury me alive. That feeling of not being able to breathe . . ."

I put my hand on her leg, noting the line of tape stickum on her neck. Hysteria wouldn't have surprised me. Her composure did.

"There was a fire. They built it so close to the cross, I thought she was going to burn me, the way Catholics burned people in old times. The White Lady was speaking Latin, all dressed in her robes, carrying a crucifix she said would purify my evil. Talking like I was the evil one, not her."

"You really do believe she's the Maji Blanc," I said.

"Yes."

"But you won't say the name."

It was more like a nervous reflex, the way Norma shook her head. "No. The Widow is what I call her. In my own mind."

"You're still a believer. After what she did?"

"How can you not believe something you

460

know is true? When the sun's up, she's just a mean rich woman. After dark, though, things change. You don't live on this island, but I know. The Widow, she has power. Six people watched me roast by that damn fire. Stood around me in a circle, because that's what they were told to do, and didn't lift a finger. That's how bad she scares folks — and I'd given some of them men massages."

I said, "Guests?"

"Two of them, yeah. She has some strange ones that come here four, five times a year. Crazy, sick people — but rich. The kind who'd pay anything to watch what she did to me tonight. Like I told you, I've heard the rumors. But my God!"

Always men guests, Norma told me. Toussaint tolerated women, but she liked men.

"That's why there're cameras in all the rooms. The Widow picks her favorites, watching on a monitor, and they don't even know they're being watched. She gets sort of bouncy and excited when a new man gets off the helicopter. I'd bet she's seen all of you there is to see. There's a camera over there in that clock radio. There was a towel or something over it, but I unplugged it, anyway."

I felt a creeping uneasiness, imagining

Toussaint in her nun's hood, smoking a cheroot, paintings of orchids everywhere, studying me as I stripped to take a shower.

I said, "Fabron and Wolfie were there?"

She nodded.

"What about a couple of guys name Ritchie or Clovis?"

"How do you know those two? They're the ones tied me up."

"They hang out at a bar called the Green Turtle," I said, as if that's where I'd met them.

"Um-huh, the Turtle Bar, along with all the other no-goods on this island. Those two, they're gangsters. Only come up here when she needs something bad done. Fabron and Wolfie, they showed up late. That made the Widow mad because she'd already stuck the needle in my arm, and it caused her to drop the tube when she looked to see who was coming."

I said, "Tube?"

"Same as the plastic IV tubes they use in hospitals. The Widow picked it up, me with that needle in my arm — didn't even wipe the dirt off. Then the bitch drank my blood, like sucking it through a straw. The whole time, her eyes were watching me, wanting me to be afraid, like that was something she could feed on, too."

Norma gulped the last of her water, already looking around the room for a fresh bottle.

I checked Norma's eyes, tested the elasticity of her skin, scrubbed her arm, then coated the needle mark with disinfectant from my shaving kit.

Norma appeared all right physically except for bruises on her wrists and a tape burn on her face. There were no symptoms of debilitating blood loss. But the psychological trauma had to be significant — she'd come *this* close to going over the cliff.

I had told Beryl and Senegal to leave on the morning helicopter, but now decided it was too dangerous to wait. Time to call in a charter helicopter large enough to take us all off the mountain. I stepped outside and tried to raise Sir James on the VHF. Moved to different parts of the quadrangle to get better reception. No luck.

As I locked the door and returned to Norma's side, I felt an odd, dreamy dizziness as she spoke to me, saying, "It's a sick feeling, watching that witch drink the life out of you. Her with her makeup like some child's doll, and that white hood she wears. The way her eyes stared at me when she sucked the tube — enjoying how scared I was, and full of hate, like I was dirty. But she was the one with blood on her face. And breath so nasty, bugs could feed on it. I pretended to pass out. Maybe I really did for a few minutes."

Norma had already told me she'd hidden in the woods until the dogs started going crazy — "They sounded so close, I thought they'd broke through the fence where it cuts close to the Lookout. That's happened before."

I knew the spot. I'd left Wolfie there.

Now she was backtracking, filling in the blanks as I asked questions. I found I had to concentrate to follow along.

"When I woke up, my mouth and hands were taped, and I was wrapped in some kind of heavy sheet. I heard voices — men's voices. One sort of sounded like you. But when I got loose, there was no one around." She leaned to look into my eyes. "Is that how you knew Fabron hurt me? Was it you I heard, Marion?"

I found it oddly touching that she called me by my first name. I said, "No. You must have been . . ." I had to struggle to find the word. ". . . hallucinating."

"I don't think I was dreaming it. I know Fabron. That man wouldn't've just gone off and left me unless someone scared him away. Not with me naked, the two of us alone. After all the times I told him no? He would've taken his time and made me pay. He's raped at least two guests since he's been here, but no one did anything because he's one of the Widow's favorites."

The light from the reading lamp had become piercing. As I turned it toward the wall, I was struck by something subtle but significant: Norma had kept the sheet primly over her breasts while we'd been talking. Used one arm, then the other, to cover herself when using hand gestures. Her determined modesty was so . . . decent, so admirable and consistent, despite the trauma she was dealing with. I found myself wanting to reach out and stroke the woman's hair. I did.

Norma monitored her own eyes, as well as the eyes of others. A look from her meant something. She gave me a look now, saying, *Marion? You're acting sort of strange all of a sudden,* but she let me continue stroking her hair. "Are you feeling okay?"

I felt a slow, wide smile fill my face. "I'm fine. I mean it . . . I feel great. Really great, in fact. What I'd like to do right now is —" I stopped. What the hell was I saying?

I didn't feel great. It was impossible after the night I'd had. If I wanted to picture it, I could see Fabron shrinking into darkness. I could see Wolfie's face go white as I lifted him over the fence, hearing the mastiffs charging through the forest toward us.

I put my hand on the bed and stood. I didn't feel dizzy now, just . . . strange. Happy, but also like I wanted to cry.

Cry?

I hadn't cried since childhood. What was wrong with me? I sat and looked at the carafe of iced tea. I'd given the bottle of water to Norma. I'd drunk tea, nothing else. The explanation assembled itself slowly: *The tea . . . I feel this way because there's something in the herbal tea.*

My glass was nearly empty. I held it up. "What's in this stuff? I'm starting to feel drunk . . . only not really drunk, just high . . . and warm."

"It's what the monks used to make, only weaker. The name's Divinorium. They make it from those blue flowers you see all around, plus a special orchid. It's the regular drink we serve in the spa all day. They brew it in the kitchen. It's purifying herbs with a little honey."

I stood again, seeing halos over the lights while colors strobed behind my eyes. "It can't be the same drink."

Norma took the glass, sniffed it, then tasted. She took another drink before she said, "You're right. This is stronger. It's good —" She drank again. "— but it's been brewed a lot longer. Maybe something added, too. I wouldn't drink any more if I were you." She thought about it, then said, "I wonder why the maids put this in your room."

"It wasn't here when I left. They don't put it in all the rooms?"

"Not as strong as that, they don't. Just the little bit I had, I can already feel."

I said, "Wait here a second."

I went to the bathroom, turned on the shower to cover the noise, and made myself vomit. I thought it would help. It didn't.

"Marion? How long are you going to stay in there?"

Norma's voice. Startling. I'd lost track of time. I searched the walls, the ceiling to confirm. Yes, I was still in the bathroom.

I'd made myself vomit again, ran cold water over my head. Now I was looking in the mirror, brushing my teeth. A stranger looked back . . . then blurred . . . then my own face appeared. My emotions oscillated in synch, sad . . . happy . . . sad . . . happy . . . introspective.

I studied the scratches on my face: four plowed rows of missing skin. Fabron had taken part of me with him when he fell into the sea. The combination of flesh and death, the orderly geometrics of my wound, struck me as indefinably profound. Then Fabron came into my mind. His wild eyes, the way he'd screamed for his mother as he fell.

I felt sad, thinking about his mother. I'd once had a mother. A father, too. Video of a boat exploding played in my mind as the name of my parents' killer turned to ashes in my lab.

What did it matter? Everyone died. We all left behind family to deal with the pain, to reassemble broken pieces. It was cruel. Abandonment. Maybe I would write a letter to Fabron's mother and break the news her son wasn't coming home. A mother deserved to know. An anonymous letter, couldn't use my name . . . maybe invent a nice thing to say about her son because it would ease the mother's pain . . .

Say something nice?

I took four deep breaths . . . held each for four seconds, released them slowly . . . and the fog cleared for a moment.

Why would I write a letter that eulogized a rapist? Fabron was an asshole, a sadist, a menace. It's the drug. Remorse is irrational.

Irrational — the right word. Yes, the drug again . . . effects getting stronger.

I forced myself to focus on what was rational. I was like a drunk climbing a ladder, giving elaborate attention to the rungs. Okay . . . why is an emotional reaction to Fabron's death irrational? I managed to recall another maxim hammered out on a long-ago jungle night:

Unless a man is in mortal danger, hitting a woman is contrary to evolutionary design. The man should be confined for the welfare of the species. A man who rapes a woman breaches the laws of natural selection. He should be euthanized to protect the integrity of the species.

Laws of nature have no pity. Fabron got what he deserved. Same with Wolfie, the dog fancier.

I clung to that rational thread. It was like walking a tightrope as my brain struggled to distance itself from the effects of the drug by recalling what I'd read about MDA. There were similarities.

The drug doesn't increase motor activity like most stimulants, it suppresses inhibitions . . . causes feelings of affection even between strangers. Produces a warm glow that radiates into the penis or clitoris.

I had all the symptoms — some getting

stronger even as I reviewed them. The effects of the drug would pass, I told myself. All I had to do was wait it out.

I leaned over the sink, washed my face, knotted a towel around my waist, then returned to the bed, and stood facing Norma as she said, "I have to go. Can I borrow a shirt and maybe those sandals? I have to be down the mountain before it gets light."

I said, "You're staying here."

"I thought you'd tell me to go away. Now you don't want me to leave. Funny thing is, I almost didn't come. I knew the rooms you'd been assigned, but I thought the English woman was here, and you were over there. I finally figured it out."

I said, "Senegal Firth is an incredible woman," and knew it was the drug talking. "You're both incredible women. She's got to meet you."

Norma said, "Uh-huh," the way people do when talking to a drunk, and put her bottle of water on the nightstand. She looked up . . . let her eyes move from my face to my feet, then to my face again. "You're all scratched to hell. Why don't you tell me the truth? You scared Fabron off. I heard men swearing and fighting. I'm thinking it was you. You saved me. The only reason you'd lie is if —" She paused, her attention inward, putting it together. "— the only reason you'd lie is to protect me. Or protect yourself."

I was thinking: *My God, the woman's brilliant. Brilliant and beautiful.*

"Marion? Be honest. Were you at the Lookout tonight?"

I nodded. "Where I saw the boats recovering your nephew's body."

The woman flinched. "Did you see Fabron?"

"Only for a minute or two."

"You didn't stand there arguing with him? I know I heard men arguing."

"I didn't stand on the cliff with Fabron. I swear."

"A lot can happen in a minute or two at that place," Norma said, eyeing me as she thought about it, probably picturing different scenarios, seeing herself wrapped in the carpet, the long drop to the water. She let it go, now thinking of her nephew.

"Paul," she said, still inside herself. "That poor, sweet boy. He never got his chance in life. Had a daddy who stole orchids for money. He came to a bad end, too. It was like it was in the boy's blood."

I thought, *Was the boy's name Paul or Rafael?* But then Shay came into my mind, a woman troubled by her own blood linkage to a brutal father. Dexter Money would have

471

lined up Fabron, Wolfie, Ritchie, and the others and shot them without remorse — but not because he loved Shay. Dexter had a killer in him. Some people are born to it.

"I'm sorry about your nephew."

"You showed that. You're a good man. I think I owe you more than you'll ever tell me."

I was patting the woman's leg, reassuring her, but also feeling her thigh, skin taut beneath the sheet, and thinking, *Such a sensual body,* seeing her face, the way her eyes converted light into liquid amber.

"You're gorgeous. One of the most gorgeous women I've ever seen."

She said, "Uh-huh," again, but I saw the flush of a woman unaccustomed to compliments.

"Did they try to kill you because you warned me this afternoon? It was sweet and brave of you to warn me, Norma —"

"That's not the reason," she said, looking at her hands. "It was something else. Can we not talk about it?"

I was stroking her hair again. Couldn't help myself. "Whatever you want. I want you to be happy . . . and safe. You deserve to be safe."

The woman smiled. "I don't know if that's the Divinorium speaking, or you. But it doesn't matter. Drunk or sober, it's a damn short life, and you've got to take comfort where you find it. The sound of those waves coming through the speakers — you recognize those sounds in the background?"

I tilted my head, saying, "Birds?" trying to pay attention to the sound track instead of the woman's face, and her contours beneath the sheet.

"Not birds. Listen close. It's from a tape someone made over on Saint Lucia where all the honeymooners stay. There's a few jungle parrots calling, but mostly it's honeymooners making love in the morning."

I forced concentration. The yelps and whistles of birds were redefined as the primate sounds of lovers. A brilliant idea — an idea I'd heard somewhere before. Audio pornography. Subtle, subliminal. Impossible to ignore as it radiated through the ears to the abdomen as a warm, engorging glow.

I stood, staring, stroking her hair as Norma shifted her position on the bed to face me. "You may not think therapists are experts. But I am." She grinned. "One look, and it's obvious your ching chi toxins are elevated. But I want you to understand something." Done with the joke, Norma turned her grin to a soft, sad smile that squeezed my heart. "This is different for me. This isn't a job. It's for pleasure now, Marion. Then I'm leaving. Okay?"

Norma reached and touched her fingers to the towel around my waist. She tugged the knot free. At the same time, she released the bedsheet, showing herself to me.

32

Door opens. Shadows absorb a shadow — Norma-sized. Door closes — *click* — the sound of a secret sealed.

Door opens. A figure clothed in white appears. Door closes — *click* — and displaced air floats an odor to my bed. A hooded face stands above me.

Lips where bugs might feed say: "I've been watching you. You remind me of a feral orchid — all pistil, no stamen. Yes . . . pretend this is a dream."

Norma's lips, swollen with wanting, warn me: "I don't drink that stuff because it gives me dreams."

Dream . . . dreams . . . dreaming. I drift in and out of sleep, uncertain what is real, what isn't.

I've been watching you . . .

"Men — she likes men. The Widow picks her favorites, watching them on a monitor, and they don't even know they're being watched. I'd bet she's seen all of you there is to see . . ."

I've been watching you . . . all pistil, no stamen . . .

Fingernails from a dream explore my face, then shoulders. Fingernails flex — cat claws dig, drawing blood.

"Ouch!"

Dream melts into nightmares that are old familiar scars: napalm flames, the stink of flesh . . . my index finger twitching on a trigger as, nearby, young men lay frozen in their innocence, alive, terrified, eyes fresh with homecomings; haylofts, ghettos.

The stink . . . that sickening smell, where's it coming from?

A woman's masculine voice tells me: "I am a child of the church. A disciple of the Holy Virgin. Through the sacrament of blood, I will judge the purity of your heart. Are you shocked that I crave sin?"

Touch of a rough-tongued cat licking my neck. Cat claws flex deeper.

"Get away!"

A dream, Ford, stand easy. You're only dreaming.

There is no helmsman when we sleep. The brain becomes a default computer, organizing random data into familiar patterns. Sparks leap synapse gaps; neurotransmitters arc. Chemical film snippets play on the backside of our eyes. Meaningless.

A woman's masculine voice tells me: "Desire is pain if you love the church. Pain is the path to redemption. We are born to suffer through the grace of our Holy Mother, the Virgin Mary. Spread your legs now. I want to touch you . . ."

Mary.

A familiar voice reminds me, "The only woman who impressed my mother-in-law was a dead virgin named Mary. The perfect Catholic girl — kept her knees together, but still gave birth to a saint like Michael."

A familiar voice says, "My family has done business in the Caribbean for years . . ."

A familiar voice says, "A couple of his aunts invested in Father's project. . . . I've met Isabelle Toussaint four or five times in Paris."

A familiar voice says, "I thought Shay rented the house through the Internet. But maybe she asked around for advice . . ."

Images of orchids and empty white cribs drift through darkness as another familiar voice says . . . says . . . *what?*

What does the familiar voice say?

The chain of logic vanishes in a putrid blossoming of human breath. I struggle between dream and reality, remembering: *Life conforms to a statistical pattern. Coincidence is inevitable. Multiple coincidences are not.*

White crib, white crib, white crib.

What is the significance of a white crib?

Blue cribs are for boys. Pink cribs are for girls. White cribs are for . . ."

As cat claws stroke my inner thigh, the hooded face leans to kiss my lips. Breath is gaseous, metallic-scented with tobacco, and the ferrous stink of red corpuscles.

Blood.

Blood? My blood.

Enough! I bust through dream's fog into a room cloudy with light and cheroot smoke, yelling, "Get the hell away from me!" as I roll naked from bed to the floor.

Wearing nothing but her nun's hood, Isabelle Toussaint stands aghast, her face rouge-painted like a clown. Her hands are up, fingers spread like claws, fingernails red with my skin and blood.

She screams, "You can't see me! I'm not real! I'm not real!" Then whispers, "I'm the Maji Blanc."

She slaps her hands in modesty, or shame, over her crotch, covering a miniature penis and deformed vagina. The penis resembles an infant's pinky. The vagina is hooded, the labia fused, shaped like the petals of an orchid.

She screams, "You left the dream, you fool! Why? So you can say my body disgusts you? That I'm abnormal? It's your death warrant!"

Because I understand what I am seeing, the left side of my brain overwhelms the drug-murked right side, and I tell the Maji Blanc, "You're not abnormal."

I am thinking: *Growing up in the church had to be hell for a hermaphrodite.*

Caribbean dawn, rain-forest wind. Black water floats a buoyant sun. Sun's elliptic pushes Venus, Saturn, Jupiter into the failing darkness of the Southern Cross.

Sunrise rising illuminates the blue of an old morning sea.

Parrots scream from humid shadows.

Parrots.

Parrots . . . the noise I heard as I awoke. Their wild bickering pounded a timpani skin that was the back of my brain.

I sat. I stood. I was in a cell that smelled of water on rock. Mold and rodents. A spear of sunlight touched my face. I squinted at the room's lone window. The opening was the size of a brick, slightly higher than my head.

I got up on tiptoes and looked out. I could see the stone façade of Toussaint's château.

Far below, the sea was cobalt blue. My cell, I realized, was built into the side of a hill, part of the foundation of the woman's house.

How had I gotten here? I felt like a drunk sifting through images that had survived a blackout.

Ritchie and Clovis had dragged me into the cell. No surprise that they worked for the woman. They'd . . . hit me? Yes. Clovis had used the palm of his hand. Ritchie had used fists.

I touched my cheek, my jaw. Slight swelling; some tenderness. Not bad.

I moved into the light and inspected myself. They'd left me my running shoes and shorts, but my pockets were empty, and my watch was gone. The Rolex I'd owned for years, Ritchie had taken it.

What else?

There was something I had to remember. A conversation. A detail.

Finally, the memory returned, and it scared me that I could have possibly forgotten.

Toussaint had gone into a screaming fit. Said she was going to watch me die tonight.

I had to find a way to escape.

Using my hands, I began to explore the walls of the cell. Old stone. Dense, like granite. I went from wall to wall, searching for loose stone . . . then stopped.

I heard voices outside, coming closer. A woman's voice, raspy from cigarettes and screaming.

I dropped to the floor and pretended to be unconscious. My cell door opened. Clovis and Ritchie again.

Toussaint yelled at the two men, telling them to stop punching me, stop waving that damn gun around, and put the knife away. I was conscious. That's the way she wanted me to stay.

"Are you trying to kill him? Not until I tell you to!"

I waited until the two men moved away, then stood. I said, "Thank you, Isabelle," hoping the familiarity would touch a chord. I was going to use her name whenever I got the chance. *I'm confused, Isabelle . . . You may be right, Isabelle . . . Isabelle, I'd like to understand . . .*

Killers dehumanize their victims to appease their own conscience. I wanted this killer to know that I was decidedly human.

Toussaint was under control now, dressed in her theatrical robes — purple and scarlet, decked with gold — the Midnight Star sapphire hanging from her neck. She was the all-powerful queen, two believers at her side, eager to do as they were told. But the orders

Toussaint gave Clovis and Ritchie surprised them. Me, too.

"Go outside. Leave the door open for light, but none of your damn eavesdropping. You heard me!"

They'd brought a folding chair. The woman sat, her back to the door. She could see me. All I could see was her silhouette.

"Sit down," she said. When I didn't move, she yelled, "On the floor!"

I sat, then scooted a few feet to her right to change the angle of light, but also to create distance. It wasn't the woman's breath that stunk, it was a foul combination of musk and perfume. Overpowering. She lit another cheroot, the match flame illuminating wrinkles beneath her makeup, the heavy, hooded eyes, her nicotine-stained lips.

"You think you're clever, don't you? I knew your real name even before you arrived. And why you came here. Does that surprise you?"

I was looking at the woman's distinctive forehead, her earlobes, hearing Shay's voice tell me about her future mother-in-law's six sisters — the one with a birth defect; the one the family didn't discuss because she'd been institutionalized in France.

It pleased me that I remembered. The effects of the drug were fading, but I still had to concentrate to speak without slurring. I replied, "I have no idea what you're talking about."

"Then you're stupider than I'd hoped. You've also put me in a very awkward position."

"I'm sorry, Isabelle."

"You are not! What are your two little bitches going to say when they discover you're missing? Now I have to invent an excuse to send them away. Or I could arrange for them to disappear, as well. But that's not good business, is it? They're like annuities — money and political favors I can cash when I want. Why hurt my own livestock? But I'll hurt you if you don't tell the truth."

I said, "I have no reason to lie," and nearly added, *Isabelle,* but didn't. The woman was insane, not stupid.

"What did you mean when you said what you said?"

I replied, "Huh?" as if confused.

"You said I wasn't abnormal! As if you know anything about it. You're just another little man-coward trying to save his life. You think I'm disgusting. Well, it's your kind who are disgusting! All of you — you're nothing but breeding stock. With your adolescent flirtations and absurd charades. Perfume and lies — like flowers manipulating bees.

Nothing but silly playacting. Behaving like animals!"

I was still feeling the effects of the Divinorium. There was nothing irrational about assigning the woman's bitterness to a quirk of genetics. But I felt no sympathy. She *did* disgust me, but I had to win her over, or she'd kill me. Maybe Beryl and Senegal, too.

"I didn't say you're normal. I said you aren't *ab*normal. I'm a biologist — you know that. Name a species — often there are three sexes, not two. Primates are omni-sexual as children. Boys experiment with boys, girls with girls. Some are born with omni-sexual bodies. The percentages are small, but statistically consistent."

The woman's anger wavered for a moment, displaced by curiosity. "You don't think I know that? But why would you care?"

"Caring has nothing to do with it. I don't get emotional about facts. Vertebrates produce a small number of intersex members." I touched my neck, then said, "You scratched the hell out of me."

Boom — she lost it again. "That wasn't me, you fool!"

I said, *"What?"*

"The Maji Blanc scratched you. She inhabits my body. She's a demon. And believe me, demons are as real as heaven and hell."

484

I said, "It's your hell, but it's my neck," then stood and went to the window to get air, carefully not turning my back on her.

"Your neck? As if anybody cared about your neck! Don't you understand the power of purity?"

"You're saying you do?"

"Yes. It's why I raise orchids. Did you know some orchids are self-pollinating? They aren't parasites like you people. They don't feed on filth. No need for your grotesque inserting this into *that*. I bet you actually believe I came to your bed out of desire? Hilarious! God sends the Maji Blanc to punish you. To punish you for what *you* are, not what *I* am. I'm His servant."

"His servant, huh?"

"In ways you can't understand. I film people's sickness. It gives me power — like air to an orchid. Money is the penance sinners pay for their sins. Now you stand there and pretend to *understand* me. You just want to ingratiate yourself because you're afraid to die."

I turned from the window and said, "Dying's inevitable. Getting pushed off a cliff isn't," and was surprised at the effect. She winced as if hurt.

"I've never pushed a man off the Lookout. No matter what people say, it's not true."

She was talking about her late husband, I realized.

I said, "I suppose the Maji Blanc pushed your husband," and expected her to explode.

Instead, she became maudlin. "The Maji Blanc does that. I hate her for it. But my husband died before she selected me."

It was said so softly that I had to strain to hear. Raging highs, abrupt lows — bipolar symptoms in a woman who was, in fact, three people.

"Delbert Toussaint. A week after our wedding night, fishermen found his body. The idiots in the village say I pushed him. It's a lie. Delbert jumped. On our wedding night, he saw my body. I disgusted him, and he jumped. Because of the church, he knew we could never divorce. That's why it hurts when I hear the rumors."

I said, "I'm beginning to understand."

Her anger began to cycle back. "Do you? Do you really think you're capable? Then you understand why it was *good* my husband jumped. Think about it — do you see the wonder? I was never *deflowered.* Can you comprehend the significance? A few weeks after Delbert died, the Maji Blanc came into my body. It was God's plan all along!"

I didn't trust myself to comment, so I

asked, "What makes you think your husband jumped? Did he leave a note?"

"No! But he left me rich. And he left me pure. Important people come to me now because my medicines keep them young. Potions only I know — brought from Africa by the first slaves. I have the courage to acknowledge the power of blood."

I said, "Human blood."

Her voice got louder. "Sometimes! Read the Bible: 'Unless you drink the blood of man, you will have no life.' The scripture doesn't say wine, it says blood. *Wine?*" The coughing laughter again. "It's a sick perversion of the truth. Does that offend you?"

"Yes. If it's my blood."

The woman stood, knocking over the folding chair. "I *knew* you were like the others. My clients joke that I'm a witch. They whisper I'm a vampire, but they love me because of it! For the wealthy, there's nothing left to seek but sin. People crave sin. But you pretend you don't. Liar!"

She was ranting now. "You should feel honored to be visited by the Maji Blanc. Tonight, she'll come to you again. Your blood will be consecrated. She'll say mass with the taste of your heart on her lips!"

She stomped out the door.

Physically, she may not have been abnormal. But, psychologically, she was one of the most dangerous people I'd ever met.

33

Wednesday, June 26th

Hours passed. All day, I searched for a way out, my hands raw from clawing at rock. At sunset that afternoon, I was kneeling in the corner, using my fingers to lever a slab of rock from the wall, when I heard movement outside my cell window. Heard the crunch of careful shoes on gravel, and attentive pauses. I pictured a man approaching. Maybe two men. They would be armed — Toussaint had sent them. When an executioner sends guards, the guards are cautious because a condemned man has nothing to lose.

I chose the largest rock from several on the floor, and carried it to the door.

A sound at the window drew my attention. I turned. Why would they come to the window? Then I saw a hand poke through, holding a flashlight. The beam probed the far corner where I'd opened a hole in the wall.

I lifted the rock over my head and walked toward the hand, ready to crush it . . . but then heard a man's voice whisper, "Ford. Are you there?"

I stopped, still holding the rock as the light swept over me.

The hand withdrew and Sir James Montbard's face appeared in the window.

"James?" The effects of the drug were long gone, but I felt like I was dreaming.

I dropped the rock and shielded my eyes from the light as he said, "Under the circumstances, old man, you can call me Hooker." A moment later, he added, "Congratulations, Dr. Ford. I think you've found the Misericord. Excellent work."

"You scared the shit out of me!"

"Would you prefer I leave?"

"I can't believe you found me."

"Find the guards, you find the prisoner. Yours are making a circuit around the old girl's house about every twenty minutes. Two of them with those damn, brutish dogs. Now one's gone inside, so I decided it was time to act."

Montbard's attention returned to the architecture of my cell. "This *is* the Misericord. I'm sure of it . . . monastery ruins; once a separate structure . . . clever, how they've incorporated it into the château. Part of the foundation. Ford, I think you have the makings of an archaeologist."

I said, "Get me out of here. The woman's insane. She's planning to —"

"Steady on, Ford. I'll have that door open in two shakes."

I heard the metallic tick-tick of burglar tools probing the lock, then the door swung open. Again, I shielded my eyes as Montbard stepped into the cell, then closed the door until only a splinter of dusty light filtered in. He was wearing a navy blue blazer, ascot, and dark slacks, as if he'd just stepped off the *Queen Mary*.

No, I wasn't dreaming — nobody in my dreams would ever dress that way. I said, "Are the girls safe?"

"Yes, yes, Senegal called this morning from the airport. Humorous, really — Beryl and Senegal hated each other instantly, as women often do when getting acquainted. Now they're already fast friends.

"They're both worried about you. Senegal, especially." His eyes had adjusted, and he turned to look at me. "Took most your clothes, did they?"

It seemed important to match the man's cheery attitude. "My watch, too. You're lucky you weren't around. I don't have your style."

"Fortunately, I agree. Precisely the reason I stopped at Jade Mountain and collected some of your things. I hope you're not offended, Ford, but there are places in the world where khaki shorts simply aren't acceptable after sunset."

He tossed me a backpack. "Looks like I should've brought a first-aid kit, too. Nasty-looking scratches on your neck. Worked you over pretty good, did they?" He drew the Walther from his shoulder holster and peeked out the door, gun by his ear. "Madame Toussaint must have something special planned for you. I'm surprised to find you alive."

It was because the Maji Blanc wanted to keep me alive and fresh for tonight.

The Maji Blanc — that's the way I thought of Toussaint now. An insane woman who masqueraded as a succubus to excuse her own sexuality. Gave me chills thinking about it, which is why I'd spent the day like a mole, feeling my way from rock to rock, hunting for a way out. Montbard had mentioned hidden passageways. It wouldn't be the first time a tunnel had saved my life.

Inside the backpack, I found slacks and a shirt and the dinner jacket Bernie Yager had insisted I bring. I also found my SIG Sauer 9 mm, which I'd left in the suite on Saint Lucia. I checked the magazine and shucked a round into the chamber, saying, "I'm surprised you found this."

Montbard didn't turn from the door. "It wasn't difficult. I looked where I would have put it — bottom of the dip pool, in a waterproof bag. We can't have the cleaning staff gossiping about illegal weapons now, can we —" He held up a warning finger, then touched it to his lips. Someone coming. He pushed the door closed.

Outside, I heard mumbled conversation — at least two men — and the guttural breathing of a dog straining against its leash. Sounded as if they were approaching from the front of Toussaint's home. I could also hear a motor vehicle coming from the same direction, up the long drive to Toussaint's home. I touched my thumb to the SIG's hammer, whispering, "I thought you said one of the guards went into the house."

"He did. Maybe he came back out . . . or they've added another man."

I said, "If they open the door, you shoot the dog. I'll jump the men."

Montbard didn't reply. We waited as the men neared, close enough now to hear one say, "Who's that getting outta the van?"

I couldn't make out the response, but heard the first voice say: "Yeah, one of the maids, probably. The Widow got her a big night planned, man." Their laughter moved with them away from the house, toward the garden.

Montbard exhaled a long, slow breath, nervous for the first time. "I agree, Ford. Lethal force — last resort only. I don't need any more nightmares."

I smiled — the man was human. But I also knew I could count on him to pull the trigger. The nightmares told me he'd pulled the trigger before.

The Englishman had the door cracked again, looking out as I finished dressing. He told me there was a white van parked near the château now. Said the upstairs lights were off even though it was getting dark enough; someone should have turned them on by now. The maid, Isabelle Toussaint . . . someone.

I was going through the backpack — a flashlight, the night-vision monocular, rubber surgical gloves, rope. Holding up my old silk sports coat, I said, "I thought you were kidding about this."

"The Orchid's cocktail party started fifteen minutes ago. Would you prefer to be mistaken for a guest or correctly identified as a burglar?"

I said, "You just convinced me. Maybe that's why the house is dark — she's at the party."

"I didn't see her. But, if she's in the house, I've arranged another diversion that should lure her out. In half an hour, her beloved orchid house will catch fire. Appear to catch fire, anyway, if the timers work — no guarantees. It's not easy to find reliable detonators in the islands. I expected to be operating alone, so I went heavy on the fireworks."

"What kind?"

"Exactly what I said — fireworks. People love them in the islands, and they're easy to get. In the confusion, we'll pop into the house, nick Madame Toussaint's video collection, then it's back to Saint Lucia in time for a late supper. Your friend Beryl is absolutely stunning, by the way. I wish she would have accepted my invitation to stay with us at Bluestone."

I was putting on the jacket, but stopped. "Beryl's not staying with you? Don't tell me she came back to Saint Arc."

"Nothing I could do. She took the ferry. Supposed to meet a friend who flew in this afternoon. I overheard the friend's surname — Money. Impossible to forget. Beryl said they had a lovely place rented, and that you approved. Senegal was thinking about joining them for dinner."

Like in the old silent films: Step carefully over the banana peel, then fall down an open manhole. *Damn it.*

I could hear Beryl saying, *I bet the party boys are hanging out at the resort. They'll scout the beach house at sunset, like before.*

I said, "Shay Money is my goddaughter. Beryl didn't tell you?"

"No. If she had, I would've never allowed her to leave."

"That's why she didn't tell you. They've gone back to the rental house on the beach. Shay and Beryl have talked themselves into believing they can handle the guys who conned them. We've got to get down there."

Montbard said, "Sorry, Ford, I had no idea."

"It's not your fault."

"You're sure it's the same house?"

"Yes. Ritchie Bonaparte and Clovis what's-his-name are the ones who slapped me around this morning, then locked me in here. They talked about cruising the bars tonight. I heard them." Ritchie had taken my Rolex — a watch I'd owned for two decades — so I had to ask, "What time is it?"

"Six forty-five."

The sun was setting now. "And you set the detonators for . . . ?"

"Seven-thirty, but I used bloody egg timers — all I could manage — so it's not exact."

I said, "Screw the videos, we've got to get down to the beach. There's too much at risk."

Montbard remained matter-of-fact. "Yes, there's some risk, I agree. But there's even more risk if we don't get the tapes, not only for Senegal and your friends, but for dozens — maybe hundreds — of others. We'll never get this opportunity again."

I thought about it. *Damn.* I hated that he was right. I said, "Okay. Then let's make it quick."

"Of course! The entire operation should take less than an hour. I suggest we move to the back garden and wait for the fireworks. When the old girl rushes out to save her precious orchids, we'll have a solid block of time to search the house."

I took the flashlight from my bag and shined it on the wall where I'd been prying rock with my fingers. "No need to wait. I found one of your passageways. I think it leads into the basement of Toussaint's house."

The Englishman went to the opening,

knelt, and levered another rock free. "By God, you're right." He shined his light into the hole, then stood and removed his blazer. "Doesn't look more than a few meters to where it exits. Rather narrow, though. A damn tight squeeze."

I told him, "Heretics were smaller in those days —" then paused, head tilted, hearing men's voices again, and the choleric rasp of a dog. Waited for several seconds, expecting to hear the jangle of keys. Instead, the voices faded, moving toward the front of the château. I continued, "Can you figure out a way to jam the door, so they can't open it from the outside?"

He nudged the door closed with his knee. There was a metallic click. "Already done."

I said, "Then let's move. Isabelle will be sending someone for me soon."

"Isabelle? On a first-name basis, are we?"

I told him, "I'll explain later," as I got down on hands and knees and pulled away more rock so my shoulders would fit through the opening.

34

The Maji Blanc's château was built over the ruins of what Sir James Montbard believed was the original monastery. He said the architecture was older than the ruins where previous monks had lived and died. Told me this after scrutinizing masonry and twin columns that bordered steps leading up to a stone landing. He had also brought his grandfather's journal — yellowed pages bound in leather.

The hidden entrance inside the château, I guessed, was just above the landing, where stairs disappeared into a modern section of basement. The modern section was walled off with brick and sealed with a steel door.

I'd already checked the door. Snapped on surgical gloves before I tested the knob. It wasn't locked, but I didn't open it.

Montbard wanted to search the oldest section first. We used flash-lights. We whispered. Sometimes, we heard heavy footsteps overhead, and the occasional tap-shoe scrabble of a dog's claws on a hardwood floor. Maybe Toussaint was up there stomping around, restless, moving from room to room. She sounded heavier than I would've guessed.

The western section of the monastery was intact. Montbard panned his flashlight slowly along the walls and remnants of two doorways before whispering, "The pointed arches . . . the tracery, everything — the way it's laid out — all typical Gothic architecture. The dry stone masonry could be older. Just as Grandfather described it."

I wanted to locate the tapes and run, not talk, but the man had switched into archaeology mode. "The Gothic dates from the Middle Ages — twelfth century to the early fifteen hundreds. Remember the rhyme about Columbus sailing the ocean blue? Work on this monastery could have begun before 1492. A hundred years or more."

I thought, *Uh-oh,* thinking about the article on the Templars, their missing ships and treasure. I said, "Hooker, let's stick to business."

Montbard was standing between the twin columns, using his flashlight, scanning ornate carvings of monks praying, sheaves of wheat . . . a cross with four equal arms. He held the light on the cross for a moment, then moved it to the base of the column. He whispered, "This is what I'm talking about. Have a look."

I knelt and used my own flashlight, seeing monks . . . oak clusters . . . a carpenter's square . . . a silver-dollar-sized seal etched in rock, so worn I couldn't be sure, but it might have been a skull and bones, the eyes oddly misaligned.

"It's similar to my ring."

"Maybe."

"My grandfather gave this to me. His grandfather gave it to him. There's only one other place I've seen that symbol carved in stone — in this hemisphere, anyway. An ancestor of ours was among the first —"

"He was a Templar," I said. "I read the article. But I didn't come here to prove your theory of relentless motion."

"Quite right. Just five minutes. That's all I ask. This stairway —" He used his flashlight to show rock steps concave from centuries of wear. "— I know without looking there are three flights. Three steps, five steps, then seven steps. Those numbers are significant." As if reciting by rote, he added, "Between two brazen pillars . . . a door strongly guarded," whispering to himself.

I said, "Is there something in that journal

you're not telling me about? What the hell are you after?"

"History," he said. "The truth."

I told him, "Good luck. Take five minutes, take five hours. I'm not following you."

He sound chastened, not relieved, saying, "I won't let you down. Promise. We'll search separately — might be for the best. Remember our signals. Use the flashlight."

I said, "I remember," and left as Montbard started up the steps.

I opened the steel door just enough to peek into the basement's modern section: well-lit office, air-conditioned, a desk, file cabinets, a computer, paintings of orchids on every wall. The room was small enough. I could read the signature of the artist: *Georgia O'Keeffe.* There was another stairway, and a wooden door — maybe a bathroom, maybe a closet, or an adjoining room. The door was closed.

On the desk was an ashtray full of black stubs, the smell of tobacco strong. Toussaint had either just gone up the stairs or she was on the other side of the wooden door. I waited, still hearing footsteps overhead, then I slipped into the office and used a book to block the steel door from closing.

Yes . . . the woman had just left. She'd

been working, very busy. A drawer was open, papers scattered on the desk. Receipts and bills, letters addressed to her post-office box. A book, *The Pictorial Encyclopedia of Oncidium,* lay open next to the computer.

One of the envelopes caught my eye. It was addressed by hand. On the upper left corner, the return address read: *Mrs. Ida Jonquil/Cape Coral, FLA.*

I looked in the envelope. Empty.

Ida and Isabelle: two sisters staying in touch, looking out for the welfare of the family's good name, and their saintly progeny, Michael.

Near the desk was a wall safe, door open. Big — almost as large as the painting that had covered it but was now on the floor. From where I stood, the safe looked stuffed with blocks of cash. I glanced inside as I passed: euros and U.S. dollars, not the Monopoly bills of the Eastern Caribbean. Tomlinson had nailed it: Blackmail was a boutique industry on the island, and business was booming.

Covering most of the opposite wall was a rotating file made of aluminum and steel. It was unlocked, doors open, like the safe. The file reminded me of a Ferris wheel. Its contents were efficiently organized, alphabetized with names and dates. The contents illustrated changes in technology over two decades. There were reels of 8 mm film. There were full-sized cassettes. There were minicassettes like the one Wolfie had given me. The woman had been in the blackmail business a long time.

I looked at the wooden door, ears alert, checked the stairway, then began to flip through the rotating racks. Tapes were stored like books, spines out. I recognized a few names: the wife of a former French president, the South African industrialist Sir James had mentioned, an actress, a rock star. There were a couple of surprises: an evangelist who was often in the news, and a popular member of the U.S. Senate.

Toussaint had said there was power in purity, but she'd proven the opposite. Each video represented money and power. And the woman was shrewd enough to be selective. There were fewer than five dozen tapes.

I dropped the senator's video and the French first lady's video into my backpack and continued searching.

Shay's video was labeled: *Money/Florida-Girls/Michael's Jezebel.* Jezebel, the biblical whore. It explained why Toussaint, who preyed on the superrich, had bothered to entrap a redneck girl attempting to marry above her class.

There was nothing filed under the last names of Beryl, Liz, or Corey, but I found Senegal's video under *F.* It was cross-referenced: *Politics/U.K.*

I was thinking about the desk computer — how could I destroy its memory files? — when I heard a banging, thumping commotion overhead. Sounded as if someone was moving furniture. Then, a dog began barking. Deep, wolfish roars. I stopped and listened . . . listened until the dog went silent and the thumping stopped. I happened to be standing near the wall safe. This time, I took a closer look.

Inside were stacks of hundreds and fifties banded into four-inch bricks of $10,000 and $5,000, bank notations on the wrappers. Bricks were layered five high, five wide, from the front to the safe's back wall. Half a million cash. No . . . more.

Toussaint owed Shay and the girls money. I dropped eleven blocks of bills into my backpack — $110,000. Hesitated, then took another. Expenses.

There were two steel storage trays in the safe. One contained legal documents: deeds, the woman's birth certificate (Isabelle Marie Raousset-Boulbon), her Catholic confirmation papers, a faded marriage certificate — something touching about that combination. I shut the drawer and opened the second. There were gold coins in plastic sleeves, and several black velvet boxes — jewelry. I opened the most ornate box and saw a sapphire the size of a robin's egg. The Midnight Star.

I removed the necklace and held it to the light, thinking that maybe Shay deserved a special wedding present — if she still wanted to marry Michael after learning the truth about his vicious family. The sapphire glittered, revealing a blue-black world within. Reminded me of a lighted aquarium, with crystal walls that isolated; a weightless space where beautiful predators might drift. Tempting.

On those nights when Tomlinson and I discuss — debate, really — matters of spirituality, he is quick to remind me that my rigid, Darwinist's view of the world does not explain my own moral compass. It's irritating because he's right. So I've come to accept conscience as yet another of my irrational conceits. I have to live with myself.

I returned the necklace to its box, returned the box to the safe, and closed the drawer.

I wanted to take or destroy all the videos and film, along with the woman's computer. There was a lot of misery in that rotating file, but I couldn't fit all of the cassettes plus the money into my backpack. Moral compass or not, I sure as hell wasn't going to leave the money. I needed another bag.

I was looking at the wooden door, wondering if it was a storage closet or a bathroom when, for the first time, I heard a banging noise coming from the other side. I placed the pack on the floor and I drew my gun. Heard the noise again, and reconsidered: Maybe the smart thing to do was grab my backpack and run.

But it was an unusual, muted sound, familiar on some basic level. Panic muted by constriction — like that. Reminded me of the thumping sound a rabbit might make while succumbing to the patient jaws of a snake.

I walked to the door and put my ear against it. The cries of a person who's been gagged also register on a primal level, and that's what I heard. I cracked the door . . . then pulled it wide, gun raised . . . and I nearly squeezed the trigger when a woman lunged at me with a knife.

I backpedaled as she charged me. Then slapped her strong arms aside, hearing the knife clatter on tile, and swung her against the wall, gun to her temple. She stopped struggling as I looked into her eyes — liquid amber eyes, glazed with fear.

Slowly, I lowered the gun.

"Norma?"

I said the name again as her eyes cleared with recognition. *"Norma!"*

The woman stood looking at me, stunned. Then she pushed away as if ashamed, crying, "I couldn't do it, I just couldn't do it. Thank God it's you, because I need help. I just can't make myself stab her."

Behind Norma, on the bathroom floor, next to an antique tub, was Isabelle Toussaint. She lay with her ankles, hands, and mouth bound with duct tape, her white gown pulled up above her chest, panties gone. The sight of her made me wince, and I looked away. Norma had surprised the woman while she was using the toilet.

"Paul, she killed my Paul," Norma sobbed. She stepped toward me, and I let her bury her face against my chest. "That poor boy only came up the mountain to tell me his father died. But this bitch put the dogs on him, anyway. Used the same dogs to kill my son that took my husband's legs, and made him a beggar."

Her son? Not her nephew? Now things became clearer.

Toussaint recognized me. She began to grunt as she inch-wormed across the tile, pleading with wild, wide eyes. Did she really

508

expect me to help her?

I knelt, retrieved the knife, and told Norma, "Fill that tub with water." When I said it, Toussaint made a sound that resembled a scream.

It was while lugging the computer tower into the bathroom that I remembered what Norma had said about having her mouth taped. *They could've drowned me, easy.* She was explaining the heightened fear that accompanied vulnerability.

Not a bad idea. Drown Toussaint.

I put the computer into the tub and popped the cover. Positioned it under the spigot; noticed what might have been a memory board and ripped it free before I forced myself to look down at the woman.

It was painful, the sight of her. Not only because of her body, but because she was terrified. It was in her eyes.

I felt an irrational twinge of sympathy, but it passed quickly. Fabron and Wolfie had suffered ultimate terror at my hands, yet I didn't feel remorse. I felt a clinical indifference. Norma had described Toussaint looking into her eyes, hoping to see fear. How many faces had Toussaint searched with the same sick need? Being a hermaphrodite didn't give her license to make life hell for others.

Toussaint watched me as I looked at the bathtub, opened both valves full, then looked at her. "The four girls from Florida you blackmailed — one of them's dead because of you."

The woman shook her head and grunted, breathing faster.

I reached into the tub. The computer tower made a gurgling sound of displaced air when I turned it over. "Did you ever see *The Wizard of Oz*? The scene where Dorothy throws water on the witch?"

I could tell by Toussaint's frantic reaction that she had.

"What does the witch say as she's melting? Something about 'all my beautiful evil.' You're a witch, Isabelle. If I put you in this tub, would you melt?"

She made the grunting, screaming noise again, and began to snake-crawl on her back, inching toward the door.

I stepped over her and blocked her way. "But I'm not goin' to drown you. Instead, I'm sending you to hell."

She looked at me, her eyes intent.

"I've got your tapes, Isabelle. Your political connections won't save you. One of them is of the French president's wife. Even if your island cops don't care, the French cops will."

The woman's eyes narrowed.

"French law overrules Saint Arc law — but I guess you know that. You're going to prison. For someone like you —" It took an effort not to glance at her genitals. "— prison will be worse than hell."

I knelt and picked up the white robe, ignoring her muffled screams and her lunging attempt to bite me through the tape. I covered the Maji Blanc more carefully than she deserved, and closed the bathroom door behind me.

Sir James came into the office as I stood at the safe, dropping more bricks of cash into my backpack. His face was grimy, smudged with blood, his ascot gone. What the hell had he been doing? Looked like his bag was already full, too, but I said, "If you're not too busy, clean out that file. There're about twenty more videos." I would tell him about Toussaint later.

Norma was exhausted, sitting limp in a chair, and gave me a look — *Who the hell's he?* I winked, telling her it was okay as Montbard said, "You've already found the tapes? And also made a beautiful new friend, I see."

I was on adrenal overload, and not in the mood for his chivalrous bullshit.

"Yeah, I have them — no thanks to you. So get busy. Whoever's banging around upstairs could come down any second, or send one of those damn dogs —"

"Temper, temper," Montbard interrupted, an odd, sweaty smile on his face. "I was the one banging around up there. And the gentleman who required my attention is now tied and gagged, locked in a closet. Called me an 'old man,' the cheeky bastard. And his damn dog is dead — but at a price." He held up his left hand. Fingers and wrist were wrapped in a bloody handkerchief. Looked like the sleeve of his jacket was soaked, too.

"I haven't been totally useless, you see. I also have the keys to the man's vehicle — although I have no idea where it's parked." He went silent for a moment. Lifted the handkerchief gently and checked his watch — a little pool of blood had already collected at his feet. "*Hmm,* my diversion's two minutes late. I do apologize for that."

Sounding dazed and exhausted, Norma said, "We don't need his car. I came in a van from staff housing. It's outside."

I had twenty-six more bricks of cash in my pack. Norma could never return to Saint Arc, and she would need money. Corey's family deserved an extra cut, too.

Before zipping the bag closed, I opened the

steel drawer and added the Midnight Star.

Expenses.

I asked the Englishman, "Do we use the tunnel, or is it safe to go through the house?" I felt an overwhelming sense of dread. We had to get to the beach house. We had to find Shay and Beryl.

Applying pressure to his bloody hand, Montbard said, "We'll use the front door, of course. But try to ignore the mess."

35

I was at the wheel of the van, accelerating, but backed off the pedal after only a couple of seconds. It was an older three-speed Dodge, gearshift on the column, brakes soft, shocks spongy, headlights misaligned. The road down the mountain was one lane, rock and gravel. Lots of switchbacks and unmarked curves on this black and cloudless night. Any faster, I'd overrun my headlights.

Norma was beside me. Montbard was on the bench seat behind us. He'd spent a couple of minutes on the little VHF radio, trying to raise the Saint Lucien marine patrol or a friendly vessel. But there was no reception because of the forest, so now he concentrated on stopping the bleeding. The bite was worse than he'd let on. The dog had ripped cordage away on the underside of his wrist and taken part of his ring finger. Gruesome to look at. The man remained stoic, though, even cheerful, but I knew he was in pain. He would need surgery.

I accelerated through a curve, then down-shifted when I saw a security gate ahead — two men in uniforms visible inside the lighted guardhouse. I looked at Norma.

"Keep going, but not too fast. They don't stop people leaving, just people coming in."

I said, "You're sure?" One of the men had stepped out of the gatehouse, hand on his pistol.

Behind me, Sir James coughed, then laughed. "Better late than never!" I didn't understand what he meant until I looked in the side mirror and saw a dazzling snow cone of red brighten the night sky. It burst into a multicolored shower of light. A second later, a thunderous boom shook the van. A blue starburst followed, then a high, arching fountain of orange streamers.

"Fireworks," Norma said, perplexed. "Why are they shooting off fireworks? I don't think it's a holiday."

The guards must have been wondering the same thing. They barely glanced at me as I slowed and waved, using my hand to shield my face. Then I accelerated, eyes on the mirror, watching the two men stand child-like, faces turned upward at a rain-forest sky that boiled with color.

Montbard was still laughing, but his laughter had the detached flavor of shock. I said, "How are you doing back there?"

"Bloody fucking lovely," the man said, teeth clenched. "By God, our Chinese brothers deserve full marks for inventing fireworks. I do love the smell of cordite. And the white phosphorous glow of an incendiary — even these weak things — it leaves a smile on my face. Damn nice show I'm putting on. Too bad we'll miss it."

I said, "You hang on, Hooker," as Norma said, "Your fireworks? They're beautiful," sounding like a nurse comforting a patient. She was turned in her seat, looking toward the back window, but not because of the fireworks. She was concerned about Montbard. "Don't you worry. We'll be able to see them from the beach. I bet people at the resort are out right now, watching." When she added, "Ohhh . . . that was a nice one," I checked the mirror: a blue velvet starburst with silver sparklers. The Midnight Star floated into my mind.

"Ford, old man, will you promise me something? If we get to the beach house and find our girls hurt, I'd like you to promise you'll boot me down all three hundred and eighty-one steps at Bluestone. Would you mind?"

"With pleasure," I said.

Norma told him, "He's not going to touch you as long as I'm around," then slipped into the backseat, saying she thought there might be towels in the rear of the van. Montbard was suddenly concerned.

"My bag's back there, dear lady. Do be careful, won't you?"

I heard the woman grunt. "That must be what's sitting on the towels. I'll try, but it's heavy . . . what in the world's in here?" But then she said, "Got them," and pivoted back to her seat with a stack of towels. In the rearview mirror, I watched her pull the bloody handkerchief away from Montbard's hand.

"Marion? Is there a light or something?"

I kept my eyes on the road as I fished the little Triad flashlight from my pocket and handed it to her.

After several seconds, Norma said, "This is bad. This is real bad. We've got to get him to the clinic and fetch the doctor. The clinic's not far from the rental —"

"No doctor, and no clinic," Montbard interrupted. "Not on this island. We just robbed the most powerful woman around. It would be unwise to linger."

"Mister, I don't want to scare you, but I've dealt with the kind of wound you've got. You could lose this hand. And you've already lost a lot of blood."

"Then I'll lose my hand," he said. "Rather that than the local jail."

"Is dying better than jail? Because that's what might happen, the way you're bleeding. Marion — he's white as a ghost. The clinic's only two miles at the most —"

"No doctors. Sorry. I'll not discuss it anymore."

The woman made a grumbling sound of frustration and slapped the seat. She was done with crying now, getting angry. "Those damn dogs! Why are you men always so stubborn about getting help? They got teeth as dirty as snakes, but you don't care."

Puzzled, Montbard said, "You work at the place. What do you have against the dogs? Brazilian mastiffs — only doing their jobs, dear."

I said, "Hooker, she has her reasons. Okay?"

"Don't be sharp with him, Marion. There's no way he could know. It was almost thirteen years ago my man came crawling into the village, so torn up by those dogs he wanted to die. He would've rather died than live like he did. And I have more reasons than that to hate them. I wish you'd killed them all."

I took a chance and said, "I think Sir James knew your husband, Norma. You told me he was a good man, Hooker."

Montbard was confused, but said, "You lost your husband recently, dear? I'm so sorry."

"Two days ago, he finally left us. But he was never really a man again because of those dogs. He was a proud one, Paul senior. Wouldn't let me be his wife after what happened. Didn't want our son to know his father was begging for coins on the street, either. After that night, we were never a family again."

Montbard's brain was still working fine. "Ahhh," he said gently. "I *did* know your husband, Norma. A good chap, he was. I'm truly sorry. It's an honor to meet his widow."

At first, I wasn't worried about taking Ritchie and Clovis, or anyone else, by surprise. I had the brights on, the pedal to the floor, as I fishtailed down the lane to the beach house. The sweep of headlights showed the rain-forest bluff where the camera blind was located . . . showed coconut palms leaning incrementally toward a black, vacuous space that was the sea . . . showed the outbuilding where I'd jumped the guys two nights before.

But then I thought, why make it obvious? If the men were inside, they might panic. Could make a bad situation worse. So I switched off the lights, killed the engine, and used the clutch to coast the last seventy yards down the incline. I swung in behind a good-sized citrus tree loaded with Key limes, and handed Norma the keys.

"I'll be back as quick as I can. Keep the doors locked. Watch for my flashlight. Sir James knows the signals, but use your own judgment. If you think you should run, run. Don't worry about me. My boat's not far from here."

"Ford, you're talking rubbish. I'm perfectly capable of going with you. I'm a right-handed shooter —"

"That's why I'm asking you to stay here. Look after Norma. It's about time someone took care of her." When I opened the door, the dome light came on, and the woman caught my eyes, looking from me to Montbard, whose head was now in her lap. For the first time, he looked his seventy-some years. His face was as white and fragile as rice paper. On the floor was a pile of towels soaked black with blood.

I handed Norma the VHF. "If you roll

down the window, maybe you can raise someone. We need a helicopter. Don't worry about the price." I pulled the SIG Sauer and ran toward the house.

36

There was a white car in the drive. A mid-size Volvo, which made me think of Beryl. An expensive rental car in this part of the world. Or the sort of vehicle a street guy with an ego would drive.

I touched the hood. Cool.

The beach house was lit up, windows bright, upstairs and down. The patio at the rear of the house shimmered with an aqueous, swimming-pool glow. There was music — Bob Marley, again — pounding through the palm canopy, stirring leaves like a sea breeze. It muted the percussion of waves on the beach, and the last distant crackle of Sir James's fireworks diversion.

Crouched low, I jogged across an expanse of sand to the hedge. The hedge shielded the pool at eye level, but didn't interfere with the view from the camera blind above the house. I turned and looked. No lights up there in the rain-forest darkness, no sign of movement. Wolfie had produced his last film.

I moved along the hedge, gun pointed at the ground, index finger resting parallel to the trigger guard. On the back wall of the house, I could see shadows. Shadows of people standing near the pool. Because pool lights reflected upward, their shadows were huge. At least one woman. At least one man.

I stopped and tried to decipher a garbled exchange — the man saying something . . . the woman answering, but the music disassembled their voices and left me listening to the wind.

I walked faster, then heard another exchange. This time I recognized the woman's voice. ". . . if it's me you want, get that damn knife away from her neck. Stop it!"

Beryl's voice.

I ran. Sprinted toward the walkway where the hedge ended, and peeked around the corner, seeing the lime blue water of the pool . . . seeing Senegal Firth sitting in a chair next to the bar . . . seeing Clovis, his back to me, standing, holding a knife to the side of Senegal's neck as the woman sat very straight, weeping.

Beryl faced them — stood with the wooden stiffness of an actress frozen by stage fright, arms at her sides. She wore pleated white beach pants and sandals. Nothing else. In a pile at her feet were a bra, a blouse, and a turquoise scarf. Her tanned skin was darkened by the paleness of her breasts.

I pointed the pistol at Clovis's head, stepped toward the pool . . . then stepped back. The knife — he would use the knife when he saw me. He would use it to cut Senegal, or he would use Senegal as a shield to escape.

I glanced over my shoulder, wondering where Shay was, where Ritchie was, as I heard Clovis say, "Darlin', what don't you understand about this game? It's strip poker, but without cards." There was a nauseating slickness to his laughter. "I win every hand . . . or I cut this old woman's face a little. Which would be too bad, because —" Clovis got a handful of Senegal's hair. "— she ain't too bad-looking."

He yanked the English woman's head back, and Beryl yelled, "Leave her alone!"

Clovis grinned. Used the knife like a conductor's baton: *tap-tap-tap.* Beryl took a big breath. She began unbuttoning her pants.

"That's better, darlin'. You make me happy when you cooperate."

I knelt, put left elbow on knee to steady my hands, and let the man's head blur behind the precise notch-and-blade of my gun sights. I needed an opening, a few feet of separation.

Clovis put his lips close to Senegal's ear as he released her hair. "What's gone wrong with your pretty friend? First night we met, this girl, Beryl, she was eager to cooperate. Oh man, she was so eager! She ripped her clothes off. Hell, she 'bout ripped my clothes off, too. Couldn't wait to get her rich-girl hands on my sweet bamboo!"

He looked at Beryl. "You don't remember how sweet it was? How you moaned, first time I gave you what I got? Never felt nothin' like it, that's what you said. Ain't that *true*, pretty darlin'?"

The way he emphasized the word "true," I knew he expected Beryl's signature reply. Hard to imagine the Ice Queen beauty with this Peter Lorre weasel. But there it was.

He said it again. *"True?"* When she didn't answer, his tone turned nasty. "But now, instead of bein' happy to see us local boys, treating me and Ritchie right, the bitch pulls out a silly little popgun. Like she don't appreciate what I give to her. Bitch —" He pointed the knife at Beryl. "— you try to trick me, you're gonna end up turning tricks *for* me."

For the first time, I noticed the little Colt .380 on the deck near Clovis's feet. The gun I'd loaned Senegal.

I looked over my shoulder again, seeing palm trees, seeing pumpkin-sized coconuts on sand, seeing a watery darkness in the distance, but no Ritchie.

I used the SIG's decocking lever, then hustled to the nearest palm, picked out a coconut, and put it under my arm like a football before jogging to the opposite side of the patio. The hedge was thicker there, but I found an opening and peeked through.

Clovis was facing me now. He'd grabbed Senegal's hair again, but his eyes were locked on Beryl as she stepped out of her pants, showing long, tanned legs and a golden pubic shadow beneath white panties.

The man grinned his Peter Lorre grin. "That's nice, darlin'. I think I'm gonna have me some of that. Why don't you relax, have some fun with your bamboo man? Or maybe you're the type likes to be forced."

He stepped away from Senegal. I let him take another step before I lobbed the coconut toward the far end of the pool. Lobbed it like a hand grenade. It was big, oil laden, and sounded like a bowling ball when it hit the water.

Clovis whirled, then crouched. He looked at the pistol lying on the deck, probably thinking he might need it, as I crashed through the hedge and tackled him chest-high. I got a brief look at his eyes — brown, dazed, like protuberant marbles — as we tumbled into the water.

I kept my arms locked around the man as I took him under, pinning his arms to his sides. Maybe he'd held on to the knife, maybe he'd dropped it. It didn't matter.

I exhaled a slow stream of bubbles as we sank to the bottom — couldn't have been more than five feet deep. Kept my hands locked as Clovis struggled . . . waited as his efforts became panicked . . . waited, eyes open, watching the oversized bubbles of the man's ascending scream.

I stayed on the bottom and waited, feeling his chest heave as he inhaled water, then heave again as reflexes demanded oxygen. Gave it another five seconds before I pushed Clovis to the surface . . . then shoved him away when he began to vomit, unconscious now.

It was one of those kidney-shaped, decorator pools. I got a hand under his chin, walked him to the steps, then pulled him onto the deck. "Where's Shay?"

Beryl was the first to recover from the shock. "Shay . . . she left with Ritchie. Ritchie took her to the beach. She pretended she wanted sex, so he wouldn't force her. They left us with this . . . *animal*. I couldn't

527

help her because of *him*."

Beryl had her hands over her breasts, but it was an indifferent modesty. Her denim-blue eyes glazed as she focused on Clovis. I watched Beryl lower her hands. I saw her hands become fists as she started toward the man. He was lying belly-down in his own mess, still alive. I was on one knee, using my belt to bind his arms behind him.

I stood. "Beryl . . . *Beryl.* Take it easy. Don't do something you'll regret later."

It stopped her. But I couldn't tell if she meant it when she answered, "You're right. Why lower myself? He's the sicko. Not me." Icy.

"Get some rope. Or some tape — the belt won't hold. Can I trust you to keep an eye on him? I've got to find Shay."

Beryl said, "Oh yes. You can trust me," in a flat, robotic voice as Senegal wrapped an arm over her shoulder, pulled her close, and said, "Hooker taught me all sorts of knots. I'll do it."

Senegal, with her bruised cheek, hair a mess, eyes puffy from crying, sounded okay, solid. "Magnificent," Montbard had said about her. I could see it.

I answered her by shaking my head as I picked up the Colt, checked the chamber, then the clip. "No. I need your help. And

I need you to be strong." I signaled her closer, as Beryl went to retrieve her clothes. "Hooker's hurt. A dog bit him. It's his hand and wrist, so I think he'll be okay. But it's not nice to look at. He's in a van behind the house. I want you to collect all the first-aid stuff you can find. And hang on to this in case Ritchie comes back." I touched the safety, then handed her the gun.

Senegal looked stricken.

"How bad is it?"

"Bad enough he needs to get to a hospital fast. But it has to be Saint Lucia, not here. That's important. Understand?"

The woman surprised me, saying, "Then we'll take him to the plane. Right away."

I said, "What plane?"

"Shay came in a private plane with a man named Eddie. He's at the airport now, waiting. We were supposed to be there by ten-thirty. The girls were going to overnight with me on Saint Lucia."

I was thinking, *Eddie DeAntoni.* At the marina, he'd asked if I was coming to Saint Lucia alone, or with women.

"What time is it now?"

"Quarter-past-ten."

"How many does the plane seat?"

"Six, I think he said. It's very fast and fancy."

Just like Eddie.

I told Senegal, "Then get going. Tell Beryl. Leave your clothes, leave this guy, just go. In the van, there's a woman named Norma — you'll like her. She's flying with you. Shay will come with me by boat."

I used the flashlight to signal the van, then ran toward the beach.

I was almost to the lagoon, running hard, when I saw the silhouette of someone jogging toward me. There was no cover, so I dropped to one knee, gun in hand, and watched.

It was Shay. Because I thought Ritchie might be chasing her, I waited until she'd passed before calling her name. When she hesitated, I added, "It's me. It's okay. Where's Ritchie?"

"Doc?" I'd startled her. She walked slowly toward me. "Did you see Beryl and the English woman? Are they okay? Clovis is with them . . . that's why I was running, because I was worried —"

I said, "They're fine. No danger, I promise." I asked again, "What happened to Ritchie?"

I felt a chill when she replied, "Are you alone? We need to talk."

"Yes. It's just me." I slipped the pistol into

the back of my pants.

"I don't think I've ever been so glad to see anyone in my life." The girl ran the last few steps, and let me swing her off the ground as we hugged. She laughed, smiled . . . her smile faded.

"Beryl told you about Corey?"

"Yes. Was it a blood clot?"

"That's what the doctors finally decided. But what really killed her was this island. What happened here. Feels real strange to be back. Feels like it was five years ago, not just a few weeks."

I noticed that remnants of her Southern accent had returned. *D*s softened or changed to *T*s; the nasal emphasis on *strange*.

"Ritchie showed up tonight. They tell you?"

I said patiently, "Yes. That's why I keep asking where he is."

"I'm trying to tell you, okay? Beryl had this plan, a way to get revenge. At first, it seemed . . . I don't know, exciting. When we talked about it, it was like we were actresses, seeing it on a movie screen. But that's not how it was. It got real. Then it got too real. We decided, screw it, we're leaving tonight. But then they showed up. Ritchie and the other guy. While we were packing." Shay cleared her throat. "Doc? You mind if we walk along the beach? It's nice by the water."

I said, "Okay," watching her pull a pack of cigarettes from her back pocket, then light one. She hadn't smoked since she was a teen, living in Dexter Money's home.

Shay tossed the match away and said, "That's how it started. Beryl wanted to even the score, after all the hurt they caused us. Plus, for her, I think it was a way to get back at the man who kidnapped her when she was a girl. I'm guessing. She never really said. Does that make sense?"

I nodded, thinking about Beryl back there with Clovis, his hands belted behind him. What would Senegal do if Beryl asked for the gun?

Shay said, "When Corey died, that made up my mind. Revenge, hell yes. I asked Eddie, the Italian guy at Dinkin's Bay, if he'd fly me down. He's always had a thing for me. When we told him we were pulling out tonight, staying on Saint Lucia, he went to get the plane ready. That's where he is now, waiting for us."

I looked at my wrist — no watch — and hoped that Eddie would get Sir James to the hospital in time to save his hand. Maybe save his life.

I told her, "Forget about revenge. There's no need for it now. I have your video. The original. I stole it — along with the money you paid out. You can get on with your life now, so stop worrying —"

"You got our money back? Doc, that's great! How'd you manage . . . ? No, tell me later when we have more time. My God, I can certainly use it. All hundred and nine thousand?"

I said, "Plus interest. And something extra for Corey's family."

Odd. The video no longer seemed important to her.

The girl clapped her hands together. "You are the most amazing man I've ever met! I knew my luck had to change. Beryl probably couldn't wait to tell you what happened between Michael and me. We ended it for good, the day after Corey died. Getting our money back — that's the best news I've heard for a while."

"Beryl didn't tell me. The wedding's off?"

"Yes, thank God."

"Why?"

"I found out the damn truth, that's why. Monday afternoon, Michael calls me and says Ida — you remember his witch of a mother? — he tells me Ida has somehow gotten ahold of photos of me with that slimeball, Ritchie. I tell him bullshit, his mother's making it up. I tell him it's impossible — and it should've been impossible. I still had four days to pay the people here. And you had the only other copy of the video."

But it was possible, Shay told me. To prove it, Michael brought the photos to her apartment. Graphic shots lifted from the video.

I said, "So he ended it."

"No!" she said, offended I'd made the assumption. "He thought the pictures were sexy — that's how freaky he is. *I* ended it! I ended it because I thought it through logically, just like you'd do. I even went to your lab and sat on the dock. Plus, I got your e-mail with those questions. Did Michael's family have other business connections in the Caribbean? Who recommended Saint Arc? What's Ida's maiden name?

"So I started asking Michael questions even before he pulled out the pictures. He got very nervous, because he *knew.* That witch set me up, and the whole time, he knew. Fucking Ritchie sent her those prints — Ritchie or some other contact she has down here. Ruining my life wasn't enough for his mother. She wanted to bleed my bank account dry, too.

"I'm going to have children one day, Doc. You think I want Michael's blood in my babies? His sick genes? No way."

Shay didn't know about Michael's aunt, Isabelle Toussaint. That was okay. Shay had already made her decision. She'd figured it out on her own. I smiled. I admired the girl's unemotional approach. I'd assembled her caricature to mirror my own conceits.

Shay reached, pressed her breasts against my arm . . . then was amused when I jumped at what sounded like a distant gunshot.

"It's only fireworks," she told me. "Must be a holiday or something." She released my arm, and walked to the water's edge where the sand looked gray at the lagoon's black rim and where, two days before, I'd seen jellyfish adrift, and wrestled lobsters from a cave.

I watched her. I could see the glow of her cigarette. It strobed a nervous rhythm, out of place on this dark night with stars, and the steady percussion of waves beaching themselves outside the lagoon. After taking a last drag, she tossed the butt away without looking to see where it fell.

I joined her, and Shay turned to face me. Maybe it was the way she was dressed — jeans, shirt knotted at the belly button — or maybe it was the deceptive properties of tropical starlight, but Shay looked less like a business exec and more like the plain-faced teen I'd met years before. She stood looking up at me, her cheek still swollen from the accident, nose a little too thick, lips too thin, and a body that, at another time and place, might have radiated a buxom, Southern, pheromone sensuality. But not tonight.

I said, "You were going to tell me about Ritchie."

Shay looked at the sand, nodded. "He killed Corey. That's the way I'm thinking of it. And he did things to me that night in the swimming pool I didn't tell you. Things he kept doing even when I told him to stop."

I said, "You have every right to be mad. But we're talking about tonight. How mad did you get?"

"I was telling you about this plan Beryl had —"

"Shay!" I took her hand and squeezed. "Stop evading. What happened? I know Ritchie tried to force you, I know you pretended to be interested, I know you two came here, to the beach. So, for the last time, where's —"

"I brought a gun," Shay interrupted, pulling away. She turned her back to me and looked at the sky where there were stars . . . and also a plane climbing skyward, green and white lights blinking.

"Hey," she said. "Hey! That's Eddie's

plane. I'm supposed to fly back to Saint Lucia with —"

"I'm taking you by boat," I said. "You were telling me about the gun."

"Oh. Yeah. That's one of the good things about flying with Eddie. You can carry anything you want on a private plane. The gun, it made me feel safe when I was out here with Ritchie. He probably wondered where I got all the courage when I started screaming at him about Corey. I told him he was nothing but low-life trash, and how much I hate bullies. Then . . ."

I waited for a few seconds before I pressed, "And then . . . ?" wondering if she was editing her story. She often did.

"And then I took out the gun and pointed it at Ritchie's smug damn face. He tried to bullshit his way out of it. But when I pulled the hammer back, I wish you could've seen his expression. He was like, *Jesus Christ, this woman's got the balls to really do it.* I told him, 'Ritchie, you little prick, you've got five seconds to run.' Then I started counting. And . . . that's all that happened."

I said, "What do you mean?" It was like we were in her convertible again, returning from the airport, the stories slippery in her mouth.

"I mean he ran — the coward. And so I

. . . fired a couple of shots into the sand. To scare the hell out of him. Because of the fireworks, no one would've noticed." She made a sound that resembled laughter. "Ritchie won't be back, I promise you that."

I looped my arm around her waist, then slid my hand up her ribs and rested it on her neck. The gun wasn't in her pockets; wasn't in a shoulder holster. I asked, "Are you telling me the truth about the gun?" Though I knew the answer.

Shay sighed — a mewing sound of nostalgia or amusement — a sound like that. "It was a little Blackhawk .22. Daddy gave it to me when I was ten. I learned to shoot, Doc. I learned to *pull the trigger.* That's a phrase Dexter used. It meant someone it came naturally to."

I said, "Almost sounds like you miss the man."

Shay thought that was funny. Said, "Hah!" and scratched at something on her arm. "I'll despise him forever. But Daddy knew guns — that's all I'm saying. Which is why it got so he distrusted me as much as I disliked him."

I shook my head, confused. *What?*

"I told you I ran away from home?"

"Yeah?"

"That was a lie. I didn't run away. Daddy

made me leave. I may be the only person who ever scared Dexter Money. He was afraid I was gonna kill him, so one of us had to go."

The girl looked up at me. "I was out here thinking about it. How would I feel if I'd really shot him — Ritchie. Would I have a guilty conscience? Or break down crying, or go screaming and yelling to Beryl, begging her to help me cover up what I'd done?"

I said, "What did you decide?"

Shay's eyes brightened for an instant, a feral reaction to starlight. "I decided I wouldn't do any of those things. If I killed trash like Ritchie, I guess I'd feel . . . indifferent. Does that sound cold-blooded, Doc?"

I cupped the back of Shay's neck and pulled her close, so my lips were next to her ear. I said, "That asshole, Ritchie, stole my watch, Shanay. My old Rolex. Now . . . where's his body?"

Back at the beach house, I found my belt near the pool, and the little Colt .380, one round fired, the brass casing on the deck. I'd known it was no fireworks.

No blood trail. No Clovis. Beryl had missed. Or was it Senegal?

"Pulling the trigger isn't the same as *pulling the trigger*," Shay told me, huddled close for warmth, as we boated toward the lights of Saint Lucia.

She was cold and I was freezing. The wind had cut like a knife as Shay had stood guard on the beach, while I put Ritchie in the cave.

EPILOGUE

On a silver, squall-blustery morning, July 24th, I rode my bike to the Sanibel Post Office on Tarpon Bay Road, and found a familiar postal key in my box that opened a larger box, from which I extracted one bulky manila envelope. I also found one reinforced box, carefully wrapped, very thin — made for sending valuable papers or photographs.

The envelope was from Sir James Montbard, Bluestone, Saint Lucia. It would contain articles and proofs and copies of maps related to the man's theory of Relentless Human Motion. Sir James wanted me to join him on an expedition to the mangrove jungles of Central America's Caribbean Coast. "There are Olmec ruins there unknown to outsiders — protected for centuries by native Miskito Indians," he had told me. "The few real Miskito, the traditional ones, are damn suspicious of interlopers.

It would be useful to have you along — an extra hand, you might say."

The Englishman had laughed when he said that.

"The final proof we're looking for may well be there, somewhere among the vines and mosquitoes. It's not a trip for the faint of heart. You've had some experience in that part of the world, haven't you, old boy?"

"I've been there a few times, Hooker," I'd told him, amused that his Relentless Motion theory was now "ours."

Montbard said he'd finance the trip with his cut of the money I'd taken from Isabelle Toussaint's safe.

The second package was from General Forensics Laboratories, White Plains, New York. Using infrared luminescence and digital enhancement imaging, experts there had reconstructed portions of the letter from the late Merlin Starkey, the letter that might reveal the name of my parents' murderer.

The box would also contain General Forensics's bill. Expensive. That was okay. I could afford it.

I put box and envelope in my backpack, and pedaled the easy half a mile back to my lab. Squall cells were dispersing, I noted, skies turning from silver to Gulf Stream blue.

It was going to be a hot one.

Late that afternoon, Tomlinson and I exited our local rum bar into rain-forest heat and, on the three-mile bike ride to the marina, he decided it was so wonderfully, humidly, oppressively hot, that residents of Sanibel Island, and neighboring islands, would be eager to participate in our annual Summer Christmas Snowflake Fiesta.

I responded, "What do you mean, annual? We've never hosted a Christmas fiesta before. We've never celebrated Christmas in summer before. How do you come up with this stuff?" The man had been drinking.

Tomlinson watched a trio of adolescent raccoons ramble hunch-backed across the bike path, before he said, "Just because we've never done something, doesn't mean it hasn't already happened. Think about it. The timing's perfect. You weren't listening to Big Dan and Greg, and Marty at the bar? This is National Single Working Women's Week."

Yes, I'd listened, and I'd made the mistake of doubting. The guys summoned Mark, who produced a laptop computer. He went to the Internet and proved that National

Single Working Women's Week does exist. More than a hundred female members had booked rooms at the nearby Island Inn.

Tomlinson blinked his eyes for a moment, smiling. "I'm picturing a dozen bored and overheated single working women, from states with lots of vowels, wearing nothing but Santa hats on Coach Mike's Sea Ray —"

I said, "Here we go."

"— and a big Christmas tree, with stars and shells and angel hair. And presents. Lots of presents. We suddenly have a surplus of cold, hard cash, man —"

I interrupted. "What do you mean, 'we'? I don't remember opening a joint bank account." Why were people using royal pronouns to include me in things lately?

Tomlinson said, "I was the one who signed for the package when the embassy courier knocked on the door. Brought it inside the lab; put it in a nice safe place while you were out disposing of all those weird creepy crawlers. Poison shrimp — gad! — although I do kinda miss the high-voltage jellyfish."

I said, "For that, you're entitled to half?"

"No. I'm not greedy. Just a cut. I could've run, you know. Or jumped over the railing and swam for it — almost did when I saw the Fed was wearing a badge. But I stood my ground, man. It gives me a communal interest. Why is it you capitalists can't understand the whole beautiful concept of sharing wealth?" He gave it several deadpan beats before laughing, letting me know he was doing his flaky, harmless hippie bit.

The hippie disappeared, and I listened to the real Tomlinson say, "I'm thinking of Javier Castillo's wife, Anita, and the two girls. Since Javier was killed, I hear they're struggling like hell to get by."

Javier had been one of the area's top fishing guides, and a trusted friend. A good cause.

"There are a couple of other families around — mullet fishermen; some of the illegals on Pine Island — who could use a boost. So yeah, throw a summer Christmas party. Why not? We all kick in cash, and maybe have a lottery drawing. That way, when Javier's wife draws the winning ticket, it won't feel like charity."

I said, "Let me guess. You'll use your paranormal powers to make sure she wins."

"I probably could," he said seriously, scratching at his thigh. "My mojo is back, big-time. No, what I'm saying is, we rig the whole deal. Fast Eddie's an expert. Getting him involved might give him a boost, too — an emotional boost, I mean."

The last few days, Eddie DeAntoni had been moping around the marina, despondent. Two nights before, very late, I'd strolled the docks and actually found the tough guy weeping, dimples and all. He'd had a couple of passionate evenings with Beryl Woodward, but now things weren't going well. She didn't return his calls. Beryl would make a date, but not show up.

"She's killing me," he'd moaned, then was understandably confused when I assured him that that was one of the few things Beryl would not do.

I said to Tomlinson, "Christmas in July. Why not? You're sure Eddie knows how to rig it?"

Tomlinson said, "Are you kidding? How do you think he won that lottery in Jersey?"

It was true I now had a bundle of unreported, untaxed cash on my hands. Slightly less than a quarter million, after I'd split the take with Sir James and Norma, and sent an anonymous money order to Corey's family.

The Midnight Star, I kept for myself. Expenses.

Because U.S. Customs is suspicious of citizens carrying large sums, I'd had Eddie drop me on the nearby island of Grenada before he and the girls returned to Fort Lauderdale in his leased, jet-fast TBM-850 airplane.

I spent six days on Grenada making phone

calls to old contacts and making new friends at the U.S. embassy. Turned out I had some old friends on the island, too. Grenada had changed a lot since the invasion.

My old friends proved helpful. So did my old boss, Hal Harrington — once I applied the right kind of pressure. I was now in possession of a video that compromised a powerful member of the U.S. Senate. But I'm not an extortionist. I didn't use the video; didn't mention it — although I did contact the senator who, understandably, was suspicious despite glowing character references from my old friends. The senator and I began a careful dialogue that gradually became genial, and was now friendly.

For Hal Harrington, though, a call from Sir James Montbard was pressure enough.

"Do you know who *he is?*" Harrington — a man not easily impressed — had asked.

I'd told him, "No, but I'm starting to figure it out."

Because I already had everything arranged at the embassy, and it was Saturday, I had returned to Saint Lucia for the weekend. Had dinner at Bluestone with Sir James, Senegal, and Norma, too. Sir James was out of the hospital after a successful surgery, and as upbeat as ever — despite a loss that would be debilitating to most men.

"A hook!" he'd called out when I arrived. "They're going to fit me with a bloody hook. Isn't it perfect! Until then, they've given me this temporary thing." He'd waved the stainless steel prosthetic strapped to his left arm.

He was more enthusiastic about Norma. She'd stayed by his bed during the worst of it, tending to his every need. She'd given him incredible daily massages, he said.

"I think she's marvelous. I've offered the woman a full-time billet. Top pay, full benefits." After a wry look, he'd added, "But Norma says she's come into a tidy sum of money. I don't know if I should compliment your generosity, or curse you."

I didn't tell him the woman had accepted only a small percentage of what I'd tried to give. She would take only an amount equal to six months' salary — it wasn't much — and enough for a family crypt so her dead son and estranged husband could finally be reunited. She wanted the crypt to be large enough for a third. Her time would come.

I also didn't tell him what Norma had told me — that she was falling in love with the man, pirate's hook and all.

"Hooker has more ching chi toxins than a twenty-year-old sailor," she'd laughed, but wasn't joking. I could see her amber, liquid eyes now, and her smile — teeth whiter because of her dark skin. The prettiest widow I'd ever met.

Norma had chosen a seventy-year-old legend over me. It was okay. My ego was intact.

At the Bluestone dinner, Sir James told me the artifacts he'd taken from the monastery had turned out to be a disappointment. Sort of. They were pieces of the stone artifact his grandfather had stolen decades before.

"He was just a lad at the time," Montbard told me, showing me his grandfather's journal as we sat in the library, near the stone with the strange glyphs. "Someone came along, surprised him, and he dropped the thing." He'd gestured at the artifact with his temporary hook. "The Mayan glyph is unmistakable. But it's only been in the last two years that I've had time to break the other cipher — my real job always kept me hopping."

He'd taken out a sketch pad as we stood over the artifact, and showed me tracings of the glyphs. They were similar to sketches I'd made in my notebook.

I was skeptical when he added, "I think we're looking at ancient Masonic code — but not as ancient as I'd hoped. See what you think."

He flipped the page, saying, "Here's the key to the code."

There were two tic-tac-toe grids. Each square contained a letter: *A-B-C* on the top level of the first grid, *D-E-F* on the next level. Letters followed that progression. In the second grid, there were dots beneath each of the nine letters.

There were also two large *X*s, with a letter in each of the eight open triangles. There were dots beneath letters in the second *X*.

"Look at the glyphs. They're actually shapes. Partial boxes. Now look at the grid. The first square is a two-sided box, open at the left and top. It represents *A*. *B* is a three-sided box, open at the top. *C* is a two-sided box, open at the right and at the top.

"It's a simple substitution cipher," he'd said. "It's supposedly a Masonic secret, but you see it all the time these days in books and films. Each box, opened or closed, replaces the letter it contains. Understand?"

"I think I do."

I took the sketch pad and matched the glyphs to the tic-tac-toe grids. The result was a series of meaningless letters.

"It makes no sense. Did I do it right?"

"Perfectly," Montbard had replied, grinning. "But it's also perfectly wrong. The actual Masonic key — the one used for many hundreds of years — really is *secret*. The popular books, the films, the cipher they use, is actually gibberish when properly translated."

"You know this because you're a Freemason?"

"No. I know because the actual cipher key is here —" He held up his grandfather's journal. "It has been in the family forever, but it wasn't obvious, even to me.

"You'd have to be a Mason to understand that we have codes that represent codes that replace other codes. I have no idea of the meaning of half the things we learn as Masons. The language is archaic. But I finally figured out this one."

He'd flipped the page of the sketch pad. "I can't show you all of it, old boy. I'm breaking a rule, showing you this. But see what happens when I turn this . . . add this . . . then join this?" He used a charcoal pencil to change the key, then he translated the glyphs.

" 'TUBAL,' " I said, "is that a word?"

"If you're a Freemason, my boy, it has great meaning. That's all I can say."

Sir James then took portions of the broken fragment he'd found at the monastery. On it were three more glyphs. When he fitted the stones together, the five glyphs, using the new cipher key, now translated as: "MDCXV."

"Another secret word?"

Sir James said, "No. Roman numerals. It's a date: 1615."

I smiled, impressed. "It's a great find."

"Yes," he said, "but it's also disappointing. The Mayan glyph, of course, was carved long before 1615. Frankly, I expected the new section to provide missing numerals — thirteen. As in 1315. Still . . . it's suggestive. Even encouraging, in its way. I'm not done looking, Ford. By God, I'm not!

"One more surgery, a spot of rest, then I'm off to Central America. Descendants of the Knights Templar were here. What I've found proves it — to me, anyway. I'm convinced the warrior monks sailed here long before Columbus, their ships loaded with gold and jewels, and relics from the Holy Land. Their treasure's out there, Ford. Somewhere in the jungle."

The next day, back on Grenada, Monday, July 1st, I sent duplicate packages to the Eastern Caribbean tourist board, to the *Miami Herald,* and to the French DST, which is the equivalent of our FBI. The packages contained evidence I'd collected against Isabelle Toussaint. I included a letter that suggested blackmail was a boutique industry on

Saint Arc, and possibly Jamaica, too. I used data assembled by Tomlinson.

Contacting the wife of a former French president was trickier than contacting my new senator friend. So I let Bernie Yager take care of it.

The same day, I delivered a box to the U.S. embassy in Grenada. It would be transported to the States via diplomatic pouch.

It would not be the first time stolen cash and gems had entered the U.S. in that fashion. But it was the first time Tomlinson ever opened the door to a Federal agent and didn't expect to be arrested.

Thursday night while I was in the lab, gathering Corona bottles Tomlinson had emptied as we planned his Summer Christmas Fiesta, the phone rang. Surprise, surprise — Hal Harrington. He sounded perturbed, but also mystified when he mentioned the first initial of my new friend, the U.S. senator, then said, "This person thinks you're an absolute saint. This person talked my ear off about you at a certain embassy last night. I've heard this person actually got a certain state agency to release you from your contract. Why, for God's sake?"

Hal spoke of the senator in careful, neutral terms because the senator was a woman

— an attractive woman, dark-haired and fit, judging from photos. One of the youngest ever elected to that most exclusive of clubs.

"I did the person in question a favor," I told Harrington. "No strings attached. That's the truth. And that's all I can say. Hal — I may do you a favor, and come back to work. If you ask real nice."

"You're serious."

"On my own terms, of course."

"Things are going pretty well, right now. Maybe we don't need you."

"Are we already negotiating, or are you being an ass?"

"We're negotiating. Are you fit for duty?"

I brushed a hand over the back of my head. "Never better."

We talked for another ten minutes. It sounded as if the man was my friend again. Then I told him I had to go — also true.

The visitor I was expecting was a woman. Ten-thirty sharp, drinks and a late dinner, she'd told me in a familiar businesslike voice. Then she had to go. Lots of work to do.

I wanted to be shaved and dressed before she arrived, so I was headed for the shower, towel knotted around my waist, when the open box on the dissecting table, return address *General Forensics, White Plains, NY*, caught my eye once again. I stopped, checked my Rolex — 10:10 p.m. — then reread the last few paragraphs of Merlin Starkey's shaky hand.

. . . your daddy was a good man, Marion. A sight better man than your uncle Tucker Gatrell, although Tuck had a genius, which even I will admit.

If I wasn't sure you already knew what it is I'm about to write, I'd warn you it might hurt. But I am sure. Your mother was a well-educated woman. She liked music and things, art and such, and she knew all the birds, which your daddy didn't. People can get lonely inside their own heads. Maybe it'll happen to you, one day. It happened to your mother.

She had an affair with a young museum professor, an expert on plants or maybe trees, who come down here from Chicago. The museum fella, he fell in love with your mother. Your mama didn't fall in love with him. He was good-looking, I reckon, but he was a damn bad man. You know his name, Marion. No need for me to write it.

He disappeared seven months after the boat blew up and killed your parents. You couldn't have been sixteen years old at the time. The museum man was out in the swamps, slogging around with his note-

book, and he just disappeared. Murdered. I know, 'cause I investigated that murder, too.

I don't know why you blamed that shit-heel uncle of yours. Maybe you wasn't sure. Maybe something up in your head was blocking the truth. So that's why I'm writing to tell you.

You got the right man, Marion. You did it real smart. I wish to hell I was still alive so you could tell me what you did with the professor man's body. . . .

The clanging of the bell on the deck below snatched my attention away — a good thing. This was the third time I'd read the letter, but the first time I'd felt an uncomfortable surge of emotion. I was ridiculously close to tears.

I went to the porch, holding the towel around my waist, thinking, *What the hell, this is the tropics,* and looked down into the smiling face of a good-looking woman dressed for business — dark skirt, white blouse, dark blazer.

"Welcome to Sanibel," I called to her. "Ready to de-ice?"

The woman had a sense of humor, thank God. She laughed. "Looks like you already have, Dr. Ford. But the only ice I want is in

a tall glass — I hope I'm not being presumptuous."

I said, "Not at all. I've heard your voice so
often on the phone, Senator, it'll be nice to
talk face-to-face."

ABOUT THE AUTHOR

Randy Wayne White is the author of fourteen previous Doc Ford novels – *The Heat Islands, Sanibel Flats, The Man Who Invented Florida, Captiva, North of Havana, The Mangrove Coast, Ten Thousand Islands, Shark River, Twelve Mile Limit, Everglades, Tampa Burn, Dead of Night, Dark Light,* and *Hunter's Moon* — and of the nonfiction collections *Batfishing in the Rainforest, The Sharks of Lake Nicaragua, Last Flight Out,* and *An American Traveler.* A onetime veteran fishing guide, he lives in an old house built on an Indian mound, and spends much of his free time windsurfing, playing baseball, and hanging out at Doc Ford's Sanibel Rum Bar & Grille on Sanibel Island, Florida.

The employees of Thorndike Press hope you have enjoyed this Large Print book. All our Thorndike and Wheeler Large Print titles are designed for easy reading, and all our books are made to last. Other Thorndike Press Large Print books are available at your library, through selected bookstores, or directly from us.

For information about titles, please call:

(800) 223-1244

or visit our Web site at:

http://gale.cengage.com/thorndike

To share your comments, please write:

Publisher
Thorndike Press
295 Kennedy Memorial Drive
Waterville, ME 04901